Exiled on Rant

Farley Dunn

THREE SKILLET

EXILED ON RANT, Dunn, Farley

First Edition

THE SE'YAN'T CHRONICLES, Book 2

 THREE SKILLET

www.ThreeSkilletPublishing.com

Cover design by Farley L Dunn

ISBN: 978-1-943189-29-8

Exiled on Rant

—Chapter 1—

*com•pound (kəm'pound) per•son (pər'sən) n.
more than one person so fused together in
identity, lifestyle, and goals that no
demarcation is clearly distinguishable*

—*New Webster's Thirty-*
Seventh Secondary
Dictionary

OVERCADET STEPH'NI B'LTN RENHANT panted, the slippery floor forcing him to crawl toward the door. The room had never angled uphill before, and he kept sliding backwards, his hands and feet slipping out from under him. In the darkness, desperate for a handhold, he felt for anything he could grasp. A chair. A table. *There.* Someone's wrist.

"Thank you," he whispered.

He pulled himself forward, stretching his hand across the person's waist, his arm sliding across a naked breast. A woman! Shame flooded his face. He offered an apology as he tried to push himself off and couldn't. He realized to his horror he was naked also, his body engaged in a way he found repulsive and sensuous at the same time.

"I'm sorry," he groaned, as his vision went white, and he lost control. Crawling off the woman, he slipped and fumbled to the wall, searching for the light. The room flashed into brightness, painting blood everywhere, leaving the woman's sightless eyes to stare up at him, fixated on the slashes of red covering the front of his body.

Renhant jerked, his eyes flying open in the darkness, his mouth dry with fear. He grasped his bedding in his fists, only to find his sheets soaked with sweat. It was the same dream every night. That wasn't the way it happened, though. He stumbled to the toilet and threw up, as he did each time he woke from the dream.

The other bed in the cell creaked. "Another nightmare, huh? That's tough, kid. Flush the toilet when you're finished." The words were growled, slurred with sleep. Then there came a long whistle of expelled gas.

Renhant hit the button on the wall, the smell of his vomit disappearing down the drain. Sitting on the cold of the metal floor, the wall's chill penetrating his face, he wished he could go back and start over. Just one year. Just one month. Tears streaming down his face, he wanted someone to help.

Just one lifetime to live over again. He ran his hands over his hair, realizing it was as soaked as his sheets.

Crawling back in the rude bunk, he knew he wasn't alone. Jer'son was somewhere in a similar lockup. So was Barn't. They hadn't been allowed to communicate, as if they might actually be able to plan a way to escape. They were on a spaceship, for gods' sakes! At least let them have one another for solace.

Sliding hot, moist skin against the damp cold sheets was truly almost as bad as the nightmare had been. Then there was the smell from his cellmate's gas. Renhant gagged as he forced himself to lie very still, waiting until the urge to vomit once again had passed. Finally, he closed his eyes, and in the stillness, a world that had once been better filled his dreams.

"YEAH, LOOK." Renhant held up the credits. He turned and walked backwards, doing a little dance step, waving them over his head. "Fifteen credits!"

"Hey, who'd have thought that kid had that much. I figured a newbie that fresh to have maybe one or two at the most." Renhant's friend, Overcadet Fal'dera Hult Jer'son, laughed. "Did you see him beg you to take the money? And that was before you even kicked him!"

"Yeah, where's my five?" Overcadet Je'main Winterd Barn't jumped to grab it from Renhant's hand.

"Who says you get five?" Jer'son teased, waving the credits in front of the smaller boy's face.

"I'm the one who kicked him hardest. I deserve my share." Barn't pouted, his face turning red.

"Here," Renhant peeled off five of the credits and handed them to Barn't. "Here's yours, too, Jer'son. Let's go to the games room. They've got some new ones I want to try."

With echoes of laughter, the three friends disappeared

down the corridor, games on their minds, the boy lying in his own vomit in the utility corridor forgotten. They knew there would be others with money when they needed more. There always were.

JER'SON KNELT by Renhant's bunk. "Did you notice the new kid? The one behind the pipes?" He grinned expectantly. "You know, when we were borrowing that newbie's credits."

His friend sat up on one elbow. "Yeah, I saw him. I didn't know anyone else did. We should have beat him up after we thrashed that newbie. What do you think? Should we show him who's boss around here?" He let himself fall back to the bed, tossing a hard ball at the bottom of the bunk above, catching it each time it returned.

"I talked to Barn't, and he says the kid had a really bad reputation downside."

"Barn't knows that?" Renhant laughed. "He can't even decide which shower niche to use unless we point him to one."

"He says he was called up to the head rooms—"

"He was what?" Renhant sat up abruptly. "Did he rat?"

"Nah." Jer'son pushed hard against Renhant's shoulder, dismissing his concerns. "You know Barn't. He wouldn't rat without asking us first. No, he filched the kid's file—it was right there on a glass—and he's a forced inductee, had to come to the academy ship with no choice."

"So, what do you think? Is he all right?"

"Don't know." He thought so, however. Forced inductee? That sounded like someone who would fit into their little trio snug as a bug. "Maybe. I say give him a cycle or two and see if he rats. If he does, I've never broken an arm. I might like to give it a try." He laughed at that.

"Barn't okay with this?"

"You know Barn't. He'll tag along with whatever we decide. Who knows, if he proves okay, the new kid might even be one of us some day."

"If he fits in," Renhant mused. "Otherwise, we'll just work him over good. It wouldn't hurt him at all." He snickered, and then finished with, "Well, maybe just a little bit, but then that might do *us* some good."

BARN'T HELD the fingerlight to the page, the lights of the holding cell long ago dimmed. He knew he would get in even more trouble if they knew he had the small device with him, but he had to have light. He was really nervous about going in front of the judge tomorrow. That's when they'd find out just what would happen to them. With the girl dying, and then Zen'ri, it probably wouldn't be good.

He hoped they'd be kicked out of the academy for sure. That'd be fine with him. He'd just go home. Sometimes he thought he'd like that, just pack up and go home, forget about all his classes and military training.

He didn't know that he was really cut out to be a soldier like the others, not even if he did make officer someday. OverCap't Je'main Winterd Barn't. Wouldn't that have really impressed his old man! It wouldn't go over well if he came home, kicked out from MegaCorp, though.

Maybe he wouldn't go home, just get a job on a private ship, and work his way up from the bottom. There were all kinds of things a boy his age could do. He stopped and corrected himself. There were things a *man* his age could do.

He *was* a man. He had been with her that night. He knew she hadn't been dead then, because she had made moaning sounds as he had spilled his juices into her.

Barn't hit his head with his fist, slamming the heel of his hand into it over and over. Someone had to take the blame, and it wasn't going to be him. It was Renhant's fault that all this was happening. If Renhant hadn't done whatever he'd done, they wouldn't be here. *He* wouldn't be here, and he'd graduate from the academy in only a few more quarters, go home and show his old man what a jerk he'd been, telling him he'd never make it once he got here.

Once on the ship, Barn't had thought he was free from the insults. Then, his old man had decided he had to come see him at the academy, and when he'd gotten here, he'd told his insults to everyone in the dorm, making him feel small all over again. Now, he could never go home. The old man'd never let him live down getting kicked out of the academy.

Barn't ran his fingers down the file, hating using this paper copy, wishing for his glass, knowing it had been taken away with everything else that was his, taken and "held" for him until all this was resolved. He was sure there must be at least one accidental death case like theirs on the list where the accused were simply discharged.

After all, Zen'ri's death had certainly been accidental. They hadn't touched him, not really. It was just that Zen'ri was running, wouldn't listen to them, and they had to stop him. He must have tripped. Zen'ri always was clumsy, anyway. Surely they would take that into account. They couldn't really blame *him* for Zen'ri's clumsiness, could they? Yeah, maybe kick him and Jer'son and Renhant out, but surely they wouldn't do anything more than that.

Barn't's eyes starting to twitch, he came to the bottom of the list. There had to be at least one. He went back to the top; he must have missed it. Surely, not every single case was assigned to Rant. Not him, not Barn't. He just wanted to be at the bottom of the ladder on a ship somewhere. He'd even wash floors as long as he didn't have to go to Rant.

The words on the paper blurring, he wiped his eyes as he jerked across the words, running his fingers down the list once more. *There must be at least one. There has to be,* he told himself as he started reading at the top one additional time.

JER'SON SAT on his bunk in the dark, hitting his fist into his palm over and over. The slapping sound of knuckles against flesh was gratifyingly loud in the blackness.

Bofsky'd wanted to go. It was his idea. Even then they could've turned around and come back, especially at the point when they discovered they didn't have enough credits. Playing ringleader, Bofsky had found a way. One walker for all of them, sharing one at a time.

Jer'son shouldn't have listened to him. If they'd stayed on the ship, things would have been okay.

Then, there was that idiot, Zen'ri. To run like that—how stupid! They wouldn't have hurt him. All he had to do was keep quiet for a while. Now, all three of them would be sentenced tomorrow. He knew what they'd do, not like stupid

Barn't, thinking they'd just let them all go home. No way. They were all going to Rant. That's where all academy officers got sent when they broke the really serious rules. Well, they weren't exactly officers, yet, but the three of them were almost officers, would have been, too, if it weren't for Bofsky.

Jer'son continued to pound his hand, anger flooding his veins, hoping, just hoping he got on someone's nerves. He needed to vent his rage on something or someone. He'd kick bars and pound metal, whatever it took. Gods, he hated Bofsky!

"Hey, you, kid. I'm trying to sleep up here." Jer'son's cellmate shifted in the bunk, and the metal creaked with his weight.

Jer'son went nuts. He jumped up and pushed on the edge of the man's metal sleeping platform, slamming into it hard. "You talking to me? That me you're talking to, huh?" His breath coming in gulps, pent up fury painting the world red, Jer'son turned away, and equally fast, he whipped back, lunging into the man's bunk repeatedly, attacking it with his fists each time.

"Kid, go back to bed. You don't want to mess with me," the tired voice snarled.

"I don't, huh? Then you just leave me alone, you hear? Just leave me alone." Jer'son lunged forward one more time. As he did, a hand wrapped itself around his wrist.

"Want a broken arm, kid?"

He pulled back, forcing his wrist from the man's grasp, his other hand slipping and inadvertently hitting the man in the face.

14

"That's it, kid. You keep asking, so I'm gonna give you what you want." With a creaking of the man's bunk, there were quickly two angry people standing in the room. "Come on, kid. You think you can take me, or are you going to shut up and let me sleep?"

Jer'son hissed, "You can't tell me what to do," and with that, he attacked the man with both fists.

The man staggered, but the boy had no chance. While fending his hits with one hand, the bigger man kept his other curled into a fist, connecting with his inexperienced cellmate in all the places where the young man would hurt the worst. Soon, he hurt too badly to fight back.

As he lay on the floor, the man spat at him, "Now lie still. I want to sleep."

This time, Jer'son did as he was told for the rest of the night. The next morning the guard kicked him as he lay curled on the floor.

"What happened to you?" Glancing up, the guard grinned. "Oh. I know *who* happened to you."

"Damn right," muttered the occupant of the top bunk.

Kneeling down, the guard grabbed Jer'son's face in his hand, turning it, looking for damage. "Clean face. Good, this'll be an easy one to overlook." Giving the man in the top bunk a sharp slap to the shoulder, the guard called out, "Thanks. Good job," and turned to walked out.

The man's only reply was, "Go away."

THREE DIFFERENT guards pulled three different seventeen-year-olds from their last night on the academy training ship. Each was forced to stand outside a cell holding a

15

change of clothing until a shower room was ready. Then, one at a time, the boys were taken inside, and the guard stood at the door monitoring as each boy stripped off his clothes and handed them to the burly man at his side, who then searched the pockets before stuffing them into a recycle slot.

Exposed to the greedy eyes of the watching sentry, each boy was required to shower and dress in the change of clothing he had been given. One at a time, the guards delivered their packages to the sentencing chambers, where finally all three were together again.

"Guys, do you think they'll just let us go home?" Barn't whispered. His cheeks were flushed with worry. Red traced lines in the whites of his eyes.

"Grow up. How many times over the past few cycles have you read down that ridiculous list you snuck in here? Things won't change for us, Barn't. Face it."

"It might be we'll be different. We might. When things change, there always has to be a first time. We might be it." He scratched at his neck, leaving red marks as long as his fingers. They matched the color of his cheeks.

"Yeah, and Bofsky might pay his dues with us, too. Do you think that might happen, Barn't? Bofsky might decide it's not fair for him to get off while we pay his dues. Right. Like I said, grow up."

"Be easy on him. He's just scared." Renhant sat with his head against the wall, his eyes on the ceiling.

Jer'son exhaled a barking sound at the reminder. "I guess I'm not, and you're not, huh, Renhant? Just Barn't, right?" He stood, walking around the room. "This wasn't supposed to happen, you know. I was supposed to move on up and take command of my own ship. It's not like those military commanders out there passing sentence on us haven't sent men to their deaths, and then said, 'Oops!' Why do they have to do this to us when this is no different?" Jer'son slapped a bare fist against the wall.

"Because they can. Then they can feel righteous about keeping everything moral and honest when really it isn't. You and I know that, but it doesn't change what they can do. We don't have a choice. We have to do what they tell us today. We just have to make sure we agree on one thing." He sat up and leaned forward, motioning for the other two to join him. He whispered, "If this goes as bad as I think it will, Bofsky pays. I don't know how or when, but we make a pact here and now to never rest until he has paid as much as we have. Is it a deal?"

All three boys reached their hands out and shook, the pact sealed with the act. The door opened, and they turned to face the guard.

"Break it up, boys. There will be no collaboration allowed. You will be led one at time to the chambers. Please follow protocol. Nod when sentenced. No comments are allowed, whether the sentence is in your favor or otherwise. Overcadet Renhant, first. Then, I will return for you other two."

Renhant walked to the door, turning to his friends, and just looked at them before spinning around with resignation to follow the guard. Soon the other two were also taking their places as they were led off to learn of their fates.

"ALL RISE."

The three boys could see their former friend, their Judas, across the room. He looked so proud and cocky at having escaped the punishment he should be sharing.

"Overcadets Renhant, Barn't, and Jer'son, this board of inquiry has returned a verdict for the despicable actions you have initiated. You have shamed this training academy. For the willful entrapment and injury unto death of one Cadet Fabr d'Sen Zen'ri, you are sentenced to a permanent posting on Rant. A jumpship is waiting. Officers, please escort these men out now."

JER'SON FELT his mind go blank at the actual words being said. *Sentenced. Posting. Rant.* He remembered the boy, the cadet aboard the ship who had died.

"Hey, Zen'ri." The boy turned to face him, a look of wariness crawling across his face. "Remember me?" He smiled at the boy. He had attended several classes with him, but Zen'ri wasn't his type. Small and awkward, he usually got the desk chores where he couldn't mess much up.

Cautiously, he answered, "You're Jer'son, right?"

"Yes, you remembered." He put on his brightest smile. He had to charm this boy to get what he wanted. "Remember that abilities class we were in, the one where we were paired in the team races?" He looked at him, willing him to remember a race that had never happened.

"Um, I'm not sure."

"Remember, Zen'ri? We were on the same team, and you were the last one who ran. You helped our team take first. Surely you remember."

18

"I think I would if I did that." The puzzled look on the boy's face competed with what must be his desire to claim what Jer'son was offering him, recognition for a skill at which he was abysmally poor.

"You just don't remember because you know you have more important things to do, not just win *races.* You know that *thinking* is more important. Isn't that right?"

Cadet Zen'ri frowned. "I do think I remember something about that race." He looked unsure, though.

"You must, Zen'ri, because we couldn't have done it without you. Well, there's something else I can't get done without you."

Hesitantly, the boy answered. "Sure. Um, what can I do for you?"

Jer'son rubbed hands together. "I have this pass I damaged, and I need a glue that will put it back together again without it coming apart when I run it through a scanner."

Zen'ri obliged the request, even showing Jer'son the best way to apply it. What really amused Jer'son was how pleased he sounded doing it, as if he were helping out a good friend.

As if, Zen'ri. As if.

BARN'T MUMBLED, "Permanent posting? Life sentence is what it is." Memories of his father flooded his thoughts.

"Look at you! Mr. La-te-da! So, what did I come to see, a girl or an officer? I don't see any officer's bars on those shoulders, yet."

"I know, Dad. I have to graduate to become an officer."

Barn't turned from his father to face his bunk, unable to bear the drunken flush on his face.

"Don't look away from me, boy. I'm your father, and you have to do what I say. I told you you'd never make it here." His father turned to the rest of the dorm, speaking as if wanting the others to hear. "How many other fathers come here to see their sons? How many of those fathers ever got a medal for bravery? How many of those fathers set a standard so high their sons got to piss their pants just to reach it? Gods, it's hot in here. Do they have a place I can get a drink?" He grabbed Barn't's arm. "Huh, boy?"

Barn't muttered, "How many of those boys have to deal with a drunk for a father?"

"What, boy? I heard that. I am not a drunk." Louder, to the dorm, "I am not a drunk. My boy, Barn't here, says I'm a drunk, but I'm not. I just like a little one every now and then."

He can't even call me by my real name, not like a real father would. Je'main. It's Je'main.

Making sure his face was expressionless, he turned to his father. "Dad, maybe we can get you something in the officer's mess. It's right this way."

"Damn right, it's this way. Bet you're proud to be seen with your old man, huh, Barn't. I'm a real war hero, that's by god right. A real, honest-to-damn war hero." He strutted, calling out to the other cadets, "Look at me. Eat your eyes out, boys!"

After seeing you, they're probably glad their dads didn't get a special bravery medal allowing them access to the training academy where those same fathers could continue to mess up their sons' lives just as they've probably done all along at home.

Barn't kept his face straight, though. It'd be hell enough when his father was gone without being teased for being a baby, too.

Gods, he hated his father.

RENHANT WHISPERED, spitting the words angrily, "You'll pay, Bofsky. Somehow. Someday. Just wait." Bofsky had stolen something from him, and Renhant knew what it was. His pride. He remembered the sister he'd wanted to be so proud of him.

"So, my baby brother's going to follow in his sis's footsteps and graduate from the academy." Reenna Chi'lita Renhant reached across the table and ruffled his hair with one hand. "You deserve a night out on the town for this." Standing, she paid for his treat, and they stepped into the shopping arcade. "Of course, it won't be easy, Rennie, but you'll love it. The academy'll be like family after a while. *Your* family."

He grabbed her hand and led her to an arcade counter, the games involving shooting and throwing. Smiling at him, she slipped out a credit for him to put in the machine. Looking up, he was surprised to see tears running down her face.

"I am so proud of you, Rennie. No matter what happens, I'll always be proud of you. Nothing you could do will ever take that away." As she stopped right there in the middle of everything and hugged him, he hugged her back, knowing he would make her proud, would make MegaCorp proud. He would do that for his sister no matter what the future

21

held.

He would never let his sister down, whatever that promise demanded from him.

THE BOYS felt the ziptites jerk tight around their wrists. Not criminals, at least not to each other, only a tenday earlier they had been on the road to graduation, the honors of the academy theirs. Now, they were being looked upon as MegaCorp trash. Couldn't the others see them for what they really were? Officers! The short time until graduation didn't matter; this was Jer'son, Renhant, and Barn't, the same guys who sat in class, ran the drills, and joked at the mess table.

At least none of the other uppercadets would be in the corridors with them. The three of them wouldn't have to listen to the mocking calls, the whistles of derision, or the taunts made by the others who were just glad three more competitors were out of the running for the top spots at graduation.

RENHANT STOOD at his instructor's invitation. It was his third year at the academy, and this was the final day of the session. He looked at his score as the instructor raised her hands and started to clap, the entire class joining in and cheering for him.

He held his head high. He deserved this, although he had twisted every rule in the book to make it come true. His score was the highest ever recorded in her class. He had known her reputation for toughness when he signed up for her class, and he had made it his business to learn who his smartest classmates would be. It hadn't been hard, really. A planned "chance" meeting at meals, the shoulder bumped in the games room, the quick apology and introduction, and a "friendship" was formed, one beneficial at least to him.

Then, later, the friendship firmly entrenched, had come the first payment. *You're my closest friend, and I'm not as good at this as you are. Can I please borrow your study notes?* Sometimes he had to twist an arm to get what he wanted, but this was worth it.

He smiled, taking pride in the honor being bestowed on him by his teacher and classmates. Running his eyes across the room of cheering students, he stopped at one boy in the back who wasn't cheering. He paused, glancing away, remembering.

"That's cheating, Renhant. I can't give you the answers. Besides, they always watch. They'll know if you copy."

"I wouldn't be copying. I will be absent that day. I need your answers to study with, that's all. Besides, when I go in for my make-up exam, the real test'll be already over, so how could it be copying?" At the boy's doubtful look, Renhant stepped closer to him. "I really need this. You and I are friends, or at least that's what I thought. All I'm asking for is a little help here."

"We are friends, Renhant. I told you so, but this just doesn't seem right."

"You mean it doesn't seem right to help a friend. That's where we stand, huh?"

"No, that's not it." The boy looked at him pleadingly. "If I give you my answers, you'll use them just to study with, right, not to use on the test?"

Renhant smiled and stepped away. "That's right, just for studying. I wouldn't use them on the test at all. That would be cheating, wouldn't it?" He put his arm around the boy's shoulder, reassuring him they were still the closest of friends, even if they really weren't, not by any stretch of the imagination.

"LITTLE GIRL! Can't you make it like the rest of the boys?" The instructor's voice mocked Barn't.

It was his first year at the academy, and no matter what he did, he couldn't keep up with the bigger boys on his team. He looked up. Just three more pegs, and he'd be at the top, the current nightmare over.

"Don't pee your panties!" The other boys laughed at the instructor's deriding gibes.

All the other guys had been to the top, some of them on the first try. He knew his team couldn't move on until he grabbed the top peg. Frustrated, he felt his eyes grow damp. He wasn't good at this. They should know that. Every boy should be allowed at least one thing he wasn't good at. Some of the guys weren't as good at the other skills learned in their class lessons, but no one made fun of them for that. No, it was "get some extra help after class" for them. Well, no one was giving him any extra help now. Just the laughing.

He reached for the next peg and pulled himself up, his muscles quivering with the strain. He held on, sweat beading his face, and looked up. Two more pegs. Just two more pegs, and they'd quit laughing. He released one hand, opening and closing it, trying not to think about the blister forming on his palm. He reached out and grasped the second peg. With fire shooting through his shoulder, he inched his body up until he could see the top peg just above his head. Just that one was all he had to do, then he would be part of the team. They'd stop laughing at him then. All he had to do was touch it, just one quick touch.

His breath vibrating from his lungs, he opened a hand and grabbed at it, eliciting a spattering of cheers from below.

Working his way back down, barely able to keep from slipping, he dropped heavily to the floor. Standing, holding to the wall to steady his quivering legs, he turned to his team. One of them spat at him, "You almost made us lose. Even a baby could climb that. Sissy." Then, the team was gone, on to the next challenge, his efforts forgotten.

He didn't forget, though. He knew just who had laughed at him. He would always remember. He wouldn't forget them, even if they forgot him. Ever.

JER'SON KICKED the door, and again, and again. How dare they lock him in this room! He was an overcadet, a respected member of the academy. It wasn't his fault his instructor had killed himself.

Jer'son had indisputable proof that all he had done was tell the truth. Anyway, if the instructor hadn't failed him, nobody would've had to know, would they? He wouldn't have had to write that message and broadcast it on the intraship network.

He yelled through the small opening in the door, "I didn't do it. He killed himself. I wasn't even there."

Then, the door swinging wide, in walked an officer flanked by two guards. The officer walked to the table in the middle of the room and slapped a glass down on the table.

"You wrote this. We have proof of that." He spat his contempt

"If I did?" Jer'son had. It was his broadcast playing on the surface.

"Where did you get this information?"

Ah, now he knew where this was headed. He could back up his facts, because they were true. He had friends who knew. They'd been there, been with the girl, said she looked just like her father, and when they had asked her, she admitted the instructor was her father. Jer'son had to suppress a grin, though. It seemed she hadn't really wanted to admit who her father was until after a little rough "play." Jer'son knew she had also owned up to a few other top brass who'd spent time with her.

Now on confident ground, Jer'son retorted, "Check it out. The records are there at the spaceport I talked about. The instructor's daughter really is a sky-walker. Keeps the military happy when the ships come in. I even know a few captgen'ls who have been with her, even the one on this ship." He smirked. "I guess the instructor didn't know."

The officer grabbed the glass and handed it to one of the guards. "Take this and check out the kid's story. See if he's telling us the truth." Turning to Jer'son, he growled, "We have proof you were nowhere near the instructor's quarters when he was killed. It's the only thing saving your hide about now. Let's just hope your story checks out. Otherwise you'll be held as accessory, suicide or not." The officer turned and walked out of the room, the remaining guard with him. When Jer'son heard the locking mechanism click over in the door, he raised his foot and kicked it again.

It's true, he thought. *You can bet on that.* Then, with nothing to do in the barren space, he sat on the lone chair in the room and put his head on the table.

THE LIFT BLINKED red three times, and then with a sudden flash of green, the doors slid open. The three boys, hands behind their backs, resolutely stepped in. Their two guards followed, their weapons at the ready. As the doors closed, it was as if the light from the boys' world was eclipsed from around them. MegaCorp Military Academy was gone. They were leaving behind all they'd worked for. Never again would they be looked on as the future hope of MegaCorp. From this point on, they were nothing more than washed-up has-beens.

However, there was something new, a connection forming deep inside each boy. There were three of them, and they were a team. They had a pact, and that pact was stronger than what was coming up. That pact was stronger than Rant ever could be.

In the coming days, the three teenagers would need that strength. It would be the only thing to see them through.

—Chapter 2—

Twelve men walking
Came upon a tree.
Left one hanging,
I'm glad it wasn't me.

Eleven men talking
Thought they'd done right.
They didn't know
I got away that night.

—From "The Legend of
Tommy Boy"

THE LIFT STOPPED, and the doors slid open. No one moved. None of the boys wanted to be the first to take that step toward an uncertain future. Someone else's life lay outside that lift door. Not Renhant's life. Certainly not Barn't's. Most importantly, not the world Jer'son had imagined; he would not let it be his future.

Finally, out of patience, one of the guards bumped

Jer'son with his weapon. Knocked off balance, he stumbled off the lift, inadvertently leading the other two to a place none of them wanted to go. He turned just in time to see Barn't and Renhant stumbling after him.

Ahead, the airlock loomed above them as they approached, the jumpship just on the other side. At a motion from the guard on his right, Jer'son stopped, and Barn't, head down, preoccupied with his situation, ran full speed into him.

"Crikes! You little idiot!" Jer'son hissed his irritation at his friend's carelessness. "Can't you even watch where you're going?"

"Shut your traps up!" the guard on the left snapped. "You sissies aren't causing any problems here. Got that?" When the boys didn't respond, the guard repeated his question, "Got that?" stepping behind them and hitting Jer'son in the back with the butt of his weapon.

"Yes, ser," the ex-overcadet coughed out.

"You other two?"

"Yes, ser," came the boys' replies.

"Glad you agree." Snide humor laced the words. "You pissants better mind your p's and q's. Word's out about that little wussy you killed."

"Seen his picture. Too pretty to waste." His partner snorted his disgust.

"Don't let it get to you, Aain'sl. We never would have had access to that particular little piece."

"Yeah. But still." He turned to the three boys again. "Bofsky was the only man among you. One of him is worth three of you. Thank the stars this academy still trains at least

29

a few good officers to lead us into the future." The guard cleared his throat, then spat a wad at the boys' feet.

"Damn right. Men like Bofsky are what this academy needs. Ship out the riffraff like you three," the other guard seconded with a laugh.

Renhant, Barn't, and Jer'son looked at each other, knowing a different story about Bofsky, also understanding it was useless to speak up. Revenge would have to come a different way.

One of the guards whipped out a pass and held it in front of a scanner. The airlock doors immediately cycled open. "Inside, boys. It's time to get the filth off this ship. Crowd 'em up. We're coming, too."

This time, the guards didn't wait for the boys to move. Slamming into them, their weapons as rams, they pushed the boys forward into the airlock, forcing them to stumble over one another.

"Can't walk too good, huh? Lost your manhood when you lost your chance at being an officer, is that it, trash?" The guards looked at each other and grinned.

The boys regained their feet and stood, humiliated and frightened, their hands still bound behind their backs. It was plain they had no options except to take whatever the guards decided to dish out. There was no one to take up for them. As far as anyone outside MegaCorp would know, they were simply being posted to a new assignment. This would be an assignment, however, at which they would never be heard from again.

One of the guards, leaning around to trigger the ship's side of the airlock door, leaned hard into Jer'son, already sore and miserable from his beating the night before. When the man whispered into his ear, "Pretty toy," and ran his tongue along his cheek, the boy reacted.

"Get away from me, you pervert!" he hissed, slamming the side of his head hard directly into the guard's face.

JER'SON PULLED at the ziptites around his wrists, but they didn't budge. He hadn't expected they would, but in his anger, that didn't stop him from trying. It was the stink of the man next to him, the sour smell of someone who ate too many spicy foods and didn't shower often enough. The need to get away overwhelmed him.

He knew what the man had wanted when he made him stand outside his cell that morning. The way he had looked at him, the leer when he handed Jer'son the clothes, had said it all.

Later, when he led him to the shower, the man had stood there, refusing to look away. Jer'son hadn't wanted to take off his clothes, not with those hated eyes all over him. It wasn't just the bruises from his beating the night before. It was a flashback to the nights when he had first come to the academy.

As Jer'son had peeled one garment after another, the chill of the room hitting his bare skin, he had glanced at his "caretaker." A leer stared back, the grin disgusting in all its coarseness and perversity. He had turned away to cover himself, but the man barked at him, "This way, boy. I can't have you doing something I can't see, can I?" He prodded him with the tip of his weapon. Then, when Jer'son didn't respond fast enough, a hand grabbed his shoulder, spinning him around, forcing him to stand under the needle-like spray, exposed and unprotected.

Jer'son's stomach had knotted when he saw it was the same guard escorting them on the jumpship. When the man hit him in the back, forcing him forward, he had wanted to swing around and slam his arms into his face. He knew he was lucky, though, to have the second guard with them, because he was sure what the man wanted to do, would do, too, if he got the chance. One, surely, would keep the other reined in.

Then, in the airlock, the man was right next to him, too close, closer than he had to be, even in that small space. He felt his hand on him, touching his side, sliding across his clothing and touching him *there.*

Jer'son tensed. He could stand it. They would be on the jumpship soon, and the man surely couldn't bother him there. Then, the brute leaned against him, gripping his crotch in a tight squeeze, and he whispered ever so softly in Jer'son's ear, licking his face as he kneaded between his legs.

The airlock with the guards and his friends at his side melted away, and it was the training ship in front of Jer'son's eyes. In that moment, he was thirteen again.

"Yes, this is the one I told you about, the pretty one. See what attractive features he has?"

Jer'son looked up and smiled at the two men talking about him. He didn't know the one man, but the other was his activities instructor.

It was his first year at the academy, and he liked all his teachers. Most of them liked him, too, or at least they seemed to. At thirteen, nearly fourteen, now, he had grown a lot since his induction. Last tenday his dorm leader had even sent him to the barber to have his face shaved.

It made him feel special to get noticed. He was also glad his activities instructor had helped him change to a different bunk, one that was off around a corner. Now he had some privacy. His bunk couldn't be seen from the other bunks in his dorm.

His instructor had suggested the move, telling him the other boy was willing to give up the bunk, even though he wouldn't explain why. When Jer'son had agreed, a big grin on his face, the other boy had just swept up his things with relief and dumped them on Jer'son's old bunk.

That first night, Jer'son woke with a start. Something didn't feel right. Someone was by his bunk, hands touching him. He lay very still, afraid to move, hoping the person would go away and leave him alone. Yet, the person kept touching until Jer'son couldn't lie to himself any longer. The hand was no accident, and it wasn't going away.

When it was finally over, the hands covered Jer'son and walked away, leaving him to cry himself to sleep. He now knew why the other boy had been so willing to change bunks.

For the rest of his first year at the academy, he didn't know which nights the hands would return. As he soon found out, they would return often, coming up with ever more inventive things to do to the boy cowering in the bunk.

When the guard licked his face, all those memories came flooding back, and Jer'son snapped. "Get away from me, you pervert!" No man was *ever* going to touch him like that again. He would get this man's hands off him, whatever the consequences. With a blaze of red-hot fury wiping reason from his mind, he attacked with the only thing he had available, his head.

Jer'son slammed his skull sideways directly into the guard's face and was gratified to feel him let go. His moment of triumph was short lived, however. Before he could turn in triumph, he felt a blazing flash of light start at the back of his head, and in a slow-motion arc, he fell ever so gradually into the incandescent core of a fiery sun.

JER'SON STOOD proudly at the helm of a starship, and he looked through the viewscreen at the offending vessel attacking the helpless world below. His ship's weapons would pulverize them until they sent all their escape pods from their ejection ports and gave their ship up for dead. He would protect all the children on this hapless world from these vile aggressors.

"CaptGen'l Jer'son, here are the reports you requested."

Jer'son took the portable glass in his hand and swiped his fingers above it to scroll through the information. It was just as he had thought. In spite of the enemy's pleas for mercy, their cries of innocence, soldiers from that contemptible crew were attacking the planet below in the middle of the night, raping innocent women and children. He now had the proof in his hands. How could he allow that to continue?

"Gunners, lock on target." Jer'son stood and walked the bridge, making sure all gunners' fingers were poised over the red "fire" icons. "Repeat after me, men. We must protect the children."

In turn, the gunners repeated Jer'son's phrase. They had to understand they were destroying the enemy's ship because of what their soldiers were doing to the poor innocent children on the planet below. This was not a mission of vengeance, but of rescue for those who could not help themselves.

"Ser," a voice interrupted him. "There's a message coming in from the enemy ship. Should I put it on the viewscreen?"

He laughed in derision. "One last cry for mercy? Sure, let's hear it." He looked around the bridge at his gunners as the message came onboard. He had a reputation as a captgen'l of steel, and this attempt to divert his ship's attack was bound to be an over-the-top drama production. However, nothing would bend his resolve, and his men knew it.

"Fal'dera, it's your mother. It's really me, and I'm on board that ship in front of you. Please don't fire. There are good men onboard. They are trying to save the children on the planet below."

He stared, then turned to his men, his face hard. "This is the most despicable of tricks, men. See how low they are willing to go? Fire!"

Then, the scene shifting as dreams will do, he was on a tall dais, the wind whipping flags that towered over extensive parade grounds. He rose to his feet, his promotion to overgen'l making him stand tall, his pride in his ship and his men having been put before all else. As a hand pinned his new rank on his overjacket, a voice whispered in his ear, "You let children be raped for this promotion. You even killed your mother to get where you are today."

"No!" He tore the medal from his overjacket, throwing it far away. "It's not my fault. I don't want to be overgen'l. They tricked me into doing it. I want my mother back."

"Too late," the voice said.

When he looked down at his overjacket, the medal was still there.

WHEN JER'SON had yelled out, and his head slammed into the guard, Barn't and Renhant had tensed in the small space. They watched the guard, blood now streaming from his nose, raise his weapon and slam it against Jer'son's head, crumpling the boy to the floor.

The guards looked at each other over the boys' heads. The second one chuckled, remarking with a leer, "Just takes some of them longer to get used to the new order of things."

As he reached out and triggered the door, the first guard barked at Barn't and Renhant, "You two, over here and turn around." He clipped the ties off their wrists. "Now he's yours to carry. Pick him up, and let's go." Then the guard grabbed Barn't's arm and stopped him. "You. First, come here." At the look of fear in the boy's face, the guard laughed. "Don't worry, kid. You're safe around me. I only like the mature ones. It's Tan'sn over there you've got to worry about. He likes 'em sweet and tender, just like you," and he laughed as he grabbed the front of Barn't's shirt to wipe the blood off his face. Pushing Barn't away, red now staining the front of his shirt, the guard pointed. "Runt, get your friend."

As Barn't knelt by Jer'son, he looked in Renhant's eyes.

They both flinched as the guard barked, "Carry him like he's your best friend, because from here on out, he's your only one."

Stepping into the jumpship, the two friends held Jer'son between them, his arms around their necks. The second guard blocked the way to the main cabin, and he jerked his head the other way. The other direction they saw six rough slings, three on each side of what appeared to be a cargo hold.

"Set your friend down over there." One guard pointed, indicating the three across the back wall. "Drop him in the middle one. You two take the ones on either side. Hop to it. It's a full day even on this jumpship, and I don't want to be in here with you any longer than necessary." Then the guard walked up to Barn't and took his face in his hands. "Well, maybe with you, little one. But, our time is not to be, not on this trip. Later, maybe." He pointed to Jer'son. "Load him up, boys, and get yourselves seated." He reached out a hand and roughly pushed the injured boy out of his friends' arms and into the sling with the words, "Like this. Now, strap in."

The first guard walked up and grabbed a strap from the ceiling, pulling a chain curtain to the floor, and locking it in place. "See," he said. "We're safe from you, and you're safe from us. Too bad your friend there got himself knocked out. I might have kept him on this side. I might have even let you two watch." With a guffaw of laughter, he grabbed an opaque visor from a rack over his head, flung himself into his seat, and closed his eyes. "Three jumps to get to our next stop: Rant, Planet of the Damned. Enjoy your vacation, boys."

RENHANT WATCHED the second guard reach into the locker above his head. He pulled out an extra visor, hefting it in his hand and grinning.

"So, boys. I guess you don't know what to expect traveling on one of these ships." He turned to his partner with a malicious grin. "After all, the jumpships are just for the highest military purposes. Like today. The general public doesn't even know they exist. It is quite an honor to be allowed to travel in one, meaning the honoree is of quite high military rank."

"I think you've got it wrong, Tan'sn," his partner sniggered, lifting his visor for a moment. "These losers fall at the other end of the spectrum."

"But they are pretty. So, this being their first trip, and last, I might add, surely they should be given the best of accommodations." The guard walked over and made as if to offer Renhant the visor through the chain curtain. "Oops! Doesn't seem I can get this through the curtain. Hm. I guess you'll have to do the jump without it. If you hadn't been such bad boys, I'd probably let you wear one. But, no treats for the mean old guard means you three, oh, that's right, you *two* have to do without. Sorry, boys. You know, this is the only part of this jumpship that's not shielded. I hear it's pretty gruesome, or at least the yells of the detainees we transport sound that way. They won't ever tell us about it, though. Enjoy!"

With that, the guard slipped his visor on and fell into his sling.

Renhant lay still, not having any idea what to expect,

when he noticed the whine of the engines increasing in pitch. As the sound rose out of his range of hearing, he noticed the edges of his vision turning pink. His heart jerked into motion, and then he felt the pain begin. His arms and legs were torn from his body. He could feel the tendons snapping and the blood vessels releasing their hold on each other, spraying his body's life-giving energies into the emptiness of space around him. Then, when he could take no more, the globules of his blood turned to fire, pelting his body, burning his clothing from him, searing his skin until the very meat of his body began to roast. Then, he began feasting on his own flesh, consumed with a hunger he knew he could never satisfy.

BARN'T RAN his fingers in the sand. He looked up from the shore and saw his mommy standing there waving at him, his mommy from *before*, when his mommy and his dad were still together, and his dad didn't drink all day long. This would be a good vacation. He knew that.

Sometimes he came on vacation and his new stepmom locked him out of the house. He had to stay outside all day just like when he was at home. His dad never believed him when he told. His dad just believed his stepmom. After a while, his dad would start hitting him, calling him a liar.

Finally, he had quit telling. It was just what he did when his dad went away each day, spent the time outside. Not when his mommy had been here. She always let him back inside. Maybe today she would come outside and play.

"Je'main, I see you're building something in the sand. What is it?" His mommy walked to the edge of the sand and stood there, her dress blowing in the wind, her hair brown and long.

"It's a sand castle, Mommy. It'll have big towers and flags on the top and everything. I have little men and women I can put at the tops of the towers so they can look out at the sea and see the boats coming. That way if someone gets lost, the people on the towers can help the lost people find their way home." He smiled.

"That's nice. Your father will be home in just a little while, and I've prepared us something really nice to eat. Would you like that? Something really nice to eat?" His mother stood at the edge of the sand looking at him and then turning to peer across the sea at the horizon, as if she could sense something coming.

"Mommy, come play with me first, please. It's been so long since you've played a game with me. I've missed you." Barn't looked at his mother with pleading in his eyes. "Just this one time. Just today. Dad's not home yet, and I won't ask you to play very long. Please?"

His mother sighed. She turned to the house and then held up her hand to shade her eyes as she looked back to the horizon. Barn't then saw her look high in the sky.

"What are you looking for, Mommy?"

"Oh, nothing, dear. I'm just hoping, I guess. More wishing than anything else."

"Mommy, why do you sound sad?"

"I'm not sad, Je'main. I just need a rest, that's all."

She put her hands in her pockets as if it were chilly, but Barn't felt very warm out in the sun.

"Mommy, will you come play in the sun with me? It's

40

very warm out here."

She looked at him and smiled that warm smile he liked so much, the one she always smiled when she covered him up at night and told him to not let the bedbugs bite.

"I guess I could come out for a few minutes. Let me go put my other shoes on."

"No, Mommy," he cried, suddenly afraid. If she went inside, she might not come back out, and she was here, now. She was with him, and he hadn't seen her in so long. "Stay outside with me, Mommy. You can take your shoes off here. You can put your shoes back on when we're finished playing, and then you can go inside."

"Sweetie, that just won't do. I must have my outside shoes on to play on the beach. I promise I'll be right back." She ran to the house. She turned and looked at Barn't, and she blew him a kiss. He reached up and caught it. He waved it high in the air, showing her what a good catcher he was. His mother laughed and waved, standing there for a moment, her hair blowing in the breeze. He loved her so much. He watched her as she turned and walked into the house, closing the door behind her.

Barn't jumped as a huge crash came from the house. He turned to look out at the water and closed his eyes. His mommy might really be there, might still be there, if he didn't turn around and look.

The back door slammed open as his dad threw the screen door wide, yelling at him, "Where is that empty-headed woman I married? And why is this back door locked? Je'main, did you lock yourself outside again? And why did your mother have to give you such a sissy name?

41

Every time I call you, the whole neighborhood knows." He spat into the dirt, his face red with anger. "Stupid boy. When your mother was alive, you never locked yourself out of the house."

As his father turned to go back inside, an unseen window slammed shut on the other side of the house, and a few moments later, a vehicle from around the corner roared away, just as it did every day when Barn't was locked out of the house.

Barn't didn't want to open his eyes, because he knew what would be there. He didn't want to see. He wanted his mother to come back, so he just sat with his eyes closed and waited. Finally, his father came down the steps and walked up to him. He kicked him and said, "I don't know what you're doing sitting here in the yard all day. There's nothing here I can see except this grass that always needs mowing and these fenced walls closing me in. Gods above and below, I hate this place." He kicked Barn't again. "Get inside, boy. You'll never make anything of yourself out here. Besides, your stepmother finally has dinner on the table. I just can't figure out what that woman does all day. Not for the likes of me."

Barn't jerked, the vibration of the jumpship and the webbed seat cutting into his legs as they tried to bring him back to reality. The thought he tried to keep hold of was, *If I keep my eyes closed, maybe it'll go away. Just maybe.*

At first he was grateful when the jumpship faded away again. After a moment, he wasn't, not when his own personal hell swept over him once more.

JER'SON'S EYES flew open. Blearily he stared straight ahead, his breathing hard, feeling something funny in his mouth. His stomach churning, he turned and found Renhant and Barn't on either side of him.

Looking ahead of him though a chain curtain, he saw the two guards who had escorted them. One was snoring. Both were sleeping with opaque visors across their faces.

It was only then he noticed his two friends were gripping his own hands tightly, as if very afraid of something they couldn't see in the dark.

Then, with a twist of his gut, and a knife thrust of pain driving through his head, he slumped over, and he was gone again.

A MILLION YEARS later, and yet just as quickly as the nightmare had started, Renhant was back in the sling. The guards snored under their visors.

"Barn't. Barn't, Jer'son's making funny noises."

He watched his friend jerk his eyes open to the inside of the jumpship, the chain still separating them from the other side of the compartment and the two guards, one with the marks of a nosebleed on his upper lip. Turning his head, he could scc Barn't narrow his eyes at Jer'son. Bloody bubbles oozed out of the injured boy's mouth.

Barn't mouthed, "The guards?" He motioned to the two sleeping men.

Renhant shook his head back and forth, mouthing that they already knew and didn't care.

Barn't reached over and shook Jer'son. All he got was a moan. Reaching his sleeve up, he tried to dry the red spittle bubbling out of his friend's mouth.

Renhant, emotionally empty, shook his head in resignation, lay back, and closed his eyes. If this wasn't hell, he didn't know what was.

JER'SON JERKED awake, his heart beating like a drum. He turned at the sound of a caustic voice.

"How about it, boys? That jump made the others sound like girls on a sleepover. Care to share a few of the details?" At the looks of unbridled terror on the boys' faces, the guards slumped in their seats. "Thought not. It never hurts to ask, though."

The first guard stood and looked in through the chain curtain. "Hey, look, Tan'sn. We might both get a treat this trip. My favorite in the middle is back awake. I was starting to think I had to take the big one over there. I was just hoping he wouldn't be too much for me." Turning back to Jer'son, he smiled. "Hey, sweetie, how long you been awake?"

Jer'son kicked the chain in reply.

The guard leaned over to his friend. "I guess he doesn't want to play nice, Aain'sl."

"So, I guess that means we get to play rough, Tan'sn. I like it better that way." They both burst into riotous laughter.

Finally, the second guard—Aain'sl—stood up, flipping Tan'sn a set of code crystals. He reached down, unlocked, and raised the chain curtain. At the surprised looks on the boy's faces, he said, "That was the third jump, boys. When you're jumping unshielded, every jump seems like the first one. Isn't that right, Tan'sn? Wouldn't you say that?"

Tan'sn stepped over, pulling Barn't from his sling, running his hand over the boy's face. "Pretty and sweet, you know? Pick 'em ripe when they taste the best." He pushed Barn't to the door. "I wouldn't know about the jumps. I've never done one unshielded. Never want to, either." He reached down and pulled Renhant up, running his hand up and down Renhant's arm before letting him exit after Barn't. "Such pretty boys. We don't get them on this run that often. Too bad we can't stay and visit with them. We could build such fond memories together." He looked back to the second guard. "It'll take me a few minutes to check those other two in if you'd like some private time together. The station's mostly downplanet this run, so no one'll know." He winked at his friend and walked out the door.

The remaining guard stood over Jer'son and leered at him. He grabbed the straps holding the sling chair to the ceiling and leaned over to look him right in the eyes. "I asked for this duty today. I knew you'd get assigned to Rant. There was no way you three were going to walk. I've overheard the little one telling everyone who would listen to him that he'd get off, that they wouldn't send you three here. Well, guess what? You're here.

"I enjoyed that little peep show in the shower. I just wonder if we should check out some of those bruises right here, find out where they all are, and just see how good my memory is. I was looking pretty closely back there, and I don't forget much." The guard reached to pull Jer'son's shirt open, and Jer'son drew up his legs as if to protect himself from the guard's advances. "How sweet! My toy wants to play hard-to-get. Like I said earlier, I like to play rough."

With those words, Jer'son, who had been squirming in the sling as if afraid of the guard, let his legs loose like the coiled springs he had made of them. He was academy trained, and the guard should have remembered that. He shouldn't have given him such an obvious opportunity for action. Ramming his feet directly into the man's crotch, injuring the delicate body parts that he so wanted to inflict on his captive, Jer'son yelled in defiance. As the guard grabbed his manhood with his hands, dropping to the floor in agony, Jer'son climbed out of the sling and kicked the man again.

"That one's for the first time I was touched," Jer'son erupted violently, not meaning his interactions with the guard. Instead, he remembered those nights so long ago, those dark stretches lying awake not knowing if he would have a visitor, relieved when he didn't, and hating himself the times he did. Sometimes it had felt good, and that's why he'd never told, not really for his parents or because he was afraid of being kicked out of the academy, and he hated himself for that.

"That's for the second time I was touched." His boot connected yet again. It took a long time for him to kick out all the times he'd been visited that year, but he knew every one. He had relived each of those moments in his head so many times during those long nights that he could never forget a one. With each instance recalled, rage boiled inside, and with unbridled fury, he lit into the guard one more time.

This time when he yelled, "Keep your hands off me, pervert," the man did. As Jer'son walked out of the jumpship, he knew he had learned to fight back, and if anyone needed any proof, all they had to do was walk into the rear of the jumpship. There was their proof, lying on the floor, holding his degenerate crotch, moaning like the pervert he had proven himself to be. Now he had to find Barn't and Renhant. They were a team, and when guys were a team, they took care of their own. He knew that's what they'd have to do here, stick together, stand up for one another, and take care of their own, no matter who got hurt.

Jer'son stopped and called out, just to hear his words spoken aloud, "No matter who gets hurt." It sounded good to him. It sounded really good to him. He repeated the words louder, just to hear them once more, "No matter who gets hurt." They echoed off the metal walls; and somehow, they made him stronger inside.

—Chapter 3—

Caution: Watch Your Step

*—Found on sign being
removed as an old-Earth
escalator was dismantled*

JER'SON HEADED off the jumpship, his adrenalin running strong. He wanted to punch something—or someone. He recalled his Redback martial arts training—a final course at the academy he now wished he'd had the opportunity to complete—and he felt the bloodrush from the fight in the cargo flood his muscles once again. When he triggered the door, slapping the sensor hard, it opened immediately, and that stopped him for a moment. It meant there was no airlock. Clearly, they had arrived in either a land-based hangar or a shipboard landing bay. His thoughts skipped across places he'd traveled on the academy ship, and he quickly eliminated one of those possibilities. He didn't know much more about jumpships than the rumors he had heard, but one thing was obvious. Jumpships did not have atmospheric capabilities. There would be no room in the ship for both the jumpdrive and an ordinary ion propulsion drive, no matter how efficient either one was.

However, his military training told him this was no moment for self-congratulation. He and his friends had just been transported across half the arm of the galaxy, subjected to verbal and mental torture, and one of those friends had been threatened with rape. Threatened? His thoughts darkened, and he punched the side of the jumpship. It had been no threat. The guard he had left on the floor was proof of that.

Looking around the landing bay, he saw no sign of Renhant or Barn't. It seemed the guard who had gone with them had expected him to be hand delivered sometime later. Now, he had no guide, but the layout of the building couldn't be too far off what he knew, not if it was operated by MegaCorp.

He stepped through massive glassine doors leading into the facility proper, his eyes raking the area for signs. There had to be indicator markers directing people around the station. He paused, letting his training do the work. They hadn't yet arrived at the real prison, for they were off planet, and the thought of stealing the jumpship, what with being unguarded, flashed through his mind. *Home! Freedom!* Still, there were real problems with that. The most obvious was he didn't know how to pilot one. A T404 Trainer, sure. But this? He'd never had the training, and now he never would. The second was really two others: Renhant and Barn't. If he left, they were going, and he didn't know where they were. So, in order to take the next step, whatever that might be, he'd better find his friends. Better that than being separated.

Stopping at the end of the first corridor, he saw two markers. One pointed two ways, left and right. The second clearly stated that all transferees were to be kept under guard at all times. "Too late," he muttered. "Now, left or right? What's left? I'm going left." He loped down the corridor, surprised to find no one to stop him, check him for ID, or otherwise be stationed anywhere, before he remembered Tan'sn's offhand remark about station personnel being downside. It made sense to his military mind. Zen'ri's death had been unexpected, and they had been bumped out here without warning. What if their arrival was also unexpected? All this place would need would be a skeleton crew to keep it operating unless a ship was scheduled in. But, that didn't explain where to find Renhant and Barn't.

Searching, he finally came to several doors that opened at his approach. Two of those rooms showed signs of recent habitation, and one was obviously a dorm. But the location he was most relieved to find was the station-monitoring center. He had thought the station must have one of these. The academy training ship had one. He'd even manned it on numerous occasions. On any academy vessel, everything was monitored: meals; activities rooms; even showers. Unless there was an override emergency, no one could get access to some of the more private inputs, such as toilets and personal quarters, but public spaces like gathering rooms, including communal showers, were continually under observation for everyone. Only when inputs failed or had blind spots did opportunities for mischief arise. That was how he and his friends had taken advantage of new recruits to extort credits from them.

He entered the room and smiled, pleased with himself. This was equipment he knew how to operate. He sat at the console and began running his hands over the controls, recognizing the familiar layout, quickly changing and zooming various images. One screen he too quickly flipped past had something that looked interesting. Reversing the series of images, he found what seemed to be a games room. On one wall was a display of current events. He zoomed the view, and there was the explanation for the empty rooms.

Skill or Luck, the sign read. *Who Goes Home? Join in the most anticipated event of the year where one lucky person gets a free pass off this rock. Be sure to enter your idea early. All personnel posted to our lovely environs are eligible, whether downside or stationside. Your duty rotation makes no difference. You may participate.*

Then, in smaller letters he had to enlarge to read, he saw, *Must Be Present to Win.* He chortled, "Ha! Even with us coming in, no one wanted to miss out on this contest."

His eyes catching a familiar shape in a small display at the top of the wall, he pulled the feed to the main board. There in front of him were Renhant and Barn't, and they did not look happy at all. He cringed with what he expected would soon happen to him.

Another feed caught his eye, and that feed showed the jumpship's opened hatch. There, stumbling out, was his guard. Well, maybe not his, personally, but the one who'd wanted to play with him during transit, and he didn't look happy. He watched him hit a panel on the wall, klaxons started wailing, and the feeds went dark.

Jer'son groaned. He'd been found out, and he suspected he wasn't going to like what happened next.

"AAIN'SL, I won't allow you to do this. You know the rules." Tan'sn, his shoulders wide with muscle, growled as he threw his fellow guard against the wall.

"You coward. Get your hands off me, Tan'sn." Aain'sl snarled, his lip curling. "You saw what that yellow-backed kid did to me while we were loading the jumpship. All I did was lean over to key the door lock, and he head butted me. You saw the blood."

Tan'sn leaned into him, forcing him to remain against the wall, all the while whispering into his ear, "Coward? You fat slob. I also saw you groping his crotch and licking his face. The image feeds can probably even tell us what you said." He rocked hard into the man to get his attention, lapsing into the native slang of his youth. "How many flimmy repeats do I got to speak you? They don't got no eye-suck feeds in the back of the jumpship. That were your chance. It be done, now." He backed away, letting his friend get some air and space.

"How about the kid kicking me over and over, huh, Tan'sn?" Aain'sl pulled up one sleeve to show a blackening bruise. "You going to allow him to get away with that?"

"Sissy." It was the worst of insults. However, calmed, his MegaCorp standard speech was back. "You gave away your manhood to the first scumbag who wanted you, and you've never gotten it back. You forgetting? No image feeds in the cargo hold. You have no proof that kid did anything to you, and you know it."

"What about the blood, my blood? It's all over the place."

"Remember the rules. Neither Rant nor MegaCorp cares what happens in transit as long as it doesn't make it to an image feed. You broke that today. You want to be shipped downside? Why I even let you cohabitate with me, I'll never know. You are an uncouth loudmouth." Tan'sn slapped Aain'sl up beside the head. "You had better consider withdrawing that complaint, or you may be the one staying here next time."

Still furious, Aain'sl hissed, "I'll do as you ask. This time. I'll withdraw the complaint, but I won't forget what he did to me."

"That's all I ask." Tan'sn threw an arm across his friend's shoulder. "I couldn't ask you to forget. Your time'll come. Just not here and now."

"WELL, YOU'RE certainly the errant one on this station," the old man said, turning to a tray of equipment next to the examining table. "It doesn't matter, though. You'll be here a while, I guess, so what's another few moments of it as a free man? They'll be your final ones, after all. You're here until you get your promotion. That's called death, son."

Jer'son cut his eyes to the old man, refusing to let his slim grasp at hope be dashed so quickly. "I saw that sign telling about the contest. Doesn't that get people off?" His tone told of his arrogance; his words spoke pleading.

"Son, there are a hundred thousand souls on that rock down there, and six of us up here, you three included. Your chances are one hundred thousand six to one."

"Still," and Jer'son closed his eyes for a moment, his face falling, "it's a chance, someday. The sign said something about an idea. What is that about?"

"If the right idea grows in someone's mind, we won't need our contest any longer. You're fresh blood. Come up with a good one." The old man winked at him.

"What is that supposed to mean? That makes about as much sense as me being here in the first place." Jer'son snorted, his disgust coming through.

The old man stopped and looked at him through a parchment-lidded squint. After a moment, he cleared his throat. "Each idea has always failed. Most will, and rarely does anyone go home."

"If it's so hard to win, what's the point, then?"

"Continuity, my boy. Keeps us in order. Here." The man offered a hand-held razor. "Now, boy, protocol. You look pretty clean, except for the bruises, but rules are rules, and you can't change that. You can cut off all that body hair, or I will have to do it for you. Which do you prefer?"

Jer'son took the razor, remembering the video feed and how naked Renhant and Barn't had looked as they had stood, their own razors in hand. He knew he would look just the same, and like them, he would be the one to do it to himself. Turning to a mirror on the wall, he saw the old man reflected through its surface, busy at sorting items on a counter. He watched the man flick his eyes to his reflection and grin.

"Might as well get started, boy. You won't be left alone at any time here on the station, so get used to it. You'll find

Rant's not all like your trip here. Some of it, I'm sorry to admit, is even worse, but most is not."

"When do we get to the not part?" He saw the man's smile widen.

"Me, I'm glad to see Aain'sl get his due. It's rough on the kids like you when Aain'sl makes the run with them." His smile falling away, his lips pursed in momentary reflection, he looked away. "This is a prisonplanet, though, and the rules are the rules. Get to it, boy. Shower's behind me, and I'll have fresh clothes for you when you're done. They'll be prison clothes. Sorry."

"I guess it's what I should expect." He felt his remaining hope fade. "Jer'son. My name's Jer'son. What's yours?"

"Trainer. Just Trainer. Thanks, son. Not everyone asks."

In the mirror, Jer'son watched himself undress, the old man, Trainer, behind him busy at the table. Taking the razor, he made the hair fall to the floor, and as he did, one stroke of the blade at a time, the events of the day began to burn themselves into his brain. This was his life, now, and he was no longer the academy uppercadet, the toughie on campus the others feared. He was just Jer'son, a kid, and he was scared.

As the air in the room chilled his naked skin, he wasn't sure whether his shivering was from the cold or the fear of what he didn't know, or both. He wasn't sure he wanted to find out.

JER'SON STEPPED through the door and saw the backs of two familiar heads across the room sitting at a brightly topped table. Newly shaved, they weren't exactly the way he knew them, but he recognized them the same. He ran to them, grinning, and threw his arms around their necks, his heart pounding with the relief of touching someone familiar to him.

"Guys!"

Two faces turned to him, but it was Barn't who called out, "Are you all right? We didn't hear anything after our guard dropped us off. Did that man, you know, hurt you?" His eyes suddenly filled up. "I thought I would have to, I don't know, maybe kill that one guard if he touched me again. But you look all right. Doesn't he, Renhant?"

"I'm more than all right, Barn't. I took him down with a kick to his crotch and worked him over with my feet after that. He crawled out of that jumpship." He laughed at the memory. He recognized that his feeling of satisfaction was a temporary reprieve, as he looked around the room. "This seems too easy. They don't send us halfway to nowhere to just turn us loose. It feels we're riding a sun about to go nova."

Renhant nodded. "You missed the briefing. There's a contest, so only three remained assigned to the station for our check-in—"

"I know about that," interrupted Jer'son. "The contest. I saw it on a comm feed. Tell me something I don't know."

Renhant glanced at him with a frown. "That's what I'm trying to tell you. Let me finish, if you don't mind." His face had gone red, but he took a deep breath before letting it out slowly. "Sorry. It's been a rough day."

"Mine's not been exactly easy." Jer'son dropped beside him. "Or Barn't's. I guess we're all edgy."

"I shouldn't have jumped you. We all need some sleep, I think. To get on with it, tomorrow is when we get the real procedure. The station is manned by internees. So is the planet. No guards other than internees, nothing."

"So, what's the incentive for keeping the rules? Why don't the people here just take over the station and get away?" Jer'son's eyes sparkled with the prospect. He remembered the jumpship out in the bay. "Remember 5th Year Military Diversions? Oversergeant Milligan? I quote, 'If an opportunity presents itself, no matter how slim the odds, success can only be achieved by prompt and decisive action.' Anyone know how to fly an interstellar transport?"

Renhant frowned at him. "It's the food, Jer'son. Resources. Deliveries. If the station's not kept up, if the transports are ever messed with, the deliveries just stop. I think maybe that's happened a time or two, and there are people downside who don't want it to be that way again."

Jer'son sat back, thinking. "So, we just take what they dish out, let them send us down there? How bad can it be if we just try, steal the jumpship and fly on out of here?"

Barn't laughed, turning his head away from the others. "Bad, maybe. The guys signing us in just looked at us and shook their heads. Said it was a shame, sending kids, that they didn't see what the big brass at home were thinking." He looked at the others, his eyes reddening. "What's that supposed to mean, guys?"

"What it means," Renhant threw at him, "is that we stick together. We're a team, and no matter what happens, we stand up for each other."

Jer'son leaned in to finish, "No matter who gets hurt."

Like some smart-idiot guard, he finished in his head.

"No matter who gets hurt," copied Barn't.

"That's right. We stick up for each other, no matter who gets hurt." The three boys locked goals, the underdogs in this world. Like underdogs, though, they were confident they would be tougher because of it, would fight for their place, and they would do it together.

No matter who got hurt.

Breaking arms, Renhant pointed to a door off to the side. "Food, if you're hungry, Jer'son. Bunks over there." He pointed another way. "We waited up for you." He grinned. "It was sure good to see you come through that door. Want us to stick around while you eat?"

Jer'son closed his eyes, food not even entering his thoughts. First thing this morning, he had gotten up from his cell floor and showered in front of a pervert, been sentenced to prison, traveled halfway across the arm, beat up that same pervert, and now he was dressed in prison clothes. He opened his eyes with a sigh of exhaustion. "Guys, if they made a Vid of what we've gone through today, nobody'd believe it. Nah, I'm going to join you. Sleep's what I need."

As the three left the room, the lights clicked themselves off, and the room waited patiently in the darkness.

KLAXONS JERKED Barn't from sleep. He turned, putting a hand over his head. What was someone thinking? He never heard the klaxons on the ship except during drills, and those were always announced cycles ahead of time.

"Barn't." A hand shook his shoulder. "Get up."

However, all Barn't wanted was nothing more than to fall back sleep. He groaned and tucked into a tight ball.

"You heard the warning. Rise and shine."

"No way. It's my day off—" A voice nearly as loud as the alarms interrupted him.

"Inbound planetside transport docking now. Please prepare for arrival. All Rant Orbital Station access doors locking down now."

Barn't jerked his eyes open, remembering. This wasn't the academy ship. Kicking his coverings off and jumping up, he ran his hand over his head, feeling the bare skin, and he closed his eyes. Pulling open his pants, he looked. No hair there, either. Yesterday wasn't a dream.

Looking around, he saw his two friends just as disoriented, Jer'son covered with bruises.

He sat on his bunk with a sinking feeling swallowing the light from the day. Rant. This was the real deal, and he struggled to quiet the tears rising in his eyes.

Renhant called to the other two, "Hey, this door is locked. I can't get it open." He hit at it with one fist.

"It wasn't locked earlier." Jer'son picked up a loose piece of bedding, rolling it loosely and popping Barn't in the arm with one corner. He turned to Renhant and grinned. "You just aren't doing it right. Let me open it for you."

However, Barn't had already figured it out. "Everyone's back. That's why we can't get out. Did you listen to the announcement? Last night was a lull. Today scares me." He grabbed his pillow and hugged it to his chest.

They jumped at a sharp rapping on the door.

"Back away from the door." The harsh words filtered in

through hidden speakers. Another series of raps came, and then the door slipped aside. Weapons at the ready, in marched four tough-looking internee guards, one with a face that told of a brutal wound that had been poorly repaired.

"You three, you've had your vacation. Let's go. You'll be downside soon. Time to get you processed. Move."

The three youths stepped between the guards and exited into the room where they had experienced their jubilant reunion just hours earlier. Barn't turned to one of the guards to ask where they were headed. Before he could even speak, the guard slapped his shoulder with the butt of his gun.

"Just move."

Barn't did. Stepping through another door, the guards positioned themselves alongside one wall, as the boys were confronted with an examination table and an elderly medic facing the back wall. When one of the guards cleared his throat, the medic turned and laughed.

"Whoa! I see Trainer got to you before we did. Ha!" She turned back to the wall where she was preparing a series of tests and examinations for the three new visitors. "Strip," she called without turning around again.

Barn't looked at the other two, all three boys hesitating, until three of the guards stepped forward, slapping their shoulders with their gun butts. Immediately, the three boys began dropping their clothing at their feet. Barn't stood shivering, while Renhant and Jer'son crossed their arms and hugged themselves.

"Now," and the woman turned to face them, her eyes tracking directly to their bare, shaved genitals. She set a tray of instruments down, slapped the examining table with her free hand, and looking at the ceiling, once again laughed. "You three are just the naked little jaybirds, aren't you? At least it'll all grow back. I'll have to speak to Trainer again." She walked to a comm device and spoke into it. "Find Trainer. Send him to Examination A. Stat."

Walking back to the table, she shook her head. "Hazing." Fighting a smile, she elaborated for them. "Trainer likes to mark the freshies. Keeps 'em on their toes the first six months. However, it also tells everyone else who to pick on."

"Yes, ma'am?" Trainer peered through the door.

"Trainer, see these three boys?" The woman nodded in their direction.

"Yes, Medic Barkeen. They came in last night while everyone was downside."

"Why are they shaved, Trainer?"

Barn't glanced over and saw Barkeen suppress a fresh smile, angry that she knew and didn't stop it.

"I didn't do that, Medic Barkeen. They did it to themselves." This time, it was Trainer who suppressed a smile. "I just offered them the razor."

Medic Barkeen turned to the three shivering boys. "Is that so, boys?" All three nodded their heads. "All right, Trainer, you can go. Just don't touch my boys, you hear?"

He smiled. "I never do, Medic Barkeen. I never do." He backed out of the room.

Barkeen picked up a glass and looked at them. "Sixty-two standards he's been here, and he doesn't even remember why. This is his only vice, hazing you freshies. Guess that's not too bad to say about someone, is it? Makes it hard on the new recruits, though. I may have to think about requesting him to be reassigned downside next quarter. Seems a shame, though. All right, which one of you is Jer'son?"

Barn't felt slime crawl up his back, both glad it wasn't him called first, and dreading hearing his name. He watched as Jer'son stepped forward, and the medic motioned him over, slapping the table.

"Sit." As she examined him, she spoke to all three boys. "My name is Barkeen. Only one name is needed here on Rant, so only give one. Given name or surname, the choice is yours. You being ex-military, I figure you are already used to using surnames, so there we are. I'm here just like you. I was a medic on a medical transport, and a good one, too. Three society high-ups died on one of my runs, and here I am. This is what I did out there, so this is what I do here." She paused, working Jer'son's elbow, then moving on to check the bruises on his chest. "Don't try to hide what got you here. Within a day, everyone'll know anyway, and they'll use the information against you."

She stopped and turned to the other two, her expression going tight, and she slapped the top of the table with more force than seemed possible to Barn't. This time he saw tears in her eyes.

"There are some tough rovers down there. You'll have to stand up for yourselves against them, boys." She grabbed her chart, yanking it up, and flicked to a previous page. "Seventeen!" She laid it down and stood looking at them, placing her hands in her pockets.

However, to the watching Barn't, her control seemed tenuous, as if her anger might explode again at any point. He tensed for the eruption, hoping she didn't aim it his direction.

"Seventeen. You three are so young. Pretty, too." A smile ghosted her face. "I see looks of dismay on your faces. If you wish, I'll use handsome instead of pretty." Looking back at Jer'son, she added, "And a little bit of pretty," smiling at him. "There are people here who like seventeen-year-olds. Men as well as women. They'll come find you."

Barkeen returned to her examination, talking directly to Jer'son. "These bruises aren't all because you're a tough kid. I bet a few of them came from that Aain'sl. He likes 'em seventeen, tall and with pretty features like yours. I know why you're here. It's all in your chart. That chart probably tells me more than you want me to know. That instructor, your first year at the academy, he's here on Rant."

Barn't sucked in a quick breath when Jer'son flushed, his eyes narrowing to slits. He knew that look. It was one he'd seen before in his own mirror when his father screwed up his life one time too many. He hoped Barkeen watched out. Jer'son was ready to explode.

AT HER WORDS, Jer'son felt his carefully constructed self-image torn from its moorings, the old memories suddenly flooding over him once again. His feet had kicked the guard, attempting to turn loose of all those nights that year he had turned fourteen. However, now, every old memory was back, his again, never really let go.

He trembled with rage, even as his face burned with shame.

"He's bragged about that. How you laid there that year, let him come to you night after night, never fighting back, and how he even invited other instructors to go to you."

Jer'son jerked away from her hands, not wanting them on his body. He jumped off the table and turned to her, yelling, "Why are you doing this? Why are you saying this to me? Why are you humiliating me in front of my friends?" He stood there, tears running down his face, as his body shook in spasms of exposed emotions hidden away for so long he often thought them forgotten.

Barn't and Renhant, eyes wide, watched as the medic walked up to Jer'son and placed her hand on his shoulder.

"Son, for two reasons. The first is that you need to know what everyone else knows. That's a kind of power you hold in your hands. The second reason is that other people are going to do worse, much worse to you. This is the safe place to learn to deal with that. Down there, you have to make a life for yourself, and it can be a life, but it's never going to be easy. People will be cruel to you, and when they know you've let others have their way with you, they will try to take that for themselves." This time she paused, taking his face in her hands. "On any other world, this face would be a rare gift given only to the most fortunate. Here on Rant, this face may well prove to be a curse for you to bear. This is as easy as it's going to get. You will thank me later." She led him back to the examination table and slapped it again. "Face down this time."

He didn't care any longer. His worst nightmare had

been exposed, and there was nothing worse she could do to him.

He crawled on the table and ground his teeth as the medic's hand grabbed his buttocks and spread them apart. He couldn't care. His best friends knew the worst about him. He wouldn't care. He wouldn't, no matter what Barkeen said to him, no matter how awful it was.

Then, he felt pressure spreading his nethermost orifice, and in that moment, he found he did care very much indeed.

RENHANT AND BARN'T cringed as they watched Medic Barkeen pick up instruments they didn't even know existed and push them into body cavities they never imagined they'd fit into. As Jer'son's face reflected the torment of each new invasion, so did Renhant's and Barn't's, their anticipation at being in Jer'son's place as awful to them as the real thing was to the boy the tortures were inflicted on. It wasn't long before they got their turn, too, and the indignities they suffered on the table were every bit as horrible as they imagined them to be. Once their seventeen-year-old bodies were examined, probed, and gone over inch by inch, the three boys were allowed to once again gather in a line, all privacy and personal modesty stripped from them in more ways than one, ways they had never thought possible.

Her chart in her hand, Barkeen walked up to her exam-inees and smiled over the glass. "Boys," and she looked down at her information as if to reassure herself, "you are all fine specimens of seventeen-year-old manhood. No diseases, no obvious flaws, and no internal damage." With her last item, she looked directly at Jer'son. "I'm guessing you took care of Aain'sl before he got to you. Thank you, boy. That saves me a day of surgery."

She walked back to the table and laid her glass down. Without looking, she called out, "You may put your clothing on."

After the scramble of cloth sliding over bare skin, the slapping of shoes against cold feet, and the snaps of metal clasps closing, she turned.

"We have one more procedure to perform. This one will hurt a bit, so be prepared. I also want to share one more thing with you. At the academy, you boys were months from graduation. You have many skills. Be strong, but don't be overconfident. Stay a team.

"You've never seen your official academy records. By the time you get to the surface, everyone on Rant will have. You deserve that same heads-up. Your lives are all in there, boys. Every time you boys peed, your mother, Barn't, and your drunken father as well. Renhant, your sister killed on Trikeen, just twenty-four standards old, and the honors you cheated to earn. Every credit you exhorted from underclassmen, and even the sky-walker and Zen'ri. Boys, you know nothing about Rant, and Rant will know everything about you. Got that? It's important that you do." The boys nodded their heads, clearly not trusting their voices to speak. "Good. Guards, take them for ID."

As the boys exited the room, accompanied by the armed guards, they watched her turn back to her work, her best efforts to help the boys theirs to do with as they would.

66

THE BOYS WALKED down the corridor flanked by the four guards. Their freedom of the evening before just a remembered illusion, they cringed each time someone passed, feeling that the doctor's probed and invaded body parts were out for all to see. Sometimes, those they passed looked their direction, and other times they didn't, caught up in their own torments, desires, or plans. The expressions on the faces showed those emotions, but never the ones the boys so desperately needed to know. Hope. Happiness. Contentment.

Rounding a corner into a narrow corridor, the boys were herded into a noise-filled room. Behind a counter was a series of machines being run by a variety of people, both male and female. A woman turned to them.

"Freshies, huh?" She laughed. "How'd I tell, you're thinking. Easy." She removed her hat and ran her hand across her hair. "Get it? Shaved heads. You freshies are all so gullible. Buck up fast, boys. That is, if you want to last down there. Maybe, if you do, I'll see you again. Get a transfer back to the station. Took me ten standards to get back up here. Best thing I ever did." The woman laughed. "I'd tell you my name, but I won't see you again, probably, so I won't. Won't ask yours, either, so don't bother telling me. I'll just forget. Besides, when I hear the feed telling what happened to whom down there, I don't want to connect any names. It's easier that way."

Putting two machines on the counter, she said, "We've got two procedures here to do. One on the shoulder, and the other on the back. Shoulder's not too bad, but the back's gonna hurt. Get ready for it."

Reaching out and grabbing Barn't's arm, she pulled him up to the counter. She pushed his sleeve up over his shoulder. Pausing, she questioned, "You friends?" When they nodded, she asked, "You want consecutive numbers or random?" Seeing their eyes widen with perplexity, she went on, "Consecutive's easier. People who don't know one another don't like that, so, since I'm a nice girl, I dial up randoms for them. You guys? I'm doing it the easy way." She pressed one of the machines to Barn't's shoulder and held it there. Just as Barn't was about to cry out that the machine hurt, the woman removed it, leaving a series of stripes and circles embedded in the skin. "No ink, just the impressions. You've now got eighty-two thousand microscopic metal pins in there. You can't dig 'em out without cutting half the shoulder away. That's why we don't put them low on the arm anymore. Too many one-armed creeps trying to get offworld. Not too many of the women ever did that. Now pull your shirt up and show me your back. This one's going to hurt. Bad."

Barn't gasped as the woman pressed the second machine to his back. "Gods," he choked out. "Arrgh!" He stumbled forward, his shirt falling back down as Renhant and Jer'son steadied him.

"Hey! I told you it was going to hurt. Now, that was a tracker, shot directly into your lung. It's harder to get out that way. You'll never know it's there; just don't do anything that makes you breathe hard for the next tenday or so. Gives it a chance to heal." She laid the tool down and smiled. "Next?"

Jer'son and Renhant both broke into a sweat, and without thinking, each pointed at the boy standing next to him. They both got their turns, and it did hurt every bit as much as the woman had said it would.

Just like she said, it was a lot.

—Chapter 4—

When traveling through an unknown land,
the friend of a friend should be considered a
friend. After all, who knows if another friend
will arise from the sands? Allah be praised.

—Translated from an Arabic
scroll found on old-Earth

AS SOON as the last of the three boys had his lung loaded, the internee guards dropped their weapons, shaking hands with each one of them before walking away. Confused, the boys looked at the girl behind the counter.

She shrugged her shoulders. "It makes a difference to some of us. Without the trackers, you're free, even if you have no way to get off this station. You see, you could be free, because if you got off, you couldn't be tracked. However, once you're loaded, that is, the tracker is in your lung, you're one of the family, so to speak. You'd have to have a lung removed to get rid of that." She turned to put the machines away, taking her time before glancing up. "There has been gossip of people doing that very thing. You three look like smart boys. Play along to get along. Life's not that bad here, not if you follow the rules." She laughed. "The trick is to find out what they are before you're dead." Then, she turned and was gone.

Barn't turned to the other two. "I'm getting lost faster than I can fall down. What do we do now? What's more, this thing she shot in me hurts!"

"Join the group." Renhant looked at Jer'son, seeing it in his eyes, too. "We all hurt. I think that's part of the learning curve. Look, guys. We have to find out fast what we're supposed to do, and whatever happens, make sure we all stick together. We have to take up for each other, and never let another one of our group down. Got it?"

"Yes," came the chorused reply.

"Good. Follow me, and take no funk from anyone." The three of them walked out the door with as much bravado as three bald-headed seventeen-year-olds with pain shooting through their lungs could show.

"Hey, freshies, welcome!" A hand patted them on the back.

"Got a bridge if you're interested," and a laugh followed them.

"Chrome ain't good when your head's made of wood. Grow hair *here*," and someone pointed to his crotch.

"Mess hall?" Renhant yelled back at the last one, and he got a reply.

"The other way and down one level," came the assured response.

"See? Let's go get food." Renhant led the others down

the corridor looking for a lift or even stairs. Pretty soon, it became evident there were none. "Did I hear him right?" he quizzed the others.

Jer'son, quiet since the examination, finally spoke up. "I think we've been had, but let me ask." He reached out and touched a passing arm. The person jerked as if electrified.

"Don't you dare touch me!" The woman, dark-skinned, with hair the color of blood, barked her rebuke even as she looked their direction. The whites of her eyes weren't white at all, but yellowed, and she narrowed her lids. "Oh, freshies. The new ones from last night." She frowned. "Learn it now, freshie. You touch the wrong person, and it'll get you killed. Really dead. You know what that is?" She slapped his arm away. "So! That's your free advice to get you through today. What'd you need? Hurry it up." She made as if to move on.

"Down one level. How do we get there?"

This time she laughed, showing brilliantly white teeth, one with a glittering stone embedded in the surface. "What's down one level that you need?"

"The mess hall."

"The mess hall? Boys, there is no 'down-one-level' on this station, unless you want to be outside in the cold blackness of space. Now, how would you ever get anything to eat there?"

Jer'son, now humiliated, struggled out, "Then, where?"

"Turn around. See that door right in front of you?"

"Yes." He cut his eyes to Barn't and Renhant before looking back at the woman.

"Walk through it, and presto, you're there."

"Thanks," all three boys chimed.

She started to walk off, calling back, "Don't thank me. It closed a few moments ago. Try it again at midmeal." She pressed a glowing stud into her ear as she rounded a corner.

They walked to the door anyway. It slipped aside, and inside, the ceiling glowed with blue light. Red washed the floor, and the back wall was shuttered. White, unadorned tables filled the space, each one surrounded by simple stools.

"Looks like any mess hall on any ship. Depressing." Renhant stepped inside, and his skin took on a purplish glow. He motioned, and the others followed him in. "We might as well. We have no place else to go."

"That was mean of that first guy to tell us that," Barn't moaned, as he fell onto a stool. He crossed his arms on the table, dropping his head to rest on them.

Renhant took his hand and rubbed it on his head. "We're freshies, Barn't. That's all the reason they need. Get used to it."

After a short silence, Jer'son cleared his throat. "Guys," he started, and then stopped, looking at his hands as he picked at his nails. His friends looked at him, waiting for him to finish.

"Yes, Jer'son, what?" Renhant prompted.

"What that medic in there said . . ."

"About what, Jer'son?" Barn't interrupted. He worked at a rough seam in his clothing, and he pulled a long thread loose.

Renhant whispered, "Shut up," and made a jerking

73

motion at his own crotch. Barn't's eyes opened wide.

"Guys, it wasn't exactly like she said."

"You don't have to tell us anything about that. We can forget it like it never was." Renhant glanced away, keeping his eyes on the floor.

"I want you to know."

Renhant took a deep breath, letting it out as he made a face to Barn't that Jer'son couldn't see. "You really don't have to tell us. Really."

"Please. I've never told anyone about it. I didn't know anyone even knew, and now I find everyone knows. Crikes, it was only four standards ago. I was only thirteen when it started. I still remember every night of that year like it happened yesterday." He looked at the two boys sitting with him, his eyes wary. "If you don't hear what really happened, you'll always think I wanted to be there, that I asked him to do that to me. I didn't, guys. I promise. Will you just listen, at least? Then you can pretend I never said a word of it. Agreed?"

Renhant glanced from Jer'son's distraught face to Barn't's nervous one. He made a decision.

"Barn't, we're all each of us has here. If we're not here for each other, no one will be. Okay?" When Barn't nodded his head, Renhant motioned to Jer'son. "The floor's yours. Until you say stop, it's whatever you want to tell us with no judgments and no talking about it again, ever. Good enough?"

A cloud seemed to lift from Jer'son's shoulders as he began his version of that awful year he hadn't been able to bring to a stop and had never forgotten.

"I'd always been a big kid. Clumsy and taller than everyone else. I was always self-conscious about it, too, because it made me stand out. Even my teachers told me that they didn't like me around because I broke things.

"When my family lost our business in a MegaCorp takeover, MegaCorp offered to help my family out, give my parents money, plus jobs and all, if they'd let me join the academy. I was eleven, then. My family had money again, and we could buy food. For two standard years I listened to how our survival was because of me signing up for the academy, and how without me going in the military, we would lose our home and starve. For two years, that's all I heard.

"I was scared not to do well at the academy, so I was especially careful to make everyone like me. At thirteen, I was lucky my body had slowed down, and I wasn't clumsy any more. I did everything just like I was supposed to. I smiled at my teachers, and they seemed to like me. They had to like me, because if they didn't and I got kicked out, MegaCorp would take the money back. Then my parents would starve." Jer'son held his hands tightly cupped, his eyes staring at them as he talked.

"I had to make my teachers happy, no matter what they wanted. When my activities instructor moved my bunk, I liked being away from the others. I didn't know he wanted to do things like that to me. I didn't even know until today there were other instructors doing those things to me. I thought it was just my activities instructor, although he was always so nice to me in class that sometimes I was convinced it couldn't be him.

"That first night, I didn't really know what was happening. I just knew it wasn't right. I had never even done that to myself before that night. After it was over, I was so embarrassed. The next day, when I got up, I was afraid everyone could see I was different, that they would know what had happened during the night. In every class, I listened to what the other kids were saying, and I kept expecting them to be talking about me, to point to me, and to laugh.

"They never did, though, and that next day in activities, the instructor was so nice, just like it had never happened. By bedtime, I had even convinced myself it hadn't happened at all. Boy, was I wrong! When I woke up that night, he was already there, and I didn't know how to make him stop. While he was doing that to me, I lay there thinking of my mother and father and how I had to be at the academy, or they'd starve. I knew nobody'd believe me if I told, because the instructor was so well liked by all the cadets.

"If I laid on my stomach, he'd just pull me over onto my back. If I covered myself with my hands, he'd pull them off. Soon, I learned the best way to get it over with was to just lie there and let him finish what he was doing. Then, I'd cry, or sometimes I wouldn't, and I'd go to sleep.

"For a long time, I kept looking for everyone to notice, but no one did. Then, one day, I got up and didn't think about it. I just showered with everyone else and went to classes. It wasn't until I went into activities class that I remembered, and the instructor joked with me that day, and I didn't want to remember what he'd done the night before.

"After I turned fourteen, I guess I got used to it, and it became just a small part of my nights, something that happened and was over with, and I went back to sleep afterward. At the end of the term, I moved up to the next dorm. It stopped then.

"Guys, I didn't even know what was happening to me when he started, just how it felt, and that it shouldn't be happening at all. When I liked it, I hated myself. When I wanted to tell, I thought of my parents and what it would mean if I got kicked out. I was thirteen when it started. Thirteen. I didn't know what to do." He wiped the tears from his face.

"They wouldn't have kicked you out," Renhant said softly. "They would have sent him here, just like they did later."

Jer'son turned his attention to an errant fingernail. "I didn't know that then. I do now. After it was over, I didn't want to think about it. I was so embarrassed every time it came to mind."

Renhant tapped Jer'son's shoulder with his closed fist. "You were a kid. You didn't know. You did the best you could, and it's not your fault. Isn't that right, Barn't?"

After a threatening look from Renhant, Barn't chimed in, "Yeah, not your fault, Jer'son."

"You guys are still my friends?" Jer'son pleaded with his voice, his eyes still on his hands.

"We've just got each other, Jer'son. Who'd be your friends if we weren't? Of course, we're still your friends." When Renhant and Barn't each put a hand on one of Jer'son's shoulders, he looked up at them and smiled. More tightly than ever before, the trio was bonded to each other.

77

"FOOD." Renhant sat down beside Barn't and Jer'son, placing more food than they'd seen in days in front of them. "Cheer up, Jer'son, there's enough for all of us." He pushed the tray over as Barn't grabbed some, and then doled a portion out to Jer'son.

"No thanks," he mumbled.

"You've got to eat." Renhant broke a steaming roll in two and held it under his friend's nose.

"If you insist. Did you ask about tomorrow?" He grabbed it and began chewing on it.

"Our schedule is this." Renhant leaned in to the other two. "First transport down. That's us." As quickly as he'd leaned in, he sat back, a pleased look on his face.

"Why are you so happy about that?" Barn't gave him a puzzled look.

Renhant reached in his pocket and drew out a folded piece of paper, dropping it on the table between them. Barn't reached out to pick it up. Turning it over in his hands, he handed it to Jer'son.

"So," Barn't said. "What's that?" He motioned to the paper.

"That's paper, stupid," Renhant chided.

"I've seen paper before. I just don't use it for anything. What's this piece for?"

Renhant motioned the others to lean in, and he whispered, "I went back to the medic about my tracker, and I asked her for any other helpful information she could give me. She thanked me for asking and gave me that." He sat back once again, still smiling.

Jer'son tossed the folded paper back at him, snorting in

derision. "How's this helpful?"

Renhant laughed. "You guys just don't get it, yet. She said the first flight beats most of the people down there getting up, so we'd have a little time to settle in. Then, she gave me the name of someone who could get us set up. How's that?"

"You trust this? Maybe it's like our haircuts or finding the mess hall." Barn't looked doubtful.

Renhant paused for a moment, looking thoughtful, then said firmly, "Yes, Barn't, I do. I sure do. I trust her help one hundred percent."

"Did you find where we sleep tonight?" Jer'son rapped the tabletop, looking at his friend expectantly.

"Found that out, too. Same place as last night. That's reserved for us until in the morning. Unlocked, too." He grinned.

"Good. I'm tired in every way I can be tired, and I'm going to bed. Get me up early. I'll see you guys then." Jer'son picked up the paper he'd tossed back to Renhant. "I sure hope this information is as good as you think it is." He held it out.

Renhant took it from him and breathed deeply, for the first time showing an edge of uncertainty. "I hope so, too. For all our sakes." He slipped the folded paper in a pocket and sat back. He pushed away the food. "Sorry, Barn't. I'm not hungry anymore."

"Are we still a team?" Barn't kept his eyes on Jer'son as he walked away. The look on his face was hard. Very hard.

"What do you mean?"

"Jer'son's still part of our team?"

"Of course he is. Nothing can break us up." Renhant slipped the paper in a pocket and stood, motioning for Barn't to follow. Together they made their way after their friend. After all, there was nowhere else to go.

"JER'SON." Renhant gently shook his friend's shoulder, rocking the face still pressed into the bedding. "It's morning." All across his back, bruises had blossomed in the night, and Renhant shook his head in dismay.

One he recognized. It was the bruise around the tracker injection. The others, though, were a garden of murky blackness, smeared haphazardly across skin that had been fresh and unmarred only days before. In the medic's examining room, they hadn't been this bad—or maybe they had, Renhant conceded. Embarrassment had filled the room, and no one except the medic had looked up except when demanded to do so.

Carefully, trying not to press on any of the darker ones, Renhant shook Jer'son's shoulder again. As he did, his friend jerked onto his side, drawing his legs up as if to protect himself from an imagined touch, his eyes locking on Renhant in groggy wariness. Renhant was certain he saw fear there.

"Hey, Jer'son, it's me. You okay?" He was relieved to see his body relax.

"It's morning, already. I didn't expect it to come so soon." Jer'son rubbed his face, grinning awkwardly, the expression quickly slipping away into something else. "I just had a whacker of a dream. I guess I thought you were someone else." He relaxed onto his back, his arms casually looped over his head. Then, he jerked erect, grabbing his knees, his eyes darting around the room. "We're really here, aren't we? I had that dream, and I thought *this* had been a dream. Crikes!"

"Crikes?" Renhant laughed. "Things are a lot worse than crikes."

Jer'son rubbed the two-cycle old stubble on the top of his head, then he laughed. "Maybe it will all grow out again someday." He scratched his groin and then grimaced.

"It can't be fast enough, either. I saw that look." Renhant laughed again.

"Barn't up?" Jer'son dropped his feet off the bunk, tossing the bedding aside. The bruises had grown long tendrils down his legs, also.

Renhant pointed to the mound on the adjoining bunk, and in a burst of seventeen-year-old exuberance, they jumped on it, pushing and tickling until the third member of their trio was up and walking. Dressed, they gathered what little they had and headed toward the corridor.

Renhant chuckled.

"What's funny?" Jer'son rubbed his neck, stopping at one especially dark bruise that had crawled up one side. He grimaced, as if it was tenderer than the rest.

"Nothing, really, just that we entered this place two cycles ago, but those two cycles feel like a lifetime."

"A lifetime in hell." Jer'son winked, turning loose of his neck, and running his fingers across his head.

"You have that paper?" Barn't stood, yawning, and he looked at Renhant.

"In my pocket."

"Who is it, anyway, that we're supposed to contact?" It

81

was Jer'son asking this time. "Did the medic give you a name?"

"It's a name, sort of. Bird."

"Bird? That's a real name?" He shook his head. "I can't believe a man is named *Bird*. Maybe we're meeting a beautiful woman." Then he rolled his eyes disgustedly. "Maybe it's not a person at all. We just have to guess what *kind* of bird it is. Let's try Eagle, or Hawk. Maybe Sparrow, instead. Miss Sparrow, the enchanting courtesan, here and ready to give you the gift of your dreams: a night in paradise. I greet you, Miss Sparrow. Please don't die on me as you hold me in your arms."

"Come on, Jer'son," Barn't cautioned. "Don't make fun. It's just a name. Let's get there and see. Has Renhant ever steered you wrong?"

Has Renhant ever steered you wrong. That froze Jer'son in his tracks, and he paused as the other two walked ahead. He muttered, "Just that night with Zen'ri, the night that brought us all to this. No, Barn't, not often, but that one was a knock-your-socks-off wringer."

"Catch up, Jer'son," Renhant called, motioning with one hand.

"Yeah, fool! We'll have to leave you behind if you don't run." Barn't giggled, and Renhant immediately clapped him on the shoulder, silencing him.

Once the door to the landing bay opened, there stood their transport. It was not quite what they expected. Unlike the sleek jumpship, this one was dull and pitted, the outside showing what it really was: a cast-off, poorly maintained craft that no one wanted, one that had been foisted upon people no one was interested in. Them.

Barn't whispered to the others, "Could use a paint job," and he giggled again. "Maybe an update or two."

"Perhaps a complete renovation." Jer'son grinned. "At the academy, this would have been used for target practice."

Renhant put a finger to his lips. "We're about to ride in that thing. Be careful what you say."

"Hey, freshies, you can't get on that transport. Get back over here."

Renhant turned, not seeing anyone. He called out, "We were told to be on this transport. Why can't we go now?"

The voice laughed. "I didn't say you can't go now. I said you can't get on that transport. You haven't signed yourselves out. Get your shoulders to the reader, and then get on. Always sign out, freshies."

"Reader?" Barn't, as usual, was late tracking the conversation, but he asked a question the others hadn't. It was an important one. "Is someone there?" That wasn't a bad question, either.

There other voices audible in the background.

"Are freshies always this dense? I tend to forget."

"Yeah, it takes 'em forever to figure anything out."

"Like the trackers."

A laugh came through. *"And how much they hurt if they forget to sign out at a reader."*

Barn't called out, louder this time, "What reader?"

"By the door, freshie. Put your shoulder up to it so it can read the pins. You forget and set those trackers off, you can bet you'll sure remember the next time." Behind the voice of the unseen person, the second conversation continued, *"And*

83

they want to get there early? That's strange. Ouch. Hey! No, I'm not going to let them load just for a laugh, and that's the last time you hit me . . ."

The faint conversation devolved into a jumble of noises, unseen people apparently knocking each other around.

"Guys, look. There." Barn't glanced at the others and pointed, pulling his sleeve up and pressing his shoulder to a flat panel. It lit up red before immediately changing to green.

"Je'main Winterd Barn't. Subject acknowledged and tracker reconfigured. Subject must board first available transport to avoid tracker activation."

"Hey," Barn't said. "I don't like the sound of that."

Jer'son looked at the reader and stepped back. "You next, Renhant."

Renhant grinned and threw his palms up in the air, motioning for Jer'son to step up first. "That's a pass for me, friend."

Jer'son shot him a scowl. "I said, you next."

"All right. Not a problem. I don't like this either, but we're here and we can't change that."

"Just yet. Not just yet," Jer'son mumbled, dragging up behind him. "I just want to delay the inevitable for as long as possible."

"Then, I'm first. But I want you right after me."

Their shoulders inventoried, their passage now required, they stepped into a transport that looked as if it should have been parked on a junkheap many decades ago.

Jer'son looked at Barn't trailing his hand along the edges of torn and occasionally dismembered seats. The station had been clean and fairly close to academy standards. This was a wreck.

"So, no one cares what's out the back door as long as the lobby's pretty and polished. Maybe that's why people work so hard to get transferred back up here." Catching a glimpse of himself in the remains of a polished metal panel, Jer'son ran a hand over his head. "Freshie. We can't hide it, except maybe with a hat." He looked around, then back at the reflection.

Then he turned and grinned. "Guys, I have what might be an idea. It seems we might be the only passengers on this trip. No one else has shown up to board."

"That's good, huh?" Barn't laughed half-heartedly, still walking along the seats, touching each one.

Leaning over the back of a ragged seat, Jer'son shared his suggested solution. Renhant seemed thoughtful, but Barn't recoiled at the thought. However, Jer'son threw himself back in his seat, and reached to pull his Rant-issued shoes off his feet.

"For now, it's all we've got," he spit out. "Get on board. At least our scalps will be covered."

"You're crazy. I'm not wearing shorts on my head." Barn't threw himself into one of the seats. He curled his lip. "How can you suggest that?"

Renhant, although not yet ready to strip his clothes either, grudgingly prodded Barn't. "It might work, if we all do this together."

"If we step off this shuttle with our heads bare, how long do you think we'll survive?" Already slipping his pants and undershorts off, Jer'son immediately slid back into his pants and shoes, holding the undershorts up. "This is the only thing

85

I see around here we can use. You have a better idea, Barn't, or do you just want to walk out down there, your bare head announcing to a world of perverts that you're *new and ripe for the picking*, to quote that guard Tan'sn?"

Barn't closed his eyes and shuddered.

Renhant crossed his arms on the back of a seat and rested his chin on them. "I think we see your point. Show us how you'd do this."

"Do you think anyone else is riding down with us, or is it really just us three?" Barn't didn't even open his eyes. "I don't want to pull my clothes off if anyone else is looking."

Jer'son slapped the back of his friend's head. "Look around you. It's empty. No one wants to be there on the surface of Rant. They all want to stay here. It's just us suckers." His voice suddenly filled with determination. "I'm gonna do this, by myself, if I have to. You two keep your shorts on if you want. Not me. I'm not gonna be the fresh meat they expect, and you'd better not, either." Now out of the orbital station, and with the message from the reader ringing in his head, as well as his bald-headed reflection echoing in his memory, the anger he'd thrashed on the guard on the jumpship had begun to bubble back up under the surface. "If I get assaulted, someone will deserve what they get, I assure you that."

Renhant remembered assault training back at the academy, but he knew that wasn't exactly what Jer'son intended. It was the desperate criminals who would see them as fresh opportunities for degenerate needs. He shivered. Thank the stars for the training he'd complained about for so many standards. It might come in useful after all.

Pulling his hands from behind his head, the final knot tied, Jer'son stepped in front of the piece of his reflection he could see in the metal bulkhead. "Not bad, you think?" He reached up and tucked a small strip underneath a twisted knot, and ran his hand over his newly covered scalp. Turning to his friends, he displayed his creation. "Does it work, or am I just without my shorts?"

"Hey," Barn't admitted. "You can't even tell. Can you do that to mine?"

"Friend, I'm not touching your undershorts. You can do this for yourself."

"This might work. I'm game." Renhant stood and dropped his clothes. "If my undershorts are all I have to cover my head, then that's way better than bald. Jer'son, you may have saved us, yet." He reached over and popped Barn't's shoulder. "Drop your drawers, kid."

"Quit hitting me," Barn't wailed.

"Stop being a baby. Get those shorts off. We don't have any idea how long this trip'll last, and I, for one, don't want to be caught with my drawers down."

Barn't grinned. "If they're on top of your head, it's acceptable, though, huh?"

At that, even Jer'son laughed. Then, with a thoughtful look, he pulled his shorts, his "hat," back off his head. Holding it out, he looked at it critically, muttering, "Too clean. Looks new." Louder, he turned to the other two, now with their undershorts in hand, Barn't just slipping back into his pants. "Find something to dirty 'em up. These need to look like we've worn 'em for a while."

"We have, Jer'son. It's been nearly two days." Barn't

looked confused.

"On our heads, Bozo. Not in our pants. Wipe 'em on anything you can find that's dirty or rusty. Make 'em like we wear them constantly, never taking them off. Especially the edges. Dirty and sweaty, that's what we've got to make those perverts see. Not fresh and clean. Especially not fresh and clean."

"No?" Barn't frowned. "Isn't clean better?"

Renhant sat Barn't down and explained what Jer'son was getting at. "We're kids to these people, no matter how grown up we've seen ourselves in the past. They are going to try to take advantage of us. Remember the guards? There might be more of that; in fact, there probably will be. I think we can count on it. We have to seem as tough and as unappealing as we can. Look at Jer'son over there."

"What about him?"

Renhant dropped his voice to a whisper as they watched him wiping his "hat" on everything that might get it dirty, then wiping it on his face to dirty it up also. "He's been there. Remember what he told us? He knows and doesn't want it to happen to us. Listen to him, will you? He's a good friend, and he'll give us good advice." He reached a hand out and gave Barn't a push on his shoulder.

Louder, he went on, "So, get those shorts dirty in any way you can."

"Well," Jer'son called, "not in *any* way, Barn't." Then he laughed.

AS A TEAM, they dirtied newly fashioned headgear, faces, and Rant-issued clothing, all in preparation for a role they had little training for, but which they would be forced to play, anyway. By the time they finished, the three fresh-faced boys who had boarded the old wreck were fresh faced no longer.

They could tell when the transport arrived, the noises and subtle changes those that were familiar to men reared aboard the kinds of vessels that flew the open spaces between the stars. In moments only, they would step forth almost unrecognizable as the youths who had entered the transport just hours before. Yes, their slimness was the same, and the regular features on those smooth faces carried the same lack of years; yet the difference was dramatic. Now stood roughened men, dirtied from a life of living on the edge, unused to the casual cleanliness of a life lived aboard ship, and ready to buck anyone who stood in their way.

Inside their hearts, though, the story was very different. Ready to cast their bravado on the gameboard and face an unfamiliar world were three teenage boys, once overconfident in their ability to bully those smaller than themselves, and just now aware that they were the ones to be bullied here on this world.

Fear made them stronger, though, and running away was not an option. As the transport door opened, they stepped out into a world of heat, dust, and no one they knew.

No one except Bird.

THE DOOR jerked open, and a face peered through the shadowed opening. A rough voice accosted the three boys from the transport.

"Yeah? It's early, ya' know. This couldn't wait until the

sun comes up?" One of the boys moved aside, allowing the sun to pierce the opening. "Gads! The sun *be* up!" The man threw his arm in front of his eyes.

"Bird?" Renhant pressed his question into the opening.

The man squinted through the shadow created by his arm. "Who wants to know?"

Behind Renhant, the two remaining friends looked at each other, uncertainty on their faces. Barn't whispered, "I'm not too sure of Renhant's choice of contacts. Maybe we should just take our chances."

"Barkeen sent us, said you'd help us, said she'd let you know we were coming." Renhant turned to glance at the other two, the uncertainty in his eyes an equal to theirs. With a bravado not seen on his face, he barked his frustration through the door. "Do we have your help or not?"

"Ahhug, come on in." The door swung open as the man stepped back, the darkness of the room blinding to the boys. "Close the door behind ya' when ya' come through. Already it be growing hot this morning," and he stumbled into a back room, grabbing a container of drink from a mechanically cooled cabinet.

"Thank you, ser," Barn't chirped.

"Ain't done nothing yet," he muttered. Then he turned to them and barked, "Who's Barkeen sending to me, now? Bleeding heart woman wants to save the world. Ha!" He threw his head back and laughed, suddenly putting his palm to his forehead. "Ooh, that hurt." Looking at his three visitors, he squinted. "Ya' ain't the pups she said she was sending to me. What's this, some kind of trick?"

The boys just stood there waiting as he stepped forward,

walking around the trio, his eyes inspecting them thoroughly.

"Hm. Ya' three seem like the rough men I don't want in my place. That's good." Thima'son Gallagy Richter, although no one knew him by that name any longer, looked closely at Renhant's face, then licking his thumb, he rubbed the grime from the boy's cheek. With a grin, he ran his hand over the cap on Renhant's head. Laughing, he yanked the makeshift hat from the boy's head and waved it in the air, his free hand patting Renhant's bristly scalp.

"These are the best three pups she's ever sent me, bless that Barkeen. I wouldn't a known, not from two paces, and I know a freshie. These," and he shook the hat and whooped, "These be undershorts, if I be on Rant! Clever! Very clever! Ya' boys might just survive."

As the man known on Rant only as Bird turned, he paused and looked back at them. "Forgive me speech. Sometimes the old way comes to me, and I just let it out." Picking up his drink, he sat and laughed. "I'd never have known, not in a million."

Renhant, Jer'son, and Barn't just grinned.

—Chapter 5—

Safe is a relative term. You are safe in your home until a fuel source blows up. You are safe in your country until there is a civil war. You are safe on your world until an asteroid strikes.

When you begin to think you are safe, look around and ask yourself one question. What am I not seeing?

—From Blinded Eyes Opened *by Calvant De'Argosli, Angoni'st Prime 4314, F.E. (c. 2346 A.D. old-Earth timeline)*

"TAKE THEM things off ya' heads, boys. Now I can see the freshie in ya'." Bird put his container down and stared at them, looking each boy in the eyes.

"We did good, though?" The question came from Barn't, while Jer'son hung back.

"Well enough. One thing ya' must know: I know what ya' did, and I know who's looking for ya'." Bird ran his eyes over the three, and then he paused, evaluating. He stepped past Renhant and pointed to Jer'son. "Claiming ya' as his own."

Jer'son stepped back, his eyes wide. "Looking for me? Claiming me? Why?"

"Ya' be Jer'son, be ya' not?" Bird raised his eyebrows in question.

"Yeah, but how did you know?"

"It just what the man be saying. Now, I don't know what did or didn't take place between ya' two, and ya' can tell me or not, but it don't change a thing. He don't got no right to ya', no matter what. Here on Rant, each man be his own, lest the man decides otherwise. Same thing goes for the women. Keep that in mind, boys."

Jer'son stepped towards Bird, his hands pumping themselves in fists, his voice flinging itself out of his mouth. "Tell me!"

"Back up, boy. It ain't me that wants ya'. I like the skirted kind, meself. Being with ya' would kinda be like playing with meself. Not much fun in that, I don't guess." Bird retrieved another drink from his cooled cabinet. "Boys?" He made as if to offer them one.

When he saw no takers, he shrugged his shoulders and opened his own. Then, his eyes narrowed as he fixed them on Jer'son.

"Boy, I knew ya' when I looked close at ya' under all that dirt ya' tried to hide under. 'The prettiest face with the nicest smile I ever laid eyes on.' Yep, that's exactly what I

93

heard he said. Heard something else, too." He pointed his drink in Jer'son's direction. "Says ya' never complained once or tried to stop him, and he wants ya' back. Said ya' was about fourteen at the time. Pretty as a peach be what he said."

Jer'son turned around, driving a fist into his palm over and over, tears erupting down his face. "I didn't *ever* ask him to do that. *Ever!*" He turned back to Bird. "He's telling people that?"

"It be everywhere, son. Know it now. He be a'telling everyone. Here be my question, and ya' don't have to answer, 'cause it don't matter much if ya' did or didn't, as I said earlier, but knowing sure helps out around here. Boy," and he pulled Jer'son down to sit across from him, "did ya' ever try to stop him?"

Renhant stepped in, "Ser, please. He was only thirteen when it started."

Bird waved him off. "If ya' don't want me to hear, boy, tell me now, but tell me something. Did ya' ever try to stop him?"

Jer'son sat, his head down, and the tears ran down his face.

"Boy, do I get an answer?"

"Ser," Renhant tried again, and was waved off a second time.

Jer'son whispered, "No, I never did. I just—"

Bird slapped a hand on the table, interrupting the confession, and causing all three boys to jump. "That be enough for me, boy." He stood up, slapping him on the back, and grabbing one arm, he pulled him up. "Ya' had'a told me yes,

94

and I'd a called ya' a liar. Then I'd a'told him where to come find ya'. Ain't no thirteen-year-old knows how to fight that. Ya' ain't his boy, and I'm gonna make sure a'that. Ya' got me?"

Jer'son wiped his tears and his mouth screwed up into a weak grin.

"Ya' got angry real fast. That was my first clue, Sherlock. I figured no boy gonna listen to that without getting angry unless he wanted it in the first place."

"But," Renhant started.

"Nah! No buts." Bird looked around the room. Making a decision, he picked up a broom and held it out. "First things first. This place be a mess. I were up all night. Ya' clean it, 'cause I be going back to bed." Renhant took the broom from his hand, and with that, Bird stumbled back off to his sleep.

"You going to be all right, Jer'son?" Renhant put his hand on his friend's shoulder. He looked over at Barn't, motioning for him to do the same.

"Yeah. It's just I thought this was over when I was fourteen, and then it came back. Then it came back again, and now it's back once more."

"Here, doing something will help. You take this broom, and Barn't and me, we'll put stuff away."

Barn't picked up some drink containers and started looking for a place to set them, finally placing them on an empty stretch of counter. "Why'd he call you Sherlock, Jer'son?"

"I don't know." Jer'son rubbed his face, smearing the remains of moisture from his eyes. "Ask him when he wakes up."

"What do you think this is, an eating place?" Barn't

picked up an empty glass and sniffed inside. "I don't see any plates."

"Probably." Renhant reached under a table and picked up some lacy underwear. "But I suspect it's a whole lot more."

"Why do you say that?" Barn't turned to look, and when he saw what the other boy was holding, his face turned red. "I guess that might be a pretty good guess, Renhant." He reached over and got Jer'son's attention. "Wouldn't you have to agree, Jer'son?"

Even in his distress, Jer'son had to smile at that.

"BOYS, THIS be it. Ya' been here a day, and this be the place for ya' to call home each night." Bird opened a roughly made door, swiping cobwebs from his face. "Danged fool spiders. A billion miles from old-Earth, and they still got here." He looked at them and winked. "Old-Earth term, there. Miles. Ya' probably wouldn't recognize it."

"Nah, I know it. I had a bunkie named Mil's. Back at the academy my first year," Barn't bragged with pride in his voice.

"Wrong, kid. System of measurement. Distance. Miles. But it be not important. The spiders be so, though. Most won't hurt ya', just watch for the black ones and the big brown ones."

He pointed to three wide planks against the wall. "Where ya' will sleep. It be cool here at night, but at midday, the warmth will get to ya', if'n you don't open the window. Mind ya' do. And I'll get ya' something softer to lie on, but ya' will pay me back, got that? I got rooms, but they be all busy at night. Don't pay no attention to the noise."

Bird turned and winked at Jer'son. "And I only got girls here." He slapped him on the shoulder. "Just kidding with ya', kid. Get used to it. Throw your stuff on the floor there, if ya' got any. Keep away from the crowds awhile with your heads done that way. People'll do ya' up for a sucker faster'n fast. I be taking care of ya' boys. Just trust me." He turned and started back down the stairs.

"Ah," Jer'son said, once the old man was gone. "The dusty room at the top of the stairs. Didn't they make a Vid of this once? It seems like the three errant boys got dismembered."

"Tortured is what I heard."

"Nah," Barn't grinned. "Eaten alive."

Renhant winked at Jer'son. "Well, at least that last one doesn't worry me. They get a taste of you, Barn't, and they'll all run the other way."

"Not funny, Renhant. They might just get a taste of you and lie down and die. That's what might happen." Barn't chose one of the planks and lay down. "This one can be my bunk."

"Bed. They call them beds onworld. Hey! There's another room back here." Jer'son disappeared inside.

Renhant took off on Barn't, though, sitting on him, and holding his arms as the smaller boy began to struggle. "Hey, Jer'son, tell Bird I don't need a pad after all. This bunk already has one." He made as if he were about to lie down on the smaller boy, and Barn't started thrashing vigorously, pushing Renhant off.

"Get off me, you boy lover." He jerked abruptly to his feet, straightening his clothes.

97

Renhant hit him and pointed to the door Jer'son had stepped through, whispering, "Shut up, Barn't."

"Shut up, yourself," he hissed back, jumping on the bigger boy, with one hand in a fist.

"Guys, I think this is on old storeroom, for Bird's spiders, anyway." Jer'son stepped back into the room, and his face dropped at the ruckus. "What are you fighting about, now?"

"Nothing. Just stupid stuff." Barn't let Renhant go.

"Hey, let's try to get along. All we have is each other. Got it?" Jer'son looked from one to the other. "Is everyone agreed?"

"Sure, Jer'son," they replied in chorus.

"Now that we've got a place to stay, I want to go see what this world is like. How about it? A night on the town?"

"I don't know," Renhant hedged. "What if there's a problem, us being freshies? Remember what Bird said?"

Barn't jumped in, a look of undisguised anticipation on his face. "Don't worry, Renhant. Even Bird said he couldn't tell." He had that eager look that said someone else had suggested something he had been afraid to ask about. It also said that whatever Jer'son suggested, he'd be on board, because he didn't want to be left out of the action.

"Jer'son, Barn't." Renhant frowned, hesitating. "He was thick with a hangover when he first saw us. Besides, Bird said not to go out until our hair grows."

"No, that's not what he said, Renhant. He said not to go out with these shaved heads. Ours will be covered." Jer'son whipped his "hat" from his pocket. "Are you with us, Renhant? Are we still a team?"

"Why am I always the voice of reason, and yet no one

listens to me? Yeah, we're a team, and a team sticks together. If one of us messes up, we all mess up. So, yes, I'm game."

"Good," Jer'son said. "Let's get dirty."

In a very short time, instead of three seventeen-year-olds, in the room stood the roughshod roughnecks that had arrived at Bird's door only that morning.

"Jer'son, come over here and look. Right down there." Barn't motioned him to the lone window. "Look at that."

Jer'son looked out, Renhant right behind him. "Wow! Look at that. If those girls wore any less, they'd be wearing nothing at all, and that'd be fine with me. Move over, Barn't. I want to see the one in black."

"Do you think all those girls work here?" Renhant whispered.

"That's what Bird said, that girls worked for him."

"Makes me want to help Bird around the shop." Jer'son looked at the other two boys beside him. "Maybe I'll just hang around while you two go exploring." He laughed. "Just kidding, you know. We won't get any just standing here watching. Might as well go out and see what the rest of this place's like." He jumped away from the window and opened the door. "It's clear, men. Let's hit the streets."

Once down the stairs, residual heat from the day wrapped the boys. This was no ship's interior, with carefully regulated temperature and humidity; and the temperature gradient, although well down from the midday high, remained oppressive.

"Slug-sucking hot out here." Renhant coughed, and he worked his shoulders, grimacing as he did so. "Bird was right. Maybe this isn't a good idea."

"Now who's the sissy?" Barn't grinned, dancing into the street.

"You'll think sissy!" Renhant made a grab for him, only missing because Jer'son got in the way.

"Give him a break. Okay?" Laughing at each other, the tension released, and they moved forward into the night.

Passing pockets of people, some huddled in darkened corners, and most in the rough clothes of those who did what they did because they had no other choice, the boys walked on. Soon they found a few in much better clothes, and occasionally, someone would prance by in exotic attire. With their rough, homemade hats, the boys went unnoticed in the dark.

Coming upon a street decorated with a string of raucous, lighted signs, they recognized one as a drinking establishment. In front was a line of people, a few dressed very well, most not, and all waiting for the bouncer to let them inside.

"Guys, I'm so thirsty," Barn't complained, sticking his tongue out and making a gagging sound. "Too bad we didn't bring something to drink. If we ask, do you think they'll let us inside?"

"Where's your paycheck, Barn't?" Renhant smirked.

"I don't have a job. I can't have a paycheck."

Renhant snickered. "My point has been made by the little guy."

Jer'son just grinned at the exchange.

Renhant snorted, "Now who's the Cheshire cat?"

"Cheshire cat?" Barn't licked his lips. "What's a Cheshire cat?"

"You mean, what's a cat, right?" Jer'son's grin grew

wider.

"All right, give, Jer'son. What do we not know?"

"I have credits."

"How can you have credits?" Barn't demanded. "We don't have any funds to pull from."

Jer'son chuckled. "But Bird does." He didn't elaborate.

"What do you mean by that?" Renhant stepped in front of him. "What have you done?"

"There was a wad of credits on the counter. It sat there all day, so I figured maybe someone forgot it. I claimed it. After all, we cleaned for the old man. Let's spend it, guys." He pulled it from his pocket.

"Jer'son, no!" Renhant grabbed his hand.

"Why, not? If Bird misses it, we'll say oops and give back what's left. We'll promise to repay the rest."

"He's helping us. You're stealing from him. That's not right."

"What's not right is us being here." Jer'son's voice was suddenly hard. "We have to take every opportunity. This was made available, and I took it. How's this different than what we did all those times on the ship?"

"What's different is we need someone's help now. We can't lose that until we can make it on our own."

"How are we supposed to do that, Renhant, if we don't figure this place out? Like I said, if he misses it, we'll just promise to pay him back." His voice now less confident than determined, he turned to walk away. "I'm going in that establishment, with or without you."

He marched up to the line, his bravado written on his face and his credits in his pocket. He turned and motioned for the

101

other two to follow. Running to catch up, they stood in the rough-looking crowd waiting to be admitted. When they reached the door, they were told, "Move along down the street, boys."

"We have credits," Jer'son bragged, pulling the wad from his pocket.

The bouncer's eyes flashed to the credits, and then back to the boys. Pausing, the boys breathless, he dashed their hopes.

"Sorry. No prison-issue allowed. I'd take your bribe, but it'd come back to me, and my job's more important. Move on out."

Eyes followed them as they stepped aside.

Once in the street, Renhant whispered, "The credits, Jer'son. Stash 'em." He grabbed them, pushing them into his friend's pocket. "That money'll be gone into a thief's hands if you keep it out like that."

"Clothes. We need clothes," Jer'son finally decided. "Where can we get clothes?" He looked at the people passing around them, and finally grabbed one man's arm.

"Hey," the man cried, turning and spitting a black wad of sticky fluid at their feet. "You want to lose that hand?"

At the feel of something in his side, Jer'son let go. He froze as the man stood a moment, then sensing no danger, slowly put a weapon away.

"That was stupid. I almost burned you," the man growled. "Still might. What'll they do to me? Send me to Rant?" He snorted in a garish parody of a laugh.

"Man, I'm sorry. I just need clothes. Can you help?"

He looked at the three of them and laughed at what they

were wearing. "I'll bet you do, those prison-issues. Just in from the conscripts, I bet. No, don't tell me. I really don't care, anyway. Got any credits? For five, I'll show you a shop."

"Five," Barn't hissed. "No way, Jer'son."

Renhant pulled him back. "Let him deal with it. Just be quiet."

The man turned to them with a snarl. "You think I'd take you for free? This is Rant. Nothing's free."

Soon at the lighted stoop of a clothing shop, they beat on the door to get someone's attention. Inside, the shop owner motioned through a transparent section of the door for them to show credits, and she unlocked it to give them access inside.

"You intend to buy? All three?" she questioned. "What quality?"

"Something inexpensive. We are being laughed at in these. We need everything."

She snorted with glee. "I'll say you do, and I know that headgear for what it is. Let me do that for you, too." She pulled boxes from the shelves, sorted clothing, and showed them a room. "Try them for fit, but they will fit. My choices always fit."

Removing the dirtied things given them what seemed like a lifetime ago, all three boys breathed a sigh at the feel of undershorts once again against their skin.

Jer'son stood in the changing room with his two friends and laughed. "I was starting to have misgivings about giving up my shorts. I was wondering if being a freshie might have been better." Pulling the hats over their heads, they moved back into the shop.

Stepping out of an adjoining storage space, the shop owner whistled. "I am that good; that's why I get so much repeat business."

"People know you well, then." Renhant adjusted his hat in a reflecting panel.

"Non-issue is my business, boys. I do a good job, and they *come back*. However, they do me wrong, and I get them *in the back*." She laughed at her gallows humor, stressing her key words with lifted eyebrows. When they didn't catch the words she'd emphasized, she looked at them askance. "You didn't like my joke. You boys been here long?"

They just looked at each other without answering.

"I thought not. Wearing headwraps in this heat, huh? Sounds like a freshie to me. Well, freshies, at least you have new clothes. Come back if you live long enough to need more."

With that, soon they were on their way, half the credits gone.

"ARE WE having a good time, yet?" Jer'son grinned, tapping his fingers on the table to the beat of a fast song.

"What was that? I can hardly hear," Barn't yelled, the noise inside drowning out all but the loudest of voices. He held up his container of drink, giving a knowing wink. "I like this just fine. You know, they sure have good stuff in here. I don't feel thirsty anymore,"

"Barn't, after four of those, I wouldn't think you'd be feeling anything any longer." Jer'son reached to sip his own and sent up an order for another for the two of them.

"Jer'son, I don't like this." Renhant leaned close to whisper in his ear.

"Renhant, I'm beginning to think we should have left you behind." He leaned over to Barn't, pointing out a girl dancing on the floor. Laughing, he nudged him. "We'll have to ignore anyone dragging our little party down." He cocked a thumb towards Renhant.

"That man over there," Renhant insisted, nodding his head one direction. "He keeps looking at you."

Jer'son reached his hand and grabbed Renhant by the neck, pulling his face down next to his own. "The girls are that way," and he nodded the opposite direction, "not that way." When he turned his head the direction Renhant had indicated, he realized what his friend was trying to get him to see, images of a smiling instructor welcoming him to class each day, and the remembered dread of what might happen each night hitting him hard. He felt his expression of happiness melt away, his face wax in the heat of a flame. He was cold and very sober, all of a sudden.

"What? Is it Bird?" Barn't glanced around, wiping his mouth with one sleeve. "Has he come to take us home?" He giggled. His eyes were slightly glazed, and to anyone paying attention, it was clear he had drunk far too much for a seventeen-year-old.

"Shut up, Barn't!" Jer'son pulled his hat low, his stomach churning. "That's him!"

"Who?" Barn't cried out. He grabbed Jer'son's arm. "You see someone we know?"

"It's *him!*" His intoxication gone, he sagged farther into the chair. "Yeah, it's someone I know, stupid. From four standards ago. Flipping crikey, I shouldn't have come here."

"Why? Who is it?" Barn't loudly insisted on an answer, standing to look around.

Renhant grabbed him by the neck, emphasizing each word clearly. "Shut. Up. Barn't."

Then the man he'd seen was there, standing behind Jer'son, and all three boys froze. Not so old, the man had been little more than a youth himself during those days when he had worked at the academy. The past few seasons on Rant had hardened his face, though.

"I think I know you, boy. Seems like you were on an academy training ship, hm, must have been about four standard years ago." He strutted, a look of success at locating this particular boy writing itself across his face.

At the look of fury growing in Jer'son's eyes, Renhant touched his arm and whispered, "Don't. Please don't. Ignore him."

The man put his hands on Jer'son's shoulders and continued, "It seems like we got to know each other pretty well that year." Leaning down, his face next to Jer'son's, the man whispered where only he could hear, "You seemed to enjoy my visits all those dark nights."

At those words, Jer'son's erupting fury, blinded to Renhant's cautions and Barn't's confusion, exploded. He launched from his seat, his hands smashing into the man's face, displaying skills learned in MegaCorp's academy training classes, then honed on frightened undercadets. It seemed he caught his onetime activities instructor, now turned prison internee, quite off guard. As Renhant and Barn't tried to pull their friend back, his fury ripped him free time and again, pummeling the man until he finally lay still on the floor.

Jer'son, panting hard with exertion, his arms finally restrained, at last let himself be held in his friends' grasp. He spat his intentions, though. "I'll kill him. If he's not dead, I'll kill him." And he knew he would.

"Boys, it's time to be gone." Firm hands grabbed their shoulders from behind. Turning, their eyes fell as they saw the face of Bird standing there beside the establishment's bouncer. He turned to the big man. "Help me get them to the door. They will be tuckered out from their exertions."

The bouncer just grinned.

Navigating the crowded floor, the people moving aside as the bouncer led the way, the entourage stepped from the cacophony of the crowd inside to the silence of the now deserted streets. In silence, Bird led them back to the place he had that morning offered them as a home.

Once inside, he sat, his establishment quiet, the night nearly gone. He motioned for the three boys to join him. Jer'son remained standing as Renhant and Barn't pulled out chairs and sat. Seeing their friend had no intention of following their example, after a moment of indecision, they returned to his side.

"I'm sorry, Bird. We'll leave tonight," Jer'son mumbled. *Before I do something else I regret.* He felt tears growing in his eyes, and he didn't want them to fall. Not now. Not in front of his friends.

Bird exploded, "Ya'll do no such thing! Sit down, the three of ya'!" He waited until they complied, then stood, towering over them. Loudly he began, "I've been here more years than I can count, and I be forgetting the reasons why, but I was a freshie one time." He took a deep breath and continued, "Ya' took the credits, I know ya' did. Which one?" Jer'son made to stand, and Bird pushed him back down.

"Them credits was yours, anyway. They was for just what ya' did with 'em, and ya' made a good choice with the clothes, she being the best in town."

The boys looked up, suddenly aware Bird knew where they'd been, perhaps even all night.

"The little extra ya' spent having fun, well, it was worth it to see what ya' did there, boy. He had it coming, he did, and ya' gave it to him well." They could hear him chuckle. "Boys, let me see your shoulders, the mark they made there." As the boys pulled up their sleeves, Bird showed them the same mark on his wrist. "Ya' be tracked each time ya' enter and leave a building here on Rant. I didn't tell ya' and I should'a, I know." He pulled an information glass from a shelf, tapping it to turn it on. His fingers dancing in the air above the instrument, he pulled up the records of the boy's escapades. "There, ya' see. Anybody's number ya' know, ya' can track 'em. Stay inside or stay outside's the only way past it. Even a window'll track ya'. Never," Bird rapped his knuckles on the table beside him, "never give ya' number to no one. They got ya' if ya' do. Never give it to no one." He took a package out of a box and handed it to Jer'son. "For that lung. Ain't healed all the way, yet. Ya'll need to take this."

Bird turned, his hand on a chair back for support. "Me brain is tired, and me body is tired. Me speech be tired, too, me old words a'slipping in of their own accord. Boys," and before he turned his head away, his eyes could be seen glistening, "it's been many years since I sent me own boys off to die in some forgotten war, damn MegaCorp for taking 'em, but I be glad to have ya' as long as I can get ya' to stay. Your beds be ready up top the stairs."

Once he was gone, Barn't turned to the other two. "I thought he'd kick us out on the streets. Gods, that was close."

Jer'son lifted an arm and wiped tears from his face. "You think he really means it, that about wanting us to stay for as long as we want?"

"I think so," Renhant said. Then looking up at the ceiling, he whispered, "Thanks, Barkeen."

THE DOOR to the boys' room slammed open. "Boys! Up with ya'. It be a day for working. I got jobs for ya' all three. Let's be at it," and without another word, Bird summarily clumped back down the stairs.

Jer'son rolled over to see Renhant sitting already, his eyes bleary and darting frantically from side to side. "Hey, Renhant. You have that dream again?" He sat up to face him.

"I see her there looking at me, and I just want to do it with her again. She's dead, Jer'son, and I know it, and I want to do it with her again."

"You got the worst of it that night. You couldn't have known. She probably had a bad heart or something, and we didn't even know. We were just scared."

"The dream seems so real."

"Let it go, Renhant. Let it go." He lay back down, turning to the wall, and he put his hands between his knees, whispering to himself, "We all have our nightmares, only mine is walking this planet with me," and he blinked away the tears.

JER'SON SAT on the transport, the wheels underneath making the feel of the road vibrate every bone in his body. He coughed, the stuff Bird having given him making his lungs burn. He closed his eyes, the sounds of the men around him reminding him of times he had sat among other men, teenagers, really, fellow cadets onboard ship, only this time he wasn't on the ship.

He took a deep breath and coughed again. He glanced at his side, seeing a package carrying a change of clothes and some credits if he needed them. He smiled at the idea of Bird preparing it for him, muttering that he would be at the jobsite for several days, and who knew what he would find.

With the windows on the transport either opened or broken, the heat was mesmerizing, and he found himself very sleepy. His eyes closed once, and he jerked them open, rubbing his face to stay alert. Then, he felt the roughness of the transport fade once more, and drowsiness pulled his eyelids shut.

"You big clod. You broke another one." His father's disgusted expression burned into him. He tried to be careful, but his hands didn't always go where he asked them to go. Sometimes he watched them very carefully so they didn't touch something the wrong way, but then he might hit something else he didn't see with his elbow or foot.

He didn't like being here when his father was working. Sometimes when someone else broke something, just because Jer'son was tall, his father would see him and yell anyway.

"Fal'di, you just sit over there. Money's too tight for you to be breaking things. You just sit there like a good boy until your mother gets back."

"Dad, this is boring. I want to help. Please let me do something."

"If we lose this business, you'll think boring. How boring will it be sitting in front of an empty plate, never knowing if you'll get anything to eat? Do you want your mother to starve? We'll have to send you to MegaCorp just so you'll have food to eat. Your mother and I will stay here until we starve to death. Is that what you want?"

"No, Dad."

"Then sit there, Fal'di, and quit bothering me."

"I will, Dad."

Later, "Dad?"

"What, Fal'di?" It was very clear his father was irritated.

"I'm hungry. Did Mom pack my lunch?"

"Just sit there, Son. Mom'll be back soon."

"When, Dad?" He knew he'd gone too far when he saw his father step into the room.

Walking up to him, the man spoke in a quiet fury of heat. "Did I tell you to be quiet?"

"Yes, Dad." His voice quivered.

"Did I tell you not to bother me?"

Very quietly, "Yes, Dad."

"Did I tell you your mother would be back soon?"

He whispered this time. "Yes, Dad," and he braced his head with his eyes closed, waiting for the blow he knew would come. Just then he heard a door and his mother's voice. He took a deep breath in relief.

"Your mother saved you this time, boy. Next time I won't take so long to make you see you need to listen to what I say."

His father walked away from him, and he could breathe again. He listened to his father talking to his mother.

"Things are fine. Fal'di's sitting outside enjoying himself. I was just out there."

His mother replied, "I'm so glad to see you two getting along so well. That's good. He needs a good father like you." As she walked outside, she waved at him. "Hello, Fal'di. I hear you've been a good boy. Mommy loves you," and then she went back inside.

He loved her so much, and she didn't even know what happened while she was gone. If he told her, she might not love him anymore. He would try to sit very still so one would notice him. Most importantly, he would never ask for his lunch again.

He jerked awake. The sun was very bright, and he squinted as his eyes adjusted. He felt something at his side, and he remembered. It was his lunch and the other items from Bird.

He smiled.

Glancing ahead, he caught sight of the jobsite. Mega-Corp was building a new ship, and they were doing it here. Part of it, anyway. He knew how they were built; he'd had that as part of a class back at the academy. He'd just never been to a shipyard before. Pieces of the ship would be constructed, and then they would be moved offworld to be assembled. Smaller ships could be completed on the planet's surface, but the big cruisers couldn't take the strain in the gravity well.

He also knew this was where freshies started out. At least, it was where he was starting out. He would even get paid, eventually. When the part he was working on tested out successfully, then MegaCorp would cough up monetary rewards. That's how they assured quality control of the highest caliber. The corporation only paid if the work done was of the highest quality, and no one wanted to work on something that MegaCorp wouldn't pay for.

Jer'son stood to exit the old transport, Bird's package in his hand, its thoughtfulness easing old memories. He didn't know if his life would ever be all right, and at seventeen, he had a lot of life to live. Still, with Bird there, maybe he could get through this part of it.

ON ANOTHER transport headed to the same jobsite sat a man demoted for instigating a fight in a drinking establishment. He'd had problems ever since being transferred to Rant, but he knew it was never his fault. Not even the time he'd broken that one kid's jaw when the kid had told him to go milk himself and leave him alone.

It wasn't like the kid had been seeing anyone else. He'd had to start over that time, too. It wasn't fun to start at the bottom and work your way up, but that's what he was having to do one more time.

It was that fault of that new kid, the one he'd used that year on the training ship, and he wasn't a forgiving kind of man.

—Chapter 6—

"I saw it coming, and I just watched. At first I thought it couldn't be true, that things like this don't really happen to people. Then it hit, and the world came apart. I didn't even try to run or warn anyone. It just didn't seem possible it could be real."

—Survivor of the World Trade Center Disaster, 2001 A.D. (old-Earth timeline)

POOR JER'SON, Renhant sighed. *I've learned more about him in the last two weeks than I did in three standards at the academy.*

He leaned his head back, the jolting of the city's maintenance transport shaking his teeth in his head. At least he had plenty of time to think between stops, although he hadn't yet determined if that was a plus or a minus.

Something gnawed at him, though. He wasn't sure just how Barn't was taking all this, and that bothered him. He had always been a tag-along, willing to do whatever the other two suggested. He grinned as he thought of him back when they first met him. He was smaller than all the other cadets, could have passed for twelve even though he was fourteen, nearly fifteen at the time. Almost three standards ago, and it already felt like a lifetime.

Barn't was being bullied by some older cadets and couldn't get away. Renhant laughed at the reason. He refused to wear the academy-issue priv'tshorts. His mother always sent him some that he preferred; at least that's what he said. Renhant had heard rumors, though, that his mother was dead, and he was just pretending. Rumors said he couldn't let go of her.

His father did come to the academy on regular visits. That was the real reason he and Jer'son felt sorry for Barn't. That father. He was some kind of MegaCorp war hero, special decorations and everything, but something had gone bad with him. He was just an old drunk now, and the whole dorm suffered when the man visited.

One time, Barn't's dad had found a crease in his son's bunk. He had torn the covers from the bed, intending to demand it be remade to his imaginary standards. Inside the bedding was a pair of the non-academy issue shorts Barn't held as he slept, his security during the academy's long, lonely nights. When his dad laughed and held the shorts up for everyone to see, no one had wanted to look. So, Barn't's father carried them around and forced everyone to look, telling them his son was a sissy who would never make it at the academy.

That was why, when some uppercadets teased Barn't

about the shorts, and he ran behind Renhant and Jer'son for protection, they stood up for him. He'd been theirs ever since.

Jer'son, though. They'd been friends from that first year. He remembered the day Jer'son traded bunks. Renhant had been so envious for him to get that bunk, that little slice of privacy in the so-very-public academy world onboard the training ship. He remembered lots of nights before lights-out, he'd walk by, wishing he could be in that bunk instead. On some mornings, when Jer'son was slow to get up, Renhant would sometimes catch his eyes, and Jer'son would suddenly fly from the bedding.

That's why they had become friends. Renhant knew that catching his eyes every morning was something Jer'son had needed to force himself out of bed. Now Renhant knew why he had been slow to get up all those mornings. He wondered if his friend thought he had known. He hadn't.

He also remembered how Jer'son charmed everyone that first year, especially his teachers, as if he had to please everyone. It wasn't until the second year the pranks started. Then, Barn't came, their tag-along friend. After that, they let Bofsky into their group . . . Bofsky . . . may he burn in someone's hell, if there was one.

But poor Jer'son, off to that construction site today. He looked so distraught when Bird handed him that package and told him he'd be on an overnight job. Renhant did feel kind of sorry for him, but he knew it would be good, also. He thought that's why Bird picked that job for him, so he could be out of the city and away from that pervert he'd beat up. It seemed a really good idea to him, too, and he was grateful.

116

No one would know him, and the work would keep his mind occupied.

Renhant had his own work laid out for him today. He sighed again. Bird felt they needed to be kept busy, that Jer'son's plans for their botched outing had come from too much free time on their hands. The best of the three jobs had not come to him. He had been assigned to the city's maintenance transport, and he traveled with a digging tool in his hand. One of the men Renhant was working with today was called Racket, a big man who looked like he had lived a rough, mean life, and he was driving the transport. Each time they would stop, Racket would get out with a digging tool just like Renhant's. The other man, tall and thin but with seemingly endless strength, was named Cornerstone. He ran the big machine.

They had been at this all morning, and he was hot and tired. He rolled his eyes when Racket stopped the transport at yet another rough place in the street.

"Here's another one, men," he called through the broken back window. "Let's go, Ren, my man."

Renhant rolled his eyes. That had been his name the entire day. Ren, my man. He wasn't sure if Racket was changing it on purpose, or if he really did mishear when he had introduced himself. It didn't matter. It really didn't, he knew.

Cornerstone jumped down and swung the big machine out on its arm. Pulling a wired remote from a holder on the arm of the machine, at each stop he would manipulate it until the head of the big machine was just above the street's broken surface. An array of chipped, pyramidal teeth was poised to shred the ground. Pushing on the remote, the machine would punch the surface of the street until it was broken into many small pieces. Then, deftly rotating the big, counterbalanced machine so the top was poised at the bottom, he would step back for Racket and Renhant to do their part. Using very sore shoulders and their digging tools, they would spread the broken street surface evenly. Once they stepped back, Cornerstone would tap the remote, causing the flat foot of the big machine to pound the street back into a level surface. Resetting the machine and swinging it back onto the transport, they would all hop on and drive until they found another rough spot.

Finally, after an especially large damaged section where they'd had to move the transport several times, Cornerstone called out, "Anyone for lunch?" Sitting on the bed of the transport and leaning against the big machine, Renhant kept his eyes closed in the bright daylight, letting the other two make the decision. Finally, feeling a hand prod him, he glanced around.

"Renhant, look down there." He leaned over to look and saw the blue globe of a familiar world lazily turning underneath the glassine wall of the ship.

"What is it, Kien'ese?" He used her given name. It was too pretty not to.

"Don't you see it?" She took his arm, turning him. "Right there, on the top part. See where it curves out there?" She turned to look in his face, only to find him looking at her. "Silly, you'll miss it if you don't look. Those clouds are moving in over it." She reached one hand to push on the side of his face, turning his view away from her to the world below. That was her favorite thing about him, the way he loved to just watch her, to look at the shape of her face. He knew that. She had told him over and over.

"What am I looking for again?" His eyes studied the globe, familiar from his studies, but seen for the first time here today. "Point it out to me."

She reached down, taking one of his hands. Laying her hand atop his, she wrapped all but one of his fingers into his palm to form a fist. Placing her other hand underneath, she manipulated his extended finger until it pointed just where she wanted him to look.

"There." Releasing his hand, she turned to him. "Did you see it that time?"

He smiled. "I'm not sure. Do that again, and I think I might just be able to find it." He enjoyed the touch of her skin as her hand again grasped his, their arms together. He guessed wrong again and again as she used his hand to try to point out where her home was, even though he knew its location all along. He had looked it up on the glass the day before.

Laughing, she finally gave up. "How you ever passed your Earth geo classes, I'll never know."

"It's just that on the real thing like this, it's so different. One more time, and I know I'll have it. I almost saw it last time."

She looked at him doubtfully.

"Please, Kien'ese. This time I'll pay close attention."

"This is the last time," she said, taking his hand. This time he did pay close attention. He moved his feet ever so slightly until his arm just brushed the curve of her breast. Fabric slipped, skin tingled, and he felt his body respond. He stood frozen, all of his attention on her, watching her.

When she asked if he could finally see it, he softly answered her, "Just off the old-Earth country of Alaska, on the Aleutian Islands. I know."

She turned to see him watching her face. "What do you see there?" She smiled at the trick he'd played on her.

"I see a blue sky looking back at me, and surrounding it is the jet-black of the deepest space to run though my fingers." He reached his hand and brushed it down her cheek, coming to rest alongside her mouth. "I also see a beautiful girl with the most wonderful freckles I've ever counted." He smiled at that, and she reached up, pushing him away.

"Stop that. Are you coming with me?"

"Are you really going? Down there?"

"Of course, silly. My parents still live there. Even my grandparents are still alive. I may never see them again."

"Do they still love you?"

She put a hand on his shoulder and pushed him away in mock disgust. "What kind of question is that?" She turned back to the glassine wall. "Don't yours?"

He reached out and tapped the glassine, the view going blank. He leaned back against it, his eyes anywhere but on Kien'ese. "There was just my sister. She's gone, so I guess they don't. I always thought that if they had loved me, they would have stayed around. They would have tried harder not to get sick when the plague hit our world." His eyes now red, he squeezed his mouth tightly and was silent.

"I didn't know. I am so sorry. You must come with me. My family would love to get to know you." She placed one hand on his chest. "Please, Renhant?"

120

"When does the transport leave?" He turned his head to look at her, so beautiful there with him, and he smiled. At that moment, a chime sounded, a voice telling of the impending departure answering his question.

Kien'ese grinned back. "Now. We've got to go now." As she pulled his hand, a voice tugged his attention away, and he and Kien'ese turned to look down the corridor.

"Renhant!"

"I haven't changed my name, Barn't." He laughed to see his friend stopping beside him, panting, his hands on his knees, his face red.

"Jer'son says it's urgent. Hurry!" Then, he was gone, the answer to the why not even given an opportunity to be shared, only the need of the demand, its urgency.

Renhant released Kien'ese's hand. "I'm sorry, Kien'ese. I have to go," and he took off in a run. Turning and dancing backwards, he yelled, "I will come. I'll be back before the transport leaves." Blowing a kiss, he was gone even faster than before.

The joke told, the anger that he didn't find it funny, and the mad dash back to the transport left a disappointed Renhant standing at a glassine wall. Reaching out to tap it, a planet-based transport with the words *Destination Earth* on its side was seen slowly moving away from the academy training ship.

Renhant watched it with tears in his eyes and then with disbelief as the propulsion exhaust vent on one side suddenly glowed blue. His eyes opening in shock, he watched the letters on one side of the transport shatter and break free from their moorings, taking the contents of the transport along with it. In a final agony, the ship disintegrated before his eyes. Now, unable to tear himself from the scene before him, the suddenly blaring klaxons behind him went unnoticed. All he heard was the breaking of his heart.

"I thought maybe you might not want lunch, eh?"

Renhant shook his head, opening his eyes. Cornerstone stood before him, offering him a package.

"First days are long. In case you forgot about eating, I always bring an extra for someone's first day. You want?" Next to him, the driver of the transport smiled.

Renhant nodded his acceptance. "I appreciate it, and I did forget. Thanks, Cornerstone." He looked at Racket and took a proffered bottle. "You guys are all right, just all right," and he smiled at them, but in his mind he was counting the freckles on the face of a girl who was showing him a world he couldn't bear to turn his eyes to see. His eyes were already taking in the world right there in front of him, and she was the only thing he needed.

BARN'T TOOK the package he had been assigned to deliver and looked at it, turning it over in his hand, still standing inside Bird's foyer. Glancing up, he caught himself in a mirrored panel. He grimaced, not pleased with what he saw.

The slightest of the three boys, he could pass for much younger than seventeen. Always late to bloom, no matter the stage of his life, he had accepted that he would never be the smart, outgoing Renhant or the tall and handsome Jer'son. That was fine with him. It was enough that they were his friends.

He just wished he didn't know what he'd learned about

Jer'son. What if he really had liked it, what had happened that year? What if it had happened other years and he just wasn't telling? How would he know? What if Jer'son did that to *him* sometime? That guard on the jumpship had sure wanted to. Barn't didn't want to wake up sometime with Jer'son down there doing that to him.

He had never been able to figure out why Renhant and Jer'son let him be friends with them. Sometimes he wondered if they really liked him. The other two always bunked together, but never with him. He had always been forced into the next row over. When they wanted to do something, they always decided first and then asked him if he wanted to be a part. He always said yes, but that was because he didn't want to be left out. After all, what if they went and did the thing anyway, leaving him behind? They never had, but they might.

Maybe, and this made him shudder, Renhant and Jer'son even did things to each other at night. Maybe that's why he hadn't been asked to move his bunk closer on the ship. Now that he knew, sometimes he woke up at night to see where they were sleeping, and in the mornings, he wondered if they'd changed beds during the night. He looked to see if one bed looked more slept in than the other. He could never tell, but that didn't mean anything. Maybe he just didn't know what to look for.

He also knew he had to be very careful. His mother never came back. She said she would, but she never did. Renhant and Jer'son said they were a team, all for each other. They said they'd always be his friends, but he wasn't sure. What if they were lying?

123

He looked up as Bird walked through the door, and he inquired, "Where does this one go?"

"Ah, that be an easy one." Bird explained the dealer's location, close to where he had taken the last one.

Stepping from the door, he squinted in the bright light. It was always so *hot* here. He really didn't like the heat, but he couldn't do anything about that, could he?

However, he liked what he was doing because it gave him lots of time to explore the city. Bird wasn't really picky about how long he took to deliver the packages, so he thought he might want him to explore. He looked back at Bird's establishment, remembering the dread on Renhant's face when the city transport had picked him up that morning, and he giggled in glee. He also wasn't working when he explored, and he liked that even better.

One of the things he wondered about was the prison thing. Most of this didn't look like any prison he'd ever seen. Bird said he owned his place. How could he own it if this was a prison? Maybe only some of the people were in prison. They would have to do that, wouldn't they, have people to make the prison run right?

He stopped walking and looked across the street, hefting the package in his hand. This seemed like the right place. He stopped to think about the directions he had been given. Bird has said three over and four up. Or was it four over and three up? He tried to remember the way he'd come, and he realized he was lost.

They couldn't expect him to remember to count streets when he had other things to think about. This was not his fault. He would just have to walk up to the door and see if the people inside knew Bird. If they did, fine. If not, he'd just walk around and try to find the right place. It couldn't be too hard. After all, he'd never gotten lost on the academy ship . . . well, at least not for a very long time.

At the door, he knocked. After he waited a while, he knocked louder. When no answer came, he stepped back, wondering why there were no street signs. He remembered that from before he went to the academy. You found places by street signs and building numbers. He looked over at a door opening in the next building over. A face appeared, and a rough voice called to him.

"What do you need, boy?"

"I have a package to deliver." He held it up to show he really did.

"No one's there, boy. Won't be for a while. Come show me what you've got."

Hoping the man would take care of the package for the door that wouldn't open, Barn't walked that direction. When he got to the door, the man opened it wider with a grin. Barn't was surprised to see he was shaved bald.

"Who's it for, boy?"

Barn't turned it over and looked for a name. "It doesn't say."

The man turned to someone inside and yelled, "We've got a really pretty package out here. On the small side, just like you like 'em."

Barn't turned the package over, not understanding why the man thought it was so pretty. It was just wrapped in brown paper.

"How old are you, boy?" The man squinted at him, then

a second man appeared in the door, one with thick hair and a beard.

"Seventeen." Barn't stood tall. He knew he didn't look it, and that's why he wanted everyone to know.

"What do you think?" the bald man asked the bearded one behind him. "Do you like it?"

"I'll take it. It might be fun to have something new." The second man walked back into the building.

Barn't's eyes brightened, "So, can I leave it here?"

The bald man smiled. "Come on in, son. We'll enjoy keeping your package for a while."

As Barn't stepped in, the man closed the door behind him. When he clicked the lock, even that didn't trigger Barn't's concern. He just looked at the man and smiled, waiting.

JER'SON STEPPED from the transport and lined up with the others already there. Those who had come out with him, he had learned from Bird, were those who didn't have either the skills or the social ability to move up the ladder in this harsh society. Jer'son also knew that for those who chose not to participate in the jobs offered them, this society provided little except free clothing and basic foodstuffs. However, he had been assured this would be the place to start to learn how to exist on Rant.

"Armscans, here." A man waving a wand stood at the head of the line. "Day, only. Overnights, there." A hand pointed the way. Pulling his sleeve up, Jer'son walked over and put his shoulder under the correct scanner.

"Fal'dera Hult Jer'son. Registration documented for

126

current day's payshare. Documentation will be finalized upon checkout." The machine repeated the mantra with each person's shoulder presented to it.

"Sleeping quarters?" Jer'son questioned another man.

"First time?"

He nodded.

A hand pointed to an open bank of bunks. "Scan in, and it's yours. Verifies you're here and the locker unlocks only for you. Scan out and it releases your bunk to someone else." The man walked off with a surprisingly congenial nod.

"Thanks," Jer'son called to a receding back. Walking over, he chose one and put his shoulder up to the panel.

"Fal'dera Hult Jer'son. Occupant confirmed. Bunk 46. Please feel free to use locker to store your things."

"Shift is starting."

He looked up to see the man from earlier walk up to him. "Thanks." He tossed his package inside, keying the bunk to close, and fell in beside him. "Jer'son." He put out his hand. The other man looked at him for a moment, and then he smiled and matched his offer.

"Chr's."

"Zi'ggratson," someone next to him called. "That name was once known across half the arm, although it's now forgotten except in Rant's databanks."

"Ignore him," and Chr's laughed, waving the man away. "He's an idiot," he called louder.

"What do you do, Chr's?"

"Whatever they want me to do."

"How do they tell what you're good at?

"Readers. It's all in the records. They know we're here

127

because we signed in. They're already sorting us by skills. The more jobs you work, the wider your skill base, and the better your pay. People who only work a couple times a year get the minimum. Work every day, the pay might triple or even more if you've got a high-demand skill."

"My first day." Renhant chuckled. "It'll be low, low for me."

"Join the crowd," Chr's laughed, warming up. "I just can't get the hang of these latest updates. I'm struggling. Still, for pay, I'm several steps up the ladder. Here's a hint, kid. If you cause trouble, anywhere on Rant, you bump to the bottom of the pay steps, automatically."

"What about your skills, if you've got good ones?"

"It doesn't matter. This is Rant, remember? It's one of our incentives for behavior modification. Works for most people." Chr's stepped into a line. "Scan again, and they'll set you up. I'm here for at least a week. You?"

"Two days to start. I'm trying it out."

"That's smart, kid. See ya'. Just watch the toes you step on."

His arm scanned once again, Jer'son found himself in an electronics bay, a tool slapped into his hand. It was accompanied by a familiar voice.

"There, kid."

He turned to the man who'd handed him the tool, relieved to see a familiar face. "Chr's?"

"Looks like you've got some skills after all." He seemed impressed. "Where do you hail from?"

"The academy?" Jer'son was unsure of the answer he should give, but he could say that, he thought. "I was in

128

officer's training." He walked up to the console. "Hey, I recognize this. I trained on one of these. How can I tell what needs done?"

Chr's walked over and pulled a glass off a rack. "These are limited data access points." He laughed. "Known as L-DAPs. Carry one with you. Wherever you are, it picks up and displays the instructions for that station. Simple and easy."

Jer'son turned and smiled. "Maybe I can do this after all."

"They picked you, and that means you can." Chr's winked, and it made Jer'son feel good. "Go to it, kid."

"HEY, RACKET, are you feeling all right?"

Renhant turned to see Cornerstone standing over the third member of their team, currently sitting on a curb. "Can I do anything to help?"

Cornerstone held up a hand for Renhant to hold off for a moment.

"I don't think I'll make it for work tomorrow." Racket ran a hand through his hair. He sounded tired, and his voice was gravelly. "I feel really sick. This is bad." Suddenly, he paled, and doubling over, he retched in a series of dry heaves. Once finished, he grabbed Cornerstone's arm to stand. "I'm sorry for leaving you like this with no driver lined up."

"Not your worry. Let's get you back home and inside. We'll get a driver for tomorrow. Anyway, the job's shot for today. It's about closing down time, anyway."

"Thanks, man. Hey," and he looked at Renhant, rubbing

129

one eye and coughing. "Sorry for this on your first day out." He laughed roughly. "An apple a day makes the medic go away. My great-grandfather used to say that. I've never seen an apple, but I think I forgot mine today."

Renhant nodded. "Just get better." He turned to their boss. "Should we take him directly home?"

At Cornerstone's nod, they began to make their way that direction, traversing several city streets that Renhant had already begun to recognize as familiar. Upon arriving, Cornerstone motioned for Renhant's assistance, and they helped their driver inside.

As they exited Racket's abode, Cornerstone gave Renhant an appraising eye. "How are your driving skills, Ren, my man? Any good?"

"You have no idea. Nonexistent." He grinned.

The slender man pursed his lips. "Nonexistent as in not for a long time, or as in never did it?"

"Nonexistent as in, what is this?" He laughed. "I have no idea about the driving at all, although I have trained on a virtual T404 Trainer. Will that do?"

Cornerstone laughed. "We'll find out. You're in the driver's seat."

Renhant slipped in the transport. Several things looked obvious, but one thing did not. "To start it?"

"Tap the foot pad. It just goes. Max speed is very slow. You'll have no problem. It's not dangerous."

"That's what you think," Renhant mumbled. As he started off, the transport did wander back and forth for a very long way. Cornerstone just laughed and leaned forward.

"You're hired, Ren, my man. I like your driving. I'll see

you tomorrow. If you know a good man to join us, bring him along."

"I don't know anyone, but I'll keep a lookout."

"That's the attitude. I'm lucky you joined up with us."

There was more to it in Renhant's mind, though. If he had access to a transport, even a slow one like this—and during his first tenday on the planet—he might actually gain real skills, maybe even enough to get back at Bofsky someday. Yeah, he'd like that, indeed.

With that realization, Renhant's smile grew even wider, and it wasn't one Bofsky would have enjoyed seeing.

BARN'T LOOKED at the two men in the hallway, and he held out the package to them. Turning it over in his hand, he asked in a puzzled voice, "Why did you say it's a pretty package? It's just brown paper." When neither man offered to take it, he glanced to either side for a table. Ready to leave, he made as if to hand it to the man with no hair. "Where can I put it?"

The bald man smiled. "Here in the back room. Follow me." He stepped through a doorway, motioning for Barn't to join him.

Barn't entered a transitory space that had probably never been very nice. A cracked Vid screen was playing on one wall. At the back was a simple food preparation area. Several low and very well worn couches filled the remaining space

The second man, the one who earlier had come to the door just for a moment, leaned in and said, "I'd like to be first in the shower." A nod of a head sent him on his way. Soon, water could be heard through the ceiling above them.

131

Barn't frowned. He didn't know why this was taking so long. He took a step back as the first man walked up to him, not really nervous, just aware of how close the man was.

"You're seventeen, you say?"

He glanced away, embarrassed for a moment. No one ever believed he was his real age. Then he caught himself. Raising his eyes, he smiled proudly. "I look small, but I really am. I might still grow, though. My dad says he did, after he was older. The package?" He held it out to the man, already backing toward the door.

"Hold it for a moment, kid. Where are your stripes?" The man reached over and yanked up his sleeve. "You got 'em all right, so I guess you really belong here." A chuckle escaped his lips. "Should have known you couldn't be here without them."

"Hey, stop that." Barn't, taken aback at the man's forwardness, jerked away, and he pulled his sleeve back down.

The bearded man appeared, his hair wet, with just a towel around his waist, and he motioned for his friend to head upstairs.

Starting to feel distinctly uncomfortable, Barn't made a point to peer through an open window. "It's getting late. I think I'll just take this with me and bring it back later." The sun was high in the sky, but he now wanted to be gone from this place and these men.

The man put his hand on Barn't's shoulder. "Maybe you should just hold it until my friend gets back from his shower." He rubbed the top of Barn't's hat. "You know, some of us here like our boys young and sweet, but we don't get too many of those on Rant. We can't raise our own, and we can't choose our new assignees. So, we keep each other informed. A friend of ours on the most recent jumpship let us know a pretty one was on the way, but I didn't think I'd find him so soon. You may know the guard. Tan'sn."

The man leaned down to look directly into Barn't's face, and a gleam of desire leaped into his eyes. He paused for a moment, studying him, and then he grinned. "Then that new boy walks right up to my door."

Barn't felt him grab his face, fingers on one side, thumb on the other, and rub across it gently. He was frozen speechless, and he could barely breathe.

"I wonder what I'll find under this hat, a freshie, or a head of hair?" He yanked the hat off. "It *is* that freshie!" The man laughed at his performance.

His friend came down the stairs, now freshly showered. "Don't tease him." To Barn't he was gentle. "There's no need to be frightened, boy. We just don't get new blood very often, and when you're it, you have to be ready to share. Now, I think it's time to put that package down." He took it, setting it on a side table. "Let's see what we have underneath that shirt of yours."

Barn't stood in shock as the man removed his shirt and ran his hands over his arms, chest, and back. He was scared now, and he thought of Jer'son. He had known Jer'son could have said no. He'd just known it. Jer'son must have wanted it to happen. Why else would he have lain there night after night while that instructor messed with him? That's why he'd thought all those things about him, and about Renhant, too, why he'd looked to see if Jer'son and Renhant were together. That was why he'd looked to see which bed had been slept in the most. He hadn't really believed Jer'son, hadn't really wanted to believe him.

Later, in the shower, the rest of his clothes gone, the men's hands once again on his body, he remembered the sound of the lock as he entered, and he repeated in his head, *This isn't my fault. Bird didn't give me good directions. The men locked the door. They're bigger than me. They might hurt me. I'm scared.*

As the men moved him to the bed and took turns driving his face into the pillow, he closed his eyes and whispered to himself over and over, "Jer'son could have said no. Jer'son could have said no. Jer'son could have said no."

But he knew it wasn't true.

BARN'T SAT on a side step outside Bird's establishment, one rarely used except during the day. He had been there for several hours. Allowed to shower and clean himself after the men's exertions were completed, they had not been unkind, but they had let him know others were looking for him, also.

This he could not do, to let everyone who would, use him as those men had today, so he sat, the package in his hand, the world sliding by, as he entertained no thoughts at all in his head except the one. *I cannot do this. I cannot do this. I cannot do this.*

"Bird! I've found him!" Renhant threw the door back, letting it slam noisily into the stone wall at the side. It rebounded, closing with a soft click as he tore across the walk. "Barn't, what is it?" He dropped to the step and put his arm around his friend's shoulders, giving him a quick squeeze. He turned at the sound of the door. As Bird stepped across the threshold, he came around to look at Barn't in the face.

"Me word, I was afraid this'd happen, I was. I seen this look before, and now I see it on one of me own. Poor boy to have this happen to 'im." He stepped to Barn't's side to help Renhant stand him up and walk him through the door. As they stepped through, Barn't stopped and looked directly in Renhant's eyes.

"Jer'son couldn't have said no. He couldn't have said no."

"No, he couldn't, Barn't." Renhant looked away, catching Bird's eyes, and his began to water.

As they helped him upstairs and covered him up on his bed, he kept repeating that phrase over and over.

"He couldn't have said no. He couldn't have said no."

—Chapter 7—

She grinned with the plan starting to form in her mind. A few rocks wrapped up with him, and the sea floor could claim him. "Yes," she said aloud to herself as she turned back to gather some of her fresh supplies. "That could certainly work. A few rocks would take care of the problem just fine."

—Paraphrased from
*Holcum's Dynasty: The
Grandmothers*

"HE NEVER believed Jer'son, did he, Bird? All that time since the medic told us, he never believed what Jer'son said." Renhant turned raw eyes to his mentor. "I can see the little things, now. Sharp looks. Easy encouragements he didn't want to say." He dropped his head into his hands, tiredness making him numb. He sat for a minute and then looked up, an understanding of the situation suddenly clear to him, one he'd never had the chance to see before.

"Barn't's never really felt like one of us. I even thought of him as our tag-along friend. When we wanted to do something, I never asked Barn't first. Never. I always went to Jer'son. Jer'son did the same with me. We knew Barn't would go along. He was just like that."

Bird prompted, "Would ya' have done what he wanted if he'd a'asked ya'?"

"I don't know. I think so, but I really don't know. He never asked. Never."

"Son, ya' can't beat ya'self up over something that's already happened."

"Bird, after the medic let Jer'son's past out, he felt he had to tell us everything. He told us what happened that first year at the academy. See, now I realize I was there when all that happened, every day, and I didn't even know. I was right there. I was even jealous of the attention he was getting. How can that happen and a best friend not know? Gods, I walked right by his bunk every morning and every night. I looked him in the eyes, and I never knew."

Bird reached a hand and placed it on the boy's arm. "Some things scar us on the outside, boy, and the world looks and laughs. Some things just scar us on the inside." Bird paused, then sniffled. "The inside's worse. Sometimes I envy them's got the scars on the outside. Them's the lucky ones. Your friend's gonna have a hard time up there. To-night's gonna be hard, and the morning's gonna be hard, and the day, tomorrow. All's gonna be the hard thing for him, now. Be with him, boy." He took a deep breath before continuing. "It'll fade for him, what be inside, but it be public, too, and that be harder. People'll remind him, some on purpose. Hold his hand if ya' have to, do whatever it takes. There be good in this world, even on Rant. Help him see it. It just be harder to find here."

"Did you ever find it, Bird, the good here? Did it ever come to you?" Renhant leaned in, desperate with need, especially after the attack on one of his own. "We were bullies on the ship. Did you know that? We can be bullies, still, and would be if others weren't stronger and smarter than us."

"Aye, I did, and I do. That's there with the other. Your records tell it all."

"Why'd you take us in, then?" Renhant pleaded for reassurance.

Bird looked away. "Cause I found the good here, boy. I weren't strong enough to hold it, but it were mine for a time. And good it were, too." He smiled at Renhant. "I think ya' know what I mean. Ya' found it, too, ya' did. It helped ya' when ya' needed it most, didn't it?"

Renhant looked into Bird's eyes, those eyes he'd seen mist with emotion, then turn gruff with irritation, and he knew her for who she was. "Barkeen?"

"Aye, boy, and they don't come no better. Too good for me, she were, but she graced me life for a time, and I be the better man for it." He grinned at the boy and tapped his chest with a fist. "Still got me a soft spot for her, and she knows. Aye, she knows, so she sends me the likes of ya'. I trust her, I do."

Renhant smiled and leaned forward again as he told Bird something of his own experience with Barkeen. "The guys asked me that on the station, did I trust her, and I gave them that very answer. I told 'em, I sure do."

"HERE, CHR'S, hand me that big lever." Jer'son reached his hand behind him, taking the tool from his new friend. He looked at him with a confident grin. "I'm going to put it in here. When I twist, you push as hard as you can. On my mark. Three. Two. One. Mark."

"Ahhiiieee! Ahhch! It's in, my friend. Excellent!" Chr's grasped the young man's shoulder in congratulation.

"I think we make a good team, and this will be a good ship." Jer'son laughed. "Especially now that I'm working on it." He was inordinately pleased. It was the small success with the difficult installation, he thought.

"True, but this will not be a good ship for many years to come." Chr's put the lever back in its place, sitting down to rest.

"Standard years? Or Rant years? And how many are you talking about?" Jer'son didn't intend to waste forever here, and getting off Rant included learning what he could and moving on. If it took many years, it would be that long before he collected any real funds from this project. He had learned that much, at least.

"This is all first stage construction, my friend. Many standard years will pass before this can be complete. Many Rant years, also." He paused, and then seemed to completely change the subject. "You know, I used to be a scholar."

"A scholar? That is?" He frowned in puzzlement. That was a term he'd never heard.

"A learned person of much information. That's what got me here."

139

"How did information get you here?"

"I loved it so much, I took more than I should, selling it to the highest bidder. When MegaCorp decided it wanted it back, I had already spent it all. So, here I am." He sat back and laughed before leaning in to Jer'son. "I also embezzled many, many credits, and it took them years to know."

"That must have galled MegaCorp when they made the discovery."

"You don't understand the half of it. You know, on old-Earth, before there were even glasses—" he leaned over and held up one of the L-DAPs "—or space flight or MegaCorp, they built giant stone monstrosities like this to their gods." Chr's stretched his arm toward the ship. "Some appeared as solid as the rock they built them from, and others were as lacy as my ex-bedmate's undergarments."

"Out of rock?"

"Rock, my boy. Stone." He sat up and leaned forward. "Here's the deal. They didn't plan for it to be finished while they were alive. They knew the time span it took to build an edifice so grandiose. Today, if it's not complete within several local months, it has been too long. I tell you, Jer'son, the workers then would be proud to be the grandson or great-grandson of the stonemason who had labored on just a few blocks. Fifteen standard years to build the grandest star cruiser ever envisioned? Those years are not so long, my boy. Not in the annals of time." He smirked. "It will go to a great captgen'l, I'm sure."

Jer'son leaned in close, defiantly sharing the one secret that could now make his life worth living. "I know one man I would like to be on it, because if I could guarantee that, I would find a way to sabotage it, one that wouldn't be detected, and he would be gone with his dreams into the blackness of space, naught left but stardust."

Chr's laughed with the robust gusto of one truly amused. "You certainly have the grandest dreams of any I have ever met. I wish you the luck of the stars, the luck of twin stars if there are any out there with habitable worlds around them, that you accomplish your dream, and better yet, that you allow me to help you."

Now Jer'son laughed. "Why habitable worlds?"

Chr's looked at him through slitted eyes as if his point was a secret to share. "It's the people that bring the luck. It doesn't just happen."

"Then, done. A twin star with a habitable world. Shake on it." He stuck out his hand.

"This is a strange custom for me, but it's of old-Earth, and I like it." Chr's reached out his hand and struck the deal.

Jer'son felt extraordinarily pleased, as if Bofsky might indeed someday fly this very ship, and it would send him into the deepest hells that had been invented by the cruelest religions ever known to any race.

THE TWO MEN shaking hands caught the eye of one lowly day worker, a youngish man with a face just going hard, one who liked boys barely past that age when they were no longer boys, one with injuries not completely healed from a refused advance in a city drinking establishment. The man's eyes grew hard, and his plans grew thick. He wanted revenge.

He turned to the man beside him and put a question to

141

him. "How can I get assigned to there?" He pointed to the insides of the great frame of the ship.

"It won't happen, man. Only the smartest and brightest get posted there. At three to four times the pay, to be sure. Some get more than that."

"The pay doesn't concern me. Someone who works in there does."

The man beside him laughed. "Ah, I see. Revenge is what drives you hard." He looked piercingly at the onetime instructor. "How hard?"

Without expecting a successful response to his sudden proposition, and knowing that any money from this job was years away, he called his price. "A week of this job's pay."

With widened eyes, the man told him, "I think I can get you there. If I do, the pay's mine. If I don't, you owe me nothing. Is it a deal?"

"Struck in dirt." The instructor stomped his foot in the soil, leaving an imprint, his partner on the fly stomping in the same place.

Those watching knew some powerful deal had been closed, and they made sure their feet avoided the imprint in the dusty ground. A deal struck in dirt was a mighty thing, indeed, and no one wanted to risk his or her own position on the jobsite.

"BARN'T, YOU'RE with me today."

The smallest of the trio rolled over and curled into a fetal ball, unwilling to be the person he felt yesterday had created in him.

"Barn't," Renhant repeated. "I'm not taking no."

"No. Go away." A hand struck out, batting at air.

"Barn't, I'm your friend, and I'm with you today. That means you're going with me. Up," and Renhant rolled him out of bed onto the floor.

"Ow! That hurt!" With reproach in his eyes, the emotionally bruised boy sat up, rubbing his shoulder.

"That sounds like the Barn't I know. Let's move."

"I can't, Renhant." He wrapped his arms around his legs and dropped his chin on his knees, his face flushed. "Everyone'll know. I can't go out there."

Renhant dropped to a squat in front of him, and he looked at him hard. His voice was stripped of sympathy. "Did you ask those men pretty please to do that to you?"

"No!" Barn't's eyes flew open, shocked.

"Did you enjoy it so much you asked them to do it again?"

"Gods, Renhant!" He began scooting away from the impromptu interrogation. "No!"

Renhant reached both arms around his friend's neck and pulled him close, forehead to forehead, his tone quickly softened with the ardent denials. "Then you have nothing to be ashamed of. The memories will be awful, but you do not have to feel shame."

"People will think I wanted those men to do that."

"We will know better. That's what counts."

In a very small voice, Barn't said, "I thought Jer'son wanted that man to do those things to him."

"Now you know differently."

"What if people think that about me?"

"Then I'll still be your friend, and Jer'son will still be

143

your friend. Do you have any more friends on this planet you haven't told me about?"

"No."

"Then, friend, we're the only ones that count."

This time, when Jer'son stood and stepped back, Barn't got up and began to dress.

At the bottom of the stairs, Bird stood, and he glared at the boys as they came down. "How be it that this friend don't count?" Then he burst into a bright grin and put his hand on Barn't's arm. "For me serious side of things, boy, this be a tough world, and ya' must be tough to be here. Ya' got it in ya', so show them who's wanting to knock ya' down."

Stepping back, he let them pass, and then he called out, "There be lunches for the two of ya'; drinks there be, too. Gods speed ya' along and bring ya' back safely."

Grabbing the lunches and drinks, Renhant stopped at the door. Then, he grabbed four more drinks, two for his pockets and two for Barn't's. He grinned with a glint in his eye. "I was out there yesterday. More drinks are better. You think it's hot now, wait until midday."

Cornerstone threw Renhant a pleased smile when he saw him walk up with a ready partner. Aside he remarked, "Can he keep up? He looks slight."

Renhant laughed. "His height is coming, to believe his daddy. I think this work is the best way to get it."

"Ha! Ren, my man. You are after my own way of think-ing. I'm glad to have you drive for me today. Let's go."

Cornerstone handed Barn't his digging tool, although he just looked at it with confusion and dismay. Then Corner-stone patted the back of the transport to indicate where to sit.

144

Renhant's tool rode up front with him, where Ren, the man, gradually became adept at maneuvering the snail he had driven so erratically the day before.

CHR'S, JER'SON, and the other overnighters had deposited their L-DAPs back to the shelves, racks, or hangers where they belonged, and trudged back to the bunks.

Jer'son opened the package Bird had sent and spent a credit on a meat pie from a portable vendor. With the day still light, he sought out Chr's, finding him in a small group off to one side. With a rousing whoop, Chr's stood and waved his new friend over, introducing him with glowing accolades. Embarrassed, Jer'son brushed his words off with a casual motion of his hand. Then, with a flourish, the self-proclaimed scholar turned to those gathered around him.

"Now, my men, those of you brave souls who dare test war's power, I dare you to put forth your finest words in this grand hour. For this good friend, in a time of revenge now standing, has need of our assistance, so with us he is now banding." Chr's then bent low and put his finger to his lips. "It must be our secret, I think you must know, because he doth wish, up, the ship to blow!" At this, the men sitting around burst into riotous laughter.

Chr's was very drunk. Jer'son could see that, and also that his crowd was not far behind, but to proclaim such a deed so blatantly? He put an arm around Chr's' neck and pulled his face close. "Are you trying to get me in trouble, telling that aloud to everyone?"

"Not to worry, my friend. It is an old tradition. On one's first night out, we dream of ways of dismembering the old girl. Of the most creative, we take those with us and ponder their feasibility. None, of course, could possibly work. MegaCorp would search it out, and we would be out of business. Commonsense always prevails. But the dream is what keeps us. Will you listen as our ideas we share?"

"I would like that. Thank you, Chr's." His anxiety assuaged, Jer'son forced himself to relax and smile.

A rowdy group, the noise only elevated as the evening fell. Jer'son glanced overhead, unaccustomed to this gradual darkening of the sky. Sure, he grew up a groundie with a sunrise and a sunset, but it had been a long time. He hadn't yet become used to it again, and he found it somewhat disorienting. But even so, he found it gave a sense of closure to the work they'd accomplished that day.

He blinked as a container was placed in his hand, his own restrained consumption soon pulling him into the sortie, and he began to pay attention to the audacious suggestions and the equally outlandish retorts.

"My idea is to use explosive paint. It ignites in deepest space," one man cried out.

"Nah, the ion drive would do better to set it alight. Just get it far from a world you want to keep!" The laughter rang at that.

"Line the captgen'l's quarters with hallucinogenic mushrooms. He'll drive the ship into the sun."

"He'll probably just scrape it off and drink it in his tea!" The old-Earth drink was unknown to many of those around, but the context was clear, and the crowd roared.

"Put poisonous larvae in the water hold. All the men'll die of dysentery."

146

"Maybe on this world, old man. They keep medicine up there!" The men roared again.

The scholar, Chr's, stopped the series of gibes and let the laughter quiet its lazy ripples. He stood, his stance unstable, his eyes bleary. His words, however, were clear.

"Our honored guest is standing here with me, or to be more accurate, sitting here at my side with his many drinks." Chr's glanced down at Jer'son's waving hand showing one finger raised. "Oh, just one? Well, with just one drink, he is far too intoxicated to stand. So, I will point to which one he is, and I would like you to listen to our guest's rendition of how to sabotage our magnificent ship and still get paid for the work." At that, the laughter rippled again. Chr's raised his hand for silence. "Shush! Quiet, all."

"Jer'son, here." He stood and pointed at the crowd with his drink, not the least bit drunk by any measure. He barely felt a buzz. "To you who have made the best of a bad situation. To the many of you who should not be here," and he paused as a ripple of applause spread around him, "and the rest of us who should." Even louder clapping showed the sense of humor in the men. "I propose a practical solution, but one that would never be discovered." It was not his idea, though, rather something from an unsolvable classroom exercise that was given once for extra credit. He was unable to think of anything else. "It is a two-stage jimmy. First, we stymie all the escape pod doors so they are testable, but not usable. Escape pods only function when the doors are at full retract, after all."

The crowd grew surprisingly quiet as Jer'son spoke. When he paused, thinking he might have breached some unknown code of this game, a voice rang out. "The second step? What is that?"

"Easy. Although it's a basic design principle that the propulsion actuator arm must always remain engaged during ion burn, we pretend otherwise. We tweak the design to rig the propulsion actuator arm as a type of pressure relief valve, claiming it is designed to 'unhinge' itself during system overload. So that our deception would never be discovered, we even mock up a 'reset' mechanism that would 'reset' the actuator arm automatically. If ever the ship's systems are pressed hard, it will destroy itself, and no escape will be possible."

Several whispered voices could be heard, some comments uncertain, yet other voices thinking this was the joke, something so complex it could never be done. One old, cracked voice was different, though.

"Wait, wait. Many years ago, this test was run, this considered a possibility, a method of improving the ion drive's thrust parameters with only modest design changes. I set it up myself." The voice paused, as if having to think, before going on hesitantly. "A prototype was actually made. It worked, too, at first. Only too late did the original purpose of the actuator arm become apparent. The arm was originally designed to restrain the forces of an overload. We thought we could mitigate the pressure on the arm, damping the stress, allowing it to dissipate. Removing the pressure had the opposite effect, resulting in catastrophic failure." The speaker, an elderly man, turned to walk away, his voice losing its strength, as he began mumbling, "This might work, although to disarm all the escape pods might not be possible.

I had forgotten this. What else have I forgotten?"

"Chr's, who was that?" Jer'son turned to question the man at his side.

"He invented the ion propulsion drive. He was sent here to keep it from ever being duplicated. He's the only one with all the records, only it's locked away in his brain, and he can't get to it." Then, he burst into a grin. "They loved you, Jer'son. They frickin' loved you."

"LOOK, BARN'T. Hold the digging tool like this." Renhant hefted his in front of him, flipping a pile of crushed road surface back to a low spot. "This is our job. Cornerstone breaks and packs. We smooth. Sound easy enough?"

"Sure. This'll be easy." He grinned. "I just ride around, flip, and level. I can do this."

Cornerstone laughed. "Just say that this afternoon when it's hot and your shoulders hurt." Seeing a worried shadow cross Barn't's face, he offered something more soothing. "You get used to it, plus it pumps the muscles up really fast."

Barn't grinned at the prospect, then taking in Cornerstone's wiry frame, he frowned. "Where are yours?"

"*This* is my job, son." He held out the remote and pushed a button. "I have very muscular fingers." That got a grin from his young companion.

"Did you do this before you came here? Can I ask about that?" He looked at Renhant, who in turn glanced back to Cornerstone.

"Some people don't like it, but me, I don't care. It's always polite to inquire about personal preferences before questioning, though, if you enjoy living peacefully." Cornerstone continued pressure stamping the roadway as he talked. "You know what a termite is."

"Sure," Barn't answered. "It's a nanobot that keeps the comm feeds clean."

"That's only one meaning of the word. It's also a living creature. A very small creature. A bug."

"Can you see it?" Barn't studied his hand. "You think I have any on my hand? Do they eat skin?"

"Sure," Cornerstone said, finishing up the road repair, and effortlessly flipping the big counterbalanced machine up and onto the transport. "If they're hungry enough. Jump on, Barn't. We're through here. Drive, Ren, my man."

"Why do you call him Ren, my man?"

"It's his name, boy. Now, back on our conversation. Think about the termites. They're about the size of your pinkie nail." He pointed to Barn't's little finger. "A couple of them got to a planet that didn't want them. Now, these termites I'm telling you about build in the ground, and the dirt they hollow out is piled above the ground, making really big mounds of dirt. These people didn't like the dirt mounds."

"Couldn't they just push the dirt back in?"

"These termites have spit that turned the dirt on that world to concrete. That's true, to be sure. I used one of these machines I have here today and busted up those termite piles, and then I stamped the dirt back into the ground. I did that for many standard years. What do you think of that, huh?"

"I like that idea. We're not just breaking up the road, we're busting up the bugs' houses and stomping them back into the ground."

Cornerstone grinned at the concept. "Yeah, I guess we could look at it that way."

Stopping for lunch, Cornerstone pulled Renhant aside. "I like your friend. He's a good worker. Talks a lot, too," and he just bobbed his eyebrows at that. "However, he sits kinda funny. Does he have a problem with constipation?"

Renhant thought for a moment before answering, then grinned. "I guess you could say that. He was a bit impacted yesterday. He'll be fine, though. It embarrasses him to talk about it, so we don't mention it, all right?"

Cornerstone shot him a thumbs-up.

THE DAY finally over, the drunken crowd dispersed, Jer'son lay in his bunk, the warm night air filling the space around him. It was nice, the stars overhead, the work something he knew and enjoyed. It was good to be out from the city; here he felt safe. It was open, the people friendly. This didn't feel like a prison out here, not really. Sure, he was still monitored, he knew that, and he couldn't leave the planet or anything, but this *could* be a life.

He smiled, thinking of that actuator arm. He had no idea it could be a real plan, just remembering it as one that had been presented as a challenge by an instructor in one of his academy classes. It had clearly been designed as an unsolvable situation, and since the solution hadn't been required to pass the class, he'd tired of it eventually. Imagine that old man claiming to have actually created a full-size mockup, much less an actual ship. He was certainly old enough to have really invented the original ion drive.

He reached and touched the bottom of the bunk above

him. Doing so brought back memories of being at the academy. His life had been better then, or at least he would have thought so recently. His new friends from Chr's' gathering painted a smile on his face; they had liked his idea. They liked him.

With the quieting of the night, Jer'son let his mind drift, until he was soon fast asleep.

WITHOUT SO MUCH as a by your leave, Barn't dove through the broken window of the transport, landing in the cab beside Renhant. He slumped down in the seat, his face white with terror. Renhant looked at him with a question on his face.

"Is something wrong?" He watched him nod his head vigorously. "Spit it out, then, will you?"

"One of them, sitting right over there." He pointed across the street, sliding even lower. "The men from yesterday."

"You're sure that he's one of them? You know, last night Bird tried to track where you'd gone, but that building you were in was unregistered to anyone."

He whispered, "I saw them both and talked to them. I would know them anywhere. It's him."

"What do you want to do, then? This is your call."

"I don't know."

"Cornerstone will want to know what you're doing. What do I tell him?"

"You're my friend?" He looked at Renhant and away again, his eyes red with emotion.

"Of course." Renhant punched his shoulder.

"No matter what?" His voice wavered.

"No matter, Barn't." Renhant didn't know where he was going, and he suppressed a smile. He meant what he said, though.

"Tell Cornerstone. He'll know what to do." He slumped even farther into his seat, completely out of view of the world outside.

"Are you sure? Once he knows, we can't take it back."

He turned to see Cornerstone peering questioningly at him through the empty window. He looked at Renhant for a moment before dropping his eyes. "Yeah. Will you do it, though?"

"Sure." He looked back out the broken window. "I'm stopping here, Cornerstone."

"Sure. You're the driver, Ren, my man."

RENHANT STEPPED out and pulled Cornerstone out of Barn't's hearing. "There's a little more to Barn't than I mentioned earlier." He looked down the street where the man Barn't had seen was still sitting, doing something or the other, and he pointed him out to Cornerstone. "That man with the beard, you see him?"

"With the dark hair there by the wall. That him?" Cornerstone pointed with his head.

"Yeah. My friend isn't exactly constipated. Yesterday, that man and a friend—"

"No more words are necessary," Cornerstone interrupted. "I know what your friend is hurting from. I know this man. I know his friend. They are very bad people, living in unregistered houses. Traceable to the authorities, but not to us, not unless we get their number, and that is very hard to do. The authorities? They don't care unless the stability of their operation is jeopardized. One poor boy doesn't do that, so they do not care. However," Cornerstone grinned broadly, "I like your friend, and I care very much."

"If we could get his number and give it out or something, how much would that hurt?" Renhant was beginning to enjoy this.

"Very much, my crazy driving friend. If you could perhaps lose control just a little bit at just the right time, I happen to have a little toy here, used to check the transport in and out to me. It will record his number just as well. Pin him down, and if a leg breaks, my regular driver is sick today, and the bad places, they have to be repaired. So, if you do not drive so well, neither do I. So, let's go be a crazy driver. Just be crazy in the right spot, my man."

Barn't was left around a corner to wait while they went for the gold. The transport having already driven along one side of the street, the man thought nothing of seeing it moving up the street again. As it swerved towards him, he stared in amazement, the transport quickly pinning him to the wall. Cornerstone leaped to his side and yanked up his sleeve, and Renhant grinned as he began yelling and cursing. Struggling, he knew the man had no recourse when the reader was slapped against his number code. With that public, there would be no privacy, because according to Cornerstone, anyone in the city could trace his every movement.

Renhant felt a great deal of satisfaction as Cornerstone looked him right in the face and said, "If your friend stays in the city, he's next. Tell him he can count on it."

He backed up the transport, pausing around the corner to

make sure all interested parties were on board, and then they were off.

"What can you actually do with that number?" He watched Cornerstone entering information rapidly into the hand-held device.

"In fact," he answered, "I've already done it." He held up his portable reader to show the display, grinning. *Boy lover rapes children, XX09573949-OX. Have you seen his friend?* Beside it, a small animated avatar with an incredible likeness to the bearded man sat crumpled against a curb, just as they had left him. "It's already on the broadcast network. What do you think, my friend Barn't?"

Barn't smiled, "I like it very much. Thank you, Cornerstone."

"You are very welcome, my good friend."

Renhant winked at him. The word friend was an unexpected treat from Barn't's rescuer, and Cornerstone didn't even know. He leaned in to Barn't and whispered, "That makes four."

Barn't smiled even wider.

JER'SON WOKE, his second day at this job. He looked around, the morning already alive with the activity of men climbing from bunks. He smelled the growing heat permeating the air. The day would turn out to be a scorcher, he was certain. Swinging his legs over, he dropped to the ground, the food vendors already making the rounds. Pulling a credit, he soon had firstmeal food wraps to carry in his search for his friend. He had a question for Chr's about the job today.

Down the way Jer'son saw the personal facilities and the

showers. His change of clothes! He put his nose in his armpit and decided that a shower and clean clothes should be the first thing he did. Chr's could come later.

He returned to his bunk and gathered his fresh clothes as well as more credits, expecting that the showers, as all else on this world, probably came at a cost. Soon he found that as he had suspected, indeed, nothing was free.

Watching those already in the low-walled showers for a moment, not caring to be caught half complete, he planned what he must do. The time allowed was very short. His clothes were off before his credit was entered. His hair, his armpits, and his groin, then a quick wash over everything else, and the water was gone. He grinned, stepping out as he heard others cry out about the extra credit or two they must now insert.

Slipping his clothes on, he felt better already. Rolling his used things, he jogged to his locker, dropped them in, and headed out to find Chr's. As he looked in all the places he could think of, concern began to gnaw at him. Seeing others from the night before, none knew where the scholar was, although a few thought they had seen him walking with a man, maybe heading out to the job site.

He began to jog that direction, his hazy concern soon solidifying into concrete alarm. No others were at the job site yet, and why would his new friend have gone there so early?

"Chr's?" he called repeatedly.

Reaching his and Chr's' work area, he called out again, and all he heard was the silence of the shipyard. Then, he caught the muffled sound of a groan. Easing forward cautiously, their workspace from the day before bare, he saw the glimpse of a leg sprawled across the ground. As he moved forward to see, he found the wide eyes of his friend staring back; and without warning, pain erupted in his head, and his world went black.

WAKING, JER'SON felt his hands tied behind his back, and he could see his legs were also bound. His mouth was gagged and tied. Across from him was Chr's, and beside him, Jer'son's old instructor holding a long metal rod.

As he began to struggle in an attempt to reach his friend, he heard his old tormentor taunt, "You humiliated me. You refused me. Now, you get to choose. You can be mine of your own free will or watch him die. Here's a sample," and he swung the rod with all his strength, connecting with Chr's' leg. The leg crumpled, and Chr's writhed in pain.

When Jer'son was asked again, his heart knotted in his chest. Desperate, he locked eyes with his friend. The injured man violently shook his head no. Jer'son saw the metal rod flash in the air once more, closing his eyes as he heard the meaty whup of the metal impacting once again. Soon, the sounds came faster and faster, and Jer'son, his lids squeezed tightly shut, began to nod his head yes over and over in a vain attempt to stop the noise, to stop the sounds of an innocent man being beaten to death.

The cloth was unexpectedly pulled from his mouth, and Jer'son cried out, "Whatever you want, just stop hitting him."

"Open your eyes," a sing-song voice, one he remembered from the night before, encouraged him. "Your friend will be all right. We did not find you in time to stop all his pain, but he will heal. His attacker will not."

"What does that mean?" he asked, attempting to stand. With an outstretched hand raised in his direction, he was silenced.

As he was untied, his rescuers spoke to him. "It is better you do not know. We have called for your old friend from the city. He will carry you back to a safer place. You have given us good advice that we are certain we can use, and you will be rewarded in some way. I am convinced of that. May the gods speed you along."

More friends helped him to retrieve his things from his locker. In spite of his protests, each time he twisted to look for his friend, they turned him away.

"Go. One who was evil no longer walks this world. Our service to you was small in trade for the service you've given to us. Our thanks are yours for all time."

On the return to the city, even with Bird at his side, he mutely watched the barren world slide by, his mind swaddled in the memory of that morning and a man whose concern for his life had been greater than his concern for his own.

Yes, a life could be found here on Rant, but as he was learning, it could be very hard, indeed.

—Chapter 8—

"A memory can be forgotten. Movies may deteriorate. A whole library of books might burn. Records will be lost in the morass of bureaucracy. However, what you put on the Internet is there forever."

—Judge to a junior high
school class during a tour of
his chambers

JER'SON SAT under a dark cloud, his elbow braced on the table and his chin resting on the heel of his palm. Gaiety filled the space, and yet he felt it had nothing to do with him.

Renhant swung his leg over the back of a chair and reached across the table to pat his friend's face. "We're having a good time in the next room. Join the party."

Jer'son flicked his eyes to his friend's face. He pressed his lips tightly but didn't reply. How could he? To join in the celebration would be to celebrate his own failure. Couldn't anyone besides him see that?

159

Renhant prodded him. "Join us. We're having fun in there. Why, listen to old Bird. Who'd have thought?" He smiled and turned his head to look through the adjoining doorway. Glancing back at his friend, he tried one more time to pull him in. "We really want you in there," and he cuffed him on the shoulder before leaving him in silence.

Jer'son turned his eyes back to the table in front of him, tracing its marred surface with a broken nail. Each time the nail would catch, he jerked it past, the pain in his finger one he knew he deserved. He closed his eyes, thinking of Chr's looking at him, that friend he'd known for only a day, doing that for him, and another thought from a time far away crowded in.

He stood behind the door. He wasn't supposed to have gotten up this time. His mother had told him to stay in bed, but he wanted to see.

"It's that kid, Jeama. You know it is."

He watched his dad turn his eyes to his mother and back to the papers on the table.

"Jet, ours isn't the only business struggling." His mother reached for one of the papers, only to set it down again without looking at it. "It's MegaCorp."

"Woman!" Jer'son jumped as his father wiped the papers from the table in a broad, angry stroke. "MegaCorp didn't cause that crushing birthing cost. What about that time I had to replace the shop's front glass when he 'accidentally' broke it? Do you think MegaCorp caused that?"

Tears starting in his mother's eyes, she put her hand on his father's wrist, only to have him toss it off. "Jet, I've given you my mother's jewelry. You've sold it to help with the

160

costs. You have all the savings from my father. Jet," she pleaded with him, "he's just a boy."

"You don't see. He's breaking us, Jeama. Without him, we'd still have money. His schooling, the medics' visits. Where does it end? We have to live, Jeama."

The small boy that had been Jer'son watched his mother take off the shiny necklace that he loved so much, the one he liked to play with when she kissed him good night, the one she always wore, and she handed it to his father. "I love our son even more than this. Take it. Grandmother would understand. It should bring us enough money for many months."

Jer'son kept his eyes on the necklace as his father slipped it into his pocket, his tightening lips letting Jer'son know it wasn't the sacrifice he wanted his wife to make.

He opened his eyes, the noise from the other room catching his attention and drawing him in. Standing, he moved to the door, watching the merriment on the other side. He smiled as he watched Bird. There he was, that jovial man who loved life. One of Jer'son's questions had received an answer today. Soothed with the smoothness of a drink and the joy of a day gone well, that gravelly voice opened up to the sweetness of a bird's song. Who knew what woman had gifted the man with that endearing moniker? It had stuck, though, and Bird he was. Even Barn't seemed to have put aside his distress of the day before.

However, Jer'son was too upset to step in and take part, and his disgruntlement was at himself; he hadn't been here for Barn't. That bothered him almost as much as the events out at the shipyards. If they'd come and gotten him, Chr's would still be all right. Instead, a new friend had taken a hit for him, and someone else might be dead, for all he knew.

"Hey, there he is!" Renhant jumped up and pulled him into the room.

"You should have seen him, Jer'son," Barn't laughed. "He was pinched between the transport and the wall, and all Cornerstone had to do was pull up his sleeve and read his number."

"Cornerstone?"

Renhant leaned to whisper to him, "He works the transport with me."

"Ah."

"This is Barn't's payback for what that jerk did to him. Our friend was in an awful shape when he returned last night. This has been good for him." Renhant stepped away, joining in telling the tale one more time.

Jer'son smiled at the antics of the retelling, but he was intensely aware that just one day and a night away from his friends, and he already felt like a third wheel.

Yeah, a smiling third wheel.

CORNERSTONE GRABBED Renhant's hand as he held it out, a greeting given to a good friend with common opponents. It had taken several days for Racket to recover enough to return to work, and now a decision had been reached.

He put a hand on Barn't's shoulder.

"This one you brought me," he looked from Renhant to Barn't, "is a good one. I think I'll keep him, is that so?" He smiled a broad smile, remembering the boy's pleading to stay with him. "I will take good care of him. You know me. No big bad man will take my Barn't from me. I'll deliver him safely to you each day. Do we have a deal?"

Renhant laughed loudly. "No one could protect my friend better than you, Cornerstone. You have become a protector, one Barn't and I have quickly come to trust." He turned to greet Racket. "You are feeling better than just the other day, my friend?"

With a bark of greeting, Racket bowed his head to Renhant and climbed in the transport.

"Not much better, but he needs the credits. A girlfriend." Cornerstone nodded, his eyes glancing to Racket's home just off the roadway. A dark face surrounded by even darker hair peered from the doorway, and he waved before touching his fingers to his lips and blowing a kiss that way.

Renhant chuckled, his one experience with a girl having landed him here.

"I'm sorry for you to be leaving, friend," Cornerstone continued, "but with Racket . . ." He shrugged. "Only three are needed to work the machine."

"I'll find another job. Bird can look for me."

"No, you must understand. I already have done this for you." He reached into an opening in his clothing and pulled out a torn fragment of paper. "This. This is the job for you. You'll see. Go there today. Wait until midmeal, and see this man. A woman will meet you when you arrive. Make sure she's there. She will know you, I'm certain. I've spoken with them both, and they know what you can do. Trust me on this, Ren, my man. Don't forget. At midmeal."

Renhant looked at the paper, then at Cornerstone. "A good friend, that's what you are." He grabbed his hand, and without having planned it, quickly pulled him close and slapped him on the back. With a grin, he stepped away. Stopping to turn, he called out, "Thanks, Cornerstone. You are indeed a good friend. Barn't, do as well as I would have."

Then Racket started the transport moving, forcing Cornerstone to jump aboard.

THE HEAT on its way up but not yet stifling, Renhant picked his way through the scattered people already on the street. He could enjoy even this today. Barn't was safe, Jer'son's nemesis was no longer a threat to him, and his morning was unencumbered.

It amazed him how this world of people, all required to be here, none allowed to leave, not even during the contest if he could believe old Trainer from the station, had come together and built a society. Perhaps not always a safe one, but better than some.

Renhant stopped for a moment and looked around. Children. Even on the academy vessel, there were always those. Not tiny ones, of course, but ones not yet out of childhood. Also, he noticed, as his eyes caught the people up and down the street, there were very few women. But, what about Barkeen and the girls in Bird's establishment? Clearly, Renhant knew there *were* women, but he didn't see very many out on the street.

Hm. That was a question for Bird.

He moved along, seeing a small discarded metal packaging container against the wall of a building, and kicking it down the street, he grinned at the metallic ringing that echoed against the rough brown walls of the buildings. For the moment he allowed himself to be no more than a

164

carelessly dressed seventeen-year-old with a brimmed hat killing a morning on a hot, summer day, not a criminal who had been given a life sentence.

Smelling moisture in the air, he followed the street to where it led to a bridge. He walked out on the elevated structure. When he looked over the rail, he was very surprised.

"Who would have guessed on this dusty world?"

There was water underneath, no more than a small stream, really. Walking to the end of the bridge, he found a series of steps and platforms leading to the ground, where he stepped onto a carpet of wiry grass. It felt vastly verdant, green, and cool.

On this hot world, to him, the trickle was a mighty flow.

He looked up at the sky, the cinnamon of the horizon changing to smoky gray overhead. He knew from his studies that the blue he recalled of Kien'ese's world was found on very few planets. This cinnamon, an uncommon sky also, was a color to be enjoyed.

Taking the time to sit on the sloping bank, his knees angled to the sky, he ran his hand over the wiry blades of grass. *Almost always green,* he mused. Plants, no matter the color of the sky, were almost always green on all the worlds. *Chlorophyll* was the word. He was surprised and pleased to recall it, feeling somehow clever as he ran the syllables over in his mind.

He chuckled, seeing the irony in that. In spite of his academic honors, and he had earned a few, he hadn't always learned the lessons. Sometimes he had just bullied others into doing them for him. He remembered cheating his way through one class as they had studied a world with yellow and gold skies. This was better, with greens and browns. He could get to like cinnamon.

However, could he even imagine coming back to sit here as an old, old man, knowing the universe out there had gone on without him, had passed him by, all because of that one stupid night just those few sevendays ago? Moisture softened his eyes. Sometimes he felt like he was still there, and sometimes as if the academy had never been his life at all. Could it be true that just one deed happened, and here he was forever?

He reached and tore small bits of grass to toss in the stream, watching them float into the distance where he could see them no longer. With an epiphany, he scanned the skies. *No birds!* That's another thing he suddenly realized he missed. He did remember birds from his life as a boy. He had loved birds, and now he would never have them. Not on Rant.

"Hey, boy." A woman's clear voice floated down from the bridge above. He looked up, and against the brightness of the sky stood a form. Not old, certainly, and very much a woman, but not someone he had seen on this world. She seemed oddly familiar. However, against the bright sky, he couldn't tell just why. Having already seen that keeping his own business was good business here on Rant, he just nodded his head at her.

"Haven't seen you before," she continued. "This is pretty under the bridge. The big continent is better, however." She tossed something at him. "There's more women there. I'm off to midmeal." Then she was gone.

Midmeal. Renhant picked up what the woman had thrown at him, seeing it as an intrusion in the blanket of green along the banks of the stream. It was bound in a square of cloth, and without paying it much attention, it was gone in a pocket as he pulled out the scrap of paper Cornerstone had given him. Midmeal. He also had somewhere to be, so he dusted the grass off his trousers and started back across the bridge.

A RAPID KNOCKING at the outside door, which Jer'son felt quite inclined to ignore, was soon answered by the creaking step of old Bird. The door slamming shut again, a voice called out, "Not mine, it ain't. Some moping boy'd better be a'getting the door when it calls." The old man stepped in and slid a package onto the table in front of him.

He looked up in surprise. There was no reason for anyone to send him anything. His two friends were out, his new, private friend was maybe dead, and he no longer had a job. Other than them, he knew only Bird on this world.

"Well, boy?" Bird nudged it closer.

"What do you think it might be?" He picked up the package.

"Boy be hanged, it will not open itself. How else'll ya' see what's inside?" Bird sat across from him. "It might be something bad, boy, but it might be the good ya' need. Give it a try. Ya' had a hard thing, ya' did, a day ago. Your young friend had a time as hard, maybe harder, just the day before. He's out again, his wings a'flapping in the wind. Life will not come to ya' and offer itself on a plate, telling ya' which things are for the good. Ya' got to reach and grab it, boy.

167

Hang onto the good, and let the bad be carried away by the wind." Bird slapped the table. "Open it, boy. I be curious as ya' be, maybe more so."

"I think you are more of a kid than the three of us, sometimes, Bird." Jer'son found himself smiling at the old man in spite of his inner turmoil.

"Just open it, boy. I feel the good in it, already." Bird turned a grin to him, the anticipation sparkling from his eyes.

"Sure, Bird." He began to work at one corner with his fingernail.

"Your teeth'll do it better. Give it here." With that, Bird grabbed the paper wrapping with his own and tore it from the box. "Here, now. Get it open. When something good is given to ya', don't let it just sit by the side."

Pulling the top open, Jer'son smiled at the man watching his actions with such anticipation. Inside was another box wrapped in cinnamon tissue paper. The old man had to wait just a bit more as Jer'son dismantled that, also. Underneath the tissue was an elaborately decorated box with a hinged lid. Working the clasp, the lid of the box was finally free.

Jer'son chuckled and looked up at Bird. "Should I open it now?" He could see the man was beside himself with anticipation, and he made no effort to hurry the process. It was too much fun to watch him squirm.

"Such a fine box I've not seen in many a standard, me boy. The excitement be killing me. Let's see what might be inside." Bird reached over to release the catch, and the lid was up.

Jer'son looked in, now puzzled. The box was so exquisite, he had expected something delicate, perhaps even fragile. "It makes no sense to me, Bird. This is all that's in here." He laid a blank card on the table between them, sliding it partially underneath the packaging for the box.

"There's nothing else, boy?" Bird put a hand out, attempting to turn the box to look inside.

"Empty. Nothing else." Jer'son flipped it upside down and shook it.

"Check the wrapper, there. Something must be here." Bird took the paper he'd pulled from around the box and searched it, both sides. His eyes fell on the card on the table. With quivering hands, he took the stiffened paper with two fingers, turning it over for them both to see. He drew in a deep breath at the sight, and then he let it out. Handing the card to Jer'son, he whistled.

"Boy, this be ya' day, that be for sure. This be ya' day."

The card had begun to sparkle and swirl in unusual patterns on the reverse side, clearly not a simple paper card. He reached to take it, only to have it feel warm to his fingers.

"It was cool a moment ago." Jer'son looked carefully at it, frowning at the image he saw coalescing from the sparkles and swirls. It was his face.

"It sampled ya' DNA. That card now be alive, and it be all yours."

"For what?" He laid it down, removing his fingers slowly as if it might bite.

"Forever, boy. For forever."

RENHANT COUNTED the streets, the ways hard to navigate. He understood why Barn't had wound up at the wrong location. There *were* no street signs or building numbers. It

169

was all by memory, or knowing that something was so far from what was located somewhere else.

He knew he had reached his destination when he saw that Cornerstone had even drawn an identifying symbol carved into the door's surface right on his paper. He grinned. Good old Cornerstone.

He knocked first, but the door was heavy, and the sound didn't seem to carry well. When there was no reply, he rattled it, waiting for what seemed like a long time. He held up the paper, comparing the marks there with those on the door, and turned to see if any of the surrounding entrances might have similar markings he might have missed. The doors all looked very much the same, but only this one was marked in the way Cornerstone had drawn.

Before giving up completely, he placed his fist on the door and hit it rapidly three times. Pausing for a moment with his hand on the door, he thought to knock a final time, but before he could lift his hand, he nearly fell as the door opened out from under him. He nearly fell again as he saw who was inside. He hadn't even guessed at the bridge. With the light, he hadn't been able to see her well, and only a few words had passed between them.

Then, he stopped himself and let reality intrude.

He realized he was seeing what he wanted to see. His sister had been killed on Trikeen. Even the medic on the station had repeated the news to everyone. Well, to the three boys, anyway, and the guards who were listening. Back on the academy ship, probably recycled by now, were the sympathy memento and the casualty list from the battle in which she died. She had been gone, but at least MegaCorp had forwarded him her medals and awards, even if they were lost to him, now.

This woman in front of him was so like her. Only a little older than the sister he remembered, he would not have been able to tell them apart if they had stood side by side. Her height, her hair, and even the color of her skin.

Her voice would be different, though. When she spoke, he'd know the difference, and the spell would be broken. Even after eight lonely years without the voice of his sister, he had her memorized, her words stored away. After their parents were gone, she had joined the academy to ensure his financial welfare. Although she was no longer around, he would lie in bed and listen to her talk to him, even though he knew she wasn't there. He would laugh with her when she would laugh, the stories at night his alone, the laughs with her his to share with no one.

He took a deep breath, his mind regaining its grasp on the now, putting those thoughts of his sister aside. This was about a job. That was why he was here. His sister was dead and had been gone since he was little more than a boy. He was seventeen, and he had played a part in killing another boy. He was in prison. The past was the past, and this wasn't his sister.

"Good day. A man named Cornerstone sent me here to inquire about a job. He asked me to arrive at midmeal. May I come in?" He held Cornerstone's scrap of paper out to her.

"Rennie, don't you know me?" Her voice caught as tears formed in her eyes.

"Rennie? How do you know that name?" He was jolted. He hadn't heard it since before entering the academy. In the

171

ensuing silence, he thought she was going to cry.

"The thing I threw to you. Did you pick it up?"

He reached into his pocket, pulled it out, and unwrapped it. It was a toy, and he held it in his hand as his thoughts faded into the small boy he had once been. With a small arm, his fingers released the toy to roll across the floor. He missed his sister. She was his mommy and daddy since Mommy and Daddy got sick and had to go away. His sister had to go away, too. He hoped she would come back.

The people he was staying with had lots of kids, and the kids all slept in the same room with each other. He didn't get to sleep with this mommy and daddy, not ever, not even if he was scared at night. Sometimes he didn't get new shoes. He had to wait until someone else needed new shoes, and then he could wear their old ones.

He was sad he couldn't go away with his sister. She said she would come back to see him, but she must be visiting with Mommy and Daddy, because one time she told him they weren't coming back, and his sister hadn't come back, either.

He still had his toy, though. When he played with it, the noise of the toy sounded just like before Mommy and Daddy got sick. Then it was okay, because he could imagine them with him for a while. His new mommy and daddy said his sister was coming to visit with him, but she wasn't here. She might never come back, but he had his toy, and he could play with that.

He looked up to see a tall person in black clothes walk in the room. Her hair was cut short, and she smelled funny. He didn't know her, so he turned back to his toy. When the tall person came and knelt beside him, he turned to look at her.

172

She was crying, and he heard her say, "Rennie, don't you know me?" He peered at the girl in black, finally recognizing her only after she spoke to him.

Renhant paused and caught his breath, looking up, his vision narrowing to her face, that face he had so adored and been so crushed to have taken from him forever. Tears started running down his cheeks as he stood, unable to move and unable to stop them. She was *dead.* Who was this? His sister couldn't be real. He had read the reports. He still had the condolences. Or used to have the condolences.

He took a slow breath, and afraid to believe the reality before him, tested the word, "Sis?"

His sister grabbed his face in both her hands and her tears erupted to match his. "Yes, Sis will do, baby brother of mine." She wrapped both her arms around him as he tried to take it all in. Slowly he wrapped his arms around her, letting himself give in to what he knew couldn't be true. Knowing it couldn't be true didn't mean he didn't need to believe in it, though, and finally he let his heart trust in what his mind could not. He hugged her back as hard as she hugged him.

"I DON'T UNDERSTAND, Bird. A card with nothing but my picture on it?" Jer'son held the card up to the light, looking for something that might give him a clue. The swirling patterns had settled into an exact likeness of his face, and it remained warm. "What do I do with it? And this box?"

"Boy, ya' did just come down, and ya' haven't heard it all, but this be something some people down here would kill for." Bird took the card from him. "This be a pass. With this, ya' can go up there." Bird pointed to the sky where the station was located. "Ya' can come back, too, and ya' will, I hope. In these few days, me heart's grown strings that's attached to ya'."

"Why would I want to go up there? They just kicked me out and sent me down here." Jer'son took the card and laid it on the table, the image face down.

"Ya' be too new to understand. People try their lifetime to get one of these and can't. Ya' get one in just a few days. There be something someone likes about ya', there be." Bird sat back, an expression of pride on his face. "Ya' have to go, ya' know."

"Can I give it to someone else that wants to go? I like it here with you and my friends." Jer'son slipped the card back in the box and closed the lid.

"It be coded for ya' and ya' only. Should anyone else use it, it sets the tracker off, and that would be painful, indeed. Ya' have to go." Bird's expression had turned intense. "Sometimes we wait a lifetime, and no new passes be issued. They got a job for ya', or perhaps, and I can't even hope this hope for ya', but I'll say it true, a pardon there may be."

"I thought no one ever got off this planet." Jer'son stroked the top of the box with his hands. It was clear to him, now, why the card came in such elaborate packaging. It was meant to last a lifetime.

Bird stood. "That be said, true. I've even said it a few times meself. But the truth be known, boy, that one truth and another truth be not always one and the same." Turning to face the window, he paused, only slowly letting the words leak out. "This be a truth I only spoke to one other person, and that person now be in the station circling this hard world.

174

Things be not all as it would seem here on Rant. True, ya' come to Rant, and ya' disappear from the roll book of life. We be a dark hole of mystery for the galaxy. But, me boy, the hole be darker for some than for others."

Bird turned and sat again. "I were not honest with ya' and ya' friends, I were not. I said I didn't remember the why I be here. Aye, I remember it like yesterday, though it were thirty-five standard years ago. Forgive me, boy, this be still tender to my heart. I would have a cloth, or I'll stain me shirt. I'll probably even lose me words to the old way before I'm done, as if I've not already done so." He stood and took a cloth from a table across the room, and he folded it into his hand.

"I had me boys, and fine ones they were," he started. "I were so proud of them, they, there in their MegaCorp pride. The captgen'l of the ship, he were a drinker, were he, and I knew it, and me boys knew it. I urged them to get another ship, but aye. They were the sturdy shot, and they stuck to the course, rotten course it were for them.

"He'd been on the drink for more days than one, I heard, and it were target practice for the rank'n file. That drunken fool let 'em send out the drones, the guns a'firin' and all. Then, fool! He drunk the last of his load. He sent me boys, both me boys, downsides to replenish his stores. Thinking they's drones, not knowing no better, the rank'n file took 'em out as clean's a whistle." Bird paused to wipe the moisture from his face.

"I found it out, I did, and went to the high-ups to tell them the drunken fool that the captgen'l was. They closed their ranks, they did, and that drunken fool still helms today, sodden fool he be."

Jer'son prompted, "What did you do that got you here?"

Bird cut a look to Jer'son that could have sliced steel. "I done told ya'. I told the truth, and they didn't want to hear it. They didn't want me to tell no one else, either, so they shut me up. Here." He gave Jer'son a look and chuckled. "It ain't your fault, boy, and don't let me gruff manner abrade ya' any. Ya', I got nothing against. Ya' told your jest at the site, and I be willing to help when ya' get ready. Just know that, boy."

"Jest?" Jer'son looked at Bird for a moment, then he knitted his brow in remembrance. "About jimmying the ship?" His face relaxed with a grin. "Bird, I never told you that. It must have been someone else."

Bird cut his eyes to Jer'son as if caught out in the open with no clothes to wear, his barest secrets out for the world to see, but Jer'son's eyes were back on the ticket in the box. The old man licked his lips and took a deep breath.

"Ya' be right, me boy. Probably him who called me about ya'."

"Probably," Jer'son repeated. "So, not everyone's a real criminal here. Some are just an embarrassment."

"Ya' be understanding that well, me boy."

"You say some can leave? How?"

"Credits be credits, me boy, whether yours or mine. Some people only want more. Ya' give 'em enough, and ya' got power over 'em." Bird looked at his hand resting on the edge of the table, then his eyes jumped to lock with Jer'son's. "Even on Rant, there be credits to be found."

The door slammed, the unexpected interruption jerking

176

the two from their concentrations. Barn't came in, his grin stretching from ear to ear. "Guys, you'll never guess who we ran into today. We can tease Renhant when he gets in tonight. It seems that Racket is good at being just as bad of a driver as Renhant. I've brought someone home with me. You've got to see what he did." He motioned, and Cornerstone walked in.

He held up his reader with a grin. *Boy lover rapes children, XX09573949-OX. Have you seen his friend? XX09573948-OX rapes children, too.* Accompanying the words were the lifelike avatars of the two men, seemingly riding together in a transport.

"What do you think, guys?" Barn't couldn't keep his smile under control, and he began to laugh.

That brought the house down, and Bird broke out a container of his most potent drink to be shared by all.

—Chapter 9—

"Pa." The boy grabbed his dad's sleeve and tugged on it. "You didn't even check the horse's mouth. What if he's not a good horse?"

"Shush," his pa said. "He is being given to us. Boy, never look a gift horse in the mouth. It shows a lack of gratitude, and it is very bad manners."

"What if you'd had to pay for him?"

His pa smiled at his son. "That would be a different pile of worms altogether."

The son grinned and ran up to grab the horse's reins. "Yeah, that's right. Then we would have checked the teeth, the hooves, and even the shanks. Can he really be mine, Pa?"

The boy's father grinned, "That's what he's for, boy."

"Whoo . . . ie!" the boy yelled.

—From My First Ride, *by Jefferson T. Davis*

JER'SON STOOD naked before the mirror, water dripping from his bath. This was a body he'd lived with for seventeen standards, nearly eighteen now. It had been like this for less than a handful, but he remembered the in-between stages, too. Then there was the small boy he once was, those memories just fragments mixed in with the other things he recalled.

He first remembered his face about his tenth birthday. He was already tall and clumsy when he stood to blow out the candles. He saw himself, really saw himself that day. It was dark outside, and in the reflection in the window, the candles on the cake giving his face unexpected shadows, his image had made him think for a moment a stranger was outside and looking in.

Then, at twelve, he grew in places he had never paid attention to before. Suddenly, all his thoughts were centered there, and for the first time in his dozen years, he was all of him, not just his hands and his face. After that, for five full years, he lived in this body, the one he wore now, knowing all of it, his hands, face, feet, and all those parts in between.

For that one awful year at the academy, his body had not been just his. He had been forced to share. He remembered standing just like this during that year and looking in a mirror, wondering, *What about me is different because of what he is doing to me? I can't see any difference, but I know other people must.* He hid that insecurity behind cruelty, and he didn't even know why.

For those five years, he had constantly craved a woman, and just once, he had enjoyed one. That was what had brought him to this place where just under his feet, men took women every night.

A bemused expression broke across his face. All those willing women coming to Bird's place every night, and he might be leaving tomorrow. The irony? He hadn't touched a one.

"I WANT IT to be you, but I got the card that said you were dead. The box I was given even had all your medals and awards. It was on my ship, but it's gone now. How can this be you, Sis?" Renhant could not connect two such disparate sets of facts.

"Rennie, it's MegaCorp. I thought you knew where I was. If I had thought they told you I was dead, I would have fought to move the four corners of this planet to get you word." She chuckled a mirthless laugh. "But even that might not have been enough."

"But," her brother continued, "I saw the casualty list, and at the celebration given for our victory, your name was read out with all the others." He knew the facts, and his sister's story did not fit them. "You were buried on Trikeen with all the others who died. The people there built a monument to those who rescued their world. I've seen the Vids."

"Renhant," she began slowly. "I've been here four of Rant's years. There was no victory at Trikeen, because it is now a mining world. All the people who wouldn't leave were killed. By me. By soldiers like me." She looked off, heavy emotions written across her face. "We thought they were rebels. We didn't find out until much later that they were the landowners, fathers, and mothers who hadn't sold out to

MegaCorp. We wiped that planet clean so MegaCorp could strip it for its resources. It was horrible what we did."

"Still, you accomplished what MegaCorp asked. Why would they send you here?"

"We were the proof. If only one of us let it out what was done there, well, you can imagine the backlash. We were an easier sacrifice for the company than a few profits would have been. They paid a few death benefits and shipped us all here."

"Sis, I am so sorry. I thought you were dead all that time. I took it out on everyone, the cadets at the academy, everyone." His memory of that time was now an embarrassment. "For what? So the rich owners could get richer. That's what it was all about."

His sister hugged him. "I'm proud of you, baby brother."

"For what?" This time he let the tears run freely down his face. She didn't know all that he had done. "For being cruel to kids younger than me, for running from an accident where I left someone dead, and for causing the death of a fellow cadet just to protect myself? For getting sent to prison? You're proud of me? I'm not proud of me."

"I'm proud of you because you are seventeen, and you have already learned a great lesson in life." She smiled at the brother she had thought she would never see again.

"What lesson?" He wiped the tears from his face.

"For too many people, it's all about the credits. When they quit living just for credits, that's when they can start to live. A lot of people never learn that lesson. You already have. I *am* proud of you."

BARN'T CLIMBED back on the transport. He liked this job, but what he liked most was the time he spent with Cornerstone. He really looked up to him. He knew part of it was the older man helping against those men who had hurt him, but Cornerstone liked him, too. Even without Renhant, he liked him.

He turned to his friend. "Where did you send Renhant, Cornerstone?"

Cornerstone just grinned. "I've got a girlfriend. Did you know that, Barn't?"

"Huh?" Barn't had no idea what he was talking about.

"Be patient and listen to my story. It'll tell you where I sent your friend. More importantly, it will tell you why I sent him there." Cornerstone shifted positions and continued, bouncing along as Racket drove on, looking for additional rough spots to repair.

"I've had this girlfriend for several years. She's a great girl, too."

"Is she here on Rant?" Barn't hadn't been onworld long enough to appreciate the finality of not being able to leave.

"Yes, here on Rant. She told me over and over about a kid brother she was nuts over. She had to raise him after their parents died in a plague. He went to the academy. She knew that, but hadn't heard from him since coming here.

"My girlfriend talked about him all the time, almost every day. Then one day, a freshie showed up that sort of reminded me of my girlfriend. I saw her looks in his face. Odd, I thought, but not too odd. I let it go, until that freshie showed up on this very transport. When I told my girlfriend about him, well, that's when I hit pay dirt. I sent him to her."

"The freshie was Renhant, and he has a sister? I thought his sister was dead." He knew dead people couldn't come back to life.

"Trust me, she's not dead." Cornerstone laughed. "I should know."

"How will meeting his sister help him get a job?"

"That's the long part of the story. I really did smash termite houses, Barn't, but that was before I joined the military. Renhant's sister and I both got 'posted' here together."

"What did the two of you do?"

"We followed orders. Sometimes, that's all it takes to irritate the big brass. Well, my mom had died, and my dad did some checking around when I was reported killed." He winked at Barn't. "No dead body being sent home as a war casualty can certainly tickle someone's suspicions."

"He found you, though. He couldn't just get you off?"

"Nah. My dad knew he couldn't get me off this planet, so he came to me. Renhant's sister works for my dad."

"Your dad chose to come here?" Barn't was really confused. "I wouldn't do that. Anyway, I thought this was a prison."

Cornerstone laughed. "Do you really think *prisoners* could keep all this running orderly? Not on your life. We have outside help. My dad's one of them." He grabbed Barn't's jaw with his hand. "Only no one knows, got that?"

"Yeah. No one knows your dad is outside help. Does Renhant's sister know?"

"Yes. After all, she's my girlfriend. And she works for my dad."

"What does your dad do?"

Cornerstone sat for a minute as if this were a bit of a sore spot. Then he looked over at Barn't. "He runs the transportation division."

"Like, which parts?" He figured like the street repairs or something.

"All of it. The whole shebang." Cornerstone sat back and leaned his head against the big machine.

"Do you work for him, too?"

"Sure do." He looked over at him. "Now, so do you."

"That's good. So, you could get a better job if you wanted."

Cornerstone laughed with great gusto. "There is no better job. That why I sent Renhant to my dad."

"I don't get it."

"My dad is always after me to convince me to work some big, important job. I like this one. So, I'm sending Renhant in to be me."

"Your dad'll notice, won't he?"

Cornerstone rumpled the kid's hair. "For my dad to be happy, it doesn't have to be me. He'd like that, but a good second best for him is for me to send him a good guy. I can tell Renhant is the one. He'll be good at what my dad wants."

"What's job's that?"

"Running the whole shebang. He'll have to learn a bit, and he'll need some help for a while, but I can tell. Renhant is one who sees the reasonable way to do things, and he feels responsible for what he does. I told my dad, 'Father, Renhant is the voice of reason.' I think my dad liked that." He laughed again.

So did Barn't. He laughed because of Renhant, but even more so because Cornerstone seemed to like him a lot.

JER'SON RAN his hand over the surface of the box, once more pensive about the gift, feeling and yet not feeling the ticket inside. What good was it to him? His friends were here, and he would have no one up there. He had depended on them to get him through some rough times, and his friends were all he had.

That first year at the academy, he tried so hard to lie still all those nights, pretending to be asleep. Then, when it was over, he had felt so dirty, remembering the touch of that hated hand.

When the bells would ring and the lights would come up, he would just lay there, not wanting to know if anyone had seen the man at his side or had heard anything during the night. Then, Renhant would catch his eye, and he somehow found the courage to get up. Every morning, he would do that for him. Jer'son felt he was saying, I know what's happening, and it isn't your fault. This part of the day is for you. He can't touch you in the light, so the daytime is yours, the part you can claim as your own, and you don't have to share it with him. Come on, and I'll share it with you. We'll show him you can be strong no matter what he does.

Renhant, with you, I was strong. You did that for me, and you didn't even know.

He traced the design on the lid of the box, wondering just how Bird could think this compared with what his friend had done for him. With sudden anger, he flung it to the floor, watching it skitter across the hard surface to come to rest

185

under a sideboard.

"You mean more to me than any frickin' ticket, Renhant, and I don't want to go to any *station*, no matter what Bird says."

Now, if he could just make that come true.

"SIS, I DON'T get something." Renhant gazed at her, watching as she dropped small leaves into the stream. He fingered the toy that she'd tossed to him earlier.

She waited on him and smiled, and when he didn't continue, she talked to fill the silence. "I'm glad you like my little park. I'm sorry my boss was called away for a meeting, but the chance to spend a whole afternoon here is wonderful. I hoped it was you when I saw you just before midmeal, but not too much."

"Not too much? Hey!"

"If it hadn't turned out to be you, it would have broken my heart. Now, what do you not get?"

"It's you being here." He held out a handful of grass he'd collected and tossed it into the stream.

"Me being here? I told you all about that, that mining planet MegaCorp wanted. Remember?"

"No, not that. This is something else." He turned to her, one elbow on the bridge railing. "You're here. Bird has his girls, and I've seen a few more, but not very many. Even Jer'son said there were lots of men at the construction site, but he didn't see any women. Do you know why?"

Reenna laughed and looked at her brother. "Now I get it. It takes me a bit, but things do eventually soak in. Too many guys and not enough girls to go around, huh?"

186

"That's part of it, but not all." He laughed in a boyish sort of way, embarrassed. "Maybe that will be important to me eventually."

"What? I do remember you and girls. If I'm not mistaken, there were a few that caught your eye even before you went into the academy."

Renhant dropped his head, warmth rising along his neck. "Yeah, I remember that, too. I couldn't figure out what made my knees weak every time I saw them, either. Now, I know." He cut his eyes to see his sister grin.

"You know, I see. You're not so inexperienced now. I understand."

"Only once, and I'd have preferred a live one." At her puzzled look, he held up his hand to forestall any questions. "It's a long story I still have nightmares about, and I'm only telling you that much, because you need to hear it all someday. Just not today."

"Sure. Whenever you're ready." A smile played at the corner of her mouth, but she sent him a wink.

"Seriously, Sis. Where are the women?" He turned his head, making his visual scan an obvious one. "None out today except you."

"There really is an easy answer, baby brother. Anyone you asked could have told you. The men have only half this planet."

"Half? What about the other half? Who has that?"

She laughed, finally turning from the water to face a man who was obviously no longer a little boy. "Now who's being dense? The better half," and she gave that laugh he loved to hear so much.

187

He smiled. "Okay. I get it. Finally. So, it's all divided up, fifty-fifty, right? What keeps everyone from mixing?"

"Water. Serious water."

"How serious, Sis?"

"Well, there are two continents on this world. Two, that is, that are worth using."

He snorted. "This one's worth using?"

Reenna smiled. "You should see the bad ones. Anyway, the women got the other one, and it's the better one. So, I'd definitely say, it's not fifty-fifty. Sorry you got gypped, Rennie. I didn't do it. Remember, I came to join the lousy side."

"How, Sis? How did you get here and not there?"

She once more gave that laugh he loved so much. "Ever looked at a row of soldiers? They all look sort of alike, right? Well, when they were readying us to ship downside, I saw Cornerstone in a line, and I just switched sides. No one paid any attention at all. Either that, or they didn't care. Maybe both. Maybe both. You know, it was the first women who did all this." She pointed to the stream and the grass.

"I thought this was natural."

She laughed at his naivety. "Natural? Look around you. Nah, this is wastewater from the treatment plant, cleaned up, of course. It was just running into a ditch, and the women wanted a pretty spot. Nice, huh? We women have some good points."

"You sure do." He looked away, letting the conversation ease into silence.

After a moment, he picked a leaf off a small bush, and following his sister's example, flicked it away to land in the stream. His eyes followed it as it drifted away, but he wasn't really seeing it. Instead, he was thinking about women, and not in the way his sister imagined. It was the dream he'd had so many times, the one that always became a nightmare.

He still had that dream most nights. He had learned to blank it out when he woke, except the part about still wanting her even though she was dead. Sometimes he did still want her. That was the part that frightened him. Sometimes he wanted a dead woman, and how could he live with that?

"BIRD, YOU know why the three of us are here, right?" Renhant sat across the table from him. His earlier conversation with Reenna had given him an idea.

"It be in ya' record, boy, that it be. Why do ya' ask?" Bird was busy repairing a small timekeeping device, and his eyes were focused there. It had already grown dim outdoors, although the day had barely started to cool, and no one had yet lighted the indoor lamps.

"Only the part about the boy we killed is in there, right?" Nervousness about broaching the topic had him jittery.

"That be the part I saw. There be more?" Bird glanced up at the boy for a moment and then back to his work.

"Yeah, something that happened on the planet we were stationed around."

"Well," Bird barked. "If there be aught else besides the boy, then out with it if ya' want me to hear."

"There were four of us, Bird. Four of us were involved in what happened."

"Four? Where's the fourth?"

"He's the reason we got caught. He turned on us." He

saw Bird cut his eyes up to look directly in his face.

"One of them kind. Well. Dirt, I guess ya' could say."

Renhant laughed. "I think you're right about that. Anyway, we all decided to sneak down and initiate ourselves into manhood."

Bird laughed. "I be with ya', boy. Go on."

"Well, we got there and found we only had credits for one girl."

"Ah, the plot thickens, I see. Go on, still."

Relaxing a bit under Bird's banter, Renhant told what Bofsky did. "Our friend, the evil friend," and Renhant heard Bird laugh under his breath, "decided the thing to do was get one girl and pretend we were one person who wanted her four times." He rubbed his hand over the top of his head. "I had to go last."

Bird quipped, "A messy position to be in, to be sure."

Laughing, but not really getting the joke, Renhant went on. "I went in, and it was my first time ever, and I thought she was just being considerate, letting me do whatever I wanted, except when it was over, I could tell she wasn't breathing. She was dead, Bird."

The old man stopped his work and watched the boy's face. "And ya' be having the nightmares I hear from up there to the top of the stairs, then?"

Renhant felt his eyes burn. "The thing is, Bird, in the dream, she's dead, and I want her anyway. In the worst way, and sometimes it doesn't go away when I wake up. Sometimes, I need her in the day, too."

"Ah, what would ya' have me do, boy? Can I be of any help to ya'?"

190

"Um, can I have a girl, one of the ones here? Maybe to cure my nightmare?"

"Hm." Bird paused, apparently thinking. "Ya' know ya' can't cure a stomach ache with eating more food, boy. And the girls want to be paid. I provide the room for them only. Ya' have to come up with the credits. If ya' decide, I'll try to get ya' a good deal, maybe cut the cost of the room. How's that sound to ya'?"

Renhant already had a smile covering half his face. "You're the best, Bird. The best. I'll talk to the guys and see."

"All of ya' again? With the same girl?"

"I just need help with the credits, Bird."

"I'd give ya' the credits, boy. All ya'd have to do is ask."

However, Renhant was gone as soon as he said his last word, and he didn't respond to the offer at all.

RENHANT SAT in the dark, only one small light over his sleeping spot, his friends on their beds. He pleaded his case.

"I don't know how much it might cost. I've just got to get rid of this nightmare. I don't know any other way. Will you give me what you've got just in case? I'll make it good when I get a job. You know I will. Jer'son? Barn't?"

Barn't offered, "I've got a little. I haven't worked but a few days. If you can wait, I'll have more."

"Thanks, Barn't. Jer'son?"

"I'd like to help, Renhant. I worked that one-day, and I won't get the money for a very long time. So, if you'd like to wait about five local years, then I'd love to give you some." He and Barn't laughed at Renhant's moan of disap-

191

pointment. "Sorry. There's always your hand. That's what you used back onboard ship."

"We all did," Barn't snickered.

Jer'son snorted in mock derision, "Some of us more than others, huh, Barn't?" He chuckled at the lack of a reply from the smaller boy.

Renhant, counting the money, smirked. "That sure shut him up."

Barn't asked, "How'd you know?"

"Ouch, Barn't! Too much information!" Jer'son and Renhant moaned together.

"Just teasing," Barn't laughed.

"We weren't." Jer'son hooted as he leaned from his bed to punch Renhant in the arm.

"Okay, I'm gone." Renhant stood and reached a hand to darken his light. "I expect to sleep well tonight. Maybe not all night, though, just the last part." He grinned in the darkness, and through the small window, the reflection of the lights from below made it a ghostly grimace.

"Do you have enough?"

"I sure hope so!" The door slammed in excited anticipation, and he was gone.

RENHANT STOOD nervously in the darkened hallway and looked at the number on the door. His mouth was dry with apprehension, but even worse, his groin hurt with anticipation. He had felt braver when there were four of them.

Suddenly, the door opened, and he could see this was indeed the right room. He felt his face warm with need, even as the woman pointed to a Vid screen on the wall, and she reached to pull him inside. "The doors are monitored, honey. Inside and out. No rough stuff allowed. Got the credits?"

"Sure." He handed her all he had. "Is that enough?"

"Let me count it, hon." She walked to a light and flipped through the credits, then turned them over and counted again as if she might have missed some. "Oh, well. Bird said he'd pick up the rest." She turned to him, a smile finally breaking across her face. As she began to remove his shirt, she leaned in and whispered in his ear, "How old are you, hon?"

"Eighteen, soon." He stood very still, aware of her breasts pressing against him, her smell filling his senses, even as she slipped his shirt off his shoulders.

"I like what I feel," she crooned as she wrapped one leg around him, pressing her other leg against him. "Better than that old geezer that just left. You can touch, if you want." As she slipped her black lace top from her shoulders and let it fall to the floor, she pressed one of his hands to her.

In that moment, he no longer cared if it was all right to touch her. He couldn't have stopped himself if he'd wanted. He couldn't stop himself several times that hour, and the girl whispered that he was definitely much better than that old geezer.

She didn't even ask Bird for the rest of the money. Apparently, with Renhant, she felt she had gotten *her* money's worth.

JER'SON SMILED to himself, what he was doing funny even to him. The box would soon be worn smooth if he didn't leave it alone. However, it wasn't the box that he wanted to hold. It was what was inside, and the decision he needed to make.

In the dim light of the room, he turned his head and looked at the pile of covers that was Barn't, showing where he had curled up for the night. He glanced over at Renhant, the blankets only up to his waist, his arms resting across his stomach, peaceful in sleep for the first time since that awful night down on that world with the sky-walker.

Jer'son lay completely uncovered, his anxiety keeping him plenty warm. The box sitting on his stomach moved up and down as he breathed, his fingers tracing the designs and patterns worked into it. A free pass anytime he wanted to go from station to planet and back again. No restrictions, and he'd found something else out, no more checking in with the shoulder reader. All he had to do was use this pass once to embed his new status into the system.

He didn't have to stay on the station, did he? Just go up, then come right back down. That's all. He might stay a few days, sure, if he wanted. After all, now Barn't had Cornerstone. Renhant had his sister. He had no one. There was no reason not to go.

With that decision, Jer'son set the box aside and closed his eyes. With the rise and fall of his chest, it was soon easy to tell he had also joined the realm of the sleeping.

HIS DECISION didn't rest so easily the next day. Leaving felt like he was running away, a boy who hadn't gotten his favorite toy and was scurrying off to pout. When it came time to leave, he hadn't wanted anyone to come with him to see him off. He wanted to be alone, not to have people around him wishing their best. His one consolation was that the ticket had come to him. He hadn't asked for it, had in fact offered to give it away. He couldn't even do that. It would work only for him. He knew he wasn't really running. It just felt that way. That didn't mean he had to like it, though.

Holding the paper pass that wasn't really paper as he walked up to the empty station, he frowned. The card wasn't coded in any way he could tell. He held it up to the reader to no response. Unsure what to do, he pulled his shirtsleeve up and placed his shoulder to the reader.

"Fal'dera Hult Jer'son, station pass activated. Please proceed at your leisure. All transports are available for your use at any time."

He stepped back, the announcement not exactly what he had expected. Moving forward onto the transport, he rubbed his hand over his head, and he smiled. At the metal plate he had so recently used for a mirror, he now saw hair. Not much, but he was no longer a freshie, that was clear.

He looked around, laughing out loud at the idea they had used their undershorts as headwear that first night. Touching the rusted and dirty walls, just a ghost of a smile flickered across his mouth at the thought of rubbing their clothing in this filth to try to look as tough as possible. Bird had been so kind. The clothier had been less so. How would he be different the next time he rode this back to the surface of this world?

As he selected a seat that was in presentable condition, another passenger entered the transport. The doors closed, and the vibration of the craft let them know it was in motion. Without having to look up, he felt her stand beside his seat.

"I remember you. I've seen you, yes . . . no! No, it cannot

be just a tenday ago. Why, it's not even that. Maybe only a week." She raised an eyebrow, beautiful even in her arrogance.

Jer'son glanced at her, to find a willowy vixen with wide-spaced eyes. He fumbled his response. "A week?"

"An old-Earth time unit. A sevenday to you."

"I know what a week is. Thanks," he squeaked. Gods, she was pretty.

"You were on the jumpship. I knew I'd remember where I'd noticed you. When I stop and think, stuff like that always comes to me. Always. You were a freshie." She ran a hand over his head, laughing. The sound had a sharp edge to it. "Not much more than a freshie, now."

"I have hair!" That hurt him.

She sat in the seat next to him. "What'd you do to get pulled back topside? Must be a big problem to get yanked back to the station. I knew someone once who had to return. Never saw 'em again. Heard they got spaced. True or not, it just gives me the creeps thinking about it. I wouldn't worry if I were you, though. Being so soon, it's probably not your fault. Surely something they forgot to do, like run a test or something." Her look said otherwise.

"Yeah. Or something." He wanted to grin, but nervousness won out, and he sat stone-faced.

"Hey!" She turned to him, anticipation in her voice. "Let's see if we can figure it out. Like a game or something. I'll go first. Now, don't rush me, because like I said, I have to think about things, you know, process them a bit, and then they just come to me." She paused with her hand to her mouth, vamping a bit for him. "Here's an easy thing. Show me your arm. I cannot imagine them not getting someone's number rigged up, but someone I know told me," and her voice dropped to a conspiratorial whisper, "a new transferee recently got all the way to the station-monitoring center without his number being coded. We were lucky the guard he beat up finally came to and triggered an alarm, or it could have been really bad." The girl shivered. "What would you have done if you had been onstation when that happened?"

Jer'son sank in his seat. He knew who that person was, and she was sitting right next to him, talking to him. He didn't like this game she was playing, because she was bringing out thoughts he wanted to go away. Like, maybe he would be spaced, in spite of Bird's encouraging words.

"I don't know," was all he could manage.

"Let me see." She grabbed the edge of his sleeve, her movement a quick jab of motion. "You shouldn't let anyone do this, really, because someone who is really good at doing this can just glance at these patterns and get your number. The station has your number, or rather, Rant has your number, but not everyone should. At least they allow us that much privacy. No one can track us except *them*," and she rolled her eyes as she said the word. "That's bad enough, though. Here." She jerked the sleeve up to expose his shoulder. "Mark that one off your list. One down, but there are several more things they could have forgotten. Okay, next. Pull off your shirt." She sat back expectantly, and Jer'son looked at her blankly. "Come on. Off." She reached over to his waist and wrapped the hem in her fists, pulling it up to his chest.

"Wait! It does have catches, you know. I can do this

myself."

"Do it, then. Are you a little slow up there?" She rapped his skull with her knuckles.

"Ouch!" Jer'son jerked back from her as he undid his shirt. "Has anyone ever told you . . . um . . ."

She interrupted with a laugh. "That I'm pushy? A time or two. But I don't listen to them. After all, what do they know?" As he leaned forward to slip the shirt off, she took it in her hand and removed it with a flourish, pushing on his back to lean him forward. "Hey! Do you know you've got really bad bruises back here? I mean, they're somewhat faded, but some of these are huge, like you fell down some stairs or got beat up or something."

"You think I'd remember something like that, wouldn't you?" He had his head ducked, so he couldn't look at her.

She sat back as if considering an unpleasant possibility for the first time, all the while still pressing on his back. "You're not here for killing anyone or beating people up or anything like that, are you? If you are, I might move to the other side, just to give you some space and all."

"I don't guess I'd say, if that's what I was here for, would I? Then, I couldn't get you alone to do bad things to you. Besides, I'm only seventeen. How bad a person do you think I am?" He grinned to himself, his shirt in her hands, his body bent over between his knees, and not much able to attack her even if he wanted.

She laughed and slapped his back hard with the flat of her hand, causing him to jump. "Well, I found the tracker injection site. You're not here for that." She paused, a hand going to her chin. "Of course, the tracker could be malfunctioning. Rikers!" She sat back as she handed him his shirt. "I sure hope that's not it. For your sake. I cannot imagine how much that would hurt. People who've had theirs go off say it's like fire inside until they can get it reset." She looked as if she meant him to worry.

Thanks to her suggestion, Jer'son could now imagine it. He slipped his shirt back on, mumbling under his breath, "You didn't have to tell me that one."

Just then an alarm sounded, and the ship intoned, *"Station docking initiated. Please prepare to disembark."*

The girl called out, "At least that still works."

Jer'son turned his head and just looked at her. He wondered what didn't work. He glanced around at the beaten up interior of the transport. "Is riding this safe?"

She laughed. "It's all we've got, so we might as well not worry about it, huh? By the way, I'm L'Rene." L'Rene Signora Tremont—although no one had called her by her full name in all her years on Rant—reached a hand and grasped his arm, just where it held his identifying pins.

"Jer'son." He flinched when she touched him, then he remembered the way her hand had rested on his back. "You can call me Jer'son," he repeated, a goofy grin growing on his face.

She smiled back, but it wasn't goofy at all. It was hard and mean, as if she had an ax to grind, even if Jer'son couldn't see it.

—Chapter 10—

"Take the red pill to find out just how deep the rabbit hole goes."

—*Morpheus in* The Matrix

JER'SON FOLLOWED L'Rene off the transport. As she passed the armscan reader without stopping, he called to her, "Hey. You forgot to log in." He pointed to it as she turned.

"Hey, yourself, freshie, I always pass the reader. They trust you once you get up here. You'd better stop, though." She stopped and watched. "Don't mess it up, or you'll wish you hadn't."

Jer'son pulled his sleeve up and pressed his shoulder to the reader.

"Fal'dera Hult Jer'son. Pass previously activated. Please proceed at your leisure."

"Hey! It shouldn't say that," she said, stepping forward. "Let me see." She pulled his sleeve up, running her fingers down the indentions in his skin. "You *are* that guy I saw up here just a sevenday ago, aren't you?"

She glanced to his hair and back to his face as he nodded a hesitant yes. If it wasn't supposed to do that, he had really messed things up. He had no idea what to try next..

"Freshie, let's try it again. Maybe it was picking me up for some reason. A delayed reaction after I walked by or something." As she moved his shoulder back to the reader, she murmured sourly, "Is everything on this station broken?"

"Fal'dera Hult Jer'son. Pass previously activated. Please proceed at your leisure."

"Gods! That's the same as before. Something's wrong here." She looked at Jer'son hard and punched a pad on the wall. "Security to docking bay." Turning to check the corridor, she asked, "How did you do that?"

Unsure of what *should* be happening, he shrugged, perplexed. "Um, what am I doing?"

"Freshies can't trigger the pass override. How did you do that?"

He brightened and reached into a pocket. "Oh, I have this. It was sent to me in a package." Pulling the pass out, he brandished it for her to see.

Her eyes opened wide with surprise. "You have one of those? And you're a freshie? What did you get that for?"

"I don't know. I tried to give it away, but I couldn't. I was told no one else can use it but me. I'm only using it to activate it, then I'm going back to my friends."

"Wait, wait, I know who you are now." She reached to activate the wall pad. "Cancel secur . . . too late. They're here." She turned to them as they ran down the corridor doing double time. "He's official. False alarm. I'm sorry." She grabbed Jer'son's arm, forcing him to hold the card to where they could see it. His face flickered from its surface, almost alive.

The guards skidded to a stop, dropping their weapons into a non-lethal position. One reached to flip up a combat visor, rolling his eyes. The other pressed a gloved hand to his weapon, and a red light on the business end blinked off.

"Check first, next time, L'Rene."

The other man cuffed his shoulder. "Better safe than sorry." They yanked off their helmets and turned to walk away, when one of them stopped and looked back. "I know you." He nodded at Jer'son with a frown, and his words were tight. "Last sevenday. There were three of you in with Barkeen."

"Naked as jaybirds." The second man jabbed him with an elbow, and laughter erupted between them. "Come on. Let's get these stowed." He held up his weapon to his partner.

As they walked down the corridor, the guard turned to his companion. "That's him, the one. He's actually here." The other turned to look back at Jer'son just as they rounded a corner.

"What does he mean by that?" Jer'son felt he was sinking further and further into a hole of confusion.

"I don't know. Nobody ever tells me anything, it seems." She brushed her hair behind one ear, then without much more than a fraction of a pause, went on, "Now that you're here, we have to get you set up in your own quarters, one in a close-in section of the ship, if we can get them to give up a good one . . ." She didn't even look back as she walked away.

Jer'son realized one thing as she led him down the

202

corridor, hopefully to find the answers he needed. Nobody ever told her anything, because they could never get in a word edgewise. However, he was pretty sure she wouldn't want to hear that.

"THIS IS CORNERSTONE'S father? His *father* works here?"

"Of course. Who did you think?" His sister laughed.

He was taken aback at the news. The first time he was here, he'd met his sister, and in his emotional euphoria, he'd forgotten about Cornerstone's job prospect, assuming his sister was Cornerstone's only reason for sending him here. Now, the person in charge had returned, and Renhant was meeting him for the first time. "He never told me his father was here on Rant. Were they partners in a crime ring or something?" He thought of Racket's name. "Was Racket in on it, too?"

Reenna looked at her brother and laughed. "I'm serious, baby brother. I think attending that academy fried your brain. There's too big a story to tell right here, and it's not all mine to share, anyway. For now, know that this is where you want to be. Cornerstone is doing you a very big favor. Use it well." She opened the door, and just before she let Renhant step in, she whispered, "In the military, you went by your last name That's how we'll introduce you."

He nodded.

"Ser, this is my baby brother," and she glanced at her brother and smiled, "Renhant. Cornerstone sent him. I'll leave you two alone." She turned to leave but paused, whispering to her brother, "Good luck, Rennie."

A deep voice boomed from the other side of the room, "I am needing you, son, and I am glad you're here. That boy of mine's been talking to me about you."

A man, tall and angular, although somewhat gone to solid middle age, walked up to Renhant and put his hands on his shoulders. "I'm doing too much, and while I love that boy of mine, he will not consent to come in for a good indoor job, no he will not. So, he's sent me you." The man stepped back to look at him.

Renhant didn't know just yet what Cornerstone had recommended him for, but he hoped he would be able to do it. He took a deep breath and tried to look as mature as possible.

"Son, you do look a little young." The man paused and then pursed his lips. He smiled at Renhant's look of dismay. "But so did I when I started out. That boy of mine trusts you, and I trust that boy of mine. He wouldn't steer me wrong. You know what he told me about you?"

"No, ser. I hope it was good."

"He told me you would be my voice of reason. He said you could think past a situation and see to the other side of it. My Cornerstone sees things like that, he does. Welcome, Renhant. You may call me Dad." He chuckled. "Reenna does," and he gave him a wink.

Renhant laughed awkwardly. "Ser, er, Dad, what will I be doing?"

That was where "Dad" laughed. "Son, I've built fortunes on other worlds, and I've lost a woman I've loved, Cornerstone's mother. I nearly lost my son to this place, and all because I brought him up to be the very best he could be. He followed directions like a good soldier, and MegaCorp tried to destroy him for that." He walked to his desk and sat down. "I'm speaking frankly to you, you understand. You don't know me, but I know you through your sister and my son. I also know my priorities, boy, and I put my family first. I want out of this. I want Cornerstone and Reenna out of this. They're good kids, and they don't deserve to be here.

"Why am I telling you this? If you're going to be here doing what I need you to do, you need to be in the know. If you can't keep this to yourself, then Cornerstone isn't the son I thought him to be, and my plans deserve to fail."

"Yes, ser, er, I mean, no, ser." Renhant's face warmed.

Dad looked intently at Renhant. Then he spoke words that made him take notice. "I'm taking them off Rant."

Renhant felt his eyes open wide. "Rant's for life, ser. How can you do that?"

"There are ways, boy. Credits talk in many ways to many different people. I have been working to make those credits, and soon I hope to have enough. But that is not today. Let's talk about you." He motioned for Renhant to sit. "Are you ready to think big, boy? You had better, because I'm thinking big for you."

Renhant grinned. He liked Dad, and he *was* ready to think big, even if he was just seventeen standards old.

"SO, YOU'VE gotten yourself back up here at last."

The words drifted over his shoulder, and Jer'son wasn't sure they were meant for him. He tried to act preoccupied by sitting in his seat and keeping his attention focused on a cracked fingernail.

"How's Bird treating you?"

At that, he turned, and he smiled. "Medic Barkeen! I'm glad to see someone I know." Then he remembered the last time he was with her, and he felt his face burn.

"Don't do that to me." She clicked her tongue against the roof of her mouth. "I'm a medic, and don't you be put off because I examined you. You've only got what every man's got."

He forced his embarrassment aside, covering it by clearing his throat loudly. "What did I do wrong down there? Everyone tells me I must have done something really awful to be back up here so quick. Was it the fight in the bar?" With sudden realization, he leaned back, remembering the man who had attacked Chr's. "He must have died. Gods, I am so sorry. I didn't know they were going to hurt him. When that man started hitting my friend, I just couldn't let him take those hits for me. I would have gone with him. I didn't want to, but I would have. I know I would have."

He wiped at his eyes as the emotional intensity of his narration petered out; and he sat in silence for a moment, his eyes glued to the floor. He looked at Barkeen to see her peering at him with a bemused smile on her face.

"So, do you have it all out?" She came and sat beside him. "To answer your concerns, I know your friend. His name is Chr's, and he wouldn't have let you go with that man, no matter what price he had to pay. The man did die, but that man died long before he came to us. He was dead to his concern for others' well-being. Rant is better off without him. No, Jer'son, you did nothing wrong to get yourself back up here. You did something very right. You can relax about that." She patted his hand. "Now, is my Bird really doing all right? He tells me so, but I'm so busy here I rarely get the chance to go back to visit with him." Her eyes reddening, she looked away.

Jer'son remembered that first night when he had gotten into that fight, and Bird had rescued him and his friends. Back at Bird's establishment, Jer'son had accepted what he'd done, understanding that he and his friends would no longer be welcome. Bird had been upset with him for even offering to leave, and instead, he had made them all sit while he gave them words of encouragement. That was how he first knew Bird really cared. He had messed up in the worst possible way, and Bird had still wanted him there.

He smiled at the remembrance.

"Now, what was so funny about what I said?" Barkeen started to smile herself.

"I knew he wanted me there. He didn't just tell me, he showed me. You know, he's been crabby and short with all of us, but we all could tell he wanted us there."

Barkeen nodded her head. "I know him well. Maybe better than he knows himself. He's a good man, even if he has a hard time showing it, sometimes." She cleared her face as if moving on to a new subject and pointed to him. "You, my boy, are proving yourself to be quite a sensation. You are the only, and I must stress that, the only person in the history of this station to get a permanent station pass after just one sevenday." She smiled. "It didn't surprise me, though. In that examination room, I let you have it in front of your friends and all those guards. You took it and even stood up for yourself."

"I got angry." He wasn't sure how she saw that as a strength. "That got me back up here?"

She leaned back and looked at him, her expression one of appraisal. Standing, she walked across the room. "You initiated that trip to the drinking establishment." She turned and emphasized her words. "You did all that. No one else."

He also knew she kept bringing up things he wasn't proud of. "I'm sorry," he offered.

"No. Do not be sorry. On the transport, who came up with the idea for disguising your freshie status?"

"Me?" He wasn't sure if it was a good idea to admit to anything at this point.

"Firebreathing right, it was you. Those two friends of yours are wonderful boys, but they would have been picked up by some group out looking to thrash the new freshies. That took creative thinking."

"So," and he smiled with his retort, "wearing undershorts on your head is now the accepted solution to keep from being thrashed."

Barkeen just smiled at his humor. "Out at the construction site, your suggestion was inspired."

"Yeah, inspired enough to almost get my first new friend killed." He sank lower in his seat, his smile melting from his face.

Barkeen walked back to him. "Remember your first night here on this station?" She waited until he looked at her and nodded. "You did two things that marked you instantly. First, you stood up to the bully that tried to rape you, and he would have, trust me." She smiled. "You also did it in a fashion so the actual fight wasn't recorded and can't ever be proven."

"Those are both one thing, right?" He sighed deeply. He wasn't sorry he'd done that, but he hadn't paraded that knowledge proudly, either. He still wasn't sure if he wanted to be marked or not. "What's the other? And this marking myself instantly, it's good, right?"

"Very good. You are the only person who's ever infiltrated this station, and you instantly went to the most vulnerable location, and were, in fact, operating it successfully."

She stood and closed the door, then opened a panel in the wall. Reaching in, she unplugged something. "Now, we are unmonitored. I will not tell you any names, but we are working to bring this giant to its knees. We are putting trusted people in where we can bring about change. Youth is paramount, as this will not happen immediately. That ship being constructed down there is a brand new class of battleship, the first, MegaCorp's pride and glory. If we can bring it down, we may be able to bring attention to the atrocities that have been committed by that corporation in the name of greed. You have shown you have the propensities we desire. Do you have the will, Jer'son? Will you step into a small role that may someday become a very big role?" She looked at him intensely, her eyes riveted to his face.

He didn't need to think about his answer, and he grinned. "You must have had a direct feed into my conservation with Chr's. This is exactly what I want. You bet I'll do it. What's first?"

209

—Chapter 11—

"If you ever do me in, you'd better do me all the way in."

-Al Capone, old-Earth gangster

BARN'T BURST through the door, slapping a decorated box on the table in front of Bird. Dancing, barely able to control himself, his eyes just begged the old man to open it. A smile broke across his face.

"Well, me boy, what do ya' have here?" Bird pushed it back, running his tongue underneath his bottom lip.

"Look at it, Bird."

He picked it up and shook it, taking his time. Finally, Barn't reached to it, ripping the top open for him, revealing layers of crumpled packing material.

Bird held the box at arm's length before turning to Barn't. "Be I supposed to look inside?" He winked.

"Yes, Bird. Look inside. You'll like it." He stepped next to him and folded his arms across one of the man's shoulders, his eyes glued on the box. They sparkled with anticipation.

Bird reached inside and took out the contents, unwrapping the packing around the item carefully. Revealed was a small wooden creature with outstretched wings attached to a metal base.

"It's a bird. Get it?" Barn't reached forward. "It's carved by a man Cornerstone knows, and we found an old music box that plays a bird's song. To hear it, you pull out the drawer in the metal part there."

Bird looked at it, tears in his eyes. He pulled out the drawer, setting the musical bird off. Closing the drawer, he patted Barn't's arm, unable to speak.

"This is the best home I've ever had. Even when I do stupid stuff, you never tell me you don't want me. That's what the carved bird is meant to say."

"Go put it on the table there, boy. It be a special piece. May it sing as well as me own voice." The old proprietor grinned. "One day I'll be gone, and that be the only 'membrance of me ya'll have. Keep it well, me boy."

"You'll always be here, Bird. Thank you for what you're doing for us. Racket can't work today, and Cornerstone is waiting outside, so I can't stay. You know, my job and everything." He grasped his benefactor's shoulder, then released it and turned to leave the room, his face still grinning from ear to ear. "I'll see you tonight."

"Not always will I be here, me boy." Bird reached up to wipe one eye. "Me time'll come soon enough." But when he looked up, Barn't was already gone.

"GALLOPING GALAXIES! This is state of the art." Renhant turned to stare at his sister. In the weeks he'd been working for Cornerstone's father, this was his first time in the Control Core. He had no idea that anything like this existed on Rant. Sure, on the academy training ship, all this would have been pretty much standard issue, but not here on Rant. On this world of castoff people, it seemed as if everything was something someone on some other world didn't want.

However, this was *good*.

He walked to the glass table and tapped it. When it came alive, he reached out and pulled the city grid up. "Barn't. Cornerstone. Place on grid." He grinned when he saw abstract icons representing Barn't and Cornerstone roll in from the side, oscillate for a moment as they attuned to some signal, then snap into place.

"I thought you might know this setup." Reenna grinned.

"Of course, the basic concept, anyway. Any MegaCorp vessel has one like this, and probably not many have better. Will it calibrate an image of them, or is this it? I don't know how sophisticated the sensors are." Not very, he would have guessed moments ago. If they matched this, maybe pretty advanced. He smiled at the prospect of being able to tell Barn't just what he'd been doing today.

"Realtime input. Pull on one of the icons," Reenna suggested. "The best way for you to learn about it is to actually use it."

With a quick pull, the icon became an image on the glass. Reaching into the air over the table, he twisted the image, and it grew to fill the space over the glass.

"What are they doing?" He watched them pulling something from a broken portion of the street.

Reenna stepped closer, watching the scene for a few moments. Then she nodded, pointing at the tools they held. "You were with Cornerstone. Did you never repair a power cable?"

"I was only with him for a few days. We repaired rough spots in the paving." He looked up at her and grinned. "And took care of one bully."

"Shameful." But she had a smile on her face.

"Not after what he did to my friend." He turned back to the glass. "Hey, Cornerstone is going inside the ground. I can see what he's doing under there. Sis, how can I see him inside the ground? It must be a tunnel, surely. You have everything monitored, even underground?"

She wiped away the images, clearing the big glass. "Utility service access." Immediately, a grid showing the tunnel system spun out of one corner revealing the service access passageways. She motioned with one hand, and the image rose from the glass. The display was now inside the tunnels.

"Come on, Sis." Renhant turned away from the display to look at her, no longer quite so impressed. "I know you can't have all these tunnels monitored with Vid cameras. It'd take thousands of inputs. Don't tell me you do."

"Actually, none of this is real." She chuckled. "This is all glass generated."

"Oh." Renhant made a face. "I thought it was realtime."

"It is, Rennie. Real time and real action. However, it is done with sonic imagers. It's sort of like old-Earth sonar navigation."

"Sonar what?"

She laughed. "Oh, never mind. The glass takes the images generated by sound waves, and we get a really good picture of what's going on. The pictures are actually image files that look and act like the person."

"So, that's not really Cornerstone."

"It is. It's just the glass' interpretation of what Cornerstone must be doing right now based on the sound waves being generated multiple times a second by our sonic imagers."

"What else can this do? Can it pull up all the transport systems?"

"Local or planetwide?"

"Individual transport units. Like Cornerstone's."

"Of course. Any transport integrated into the system. First, however, push the access tunnels to the back, and you should find the image of your friend still in place. Go ahead and do that now."

Practiced with glass usage, the size here being the main difference, Renhant followed her instructions. As the tunnels disappeared, he noticed something he hadn't seen before.

"Sis, does it often give ghost images?" He motioned to the picture of Barn't. "Or is that a side effect of the underground imaging process. See? There are two shadow icons beside Barn't's."

"No, it never does that. Shadows just mean the person's number isn't currently calibrated into the system. We don't need the entire population to be recognized for image interpretation. Just the ones we interact with all the time. However, I can easily calibrate those." She manipulated several items on the glass, and after a moment, the images started to clear. "It takes a moment for the imager to select the proper files and transfer it to the display."

"Hey!" Renhant cried, his heart jumping into his throat.

"What, Rennie?"

"I know those two men. They're the ones who raped Barn't, and it looks like they're with him right now."

"TODAY, WE'VE got some extra jobs to do, ones perfect for a two-man crew." Cornerstone threw some cutters and splicers onto the back of the transport.

"Since Racket's playing sick?" Barn't grinned.

"Yeah. Since Racket's playing sick." He tossed his portable reader to the younger man. "Here, I've already signed in. Put this against your shoulder. It'd be a shame not to get paid for a good day's work. And Barn't!" He pointed with a grin, waving him his direction to help load additional supplies. "Don't lay that reader down just anywhere. It goes with us."

"With us?" Barn't tossed it in the air and caught it. "Okay, but why? Are we catching another bad guy?"

Cornerstone laughed. "Hardly. I need it so if I drop you off at Bird's, I can log you out there. Without logging you out, you can't receive credit for your time out with me today."

Barn't pressed the reader to his shoulder, then held it up. "Here."

"Drop it in your pocket for now. Come help me move this roll of cable." Cornerstone pointed to where Barn't needed to lift, and together they hoisted the bulky roll onto the back of the transport.

Once in the vehicle, he grabbed Barn't's knee and shook

it playfully. "Now, when we get there, you get to stay on top and feed me cable, and I get to go underground and fix the damage." He grinned. "Unless, that is, you want to be the one to go underground." He winked at his refusal. "It's kind of like being the termite. I just hope someone doesn't try to stomp my house down while I'm inside it."

"No way, Cornerstone. I'll keep a watch out." His eyes gleamed with excitement, and Cornerstone grinned back.

"I know you will, and I send you thanks from the guy who stomped a million termite houses and is probably on their do-not-resuscitate lists on fifty worlds." He laughed out loud at his joke.

Barn't grinned. "I bet they're pulling out papers and pointing to your name, refusing to help."

"That's the way I see it." He clapped the boy's knee, pushing it away playfully.

"Do we really have to go underground?"

"Of course. Well, I do, anyway. We have to replace a worn section. It keeps letting the power jump to the comm line, causing connections to go down." As he pressed the power feed on the transport, pulling away, he grinned. "Now, what if I wanted to talk with Reenna just about the time the power jumped? She might get only sound, and she needs to be able to see how good looking I am when I talk with her."

He glanced at the barely-contained laughter on Barn't's face, as he took his example one step further. "Or, and this would be bad, what if the *sound* went out? There I would be, handsome as ever, and when I wouldn't talk with Reenna, she would think I was mad at her. She might do something terrible, like come to my place and put a pie in my face." He put his hand to his chin, pretending to think. "Hmm, on second thought, Barn't, let's take that cable back to the shop. We won't need it today after all. Reenna makes very good pies."

This time Barn't couldn't even respond, he was laughing so hard.

"A moment of quiet would be nice," Cornerstone intoned with fake gravity. Reaching to his feet and shuffling items in the floor, he pulled out a dusty glass. "Here. Check our position, if you can be so kind."

"I can be so kind." Barn't brushed his eyes. Then he wiped the glass clean, and pulling up the repair site, he tracked their location. "The map on the glass says the utility service access tunnel starts here on this road." He pointed to the image he held in his hand.

"Then, I guess this is a good place to begin. Hop out and hand me the splicers and cutters. I'll need them with me." Cornerstone undid his utility belt, and he began to tuck his shirt in all the way around. As he worked it in, he explained, "If I leave it out, sometimes it's hard to hook the tools back on using only one hand. The shirttail gets in the way. Wouldn't want to drop any, now would I?"

"Have you ever left a tool in the tunnel before? I'd probably lay it down and climb out without thinking about it until the next time I needed it, and by then I'd be in a completely different tunnel."

Cornerstone gave Barn't a mock-serious look. "Why, yes, I actually have. Just don't tell anyone. I remembered it that night, and I'd promised to loan it to someone else the very next morning. In the dark I had to get up, go find the access tunnel, and retrieve the tool." He gave a dramatic shudder. "That's why I always tuck in my shirt."

With an exaggerated nod of his head, he reached for the cable, then put his hands on his hips and turned to Barn't with a grin. "Medic, splicers, please." He held out one hand. "Medic, hand me the cutters, if you don't mind. Medic, next, the cable. I go to operate on our good city. Please say your prayers to whatever gods you honor in hopes that the city survives." He chuckled and waved, disappearing into the heart of the street.

"Make the city well." Barn't grinned. With a heave, he tossed more cable off the transport, jumping down to feed it directly into the hole.

He was now, for all practical purposes, alone in a city filled with MegaCorp's most reviled outcasts, and the thought never crossed his mind.

BARN'T DIDN'T even look when the unfamiliar transport stopped beside theirs. He was doing as he had been told, feeding Cornerstone the cable. As he was grabbed from his position on the street and manhandled into an open door, the last thing he saw before the transport drove off was the cable, unwinding farther and farther into the heart of the city. In the unfamiliar transport, he sank into the seat, his panic at the sight of the two faces he had memorized on that horrific day freezing him into inaction.

"Did you really think we wouldn't pay you back?"

Barn't's eyes locked on the driver. His mouth felt like it was filled with wads of dry cotton. He was certain he would choke with every breath, and he couldn't respond. He could only sink farther into the seat.

"Did you? Answer me, boy!"

The voice cut like a knife. His mind and body frozen, Barn't found all he could do was touch his tongue to his lip to soften the dryness. It turned out to be very poor timing, for at that moment, the man sitting beside him smashed the back of his hand into the side of his face. He could feel something wet running down his chin. Somehow, in the shock, he knew he had bitten his tongue. He could taste the metallic tang in his mouth.

The man beside him growled with a degree of petulance that edged on a whine, "We were nice to you. We treated you special and didn't hurt you." Then, he hissed, "Not this time."

When Barn't whimpered, the man grabbed his foot and twisted it sideways into the air until the boy gasped and let out a yell.

The driver turned and laughed. "He does make noise. I wondered last time. All I heard were little moans. This time you'll drown me out, and I intend to make all the noise I want."

From next to Barn't came the low, quiet words, "No, we're not going someplace you'll be found. We're going someplace no one ever goes, and when we're through, we're leaving you there. Forever. Maybe alive, if you're tough. Dead, if you're not. It depends on how much fun you provide." The man laughed, and it was low-pitched and coarse. "Make us happy, and we'll all get along. Decide not to play, and we'll find ways to make you play, even if it kills you."

Barn't closed his eyes and tried to make it go away, as

219

the men just laughed. He jumped as he felt the man's hand on his pants, undoing the clasp. He didn't know everything they planned for later, but he did know what the man wanted to do right then. He also knew he didn't want it to happen.

As it did, tears ran down his face.

RENHANT AND REENNA leaped from their transport. It was no old, outdated vehicle. Rather, it was as up-to-date as the glass table in the Control Core. And fast, specially modified for travel across great distances outside of the city. Finding Cornerstone's transport unattended, Reenna grasped her brother's arm.

"Cornerstone. What about Cornerstone?"

"Yeah?" A voice echoed from inside the access tunnel. "What about me?"

"Cornerstone?" Reenna knelt and called into the space.

"Is that you, Reenna?" The voice growing louder, she moved back as Cornerstone's head popped up from the ground with a smile. "It's a boy! Surgery's successful, and the city will live. Barn't? You should've told me we had company." Seeing the stricken expressions on their faces, he called again, clambering from the hole. "Barn't? Where's Barn't?"

Renhant grabbed his arm. "He's not here. We saw his attackers on the Control Core's display. Reenna calibrated their images into the system. They were right here."

Cornerstone grabbed his forehead with his hand. "Gods, I left him alone up here!" He looked at Renhant then Reenna, dropping his tools on the ground. "Those same men? You're sure?"

"We were at the glass table. We saw you going in the tunnels, and then Renhant saw there were three icons outside. One of them was Barn't. I had the table image the other two, and Rennie says they are the same men from before. How could this happen?" Tears began to roll down her face.

Cornerstone snapped his fingers. "My portable reader! It's in the transport; I have their numbers inside. We can find them. Wherever they are, it'll tell me."

Reenna grabbed his arm. "I'm sorry, Cornerstone. They haven't triggered any building systems. None. We think they've left the city."

"We have to search, then." He ran to his transport, tossing his utility belt inside, and he glanced at the remaining tools lying around. "All of this can wait. Do you have room for me?" He pointed across the roof of his low-speed castoff at their more modern vehicle. "Yours'll get there faster."

Renhant grasped his shoulder. "Bring anything you need from your transport. We'll go together." As he jerked open the door to let Reenna claim the driver's position, he heard Cornerstone yell.

"My reader! I can't find my reader."

"Come on, Cornerstone," Reenna cried. "We'll look for it after we come back. Let's go. Barn't needs us."

Cornerstone scrambled from the seat of his old transport, excitement in his eyes. "You don't understand. I tossed it to Barn't to sign in when we were loading the supplies. It's not here. That means that Barn't might still have it on him. Reenna, get your transport to triangulate on my reader. See where it is. If it's not here where we are, then wherever it is, that's where we'll find Barn't."

221

Reenna's hand darted over the controls on the transport's dashboard display, searching for the coordinates for Cornerstone's company reader. Scrolling through all the readers the company had out, she tapped on the one assigned to him. When its location popped up, it was nowhere near their position, and it was moving very fast.

"Let's go," Reenna cried. She slammed her door, barely giving Cornerstone and Renhant time to slam theirs before she applied the power.

"I'll say," Cornerstone gasped. "I knew this transport was modified, but modified isn't the half of it."

"Thank the gods for that," Renhant muttered.

—Chapter 12—

Warning: Do not start cryocycle unless subject has been thoroughly prepped. To do so will result in permanent and irreparable damage to occupant, initiating eventual death.

—Warning on all civilian cryo pods

IF I HOLD really still, maybe it will go away. Sometimes things just go away. Sometimes people just go away. If I'm really still and really good so no one notices me, the bad things will stop.

Barn't screamed.

He hated it that he was little. Even as a child, all the people around him noticed.

"Do you think he'll ever grow?"

"He's behind all the others his age, isn't he?"

"Have you had him checked by a medic?"

"Poor boy, to be so small!'"

As a teenager at the academy, it was the same. The first

day when his dad was leaving, an instructor had stopped him, pointing to Barn't, telling his dad that little brothers couldn't sleep over in the dorm. The instructor told his dad to take Barn't home and bring him back to register in a few years.

On the first day of classes his second year, he had walked in, and the instructor had looked up and glanced at her calendar, telling the class that she didn't remember a visitation day scheduled for younger siblings.

When he got body hair, he thought the others would quit teasing him. Even after he got hair, he could never catch up. When he got hair down there, the others got hair under their armpits. When he got armpit hair, they had already moved on to chest and facial hair. He was still waiting on those. He didn't think it was possible to go your whole life with no facial or chest hair. His dad had both. Surely he would get some. Renhant had chest hair, and Jer'son shaved every day. They were his friends, except that Jer'son had gone away. Where was Cornerstone? Cornerstone said he would keep the bad men away.

Barn't screamed again.

He wanted to climb in bed with his mommy. She had always wanted him to before. When his daddy was passed out in the other room, she let him snuggle with her. Always. She would tell him stories, and they would laugh. She didn't care that he was smaller than the other kids. She always said he was his own size, and that's what size he was supposed to be. When he was with his mommy, he was just the right size, and he didn't hear the comments people made, even when they did say them. She came to his school one day, and she sat with him all day. That day no one said anything about how small he was. He asked her to come to school with him every day. He knew she wanted to, but he had to go back to school alone.

The day after, his mommy said she didn't feel well. When he didn't feel well, he wanted to snuggle. He didn't know why she wouldn't snuggle. He always felt better when he snuggled. He knew that if she had let him snuggle, she would have felt better. Then, when she was in the box, he cried when they closed the lid. He knew she would have felt better if they had just let him snuggle with her.

This time Barn't whimpered, too exhausted to scream.

The bottle that had the green stripe on it was his favorite. That was the one his mommy always made for him. When he cried, his daddy brought him the one with the yellow stripe. He knew better than to cry. His daddy didn't like it when he cried.

He reached up and played with the balls hanging above his bed. He had airplanes before, but he played too hard with the airplanes. Once, one came off, and then he only had the balls to play with.

The sun coming in through the walls of his crib was fun to play with. Sometimes little things would float in the sunshine, and he would try to catch them. When he found his thing between his legs, he was so surprised. He didn't know it was there. It was a fun toy. He played with it a long time. When his mommy came in, she smiled and moved his hand away. When his daddy came in, he yelled at him and hit his hand. When he cried, his daddy hit him again. And again. And again.

The final time Barn't made no sound at all. He was

passed out from the pain.

"WE'RE HERE, Cornerstone. There's nothing here, yet the readout says we're at the end of the road." Renhant chewed at one nail, the skin around his eyes burning. He narrowed his lids, scanning the dusty surroundings. Nearby there were patches of scrubby native flora, mostly branching shrubs with yellow-green slivers for leaves. Several taller plants— what Rant called trees—were just past. He could see them over a dirt rise. He pressed his lips together. The pressure inside his chest made him want to explode.

He was worried beyond belief.

Cornerstone looked at the reader built into the car, then glanced around outside the windows. "You are correct. There is nothing out there. Rocks." He pointed to the small trees. "Those scrappy things, but no Barn't." He slapped the back of the seat hard.

"It says we should find him right here." Reenna tapped the blinking icon on the display.

Renhant groaned. "Could they have thrown it out and gone on?"

"If they did, it'll still be here." Cornerstone made to get out. "We need to look. Even that'll tell us something."

"I agree." Renhant didn't want to find the reader without Barn't, but Cornerstone was right. He opened his door into a wave of blistering heat.

"Transport tracks, over here," Cornerstone called out. "And here are some footprints. This way!"

"Barn't?" Renhant leaped forward, calling over and over with no reply. Finally, he mounted the low ridge and saw items he recognized. "I found something!" He waved at the other two, then bent to the things. Barn't's shoes. The shirt and pants they had bought that first night with Bird's money. He ran his fingers over the fabric as it lay jumbled on the ground.

"Renhant, check for the reader." Cornerstone ran to his side, dust flying from under his feet as he came to a stop. "It's got to be someplace. In a pocket, perhaps."

"I can't." Renhant handed him the clothes as he wiped tears from his eyes.

Digging through the wadded fabric, finally coming to a securely fastened back pocket, Cornerstone found what he was looking for. "I'm sorry," he apologized. "This is as far as my reader can take us."

"Um, Renhant and Cornerstone. You need to come help me. I don't know how bad this will be." From a nearby rise, Reenna motioned them to her side. Together the trio scrambled to the bottom and untied Barn't's wrists from the tree, holding him off the ground so the dirt wouldn't get mixed with the blood running down his body. As they laid him in the transport and covered him up, he curled into a ball and slipped his thumb into his mouth.

"It seems your reader took us just far enough, Cornerstone." Renhant pulled off his shirt, laying it over his friend's tortured frame. He pictured Zen'ri, and the way he'd lain on the floor that day in the utility corridor. For a moment, Barn't and the dead cadet were one and the same. Then Renhant blinked, realizing there were tears in his eyes, and in a flash, he saw the others on the ship they'd left beaten, all for a few credits. He knew he'd never think of the things they'd done

227

aboard the academy ship the same ever again.

In the transport's cooled and dimmed interior, he reached to his friend, adjusting the shirt where it touched his wounds. Until they returned to the city, there was nothing else he could do.

JER'SON'S EYES were consumed with anger as he flung open the door. "Do you know?" he erupted to Barkeen.

She nodded her awareness of the atrocity. The news had reached her as soon as the boy had been located. "Barn't will be cared for, Jer'son. I have spoken with Bird. He will soon be with him. You are not angry alone." She paused, her expression taking on a measure of hardness. "Others feel as you do. Some feel even stronger."

"Surely he can be immersed in a cryo pod and returned to the station. He may die down there." Gods! If only he were with him. He was useless up here. Jer'son slammed his fist against the wall.

"They do have pods downside, but they aren't military. Civilian models require days of injections before immersion. Failure to do so means death for certain. Traveling here by transport is faster than the cryo injections, and death isn't certain if he comes here that way. Believe me."

Jer'son erupted even more violently, "He might die. That would be acceptable to them that he might die."

Barkeen spoke softly, "I think that was their intent. This was a punishment, not an act of desire."

"I experienced nothing like this that year my instructor came to me at night. What was done to me was painful only on the inside. Barn't has been torn apart. For what? For them to have a little fun." He paced the room, too consumed with fury to sit and talk it out. Being on the planet with Bird, his secret no longer a secret, and with his friends still his friends, he had tried to push his anger deep and had done so. Yet, this was the anger he had lashed at the guard, the incandescent rage that he had thrown on his molester at the drinking establishment. He needed to *vent* this emotion so it didn't eat him from the inside.

"Be patient. All is being done that can be done." Barkeen put her hand on his arm.

"They have facilities for him there?"

"None as good as mine, but perhaps good enough."

"I would go down there. My friends need me. Twice I've left them, and twice this has happened. Together we are strong. Apart we suffer. He needs me, Barkeen." His words finally bled from him, his bile spewed on the floor, and he sat, exhausted. In that moment of vulnerability, he let the tears flow.

"Your pass will take you there or allow you to stay here. No one will fault you either way." She rested her hand on his shoulder. "You must follow your heart."

"I would make those men suffer. I would have them know my friend's pain." He slammed his hand against the top of the table.

"They will know that pain with or without you. I know men there. Bird knows more. They will be found."

He looked her in the eyes. "I want to be the one to find them."

She concurred. "I see in your eyes that you do. Then we must help you to do so."

"I THOUGHT having company might make the trip easier for you." L'Rene forced a bright expression onto her face, burying the hard rock in her chest. It wasn't what she wanted to say. She wanted to beseech Jer'son to let her help kill the bastards that had nearly taken his friend's life. It would be fitting payment, if only in absentia, for her brother and how he had died. "Surely you can't want to do this alone."

"I told you already I didn't ask you to come." His eyes were hard, and he smashed his hand into the back of a seat, laughing contemptuously when a piece of trim clattered to the floor. "He's my friend, not yours. I haven't always given him the respect he's deserved, and I've not been there for him as I should. I'll be there for him this time. Nothing else matters."

"Well, I'm here. You can't just chuck me off into space." She looked at him coldly and laughed, no longer bothering to be cheerful. "Sit there and fume if you want, but you're not going downsides without me."

"As you wish; just don't ask me to keep you company. All I want to do is hit something." He balled up a fist and slammed it into the wall at his side. "And again." He began hitting the wall over and over, his face screwed up in fury.

She knew one thing. This was not just anger over what had happened to the friend down below. Even she could see that. Something deeper haunted her traveling companion, although she could only guess what it might be. After pacing for some time, she watched him finally drop into an empty seat, facing her but not looking at her. He was silent but not still, his anger from within erupting in small ways, his hands clenching and releasing, the sudden jerking movements of his legs, the flex of the muscles in his face. She understood that anger—not what was driving it, but that it was there. It was a blister ready to burst, and she would be wise not to step too close.

It was the same with her. After her brother's death, she had felt such anger, making sure others knew they had better let her vent it as she would. For a moment, she felt the old hatred rise in her throat, narrowing her eyes at what old Barkeen had done. It had been cruel to send a boy to a death that was certain. She choked on the rising rage, coughing harshly to cover her roiling emotions.

Unwilling to let this man see past her carefully constructed mask, she pushed the rising heat aside. She could not undo what was done, only wait for a time to make others pay. Instead, she watched the boy at her side. In his anger, a man had emerged, and she felt drawn to him, someone so like herself, someone who wanted to lash out as she did. It was clear he wrestled with demons—as did most internees on Rant—and perhaps with him at her side, she could drive her own away, and they would haunt her no longer. Keeping her face hard, she watched Jer'son drum his fingers on his legs, the fabric of his clothing softening the staccato jump of the driving cadence. His head moved with that beat. It was not the quick music showcasing the soprano of love, nor the basso moodiness of a broken heart. It was fury's driving drumbeat, the one that L'Rene was certain he intended to thrash across the surface of the planet below. She wanted to be there when he did. She hungered for the revenge she had yet to enact for her brother's death, and while this time, it may not be hers, it drew her as a lioness to its kill.

She watched silently as the drum beat on.

"AYE, ME BOY, I be here. Don't try to turn ya' head. Me boy, me heart be broken for ya'." Bird stood with a heaviness inside and stepped to Barn't's bunk. "Ya' be safe here. No one can get ya' from under Bird's roof, they cannot. Rest, me boy."

The old man sat on the edge of the bunk, the medic come and gone, the repairs done, those that could be completed by that expert's hands, anyway. The damage done to the heart was up to the boy in front of him to heal.

One undamaged eye looked at Bird, the other too swollen to see, as the old man opened his mouth and let the soft wings of his namesake whisper throughout the room, the best comfort he knew how to give. It was the sound of his soul, and Bird hoped the love it sang would begin the healing the boy so needed inside.

For Bird, however, the song was so much more.

"Dad, come outside! The day is ours. The rain is gone. You must come play with us!" Two voices echoed as one.

Three weeks of rain were now gone. Bird, not yet with that name, but Bird nonetheless, looked out at the sun breaking through the foggy haze, the tall trees just making their branches known as the enveloping mists peeled away. Those boys needed outside. They did need to run and play. How their dear mother would have loved them, to see the muscles flinging those arms and legs across that clearing she had so lovingly tended.

He turned from the window, reaching for the picture on

232

the shelf. He knew it was just old-fashioned paper in the frame. His sweet love was not in the image. She was gone, and she had left him a part of her. Oh, not here. Not in the paper he so lovingly stroked with his hand. No, she was out there, in those muscles and sinews, that hair that refused to be tamed, and in those voices that called to him.

"Dad, where are you?"

The sound drifted to him from farther away, and it was the sound of a boy's excitement in his pursuit of life, and to Bird, it was also the sound of his sweet love calling to him.

He broke through the haze, one that covered the land on yet a different occasion. As the breeze shifted the mist, he could see her, her arms reaching out to him. He stepped forward to his love, and the mist shifted again, the white stone all that remained. The flowers in his hands, ones he claimed he had brought for her, were for him, he knew. His sweet love was there in his heart, but she could never again be in his arms.

He stepped forward and knelt at that slab. Tears ran from his eyes as he laid the blooms out one by one.

Before he could rise, the sound of footsteps rang on the ground behind him. Two sets there would be, he knew. The strength of a man's hands rested on his back, consoling a father's grief for a mother they had never known. His boys were boys no longer. Men, they had become.

My sweet, they are good men, too. You would have so loved to watch them grow. I have watched them for you, and I carry them in my heart. Someday I will join you, and you will know all I have stored away for you.

Bird brushed his tears away, the lines on his face now

grown deep. Too much time had passed, and it had not been kind to him or his boys. He reached his hand out and touched the fabric in the box, the creases ones he'd once pressed in by his own hand.

These, though, were not of his doing. Someone far away had placed these things in these boxes, this one and the one he had not yet found the courage to open. Perhaps the clothes in the boxes had even been folded by his sons' own hands, to be removed from a drawer when his sons no longer needed them.

Bird rested his hand on the second box, the unopened one, the second set of unfulfilled memories and dreams too much for a father's weary heart to take in one day. Later there would be time to know these things, to be lost for a time on the road these memories would take him down.

He stood and walked out the door, pausing to look through the rising fog over his sweet love's clearing. No longer as well tended, other things had taken his spirit from him. But when the mists closed in, he could still hear those child-like voices call to him.

"Dad, where are you?"

Bird looked down, now out of eyes that belonged to an old man on a prisonplanet, as he watched over a boy, now asleep, one who needed what love he could give. The light in the room had dimmed with the coming of night, and he saw the broken boy's hand resting on his own. In a whisper, he answered that question from in the mists, one that had been called out so long ago.

"I be here, boy. I'll always be right here for ya', right by ya' side."

THE TWO MEN drove down the isolated roadway in their stolen transport. Their mussed and filthy things had been thrown in an outside storage compartment, the wet cloths they'd cleaned themselves with tossed in with the items soiled by their retribution. Now they sported freshly crisp clothing, belying the atrocities they'd slashed across the boy's body they'd left hanging to die.

Barn't was of no concern to them, other than an opportunity lost. After all, he was just one more in a sea of boys they had gone through before arriving on Rant. He would have been fun to keep around, and they had enjoyed their first visit with him, but their deepest regret was the men they knew who would have enjoyed the boy as much as they had. Now he would be lost, only a memory for the two men, a totem to stack up with those of so many other young men who had been used up mercilessly.

The air in the transport was cool, and the men laughed with each other, regaling how the boy had jumped and pulled away and screamed at their advances. Pulling a food package from a storage bin, they split the contents and began to satisfy the more immediate of their bodies' needs.

What they forgot was that the boy had friends, and the two men riding in the transport were not among them.

"THE TRANSPORT must be here. It's time." Renhant paced the dusty, hard-packed earth, unable to sit and wait. "Jer'son's on his way, and I need him."

"Rennie, you must be patient. It will arrive when it arrives. Your friend will be here." Reenna tried to catch his

235

arm.

"I'm not Rennie, anymore." He stopped, angry tears released from his eyes. He felt raw emotion well up, filling his chest. "Rennie died so many years ago."

"And?" Reenna touched his cheek, rubbing it with the ball of her thumb. "What about now?"

His words spilled from him. "When I saw you that first day, I wanted to be that Rennie again, that small boy whose life had not yet gone down my roads. For a time I thought I could be. Yet, I also know I'm someone different, someone you can't imagine. I've tripped and stumbled, sometimes not knowing where I was headed, and not liking who I was when I got there. But it's me, and I'm learning I've got to accept me as I am."

"Good for you," she whispered. "Not everyone is wise enough to figure that out."

Renhant paused, weighing his thoughts, knowing he must say what he knew to be true. "For now, for this day, I am once again that cruel, vengeful boy I was so many times onboard MegaCorp's ship. It's as if he's come back to life, stepping back into me, and he controls everything I feel and do."

"You're not that boy, though. Can you see how much more you are?" She had dropped her hand from his face, and the sun caught a gleam of moisture running down her cheek.

"I can't polish that part of me away. It's a burr that will always be me. My friends and I need to find our strength in each other. We must be that strong wall for each other, defending ourselves against all onslaughts."

"Even if it means someone's death?"

He dropped his eyes, and in a subdued voice, he shared the vow they'd made when they'd learned of their fate on Rant. "We made a promise that we'd take up for each other, and never let another one of our group down, no matter who got hurt. One of us has been hurt, Sis, and if I don't step up and take my part in our group, then we don't have each other any longer. I can't let that happen. You know I can't, not and be the man I need to be." He raised his head to look at her.

Reenna looked at him and smiled. "I don't see my little brother any longer. This is the man he was supposed to become. Go be that man, Renhant. You do that. Your friends need the man you've become."

He grabbed her and gave her a hug, then he turned as he heard the sound of the transport settling to the ground.

"THANK YOU."

Jer'son turned to L'Rene. He had yelled at her, and he had wished her off the transport. He had burned with his anger, but finally he had seen that it was not at her. That she was very pretty helped. "I think it's almost time for us to land."

"Thank you for what?" Her words were restrained and careful.

He smiled, his anger still rumbling underneath, but his newfound politeness and civility trumping for the moment. "For your silence. For letting me be rude and inconsiderate. For understanding those things were not directed at you. You've said nothing, and you've been a good friend. For that, I thank you."

"I would continue to be a good friend, if you'll let me."

This time she smiled.

Jer'son nodded at her offer and turned as the transport doors opened. He had an old friend to see and a duty to perform. He didn't know which would be more difficult.

JER'SON SAW Renhant revealed through the opening transport door, stark and rigid in the harsh glare of the sun, and he could think of nothing else. He ran to his friend and threw his arms around him, the emotions of the past day ripping him apart, then binding the two friends once again as the feelings subsided.

"How is he?" He had heard the report, but it was a day old by now. "I know what the message said, but I need to hear it from my friend."

"The medics have done their work. His body will be fine, they say. His spirit?" Renhant chuckled, remembering Bird hovering over him. "He has Bird. The old man may wheedle and cajole him, but Barn't will know he's loved."

"You're right, there, friend. Shall we go to Bird's place?" Jer'son smiled with him, the void in his own emotions also needing filled, and the mention of Bird just the thing.

With Reenna and L'Rene following, their conversations filled with the men and their problems, Renhant whispered, "You have a girl, already?" He pointed her direction. "She's very pretty."

Jer'son turned to look at L'Rene deep in a discussion with Renhant's sister. Glancing back to the friend at his side, he smiled. "I think she would wish for it to be so." He walked a moment in silence, then continued, "She was on the transport on the way up to the station when I used the pass for the first time." Grinning at the memory, he recalled his opinion of her that day. "She was the non-stop talker, and she had me frightened about what I would find when I exited the shuttle."

"As I would have been."

More seriously, "She helped me once we were there. You should know what I've found out. I can't tell you much, but out at the construction site, the shipyard, what happened was only a small part of a very big picture." He waved his opened palm to indicate everything around him. "This is going to change."

"How? Change how?"

"For the better. Not overnight, no, and not even next year. However, be patient, good friend. Today we have other goals to reach. Not everyone alive on this world will see tomorrow, I can assure you. However, for now, I wish to speak with those tagging behind." He laughed and cuffed his friend on the shoulder.

Renhant called to him, "True, friend. That's the goal I also want to reach."

"HE BE FOUND upstairs, boys. Cornerstone'll be with him now. He be in a bad way, yet, but seeing ya' will be the medicine he needs. Go up to him." He smiled at the two women. "These beauties I can handle all on me own."

Heading up the stairs, Renhant clasped Jer'son's arm, and as quickly released it. "Mind what Bird said. He is bad. When we found him, he was injured and unconscious."

"Worse than I was told?"

Stopping for a moment, Renhant looked away, his mouth

239

going hard. "He was hanging by his arms from the branch of a tree, his feet barely on the ground. He was hardly alive. Be bright and cheerful, Jer'son. Bird has done wonders, but the damage goes deep."

Jer'son nodded as he mounted the final few steps and entered the room. Even expecting it, he was shaken. His friend, Barn't, always willing to be whatever he and Renhant asked of him, was a jumble of repairs. With only one good eye, his skin bruised, and bandages covering what the medic had mended, the repairs left little to recognize. When he spoke, though, his voice was his own.

"Jer'son." The word broke. "I didn't mean for this to happen. Cornerstone was helping me. We didn't know." The final sentence crumbled into incoherent sobs.

"Hey, hey, Barn't. I didn't know that my molester would beat up a friend to get back at me, either. I didn't cause it, though. Some people are just bad like that, and you can only come back and be strong again." He glanced at Cornerstone standing off to the side, and he shot him a teary smile. "You've been a good friend to Barn't. Cornerstone, if you will, please take care of him until Renhant and I return. I can promise the both of you that these men will cause no one any pain ever again."

"Jer'son, are you going to hurt them?" Barn't's words were whispered, and then he continued in an even smaller voice, "Will you kill them?"

"No, Barn't." Jer'son laughed reassuringly. "I've a better plan. I intend to let time do it."

"BOYS, I'VE called in the reinforcements. Been here a long

240

time, I have. Favors, I be owed, and a few I've demanded. Would ya' like to be the ones to do the honors?" Bird grinned at the prospect.

Jer'son smiled back. "Bird, you haven't! I only mentioned this to you to let you know my thoughts. I would've done this on my own, you know. You didn't have to be a part of this."

His grin instantly wiped from his face, Bird slapped the table, and the items on the top jumped. "Blast me moons, ya' be not taking this from me. That boy up there," and he pointed to the ceiling, "be like me own son. You think I'd not do this for me own son?"

"Bird, not even a mother could show as much love for Barn't as you have. He's needed you his whole life, whether he knows it or not. Thank you. I will not take this from you." He squeezed the old man's shoulder. "But we get to push them in, right, Renhant?" He looked at his friend and nodded his head.

Renhant just grinned in agreement.

JER'SON STOOD at the dock as Renhant made his request. "We have two cryo pods to ship offworld." Just behind them two civilian pods crowded the back of Cornerstone's old city transport.

"Ser, we have no record of a planned shipment of pods. Usually we know several days out. Prisoners being shipped to holding facilities require several days' preparation before insertion in the pods." The wind whipped the hair around a craggy face, the lines telling of years spent on Rant. The shirt that served as a uniform was as well-worn as the face. However, the glass he held in his hand glowed with information.

Renhant smiled. "This was sort of a rush job. We had to start the cryofreeze rather suddenly, and there was no time to preschedule the shipment."

"A rush job, ser? Doesn't that run a risk of nonresuscitation?" The man frowned, but it spoke more of boredom than true concern. His fingers manipulated a section of the information floating above the glass, and colors danced.

"We understand that, but it was a risk we felt it was important to take." The response had a humorous lilt that could no longer be held in.

As they walked away, both Jer'son and Renhant laughed. Unknown to them, in a room at the top of the stairs, a broken and bandaged boy suddenly laughed out loud, startling those around him. Those watching Barn't didn't understand why, and perhaps Barn't didn't either. However, they could all see the immediate improvement in his mien, and that was all that mattered.

—Chapter 13—

"Parents, it is ten o'clock. Do you know where your children are?"

—Public service announcement from the Twentieth Century A.D. (old-Earth timeline)

REENNA SNAPPED her pack shut, the military-issue fasteners drawing up with a firmness not even lasers could undo. This had been a hard campaign, and her team had suffered losses. Many losses, but that had been expected. In the early briefing sessions, it was made clear to her troops that this team of rebels was attempting to oust MegaCorp from its mining operations in order to secure that real estate for its own means and ends. The rebels were making a sympathy play by posing as an indigenous population. The troops were not to be misled by what they saw. It was all a setup to break the morale of the troops sent to drive the rebels out.

Her team had not broken. They were surprised at the complexity of the rebels' ruses, even to the extent of constructing elaborate Potemkin farms, complete with fields and grazing animals. That made no difference to her team. She taught them to be ruthless. Pictures on the walls of the farmhouses? Manufactured families. Animals in the fields? Convenient food sources. Elaborate roadway systems? Military transport avenues. There was no ruse on Trikeen that she did not see through. When her troops doubted, she set them down and worked it out for them. Of all the support troops brought out to defend MegaCorp's interests, her team was the only one that had no defectors, and she was confident her leadership played a huge part in keeping their morale strong.

With pride, she had volunteered her team to wipe out the last remaining pocket of rebels. By all the stars, the rebels had fought as if this really were their world by right. However, the true rights of ownership were vindicated, and the rebels were vanquished from the planet, leaving MegaCorp to reassume its mining operations.

Loaded on the final troop ship to depart the reclaimed world, Reenna was uncomfortably aware of the decimation in numbers this campaign had wrested from them. She was even more surprised when she awoke from her slow-sleep bunk to find herself being coded as a criminal on the prison-planet Rant.

"BARN'T, LOOK at me." Jer'son turned his friend's face to him. It had been time enough for some of the bandages to come off, but the bruises still glared angrily. Both eyes were now exposed, although the one was swollen and black. He was still a mess.

Barn't tried to shake his head, but with a yelp of discomfort, he settled for a second-best answer. "No."

"We need to get you offworld to a more secure location. This will always be a dangerous place for you. No matter how many times we strike back, you will be a target for the most depraved of these people."

"This is my home. I live with Bird. I won't leave." Barn't was as emphatic as he could be in the confines of his remaining bandages.

Bird stepped up behind Jer'son. "I wish I could support ya', me boy. I do like having ya' here, and all. It be ya' safety we must worry about. Sometimes that be the path we must take, whether we want or no." He reached out and laid a hand on the boy's leg. "Sometimes the easy path be not the path to take, me boy. Sometimes we walk the hard ways of loneliness and separation because them's the ways that take us to where we need to go. This be your time to learn that lesson."

"But—"

"No buts." He wiped tears from his eyes. "I can't say I be glad to see ya' go, and I want ya' to come to see me soon, but I will see ya' gone for safety's sake."

"Bird, you can't send me away. I'll be more careful, I promise. Cornerstone will be my guard. He will. It was just that Racket wasn't there that day." The tears now running down his face, Barn't turned to Jer'son. "Jer'son, tell him. I can't leave here. I can't leave Bird."

"Boy, ya' will leave, ya' hear?" Tears also began pouring down the old man's face. "I won't have another dead boy on me heart, I won't at that. That'd be breaking me in two, it would." Bird turned and stomped down the stairs without waiting for a response.

"Jer'son, why won't he let me stay? Doesn't he care about me?"

"It's because he does, Barn't. It's because he cares very much about you." Jer'son looked out the window at the gray sky, remembering Bird's tale of two sons and a drunken captgen'l sending them to their deaths because he had run out of liquor.

JER'SON SAT with Renhant and Cornerstone in the back room at Bird's establishment. Bird hoisted a metal container of liquor onto a cart, on the face of it ignoring them. It seemed an ordinary evening of friends gathered together. However, the door was closed, and the blinds were tightly drawn.

"Boys, ya' be safe from the eyes and ears in here, ya' be. Don't worry ya' none, because none'll hear or see ya'." Bird stepped out and gently shut the door. Overhead, the raucous sounds from one of the girls' rooms served as a disguise for anything they said tonight.

Renhant grinned. "I told you old Bird's the best there is. Now, Cornerstone, tell him what this is all about."

Jer'son looked back and forth between the two, confused. He was already involved in some sort of subterfuge onboard the station, and this had the ring of something similar. But for everyone he knew onworld to be involved? It was incredulous, at best.

Cornerstone leaned forward. "I know Renhant and trust him. Renhant's sister, Reenna, is part of the reason for that trust. Now I've bonded with Barn't, and gods help me, I regret my lapse in protection, thinking him safe for the moment, and then having him suffer the way he has." He paused, staring into his hands, the silence growing long.

Jer'son could guess what he wasn't saying. He didn't know Jer'son so well. Was it safe to confide in someone who was a total stranger to him?

In a sudden move Cornerstone glanced up, locking eyes with him. He spoke, and his voice carried an assurance that could be cut with a knife. "I know Renhant trusts you completely. For that reason alone, so must I."

"He knows our story, Jer'son." Renhant nodded as if that told it all.

"Rant is a prisonplanet, that's for sure." Cornerstone paused, taking a deep breath. Then, his story plunged ahead. "Throughout this arm of the galaxy, just to say the name is to invoke dread and foreboding. When someone comes here, they never leave and are never heard from again."

"Too true," Jer'son agreed. "At the academy we called it a permanent posting." He chuckled. "But we all knew what it really meant. So?"

"So, we live here on a world of criminals, many of which are trusted enough to come and go between the planet and the station, even building MegaCorp's war machines."

"I know some of what you're telling me. A number of the more trusted people were sent here simply to get them out of the way. Bird, for one."

"So, you know that story. Good. That makes mine easier." Cornerstone drew his chair closer as if to keep the confidence he intended to share just between the two of

247

them. "Renhant's sister and I were on the same military campaign. When we were successful, and by that, I mean achieving MegaCorp's goal as stated in our directives, we shipped home, so we thought, only to find ourselves here, and our former selves reported as casualties of war."

Jer'son glanced to Renhant with a frown, pausing a moment before jerking his eyes to Cornerstone and back again. "So, there was no mix-up or something like that? You thought your sister was dead for years, and all because MegaCorp wanted her to disappear?"

Renhant nodded his head.

"I am so sorry for those years, my friend."

Cornerstone continued, "How do you think the infrastructure here gets maintained?"

"People like Medic Barkeen on the station, gravitating to jobs that use their natural abilities?"

This time Cornerstone laughed. "Not even close. Try outside contractors."

"Like who? What jobs use outside contractors? Do you mean the shipyard?"

"That's a prime example. Do you actually think the prisoners could develop the log-in system we have, be trustworthy with untold riches in materials and supplies, or be trusted to turn all that back over to MegaCorp?"

Jer'son hesitated, not wanting to denounce what Cornerstone was saying, but this was outside anything he'd ever heard about Rant. "Do you have any proof?"

"Absolute and definitive!"

Cornerstone and Renhant grinned at each other.

"Come on, give. You're making me pull this out of you."

"His father, Jer'son. Cornerstone's father. He's here." Renhant tapped the table to make his point.

"And? How does that prove anything?"

Cornerstone smiled. "My dad has made fortunes on other worlds. When he found I was sent here, he refused to lose me to oblivion on this hellhole. He joined me."

"He just came here? And no bells or whistles went off? If he could do that, then why can't we all just get up and leave?"

"It's not quite that simple." Renhant scooted his chair forward, commanding the conversation for a time. "Cornerstone's dad took on an outside contract to run the planetside transportation department." He elbowed Cornerstone with a grin. "Then, instead of sending in a company representative, he came himself. He has to pose as a prisoner so no one is suspicious."

"He did that for me." Cornerstone nodded, and he fought a smile for a quick moment before letting it spread across his face.

Renhant continued, "Can you imagine what would happen if some of these hard-core cases here, and we have them, as we've experienced, discovered some of their cellmates aren't prisoners after all? They'd be held for ransom, probably for passage off planet. As it is, everyone here 'knows' no one off this planet cares about what happens here, so we are forced to work out problems among ourselves." He laughed. "That's not likely without help."

"So," Jer'son interjected, "Cornerstone's father just decides to come here posing as a prisoner. What about the lung tracker? The arm numbers?" He could see people being sent for political purposes, but outside contractors? In spite of everything he'd ever believed about Rant? "I need deeper explanations than what I've received so far."

Cornerstone held his hand up, palm out. "You are right to ask. The numbers, yes. The tracker, no. He can leave anytime he wishes."

"How? Go to the station and leave on a jumpship? People would catch on if only a few people did that, and it's hard to imagine someone taking a position here if they knew they could never leave, no matter how good the pay."

Cornerstone looked at the floor a long time before answering. "This is something no one except my father and I know. There are surely other people on the planet who are also outside contractors, but neither my father nor I are aware of them. We are certain that my father cannot be the only one, but those secrets, if they are here, are very closely held."

"And that means?" Jer'son felt jittery by this time. He was unsure just where this was headed.

"My dad has a private ship." Cornerstone looked up.

Both Renhant and Jer'son responded in kind, "A ship?"

Cornerstone laughed. "This is why I'm being so secretive." He waved his hand at the precautions, the sealed windows, the ceiling with its sordid noises. "I have never spoken of this, and only my dad and I know this, not even Reenna." He glanced at Renhant as a warning. "A ship with off-world capabilities."

"Here? On Rant?" Renhant questioned again, disbelief written all over him.

"He could leave and take you?" Jer'son looked around the room. And the man was still here! "And yet you choose to stay. Why? Renhant's sister? Take her with you."

"I don't choose to stay, Jer'son. The trackers, even yours with your station pass, serve multiple purposes. They track us, sure. They also provide a constant low-dosage contraceptive. No children, ever, as the trackers are rather permanent. Finally, and this is the important one. Unless constantly reset by the broadcasters here on the planet, they self-destruct within about a thirtyday. I can't leave, and neither can Reenna."

"Surgery? Can't they be taken out? Haven't people tried that?"

"Of course, but no medical facility here will do that. Try it without one. Death from internal bleeding or infection is not pleasant."

"Offworld. Go somewhere else to have the tracker removed."

"Trust me, these are good questions. I can see why you were given a permanent pass and pulled to the station. We have asked ourselves these very questions. Just think, if MegaCorp will send an entire military battalion to this place to protect their illegal takeover of an innocent planet, what will they do to a doctor who removes a tracker from the lung of a Rant internee?"

"I see, I think. The price must be very high to warrant the risk."

Cornerstone smiled. "My dad is working to earn that price, for me and for Reenna. When he has earned it, Renhant will be in place to cover our disappearance. Leaving my friend here is not what I would wish, but we will leave him very prosperous."

Renhant grinned. "I'll still be the outside rep, and you should see the toys they have, not like the junk all over the rest of Rant. I think I could tolerate it here with a little thirtyday vacation every now and then."

Jer'son looked at Cornerstone, smiling. He tilted his head, indicating Renhant. "Do you know what you've done? You've created a monster."

Cornerstone looked at him and laughed.

"TELL ME about your girl, Jer'son."

"My girl, Barn't? Now, just what is that supposed to mean? I don't have a girl."

"That's not what Renhant and his sister say." The bandaged boy worked very carefully to get his legs off the bed, only grimacing in pain a few times.

"So, good friend, tell me. Just what do Renhant and his sister say?" Jer'son stood back and crossed his arms in mock irritation, and yet, a grin turned the corner of his mouth.

Barn't, finally sitting, looked at him. "You won't make me use that pan again, will you? I really want to get up and go." He reached out his hand. "Help me, please."

"So, just what do they say?" Jer'son chuckled, offering a hand but keeping it just out of reach.

"Please, Jer'son. After."

"Okay, I give in. After, but that sounds like a promise to me. Is it?" He reached out to offer his arm.

"I guess so. Just hurry, or I might not make it. I've got to go now. Hurry, Jer'son!"

"Just a few more steps. Are you going to be all right in there by yourself? Or, do you need me to come in and hold it for you? As ill as you've been, your aim might be off."

"Gods, Jer'son. No!"

Jer'son laughed at the distress in his friend's voice. "I'm out here waiting, just in case."

"Don't listen, though. I do like a little privacy."

"My ears are plugged, Barn't."

"Just step back, won't you?"

"I will, but not too far."

"Gods, Jer'son. I thought you said you'd plug your ears!"

"Sorry, Barn't. They're plugged, now."

"Thanks."

"You're welcome."

"*Jer'son!*"

After a minute, the sound of water filtered into the room; and Jer'son saw the door opening and remarked, "I give in, Barn't. Oh, there you are already. It's too late to plug my ears now, I guess. Sorry." He couldn't help but laugh at the distress on his friend's face. "Now, you have to tell me. What's this about a girlfriend?"

Barn't eased himself back onto his bed. Looking at Jer'son, he grinned. "That girl, L'Rene, has been talking to Reenna. It seems she volunteered to ride downside with you."

Jer'son winked back. "And do you know what we talked about the whole time? Nothing."

"Nothing? What does that mean? Nothing?"

"Exactly that, so don't get too excited. I told her I didn't invite her, and we spent the whole ride without another word."

"Will you talk to her going back up?"

253

"I don't know, Barn't. Are you going to cover your ears?"

He grinned. "Of course!"

L'RENE SAT on the transport, accompanied by the two men heading to the station. All were ready to leave Rant, and all three had good reasons for being allowed aboard. L'Rene and Jer'son each had their station passes. Barn't was leaving on a medical visa approved by Medic Barkeen.

"Jer'son, I only want to stay on the station until I get better." Barn't called his words plaintively. He sat facing one end of the transport, and it was difficult for him to look around. He couldn't see the other two. "I want to be back with Bird as soon as possible. Jer'son?'

At the other end of the transport, Jer'son sat focused on someone else. "Tell me, L'Rene, if you want, how did you get here?"

"Ooh, that's a tough one, Jer'son. You sure know how to pull the hard questions out of the bag." She put her arm on the back of the seat next to her and looked directly at him. She remembered the reasons. They were the demons she slept with each night. During the day, she managed to keep them nicely tucked away, though. She would not bring them out now, and to cover her feelings, she smiled brightly at the man sitting next to her.

"Another one, then. Where are you from? Am I allowed to ask that?" He smiled at her, brushing his fingers along the side of her arm.

"Ever heard of a planet called Trikeen?"

"As in Reenna's Trikeen?" He raised his eyebrows.

She laughed, making sure it was pleasant and clear. "Yeah, she told me about that. She's here because they wiped us out, and I'm here because we weren't wiped out." However bright her laugh, with those words, her stomach turned, her emotions making connections deep inside. She knew it as a tightening across her chest, and she thought it was aimed at Reenna. She wanted it to be aimed at Reenna, and Cornerstone, too.

"So, are there more of your people here?"

"I'm the only one left. That was our world. Our family had been there for generations. It was a farming world. MegaCorp found something or the other they wanted in the soil, and they just came and took it. Those that wouldn't leave, they brought here. I was only fifteen. How much sense does that make?" She remembered, also, her brother, but she didn't talk about him anymore.

"Actually, knowing Reenna's story, quite a bit. No one could be allowed to give away the big corporation secret, so they just buried it."

"I've never summed it up that well before. Very nice. I do see some of what they see in you. You got both your questions answered, and I fell for it. Can we talk about something else, though?" She looked away, wanting to find something in this man, and she didn't want the past to get in the way.

"Who?" Jer'son sat up. "You said they. Who are they?"

She was relieved at the change of subject, and she ran with it. "Honestly, Jer'son, you are the talkative one this ride. Last time I couldn't get you to say a single word. Now, you won't shut up. When I talk all the time, it's just to fill the space. However, I can be a little quieter when someone else talks to me."

"You said they. Who are they?" He studied her face, as if he could read the answer there.

"They are just whoever is in power." She looked at him as if she didn't understand the question. In reality, she knew she had made a slip she couldn't retract.

"So, you won't tell me," he said.

"Tell you? There's nothing to tell. If there was, I'd know, believe me."

"It's just that someone up there wants me for some reason, and I'm not really sure just what I'm supposed to do."

She snorted. "You'll get a job, just the same as the rest of us, and you'll get some schooling if you want, and you'll help the station function better. Mostly that's what we do. We monitor shipments, and of course manage the planet population and where the people go after they arrive at the station."

"Where the people go? You don't send them all to the same place?"

"Of course not. Some of the internees are truly horrible, and others who aren't so bad get the better places." She laughed, thinking, *How cute, even if he is a bit of a fool.*

He chuckled, looking at the ceiling and rubbing his head. "Like the one I was at?"

"You know, I never had to stay down there." She was changing the subject, and she knew it.

"What? Never?"

"When I came here, they were short a position on the station. I happened to have those skills, and there I was. Just being on the station means having an automatic station pass, too, so sometimes I do the dirty work. Planetside runs." She turned her head for a moment, a pained look flashing across her features, then the look quickly shifted, with only the edges showing the remembered pain of her brother's memory. He had gone to the planet, and she sometimes searched for him, even though Barkeen had proclaimed him dead.

Jer'son readjusted his knee to let it rest against hers. He grinned when she didn't move away. "You know, I'm surprised they let you stay on the station."

"Hey," she said, frowning. "What makes you say that?"

"I would think you would wear out the comm system."

"Huh? The comm system doesn't ever wear out."

"Neither does listening to you." He grinned and his face began to turn red.

"That's sweet, Jer'son." She laughed, pleased he had believed her story so easily. He wouldn't have liked her if he'd heard the real one. She leaned over and gave him a peck on the cheek.

"Hey, guys," Barn't called. "Remember I'm up here."

CHR'S LAY still, his leg splinted. He so wanted to shift positions, but with the cracked ribs, *three* of them still not healed, it hurt just to breathe. He looked at the dark of the covering above him, the ceiling just a dusky shape against the blacker sky. He had to stay under this old pavilion or risk being seen by the obsat that circled the planet. He knew there was no privacy in the city. They tracked you if they suspected you. Those crikin' sonic imagers kept them aware of everyone in the city; they could even extrapolate what was

257

going on from predetermined behavioral algorithms. Out here, it was just the sats. He could hide, here.

If that pervert from the kid's past hadn't jimmied things up, they'd be well on their way to initiating modifications to the plans for that new cruiser. Oh, he knew it'd be years before the results came to fruition. He'd told the kid fifteen, but it could be as few as twelve or as many as eighteen.

At least he'd been able to get Barkeen to have the kid transferred to the station. Just in from the academy. How lucky could they get, and seemingly smart, too! Over the years, Barkeen had set up a lot of the freshies with Bird, but this one just might be the best she'd ever sent. They had needed the latest knowledge and the up-to-date academy training to help with the modifications on the plans. Keep the kid, and it was all theirs.

Too bad Barkeen didn't want Bird to know everything, to be allowed completely inside the loop. Plausible deniability, she always called it. She still had a soft spot for that old man. Once Bird was gone, and at his age, who knew, who would be able to evaluate the freshies, then? The moons help them when Barkeen was lost. If that happened, Mega-Corp was the winner.

Emergency escape cryo pod doors and that actuator arm. It was genius, and even the old man had come through to confirm it. They'd discussed it more after the kid had gone on to his bunk. They figured they could pull it off, even if jimmying all the pod doors might not be feasible. Still, most of them might be enough. An overload subroutine could be set up where testing one or two or even a whole level would allow them to operate properly, but in a full abandon ship scenario, all the pods would try to cycle on simultaneously. It would be easy to rig that, to initiate a cascading shutdown, and it would never be discovered in a routine test.

What a friggin' lucky strike that actuator arm idea was!

Now if they could just get inside the old man's mind. Sometimes he was as clear as a bell, but those times were getting fewer and fewer. How much time they had left, he didn't know, and that frightened him. He didn't want to spend the rest of his life on this rock. How much did one man have to pay for a few stolen MegaCorp credits? A lifetime? It wasn't fair, but fair didn't matter anymore. Bringing MegaCorp to its knees did.

In the darkness, his thoughts began to ramble . . .

If that kid turns out to be the gold mine we think he is, all this pain will be worthwhile, and what the hell is a gold mine, anyway, and where is the morning? I need to shift my leg, and great gods, I need to pee.

"THERE HE IS, the boy from downsides." Medic Barkeen paused as Barn't gingerly stepped through the examining room door to her familiar voice. "My, you did get yourself banged up, didn't you? Let me see just how bad the damage is." She helped him onto the table, giving him a hand as he removed his clothing. "Move as little as possible, and I'll be very careful. Lift your leg a bit. There. Now, roll over."

She thrust one arm forward, a shiny instrument plunging deep into the boy's anal cavity. His eyes teared up, and he gasped as she abruptly removed her instrument.

"Oh, there, that didn't hurt too much, did it? Now, if you'll just roll back over, and don't worry, son, I've seen it all, including yours, if you'll remember, so let's just get these clothes back on. Is that all right?"

"Yes, ser," Barn't answered in the smallest voice he had.

"I'm Medic Barkeen, remember, but Barkeen is just fine. No 'ser' needed. How's my Bird doing?"

"Your bird?" Barn't turned his eyes to catch hers.

She stood back and looked at him. "You've forgotten that man already?"

He turned red with embarrassment. "Oh! I thought you meant a real bird. I didn't think you meant Bird. I'm sorry. He's fine, I guess." Then he had to stop talking when his eyes flooded with tears.

"Oh, my, I didn't know I was opening the waterworks. Are these tears good or bad? I know that Bird, the one you stayed with. He did sing for you?" With that, Barn't squeezed his eyes shut and sobbed. "Well, I'm pretty sure that's not from Bird's singing. He usually gets very favorable responses. So, I'm counting on you missing him very much. Can I get a nod or a shake of the head? Good! That's how I feel about him, too. Let's sit you up. There." She helped him put his shirt on. "I'll be right back. I'm walking over to get my chart." Stepping brightly across the room, she reached up on the shelf to retrieve it.

She turned, and the scene she saw was totally different. Her eyes looked across a sea of children. Did no one check that planet for carcinogens? Those parents, they took their *children* into that. How horrible it must have been to watch their flesh and blood sicken and die! So many to rescue and only this one transport came.

Barkeen's eyes filled with tears as she thought of all the

children they'd left behind. To remember making her way through that makeshift ward, marking the children as salvageable or not, then having to stop when she reached her quota. Oh, if only they'd known it was so bad, maybe another transport could have been commandeered.

She walked among the ones she had so hoped she could save. There, that little girl with the dark eyes. She had been looking around just yesterday. Now, all she would do was stare straight ahead. That other one. She knelt by the boy, perhaps fifteen, his red hair falling out in clumps, as he smiled and motioned at her.

"Yes," and she looked at his name on his bed, "Frank'l. Are you feeling well, today?"

"Thank you." His cancer-ridden throat barely managed to croak out his words. "You came to save us. Thank you."

Barkeen reached out to stroke the hair remaining on his head. She turned at a touch on her shoulder. Standing, she followed the medic who motioned her along to an office. Closing the door, the medic whispered to her frantically, "Barkeen, you must go upstairs. They are demanding the head medic, and that's you. They will speak with no one else. We fear for the lives of the three old ones. Without the cryo beds, I'm afraid they will not make the trip for their treatments."

Barkeen hissed, "They knew that when they diverted this ship. We are a mercy mission transport, not even a real medical ship. We're not equipped with cryo beds. We're also not equipped with a rejuv ward. No matter how much money they have or how well connected they are, they should not be on this ship. We informed them of that before we diverted.

You know that."

"If you could go to them, we might be able to find them some sort of treatment and enable them to at least live until we reach our destination. If you would just see them."

Tears flooded Barkeen's eyes. "We could have saved every one of these children if we hadn't been commanded to divert to accommodate those leeches up there hobnobbing at the capt's table. We would have already reached our destination, and these children would have already received life-giving treatments that could have cured every one." She turned from the medic beside her. "To trade all of these children for those three relics? I will not go. These children will die because of the presumptiveness of those *fossils!*"

"But Barkeen, they will see no one else. They say it's beneath their station."

Barkeen set her mouth. "Then they will see no one." She walked back to the children, knowing there was nothing she could do, and she consoled them as best as she could.

She took a deep breath and realized only Barn't was there with her. *Gods, will the nightmares never end?* For the boy's sake, she managed a semblance of a smile. "We need to get you a place to sleep, boy. I understand you and Jer'son are good friends. Is that still the way it is?"

Barn't smiled. "Yes, Barkeen."

"Well, then." She checked her glass, flipping through several categories of information, settling on accommodation assignments. "It seems as if he's been assigned a single. How about if we bump him to a double and give you the other bunk? Would that suit you?"

Barn't smiled even wider. "Yes, Barkeen. That would

suit me just fine."

"HEY, WEASEL! I've got my stuff and your stuff here."
Jer'son flung the door open, both his hands full. He looked
around, his eyes wide. "This room is big. My single was a
closet with a bunk. This is a real room. A desk and an information console with its own glass. Now I don't mind having
you here. My own glass! That's worth putting up with even
you." He grabbed a pillow off the top bunk and held it over
Barn't, trying to wrestle it to his face while Barn't kept
pushing it away.

Barn't yelled, "Ow, Jer'son. I think I just broke a bone
again. Stop!" When his friend jumped back, a frightened
look on his face, he just laughed. "I never had any broken
bones in the first place."

He curled up to protect himself as Jer'son came at him
again. Struggling and rolling on the bunk, he begged for
mercy, erupting into repeated gales of laughter when Jer'son
refused to surrender his attack.

Finally exhausted, the wrestling having pulled their
seventeen-year-old energies from them, the two boys sat on
the bed, the pillow between them, and enjoyed each other's
company. Tomorrow might demand they be men again. For
tonight, though, they were content to forget that they were
on an unfamiliar station orbiting an unfamiliar world where
three men were dead because of them. They had to live the
lives they had been given, and for this one night, they lived
it as the boys they really were.

—Chapter 14—

"No one knows just what the driver was thinking. The overpass is clearly marked at eleven feet, four inches. He peeled the entire top of his truck away, releasing thousands of live fowl to flood the highway. Thirteen other drivers were killed due to the birds blocking their vision."

—*Twentieth Century News Report, old-Earth*

BARN'T COUGHED. Wiping at his eyes, he squinted, trying to see through the smoke filling the corridor, but even the red emergency lighting along the floor provided only the dimmest glow to guide him along his way. He couldn't go back; he knew that. The corridor there was blocked by debris.

He had run so far. His muscles burned with the agony of trying to get *away*, and tears came to his eyes. The smoke burned when he blinked. He reached up to rub his eyes with his hands, and when he looked down, he saw moisture-streaked blackness dripping from his fingers.

He turned to his side to see the blackness running down the corridor wall, puddling at the floor, and reaching out to swallow his shoes. Smoke rose where the soles of his shoes pressed against the floor. This part of the ship would be the next to go; he could tell that. It was time to run again.

His heart thumped in his chest to the rhythm of his shoes against the floor. The next corridor would be safe. It had to be safe. If he could just get past the smoke, find a place where the lighting worked so he could see, so he could tell where to go, then he knew he would be safe.

He turned his head and could see the tracks of his shoes, the smoking remains of his soles melting away with every step. The walls had begun to glow with the intensity of the destruction. He knew he must get out of this corridor, out of this ship.

He rounded a curve to see part of the wall retracting into the ceiling. Inside was an escape pod. He would be able to climb inside, and he would be safe. The pod would carry him to the nearest celestial body able to incite its internal guidance system. He would then he rescued.

He glanced around, his chest tightening in fear. The emergency lighting had grown brighter, but the panel was rising too slowly. No, he was mistaken. It was the walls and the ceiling taking on the red glow of the lighting strips along the floor. They were melting. He had to get in the pod, and it had to be now.

He tried to leap forward as the pod's access panel finally disappeared into the ceiling, offering him the safety of escape. However, his shoes had melted to the corridor floor. *No*, he screamed inside. Then, he saw a man climbing out of the escape pod, and a second after him. They grinned luridly. As he recoiled in horror, he recognized their faces, and he realized he was naked.

"No!" he screamed out loud this time.

Jer'son's feet landed on the floor beside his bunk. "Shush, Barn't. You can wake up, now. It's not real." Hands pressed against sweat-covered shoulders, forcing him back to his pillow. "Lie there, my friend. You're safe."

Barn't jerked, the realization that he was no longer in the corridor releasing the dream's hold. He drew in a deep breath, and after a moment, he exhaled. His voice shook. "It was bad this time, Jer'son. Really bad."

"Do you want to talk about it?"

"I couldn't move. The ship was burning, and my feet were stuck to the floor. I couldn't reach the escape pod. Then, the same two men climbed out of the pod, and," he gasped out a sob, "I had no clothes on."

"Barn't, they're not here now, and they can never be again. You're safe."

"I know that, but it doesn't feel that way right now." He turned to look at his friend, barely a dark shape in the blackness, yet his features as clear to him as his own hand in the depth of night. He *knew* the man at his side. Friends for nine years, on this station for five of those, Jer'son had been there for him every step of the way. He grabbed his hand. "Thank you, Jer'son. You're the best friend I could have ever had."

Jer'son laughed and stood. "That's what all my friends with recurring nightmares say. I guess I should get used to it. I think you're over the worst of it for tonight. Sleep well, friend," and he leaped back onto the upper bunk.

Quietly, so as to be unheard, Barn't whispered, "You don't know, Jer'son, just how good a friend you've been to me. Thank you for that."

"HOW WAS his night last night?" Jer'son's second-in-command, Mi'Kail Tranderkov, turned to the station's operations overseer. He grinned. They didn't often get assigned concurrent duties, and he was glad for the chance to spend the day with his immediate superior. "After that late night you had with L'Rene, I figured you might have slept right through his nightmare phase just this once."

Jer'son flushed, and Mi'Kail fought back a smile before looking away. Even though it was common knowledge about him and L'Rene, whenever it was mentioned, the man always seemed to come off as embarrassed, even though they had been together four years.

"Has she given you her room code yet, or do use your operations center overrides? Better yet, when are you going to move in with the girl? She's a beaut, and there are other fellows waiting in line to take your place," he teased, "as if they've even got a chance with those looks of yours." He peered Jer'son's direction, amused to see the red hadn't faded.

"This face hasn't always brought me luck," Jer'son muttered, as he grabbed his glass and twisted his fingers above its surface to turn it on. He threw a quick glance at his co-worker. "Do you intend to chat all morning about my personal life, or can we get to the day's business?"

"Well, hope breeds eternal for the other men on the station, so I hear. Hey!" He rolled his chair around to look at Jer'son. "I'd like to be first in line. I'm not seeing anyone right now. Are you ready to open the field?" He reached up just in time to grab the glass being thrown at him. "You should be glad I'm a quick catch. You'd be out the cost of a new one of these, otherwise."

"You know why I don't move in with her." He reached to his console, triggering the first of the day's commands; and the displays spread about the room lighted up like solar flares. "The nightmares. He has them every night."

"You might lose her. Give a girl enough rope, and eyes will rove." Mi'Kail said the words lightly, but there were still old stories about L'Rene floating about the station, and he didn't want his friend hurt. Jer'son seemed to be enamored of the woman, and L'Rene hadn't had an episode for a very long time. Before Jer'son had come along to settle her down, she'd been quick to play the field, not always leaving her beaus undamaged.

"Can I get a break, Mi'Kail?" Jer'son paused and looked at him, shaking his head.

"You know I only tease about being interested himself." Mi'Kail stood and tossed the glass to land at Jer'son's side before reaching up to tap at a display that blinked red. "You'll want that."

He jumped when Jer'son clapped him on the shoulder. "You really think L'Rene would have you?" Jer'son squeezed his shoulder playfully. "You must think you've come up in the world."

Mi'Kail leaned forward and tapped the counter directly

in front of his superior. "Seriously, if you care about that girl, is Barn't worth the risk of losing her? Are you willing to trade one for the other? I mean, he's a good guy and all that, but look at it from my point of view. He's twenty-two standards, and strapping big. I wouldn't have believed it five years ago, but I guess it's the food up here, either that or Barkeen's slipping him growth hormones."

"Don't let him hear you say that." Jer'son chuckled. "He runs in the arena, already beating some of the fastest competitors, and I even think he's started resistance training."

"You suppose it's possible he's still growing?"

"I think he's settled in. He always said his dad told him he'd do this, get his size late." Jer'son walked to his workstation, the control center of the entire habitat, really, and wiped his hand above the sensors, triggering the remaining displays to come up. "We've been through a lot, Barn't and me." He looked up at Mi'Kail and grinned. "Did I ever tell you about the time on the academy ship that he was being picked on by these uppercadets . . ."

Mi'Kail grinned. He'd been told, and more than once. However, he didn't mind listening again. The story was a good one, even if the punch line was at Barn't's expense.

CORNERSTONE STEPPED through the glass doors to see his mother sitting on the veranda. Past her, his father was swimming his daily laps in the pool. Farther away, the ground dropped off, stretching to the line of trees in the distance. He was home just for this weekend, and then he was scheduled to be back on the academy ship.

He felt guilty. The other cadets didn't have rich fathers

to pull strings to get them passes home whenever some special event came up. In reality, his father hadn't wanted him to join the academy in the first place. Gods knew, his family certainly didn't need the money from MegaCorp, but this had been something Cornerstone could do on his own. His family connections hadn't set this up, opening this door, or pulling that string to get him advancements onboard the academy ship. It was all Cornerstone's hard work that got him somewhere at the academy.

He paused, glancing down at the paving stones, imported at gods knew what cost all the way from Earth, wherever that was, and he grinned. Except this, today. Even with his son turning into a man, his dad could still pull the strings, and that he had done. Cornerstone did hate it, but he also enjoyed this chance to see his mom.

He would admit, his dad, too. He had just needed the chance to do something without a leg up from a wealthy father. He glanced up to see his mother waving at him.

She called, "Sam'elton Welt'n Rhnnesty the Third, get down here and kiss your mother."

This was the one thing he missed most. It was so good to hear her voice call to him. For the first thirteen years of his life, he had heard his full name spoken aloud just that way first thing every morning, and her voice brought back the best parts of his childhood. He pressed a kiss to her cheek. "Good morning, Mother."

Before he could back away, she reached a hand to his head, pressing the side of his face against hers. She stroked his skin for a moment and then spoke the second thing he had also heard every morning of his childhood. "You are my cornerstone. You know that, don't you? You are my cornerstone."

Cornerstone's eyes opened, and he felt dampness in them. Carefully, so as not to wake her, he turned to Reenna at his side, her profile beautiful as he watched her sleep in the dimness of the early dawn. He continued to watch as she blurred into a hazy outline, and for a moment, he once again looked into that face that had pressed for a moment against his so long ago.

If I'd only known I'd never see her again.

Life hadn't offered him second chances, though, and he let his arm slip around Reenna's waist. Soon, they would be free, and no matter the price, it would be worth everything it cost, even if it was indeed everything.

CHR'S WATCHED as the shipping carton was removed from around the massive part. It was one of two propulsion actuator arms, and his heart thrummed with excitement. This part wasn't special, but what it was planned to do would be. Now, if he could get the old man to come through with his information on how to sabotage its installation . . . but that had become increasingly difficult. The knowledge was stuck in the forgotten recesses of his brain.

He stepped from the receiving hangar and out into the bright sun. He winced at the pain in his leg. It still gave him trouble after all these years. However, if this worked, it'd be worth every time he'd cursed this injury. He held a hand to shade his eyes and pressed ahead, his limp more pronounced with his haste. He didn't know how much longer the old man would be with them, his health having suffered on this harsh world, and Chr's also knew that any moments lost with him could never be regained. The old man's knowledge was crucial to this plan.

Stepping into a massive warehouse, he opened a door into a small storage unit at the back, one especially constructed for one purpose. The old man lay inside, still in bed, propped against several pillows, his eyes open and staring. Would this be one of his good days? Chr's certainly hoped so. He pulled a glass from a shelf and placed it in front of him.

Whispering as he activated the images inside, he roused him. "The propulsion actuator arm. It's here." The old man's eyes gradually tracked to the sound of the voice in the room with him but remained as blank as ever. When he was like this, Chr's knew to play his only trump card. He didn't know all the man's story, but he knew this would break through the fog at least for a few moments. A few minutes a day might be all the old man could give, but he would take whatever he could get. He had no other option.

"Your daughter is waiting on you. Do you want to see her? We need to work on the ship so you can go see your daughter."

The man's face lit up with the expectations of the suggestion, focusing on the glass' images in front of him. "Yes, yes. We should do that. Where were we? Yes, right here."

Breathing easily for the moment, Chr's stepped from the room, motioning another man to step inside to help monitor. At least here, the old man was hidden from the obsat's view. They thought he was dead, although he might well reach that goal anytime. If he could only give Chr's a few more days, just a few more, the plans would be complete.

The dust kicked up from underneath the soles of his boots, a hazy afterimage hovering in the thick air, as he walked away, one foot firmly planted, the other just a half imprint anyone watching would have seen as an old injury that left a slight, but permanent limp. To Chr's, his limp was more. It carried the memory of that morning those five years ago when he had thought it was worth it to save one seventeen-year-old kid. He would have done it even if he'd known then he would carry the memory of that morning deep inside of him, his leg his reminder every day. For what that kid had given them, no price would have been too great.

DAD HELD a sheet of paper with Renhant's handwritten name at the top, the rest a series of entries that only he could decipher. He intended it that way, as it was safer, for Renhant as well as Cornerstone and Reenna.

He laid it carefully on a stack that was off to the side and smaller than the rest, pausing to gaze across the piles he knew as well as he knew his own face. Not even his son guessed at this. It was his true desk, the one in his secret room that no one ever saw, all his private records written and stacked in neat piles of old-fashioned paper. He had to hide everything. No one had ever been allowed to know the secrets of his ultimate goal, nor could they. It was far too important.

Walking to the huge door of his very secure back office, he turned the lock, let himself out, and twisted the lock once again, the old-fashioned key slipping into a pocket. Sometimes the old ways were the best. No one would expect valuables to be kept safe with something so simple, even if a thief might not recognize his valuables as such. They were valuable only to his son, Reenna, and himself. In spite of that, they were worth more than life to them.

Dad now walked through his main office, the public one where his official business was handled, and he spoke to Reenna.

"I'm expecting an ultra-confidential package, personal palm-approval delivery only. If it arrives today, please let me know. If I'm away, I'll cover all expenses for the courier to wait until I return." He paused a moment, then with the burning of tears in his eyes, he leaned in and spoke to her in a low voice. "Begin to prepare, my dear. Have my son do the same."

Reenna shifted her eyes to his, and then as quickly returned them to her work. "Thank you, Dad. I'll let Cornerstone know."

Dad returned to his public office and sat at his desk. Renhant was running the show now. His own position was a formality, only. Knowing he really had nothing at all to do, he lingered at his desk, studying each item adorning its glossy surface. This was his official throne where he had performed the duties of transportation chief, managing an entire continent. As far as this world knew, he would continue to do so.

Yet, if this expected delivery should contain the reply he so hoped for, his life would change. And as far as this desk, it would remain here, but it would never be used again. Renhant had his own, far grander office. With that, why would any functionary desire to trudge down to this ancient room just to meet with the old man who used to run these affairs first-hand? No, his door would remain closed, his calls returned by his trusted assistant, and gradually he would fade from people's memories. That pretty secretary who had worked for him? Why, this was the poorer half of this world. Why would she want to stay here? Not after her companion was killed when his old transport exploded at the edge of the city.

Dad was jarred from his ruminations by a gentle voice.

"Dad? Your delivery is here."

"Thank you, Reenna. Please send the courier in. I'll take care of this now."

With a press of Dad's palm on the acknowledgement glass, the courier was back out the door. Stepping through to his back office, the key once again locking the door, Dad broke the seal. Inside was the answer he'd hoped to see.

Dear Ser: I understand your desire to remain anony-mous. I appreciate you allowing me to do the same. I am acknowledging the arrival of the sum on which we agreed. I am prepared to extend my private medical facilities for your use at your convenience. I will be the only one in attendance, so please be assured your confidentiality will be guaranteed. All records will be disposed of upon successful completion of our agreement. Sincerely, Your Associate.

Dad looked up and smiled.

IT HAD BEEN close to a dozen standards, but one memory haunted Medic Barkeen more than all others. The Dispos-sessed of Trikeen.

Everywhere they had gone on the ship, they had left the

275

stain of their world. Oh, she had quickly recognized that these were not the bad people MegaCorp had portrayed them to be. These were the children of landowners who had refused to give in when a corporation decided it would take what it wanted no matter who got stepped on in the process. These were the Children of Trikeen.

They had been summarily dropped off at the station in waves, most wearing little more than rags for clothing. Many had not eaten in days, to judge by their appearance.

"Oh, my! How can they do this to you?" Barkeen walked into the examining room to see to the remains of the final influx of enforced immigrants. Why, this girl could barely be fifteen standards old. She was surely not a criminal. Barkeen looked at her glass, the chart within telling her all she needed to know. This girl and a brother. Oh! She looked at the girl, her heart breaking for her. *Does she know?*

"Come on over here, dear, and we'll check you out." Barkeen patted the table, not caring if the filth on the girl's clothes rubbed off on it. Glancing over to the two guards grinning in anticipation, she barked at them, "This is no dangerous soldier for you to have to keep in line. Leave, now! Wait outside the door." She was gratified to see them step away, the girl's privacy assured.

Barkeen remembered the boy. It had broken her heart to see him walk in that door. *Damn that Tan'sn!* The boy had been one the jumpship guard had found attractive, one he had taken and used between jumps to this world. Repeatedly, it seemed. It had taken some time for her to repair the damage he had done.

She had so wanted to help him further, to keep him off

the world below, the boy not much more than that, a boy. However, the rules were neither hers to make nor hers to break. His records showed he had been instrumental in the decimation of a MegaCorp installation, and she had been instructed to send him downside on the earliest transport, not even given enough time to try to send him to Bird.

This girl, though. Her only crime had been to be on Trikeen when the place was wiped clean. Her parents dead, there were only the boy and girl left. Barkeen instructed the girl to remove her clothes as she pondered her options. Turning to the comm device, she requested Trainer to attend to her in Examination C.

"Excuse me, dear." Barkeen touched the girl gently on the knee. "Please hold this over yourself while I speak to this man." Handing the girl a blanket, she stepped to the door.

Releasing the mechanism, Trainer stepped inside. "Yes, Medic Barkeen?" He glanced around the room, and his eyes opened wide. He grinned. "Oh, I missed one, did I? Are you going to leave me with her?" He pulled a hand-held razor from his pocket.

"Put that away unless you want to be transferred downside, stat. You hear me, Trainer? You keep your hands off her. I need you to run an errand for me. There was a girl needed, up in affairs. See if that position's been filled. Stat, man." She turned, the door closing as Trainer cut his eyes to the girl and her hair one last time.

This was one girl who would not go down at all, not if Barkeen had anything thing to do with it. She resumed her examination, finding the girl had been left unharmed, the guards transporting them this trip finding their fun in the boys, alone. Her examination complete, Barkeen handed the girl a fresh suit of clothes and pointed to a shower just to the side of the table.

The shower quickly finished, soon Barkeen heard the question, "Where's my brother? We're twins, you know."

Barkeen turned. The girl was quite pretty all cleaned up. The boy might have had these same good looks if he hadn't been abused so. She would never know.

She wiped the table and motioned for the girl to sit.

"Dear," Barkeen paused, not sure how to tell her. No doubt this girl had experienced trauma the medic could only imagine. Now, she had to go through one thing more. "Your brother has already gone down to the planet below. He left two transports ago."

"No! I promised to stay with him. You must let me go!"

Barkeen grabbed the girl as she threw herself toward the door.

"No," the girl cried. "Brackie cannot be there without me. I saw what they did to him on that ship. I must protect him."

Barkeen hugged the girl, understanding her anger. "I'm arranging you a place here on the station. You will not be going to the planet's surface, not for a time." She knew of what would happen to the boy. Her work with him would all be undone within a fortnight, and if he was lucky, he would die quickly. She knew she did not dare tell that to the girl. Let the girl be angry with her. She had taken worse. She had taken much worse.

As the girl sobbed and beat at Barkeen, her threats to get even aimed at the person who was trying to help her,

Barkeen could only see the endless sea of children she had been unable to save.

When the guards escorted the girl to her final procedures, Barkeen turned her attention to her chart. She realized she had never called the girl by her name. L'Rene. She should have done that. She should have used the girl's name.

"WHY THE TEARS, my love? This is what we've worked to achieve for years. The plans are set, and in one day, we'll be gone from this place." Cornerstone sat on the bed and hugged his precious Reenna. After a moment, he separated and held her face in his hands. "True, we've found warmth and beauty here. This has also been a place of hardship and loss. Why do you cry?"

Reenna forced a smile to her face as she wiped her tears away. "I'm about to lose him all over again, you see. All my life I've lost my little brother. When he was small, I lost him because I went to the academy. Then I lost him when *he* chose to go to the academy. Then, I truly lost him when I came here." She looked at her hands, finally reaching one to wipe at her eyes.

Cornerstone watched her, enjoying her beauty as she worked through her turmoil. He took her hand in his, pressing it to his lips before dropping it away. "He's here. We're here, still."

She glanced up. "He's only really been mine for these five years, and now I'm about to lose him again." Tears once more welled up in her eyes, and Cornerstone pulled her to him, holding her tightly.

"You're not losing him, dear Reenna. You will always

279

have the brother you found. He will always be yours. Treasure your five years. Keep him in your heart, and he will come back to you. Just trust him, and trust your heart. Can you do that?"

She wiped a tear and tried to smile. "You see people, Cornerstone. You know that? You look at people and situations, and you see through them to the other side. How do you do that?" She laughed raggedly. "I see the now, and I get so bogged down that I cannot find the other side."

"We are who we have to be, Reenna. If I were any different, would your love for me be the same? And if you were like me, why would I want to love myself?"

At that she laughed. "I get it. I really do. I will miss him, though."

Cornerstone took her chin in one hand. "If you didn't, my Reenna, you wouldn't be my Reenna, and then how could I love you as I do?"

RENHANT TURNED to the information on the glass. There it was, the first of the reports he would have to post today. A transport destroyed. A team needed to clean the site. He knew the transport wouldn't be missed. It was old, had been old when he'd come to this world five standards before.

He pushed aside a second frame of information that had been left by Dad for his eyes only. He wasn't certain what it meant, stating simply, *Racket is a friend.* He remembered that first day with Racket and Cornerstone, the heat of this world taking his energy away, and the extra meal brought by Cornerstone's own hand. And driving that thing!

He laughed into the room, his enjoyment in his memory

280

one truly felt to the depth of his bones. It had just been an old transport, he knew. It would be simple to note on the report the death of the driver. Things like that were easily overlooked here on Rant, life not being revered as it often was elsewhere.

That sister of his. Her, he would miss. He was reminded it was time to leave his office for a while. It was time to walk to a small park with a bridge and a stream. It was wastewater, really, but it did make a stream, and there was real grass. He knew he would find no birds decorating this sky that sometimes faded to a beautiful cinnamon near the horizon. The lack of birds he hadn't been able to get used to. Nothing flew, no factories pumped their noises skyward, and there were no ships flitting through the air. There was only the daily transport to the station.

Renhant stepped to the far end of the bridge, and with a remembered motion, placed a foot on the grass that ran down to the water's edge. Sitting as he had that day so many years ago, he stared at the sky, absently reaching and breaking off the bits of coarse greenery under his hand. Soon, in the distance, for someone who knew just where to look, there was a bright speck on the horizon. As it crawled into the sky, it quickly became invisible against the glare of the sun.

Five years ago I saw you, Sis, standing on that bridge in the glare of the sun, and I didn't even know I had found you. Now, I see you once again against the glare of that sun, and I know it's good-bye. I know which is harder, Sis. I really do.

He reached to wipe the tears from his eyes, and for a moment he stood, his hand holding those broken bits of grass

281

in his opened palm. It was time to go report a broken-hearted lover who had decided to try her life in a better part of this world. Before he did, though, Renhant stood on that bridge, and one by one, he dropped the torn fragments of his grass in the stream, watching for a rather long time as they disappeared into the distance.

—Chapter 15—

"How long has it been?"

—Rip Van Winkle

WHERE HAD he come from, that man on the other side of the room? Jer'son studied him appraisingly, tall and broad shouldered, a favorite of the girls on the station, the women doting on him. His hair fell rakishly across his forehead, nearly covering one eye. One of the women told a joke, and he laughed. His eyes twinkled, and his good mood was indeed infectious. At least the women with him seemed to think so.

The women were attractive enough, even if several of them were hard around the edges. Jer'son knew the internees on the station had pasts—all had been sentenced to a lifetime here—but those who lived in the confines of the metal moon orbiting Rant were the best of the lot. Most of the station crew were dissidents or embarrassments, those with no personality axes to grind.

That first night they had stayed here, finding only three

crew aboard, how like their ship it had seemed, except for Trainer, the old rascal. It seemed a lot of freshies had been shaved by their own hand, even since Jer'son had been aboard, but no longer. Trainer had finally lived out his span, and another spot had been opened up to offer to yet one more lucky planetside volunteer.

With Jer'son's placement on the station, poor Bird had seen his quota of boys trickle to just a few, those that seemed like good boys, too young to be on Rant, and their crimes small or nonexistent. He was old when Jer'son and his friends had been rescued, and five more years added to his frame had exhausted his body. He still lived, but barely. That newly tall boy, confined to the station for the past five standard years, would have to be told. It was something he didn't look forward to. Barn't would want to see him, and if he went back to Rant, not even Barkeen would be able to get him back up again.

He rubbed his arms with his hands, jerking his palms roughly over the cloth. Gods, he wished it hadn't come to this, not at this time in Barn't's life. Physically, he was strong as a gunship. Emotionally? The nightmares never stopped. However, whether he took it well or not, it was time to let him know. He would grieve and let it go, or he would not. He shook his head, remembering the small boy he and his friends had rescued so long ago. This would tell if he was truly the man his body claimed he had become.

"Barn't!" He waved when he looked his way.

"Jer'son! Wait right there!" The broad-shouldered man, no longer the slender boy of the past, leaned over, kissing one of the girls on the cheek, and then loped over to his friend.

"So. Not the little boy who doesn't get the girls, I see."

"What do you think of her?"

"Well, it depends if you're talking about the light-headed one or the dark-headed one. They both have their qualities." Jer'son pushed his tongue against his cheek, pretending that the contemplation of the differences in the two girls occupied his thoughts completely. Barn't wrapped an arm around him, his fist finding a place just under his breastbone, and he pushed until Jer'son laughed.

"Well?"

"Very pretty, Barn't. She is very pretty. Do you like her?"

"That and maybe more." He grinned at him.

Jer'son laughed. "That's the kind of look I like to see from you, my friend." More seriously, he turned and stopped him in the corridor, putting a hand on his shoulder, and rapping his knuckles lightly on his chest. "Does she know?"

The smiling young man looked away, his mood instantly deflated, and his happy look gone. "Just put a needle in my balloon, Jer'son." He worked his mouth in irritation.

"I have one more needle for you."

"Can't it wait?" He glanced back into the communal room, and with a quick, bright smile, he waved. "I think we're meeting later to tour her quarters." Looking back at Jer'son, his expression once more fell away. He was annoyed and not trying to hide it.

"It's Bird, Barn't. I've been talking to Barkeen, and she thinks he's about at the end." He studied his friend, looking for the maturity he hoped . . . no, *needed* to see in his eyes.

"Did Renhant go to him?" Barn't caught his breath and leaned back against the wall, his eyes suddenly tense. "I would have."

"He's with him now."

"Can I go down to see him?" He held hope in his voice. "He saved me, Jer'son. He was there for me and took care of me. My own dad didn't do that."

"I wish you could." Jer'son grasped his bicep, surprised at the firmness there, and squeezing it once before letting it go. "It's not safe for you."

He jerked away, sudden violence in his movements. "You wish I could? Is that all you have to say?" His eyes glistened, and he sniffled. The violence was gone as quickly as it had shown itself, and only a little boy remained. "I can. I just go out there and get on that transport. I can go, Jer'son. You just don't want me to." Tears erupted across his smooth cheeks as he slid down the wall to sit on the floor. His voice cracked. "I could go. Bird would want me to."

"Do you really think that Bird would want you there back on the surface? You know you nearly died there. Do you know Bird's reason for being here on Rant? Has anyone ever told you, Barn't? I don't think so." He stopped, furious, and looked up at the ceiling, tracing its pattern of lights with his eyes. He found himself unable to look at the man, *the boy* on the floor, barely able to retell the story. He steeled himself and continued, his eyes looking anywhere but at Barn't. "That man down there who saved you did nothing except lose his two sons to a drunken captgen'l's stupidity. Then, when he tried to expose the man, he was stuffed here to shut him up."

286

"Then I should go."

"Grow up, Barn't!" Jer'son's eyes jerked downward, and he barked his next words, his tone harder perhaps than it should have been. "That's what Bird's done for you. He's kept you alive, and that means more to him than anything you could do, including going down to that planet to say good-bye."

Barn't wrapped his arms around his legs. "You don't know. You never knew what it was like not to be loved by your father. You just don't care!"

Jer'son froze, remembering his own father, how he'd wished Jer'son had never been born, had blamed him for all the troubles he'd faced, for his family's failing fortunes, and how Jer'son had lain there that first year letting that instructor come to him night after night, afraid they'd kick him out of the academy if he told, how he had cried, certain that letting himself be molested was the price he had to pay for his family, and not understanding until a lifetime later that no one should have to pay that high a price. In an explosion of fury, he stepped forward to stand directly over Barn't, and for a moment he no longer cared. He slung his words across the top of his friend's bowed head, angry, and not knowing or caring if the hurt in his words was for Barn't or for his own past that he could not change.

"So, go. Go, if you want. You're right. You can go get on that transport. You can fly right out of here. No one will fault you. Not even me. I'm releasing you to do whatever you want to do. Go be Barn't. Go be free. You don't need me anymore, and I guess I don't need you. See you, friend. Come back and visit when you get time. Oh, that's right,

Barn't. You won't be able to, so maybe in another life."

He turned and walked away, leaving Barn't and his tears in a lonely corridor with no one else around.

JER'SON LAY on his bunk fully clothed, his anger at Barn't and his anger at himself for what he'd said still consuming every part of his being. The door to his quarters opened, leaving a small amount of light to enter the room. He felt a hand on his arm and jerked his head around, only to see Barkeen standing at his side. Her eyes were rimmed with the tears of a love lost, a love that had been found and misplaced in the pursuit of a higher goal, and then truly lost forever.

"I didn't have time to say good-bye to him. He's gone." With those words, she departed the room.

Jer'son lay there, the ceiling his only thought, his only focus, as he wished the world away.

"YOU CAN do this?" Jer'son leaned against the examining room table, his words baring his desperation. He had come to Barkeen with an impossible request, but one he hoped was in her power. His need to *react*, to *do something*, over-whelmed him. "For both of us, Barn't as well as me?" Even in his anger over Barn't's refusal to accept his responsibility toward old Bird, he would not exclude Barn't, not in this.

Barkeen motioned him to a storage closet and followed him inside. "All is monitored," she whispered with a finger to her lips. "Be careful what you say. I can no longer unplug the feed. They've taken that from me. However, we can talk quietly in here and be safe. Yesterday, I would have told you no without a second thought. Today, my reason for going on is dead, truly dead. I am old, Jer'son. I have worked long to bring this cursed place and the corporation that runs it to its knees. I know now that I will not live to see that end, but you will. For that, I will do as you ask."

"Good. When do we start? I will need to locate Barn't."

She smiled. "It's not *that* easy. There's something else you must know. Five years ago you made a suggestion about how to sabotage the cruiser being assembled on the planet below."

"That night with Chr's? It's been a very long five years. I'd forgotten. I've never heard what happened to him. And?" His patience with intrigue was thin, and he wanted Barkeen to get on with his request.

"Chr's recovered and is implementing those suggestions."

"Ha! Maybe I did something right on that world down there. So?"

"That's why you're here. That's why I sent you to Bird. That's why everything has happened. You. You are our hope, Jer'son. Bring MegaCorp to its knees." She reached to smooth her clothing, waiting. For what, he didn't know. Finally, she looked up with red-rimmed eyes.

"I can't even treat my best friend with respect. How can I be your hope?" His eyes flooded with unwanted tears, torn inside at the turmoil Barkeen stirred up in him. He wanted what she offered, but he was not the man she wanted him to be. He stood for a moment, and he looked at the ceiling as he chewed his bottom lip between his teeth. By the gods, he wanted that.

Barkeen patted his chest. "This will be gone. Your

289

friend's, too, if he is willing. No one else's." She stood a moment, her hand on his chest, then she reached in her pocket and handed him a small syringe. "At the injection site for both you and your friend, there is one dose each inside. It's a locator chemical that will make the tracker easier to find. Have it ready, but use it only when I contact you. The chemical signal fades after a time. Once this is done, you must stay on the station as if I have done nothing. For this, you must help Chr's if he contacts you." She shook her head. "I cannot contact him to let him know of what I have offered you. Bird always did that for me."

Jer'son remembered a conversation from five years ago.

"Jest? About jimmying the ship? Bird, I never told you that. It must have been someone else."

Jer'son smiled through his tears. "Bird let that slip at one time. I just never put it together before now." He wiped his eyes on his sleeve. "How can I help Chr's?" Whatever it was, he would do it for Bird.

"Just be ready, boy. Be ready. You will hear from me when I can take care of that." She patted his chest one more time. "Just be ready." She opened the door, and as she exited, her weary frame no longer carried with it that brisk, efficient step Jer'son had admired five years ago.

He understood exactly what this was about, why she had agreed to take the tracker out of him. It didn't matter what they did to her any longer. Her Bird was dead.

—Chapter 16—

Objects in Mirror Are Closer Than They Appear

*—Warning on old-Earth
personal transports*

BARN'T SAT UP in bed and rocked back and forth. He'd had another nightmare. They weren't getting better. They were getting worse. In the darkness, he wrapped his arms around his chest and wondered what he'd done wrong. This wasn't the way he'd wanted it to be at all.

"Barn't? Are you awake again tonight? Come on and lie down. You'll be tired in the morning."

"Okay, Y'rae. I'll lie down in just a moment." He felt her place her hand on his back, rubbing it from side to side. After a moment, she stopped and took a deep breath.

"Sure, Barn't. You take your time," and she turned from him to roll over.

Barn't just stared into the darkness, remembering that night after Jer'son had told him about Bird. Just remembering made him want L'Rene again. He'd only gone to find

Jer'son. Then it had turned into so much more. Even in the darkness, he still felt the touch of her leg against his. He remembered his thoughts as she pulled his clothes from his body.

This will teach Jer'son.

He had wanted to see Bird, that's all. No one else understood what it had been like having a father like his. No one. He'd needed a real father, and Bird had been that father to him. That was more important to Barn't than anything, even living on the station.

He would have gone, too. He would have done just what he'd said to Jer'son, would have gotten on that transport and seen Bird. Bird might have told him he should have stayed on the ship, but he might have said thanks for coming. Either way, he'd have been glad to have Barn't come to see him, to have him say good-bye. Bird would've liked that.

He remembered L'Rene's hand sliding along the curve of his buttock. His heart had jumped in his chest, and he'd been ecstatic. He had wanted to parade it in Jer'son's face, and his thoughts had consumed him.

Wait until he finds out what I've done.

He told me to do whatever I want. Well, I will do whatever I want. If I want to transfer down to the planet, I'll just do that. He can't stop me. Renhant's down there. He'll help me find me a place to stay. He'll give me a job. He runs the whole transportation system. Why, I could get a job just like Cornerstone. I liked that before. It'd be fun to run that machine, just like when I was stomping termite houses into the ground. I'd make them flat, flat, flat, and then I'd go find another one. I might even crawl into those tunnels underground just like Cornerstone did. I'd hook up the wires right, and nobody'd ever get just their picture or just their sound. People'd say, Barn't did that, and that's why it works so well. That's what people'd say about me.

He traced the cup of L'Rene's breast with his fingers, gripping it in his hand. *Won't Jer'son be surprised?*

I'm not even in that room with him anymore. I took everything of mine. Jer'son'll have to move. He'll have to go back to a single room. He won't even have his own desk and glass. He won't know where I am. I won't talk to him or leave him a message.

He'll try to find me, and I won't be where he looks. I won't care if he worries. He told me he didn't need me anymore. He'll find out. He'll be sorry I'm gone. He'll wish I was back, but I won't be, ever again. He'll come to me and ask me to go back to his room, but I won't. I have somewhere else to stay now. He just thinks he doesn't need me. He'll see now that I'm gone.

His lips found the curve of L'Rene's mouth. *I bet Jer'son does this every night.*

He'll see. He probably doesn't even think I'm a man. Well, he should remember, I was with that girl, too. I went in that room, and I did that, too. Even with their leftover slickness already down there getting all over me, I did that, too, and I even left my own stuff down there for Renhant. That was funny. Renhant got everyone's stuff all over him.

It just wasn't funny when Renhant said she was dead. I never saw her dead. What if she really wasn't, and we just thought she was? What if that kid on the ship hit his head and bled so much because we didn't know that girl down

293

there was really just asleep? She could have been asleep. She really could. I bet that was it. She wasn't dead at all. I didn't have to come here. Jer'son was the one who went back and checked. He's the reason I'm here. He should have checked things better, then I wouldn't have so much trouble.

Barn't ran his hand down the curve of L'Rene's back and pressed it against her buttock. *I bet Jer'son doesn't even know where I am.*

When we got to this planet, Jer'son went away that time, and I had to go out by myself. He wasn't even there when I came back. Renhant and Bird were there. They took care of me. Then, Jer'son ran away to the station, and I was alone again. He could have taken Racket's place on the transport, and then those men couldn't have found me. He wouldn't stay around when I needed him. In the corridor, he just walked away. I was there hurting and crying, and he just walked away, and I waited and waited, and he never came back. I wanted him to come back, and he never did, and when I went to find him, he wasn't in his bunk, and I didn't know where he was, but I knew he didn't want to see me anymore. He told me to go if I wanted, and I couldn't come back to visit.

Barn't felt his leg slip between L'Rene's. *I bet Jer'son hates me when he finds out.*

Jer'son had a pass. He could've gone to see Bird. He didn't want to. He came to tell me, so he wouldn't have to. Barkeen didn't even go to see him. She said she loved him. She didn't go to see him. He died all alone. Only Renhant was there. Renhant didn't love him as much as I did. Renhant moved away. He was down on the planet with Bird, and he didn't even stay with him. Maybe Bird would have lived if Renhant had stayed with him. It's all their fault that Bird is dead.

Barn't gasped as L'Rene's warm place took him deep inside. *If I died right now, that'd serve Jer'son right. Then he'd know. He'd know what I've done. He'd be sorry what he said to me.* I might go the planet. I could go live in the desert. I could live a long time out there, I bet. Then, when he came to look for me, I would hide from him, and he wouldn't able to find me. Then, one day he would find me, and I'd be dead. He would be so sad that he would never go back down to the planet at all, because he'd always think of me.

Her breasts sliding under him, Barn't's body began to move of its own volition. *I hope Jer'son kills me when he finds what I've done.*

Then, Barn't couldn't think about Jer'son any longer. When he finally crawled off L'Rene and lay back in the bed, he had only Y'rae at his side. It was L'Rene that pumped the throb of desire through him, and he wanted her once more in the worst way.

L'RENE HAD seen events that night very differently as she held her arms around Barn't. Once she had his clothes off, his arousal had been a fury of passion she hadn't thought possible of him. There had been no tenderness; in fact, quite the opposite. He had torn at her, as if there was something driving his passion, some anger that controlled the beating of his heart as well as the rhythm of his attack. It was that, too, an attack. Not love, that was for certain. However, she was quite practiced at this—although never before with Barn't—and she could wait on him for however long he took.

As he pressed himself to her in a violent spasm of thrashing arms and legs, she pulled him tight, exulting in what she had wrought. When he finished, relaxing in her arms, she lay there until his breathing slowed, running her hand over his skin, the sweat of their exertions mixing together. Somehow, even her own demons felt lessened after the violence of the encounter. She was very pleased. She started to squirm out from under him and was relieved as he rolled off her.

"I thought you told me this was your first time." She looked at him, doubting his answer even before he spoke.

"Second time," and he grinned. "Once when I was at the academy, but I don't think it really counts." His cheeks were flushed with the remains of his passion, and one hand reached roughly to her, clearly not finished. He grabbed her hard. "Again?"

"Are you sure you haven't been with more than just me?" Even as she spoke, she pushed him away. His hand on her made sure of that.

"Absolutely."

She smiled broadly at that, laughing lightly at the need she still saw in him. He would have to work that off elsewhere, because she had company coming. It was time to wrap this up. She pulled a moistened cloth from an opening in the wall.

"How did it compare?" He looked at her expectantly.

"Compare? To what, Barn't?" Her attention had already turned to cleaning up, and she glanced at him with a frown.

The boy at her side no longer interested her.

"You know. To him."

At that she laughed loudly. "So, that's what it's all about. I get it, now. I guess no one needs to know about this, huh?" She took one of his hands and kissed it, winking at him. "Barn't, if you can keep this to yourself, I want you to come back often. Real often."

He grinned broadly. "I can keep secrets very well, especially for this."

"Now, get out of here. Jer'son'll be here any time, and I want this place ready for his turn with me."

"Thanks, L'Rene. I'm gone." Barn't started pulling his clothes on as fast as he could, smiling from ear to ear.

IT WAS JER'SON who misread all the cues that night. He told himself he had looked for Barn't, not finding him. He also knew he hadn't looked very hard. He had been too angry. Now, he was surprised to find him in the corridor, fastening his belt just down from L'Rene's quarters. That familiar lock of hair covered his eyes, and Jer'son grinned. He touched his friend's shoulder and grabbed him around the side in a familiar, teasing way. Barn't glanced up just in time to hear him speak.

"Barn't—"

"Not now, Jer'son." The young man's face went pale as he ducked his head, and his neck turned bright red. He stumbled, one foot slipping out of an untied boot. He grabbed it in one hand, and running, he was gone down the corridor.

Jer'son watched his receding back and shook his head.

He now understood why he had been so emotional earlier. He was bound to be sick to be perspiring that heavily. His hair was soaked and so was his shirt. Oh, well, he was a big boy who could take care of himself, and his breath quickened at the thought of seeing L'Rene tonight. She was exactly what he needed to make him feel better after that fight with Barn't. Afterwards, he might check on him, but not just now.

Then, he turned and headed back down the corridor, his thoughts quickly shifting away from Barn't and his foolish, self-absorbed troubles.

CHR'S LOOKED through the shipping manifest. The old man had come through before he died, although just barely. Some days he had felt guilty about telling the old man he could go see his daughter, but it did brighten his days, and it had given him a purpose.

He also knew that no matter what he'd told him, the old man never would have gotten away. Which was better, for him to sit in a daze for five years, or to have at least a few minutes each day when he believed things might get better? That was Chr's' consolation for his lies, and it sometimes worked.

One thing he knew he had to do was get these modified plans into the right hands, and to do that, he had to find ground transport. The modifications had to be filed as part of the initial set of plans. The parts were going up in the next two days, and the amended plans had to be there before the parts were delivered. When the ship was finally finished, if the original plans and all addendums didn't match the actual construction, the inspectors would surely begin to look more closely.

Besides, they would inspect these first few shipments most strictly. If these matched well, inspections would loosen up later. They always did. Now, if he could get to the city, he might find a way to get the information up to the station.

He walked outside to the jobsite armscan overseer. He handed him a cooled container of intoxicant as a bribe.

"I need to get a transport to the city."

"Hey, sure." The man took the container and hefted it before sliding it into a pouch at his waist. "The next transport is three days. Last one has gone today. Tomorrow and the next are holidays. Try then. Sorry."

Chr's laughed, reaching to playfully punch the man in the shoulder. "There's no way to get a transport out before then?" He looked at the pouch with the wasted drink, nodding suggestively. He now regretted the credit to buy it.

The overseer laughed. "It's a holiday. If you were dying, then they might send a transport. You look pretty healthy to me. Sleep off whatever's bugging you."

Chr's frowned at the news, but as he walked away, an idea came to him. He groaned at what he knew came next. "It looks like I have to get beat up again," he muttered to himself. Looking for the biggest worker heading into the nearest drinking establishment, he followed him inside.

"Hey, buddy. You're in my way." He shoved the man. "Who do you think you are to come in here and get in everyone's way? Move it."

The man turned and looked at him. "Ah, you're just drunk. Go to your bunk and sleep it off."

However, Chr's needed a transport. "I've already been

told that. So what," he yelled. "You're fat and in my way."
He slammed the man in the stomach with his shoulder.

"Oomph," the man said, stumbling at the onslaught.
"You should really leave me alone. Go away." He patted a
long club hanging from his waist, only a quick-release clip
away from action.

"You're the one taking up all the room. Why should I get
out of the way?" This time Chr's rammed the man's stomach
even harder, making him stagger on his feet and nearly fall.

At last, losing his temper, the man roared at him and
threw him across the room. "Have you had enough?" He
stood with his hands on his hips and anger painted on his
face. The club was raised in one hand.

Chr's pulled himself to his feet, straightened up, and
steadied himself. "I'm still standing, aren't I?" With that, he
hurled himself at the big man once more.

This time the man wasn't so gentle. When he finished
with Chr's, someone had to wipe the blood from his face.
When the big man walked up and stood over him, he asked
again. "Enough?"

Chr's replied, "Sure. Thanks."

When the after-hours transport came, the overseer
greeted it, directing it to the injured man. As Chr's was being
loaded, he looked at him. "Aren't you the same guy that . . ."

Chr's interrupted, barely able to wave him away with one
hand, "Yeah. Don't ask."

Inside the transport, a driver, one who was there only
because the regular crews had all gone home for the holiday,
asked, "Hey, what happened to you? You look like a really
big man got the best of you."

Chr's laughed. "It does look that way, I guess. By the way, my name's Chr's. I'd offer to shake, but as you can see, my arms are in a pretty bad way. I bet you don't even know what that is, to shake." He laughed. "An old-Earth custom. A kid I once knew got me to using it. About five years ago."

The driver looked back at him. "Yeah, I know what it means to shake. I also have a friend who knows that custom. Five years, you say? A kid? By the name of Jer'son, you say?"

"I didn't say," Chr's replied. "How do you know his name?"

Renhant laughed. "He's my good friend."

"IF IT'S FOR me, tell them I'm not in today." A delivery was at the door, and Jer'son yawned and rubbed his eyes, pushing away a steaming container of the strongest beverage his subordinate had been able to procure. He coughed before taking out a cloth and working it across the back of his neck.

Mi'Kail eased out of his chair and ambled that way, laughing as he triggered the door. "Yes?"

"Delivery for Ser Jer'son. Palm on the glass, please."

"Ser Jer'son?" Mi'Kail glanced with a grin to see his co-worker sipping his drink, and he chuckled.

"On the glass, please." The courier, a thin man wearing a goatee and a most unusual prosthetic, wire eyeglasses, and looking all the part of a Rant internee, held it out with a bored look.

"Sure." Mi'Kail palmed the glass and took the package from the courier. He glanced at it, saw the medic's symbol on it, and turned to Jer'son. "Hey, ser. Are you all right?"

"Look at me, Mi'Kail. They don't come in any better shape than this. Why do you ask?" He took a deep breath and pushed his beverage container away. His eyes were black with lack of sleep. "Nasty stuff."

Mi'Kail walked up to him and draped his arm over his neck. "This is from Medic Barkeen. I've worked up here with you for a long time. Three standards, maybe four. So, I guess I must know you pretty well. I also know you've been looking tired since the kid dumped your quarters."

"I'm tired, huh? If that's all it is, I guess I'm pretty lucky." Jer'son tried to smile. He *was* tired, but it wasn't just Barn't. It was Barn't, and also Bird and L'Rene. It was his life, and everything falling apart. In addition, he had been waiting on word from Barkeen, and that had been worse than all the rest. "Let me have that package. I'll make it an early night, tonight. How does that sound? For now, let's get that maintenance glitch from the outer ring addressed. Either that, or we'll be shuffling quarters for the next sevenday."

"Not so fast." Mi'Kail set the package on a spare console, and he hefted himself easily onto the counter in front of Jer'son, one leg hanging off the edge. "When Barn't took off and you went downhill, I just chalked that up to stress—"

"And now it's not stress?" Jer'son didn't really want to go wherever Mi'Kail was headed, but he *was* as tired as the man had suggested, and he didn't have the energy to divert him. "Tell me what's wrong with me, Mi'Kail, and then I'll take an early night, anyway. Tomorrow, all will be right with me, and you'll feel a fool for whatever you're about to say." He motioned toward the package before another yawn caught him, and the hand wound up in front of his mouth, covering it.

Mi'Kail paused and cleared his throat as if considering whether or not to continue. Then, he barreled ahead. "You and L'Rene used to be a sure thing, and now I hear her eyes are roving. Are you certain everything is good between you and her? Better yet, is everything good with you?" Standing, he scooped up the package and tossed it to Jer'son. "Empty, it feels like. Enjoy." He walked back to his console.

"So, are we good?" Jer'son glanced at Mi'Kail's back for a moment, then shook the box. The package did feel empty, and he triggered the top to find it only contained a scrap of paper with some writing on it. He frowned. He looked up when his friend started speaking again.

"You know, Jer'son, I think of you as a friend, and that means I care. I want you to know that. You need help? You know where I am. Good or bad, right or wrong." Mi'Kail tossed a striped cleaning cloth his direction, laughing when Jer'son dodged and still managed to get hit in the face. "You're a good guy, and I'm on your side. Let me help. That's all I ask."

"Thanks, I guess. I'll keep that up front. Be aware that if I happen to interrupt a little of your off-the-job fun late some night with my distraught plea for assistance, you offered." As he picked the cloth up and tossed it on the console, he grinned to show it was no big deal. However, turning over the paper in the package, he found something that was quite a big deal, indeed.

Jer'son. Examination A. Stat. Barkeen.

"Sorry, Mi'Kail. Duty calls." He triggered the door and was out of the control room before Mi'Kail even had time to turn in his chair.

"BARKEEN," Jer'son panted. "Yes?" He stumbled in from the corridor, barely able to breath.

She looked at him askance. "Maybe you should rest a bit. You look a bit off." She walked to him, placing her hand on his forehead.

"It's okay," he gasped. "I just ran all the way. Can I get . . . a chair?"

"Ran?" She looked at him hard. "For the star's sake, why?"

"Your message said stat." He bent over, resting his hands on his knees, more winded than he had felt in a dozen stan-dards, probably since first entering the academy.

She smiled at that. "My new helper's idea. She likes to use new terms. She puts stat on everything."

"Wow," he replied. "Nice."

"Come with me," she motioned. He followed her into the storeroom where she closed the door. She was suddenly all business, and she spoke quickly. "Tonight. Lights out. Two hours past. You and the friend. Remember what I gave you before? Use it before coming. Do not be late." She made as if to open the door.

"Wait. The friend. That may be a problem."

"It must be two. I have prepared. For only one, they will suspect. You and the friend. Go." With that, she shooed him out of the storeroom and out of her examination room.

Jer'son stood in the corridor in dismay. He hadn't seen Barn't in several tendays. He had been so tensed up about their confrontation over Bird that he'd only seen L'Rene a few times, and she'd acted very distant those nights. Mi'Kail had been closer to the truth than Jer'son had let on. Now he had to find Barn't, and Barn't didn't even know Barkeen had offered to do this.

One thing was for certain, if he couldn't find him, they'd both be stuck here forever. And since they weren't speaking, even if he found him, it might not change that at all.

Great gods! Could things get any worse?

MI'KAIL ADJUSTED the ship's optical feeds and watched Jer'son step out of Barkeen's examination room.

When Jer'son had taken out like a thruster with a disabled governor, he'd run through the last few minutes in the control room feeds, finding one that picked up on the message he had pulled out of the package. He hadn't been able to get all the words, but all it took was enough to make an educated guess. By the time he'd pulled up the feeds for the med center, Jer'son was on his way back out again. The confusion on his face was obvious.

Mi'Kail checked his boss' entrance and exit time at the medic's, and he knew his brief time there couldn't explain why he'd run all the way. After a few minutes, he wiped his search from the records and sat for a few moments thinking. Nothing about this seemed right.

In his past life, the one before Rant, he had learned how to see when something was going on although nothing seemed to be. His wife had taught him that. For several standards, now, he had worked with Jer'son and felt he knew him well. For some time, he had suspected that there was some mysterious intrigue bubbling just under the surface. He

305

hadn't been able to identify it, but after this, one thing was for certain. It involved Medic Barkeen, and it was something bigger than just a random checkup. He trusted Jer'son, with his life, if that's what it took. He was a man who took care of people. Mi'Kail always ribbed him about his crazy friend, but it was just that, teasing. He would take a friend who'd stick up for him like Jer'son did with Barn't any day.

Now, his mind was working, and he had several ideas jumping through his thoughts. Barkeen had sent the message. Then there was L'Rene, scum, even if he had teased otherwise. And Barn't. Poor, pitiful Barn't. Sitting up straight, an epiphany slammed into Mi'Kail like a pilotless freighterbarge. He hit his head with his hand. *L'Rene and Barn't!* How could he not have seen it? He was an idiot. To hell with being a good friend who minds his own business! Jer'son was going to get his help, whether he wanted it or not.

Locking up the workstations and keying the door to keep out all comers except those with full station permissions, he left the room with a quick step, determined to keep the fate that had doomed him to Rant from being foisted on his good friend. Jer'son deserved better. To that end, Mi'Kail was off to another part of the ship, one where he was pretty sure Jer'son's crazy "friend" could be found. If he found him where he thought he might be, he planned to set him straight. Really straight.

Nobody messed with Jer'son. Not with Mi'Kail around.

"SO," AND RENHANT laughed again. "You got yourself beat up just to get a ride into town, and I had to come get you because no one else was on duty. Now you happen to be the man my best friend caused to get beat up the one day he worked here on Rant." He helped Chr's out of the transport. "Are you sure you don't want a medic?"

"Please," Chr's implored. "My injuries are of secondary importance. I must get something to your friend as soon as possible."

"To Jer'son." Renhant chuckled. "Can't you just send it up? I'm sure the normal channels can get it up there just fine, especially if it's just information. Otherwise, ship it by courier."

"You don't understand. Your friend and I haven't spoken since that day five years ago." He paused, and his eyes looked tired. "I apologize. I must weigh my options, and I find them very limited."

"On this world, all options are limited." Renhant waved his hand dismissively. "If you haven't spoken in five years, how do you know so much about Jer'son?"

"I'm being cautious in how I speak to you, please understand. There's danger in what I say. For me it's certain, for you, probable. Should I continue?" At Renhant's nod, he went on. "Each time we've been in contact, it's been through an intermediary. Someone on the station is also working with me. It is she I have used for my information. Now, however, my intermediary is gone, and I must get my information directly to the station."

Renhant breathed, "Bird."

Chr's gasped. "You cannot know that."

"Bird!" Renhant laughed. "Of course. Too many things fall in place with that one thing. That old rascal. No wonder.

That's why Jer'son got snatched up to the station so quickly, and why Barn't followed, and Bird suddenly kept almost no boys after we came through."

"How can you know this?"

"A wise man once said he always put his family first. He also said I could see to the other side of things, and I was his voice of reason. Gods, here I listened to Bird talk about contacts and favors. How could I have been so stupid?"

"You'll help me?"

"Just what are you trying to do?"

Chr's took a deep breath, holding it for a very long time. Then, he let his words out. "Bring MegaCorp to its knees."

Renhant laughed. "It would seem I have no choice, then. I must help you. First, let's get that package up there, then let me see what else I can do. I know people. Helpful people."

He enjoyed seeing a smile grow on Chr's' face.

BARN'T LAY in bed, being careful not to wake Y'rae. He'd never intended to go to L'Rene but just that once, hadn't really been sure he wanted to do anything, especially not that. At first he had been looking for Jer'son, then he had just wanted to *hurt* him like he was hurting.

Then, when she started taking his shirt off, and afterwards, hers too, from there it just felt so good, not like on the planet that time, but different, stronger, and not a game, not a game at all. L'Rene seemed to really want it, like it was something she had wanted for a long time, and then, even though he had told her he wanted to come back, he'd seen Jer'son just afterwards in the corridor.

Jer'son had stopped him and even talked to him, but he was afraid to speak with him. What if he could tell? He wasn't even through wanting her, even though she said Jer'son was on his way. Then, he had seen Jer'son, and he was still thinking about L'Rene and how her hair had smelled, how she'd moved against him, and how he wanted that to happen again, and then there was Jer'son speaking to him as if he was still his friend. But Barn't knew what he'd done, and he wasn't Jer'son's friend anymore, not after L'Rene.

He'd known right then he wasn't going back to see her. He'd been mad at Jer'son, but he wasn't mad any more. He'd taken his things and already put them in Y'rae's room. That's what he'd do. He'd be with Y'rae.

That night he'd had a nightmare. He'd tried to tell Y'rae, but she didn't want to listen. So, from then on, when he woke at night, he just told her he talked in his sleep or liked to think at night. He didn't even do it with her all the time, and it wasn't anything like it had been with L'Rene.

One day he saw L'Rene in the corridor, and he remembered what it had been like. When she took his arm, he went with her, and it was good like the first time, only he didn't think about Jer'son the whole time. Sometimes he thought about the men that did that to him, and then he got really angry. That's when L'Rene said she especially liked him being with her, and then the nightmares got worse, and he needed Jer'son all over again.

Gods, he was lonely!

Finally exhausted, Barn't fell back against his bedding, and after a short time, the darkness became silent once again, with only the quiet movement of air to mark the passing time.

"YOUR REVELATION about Bird has gotten me thinking, Chr's."

Chr's laughed at the misconception that statement portrayed. "My revelation? I said nothing. You said it all, although it's all as I know it. You certainly can see through to the other side of things, my friend. What have you been thinking?"

"A cryptic message about an old friend. I think I'll get in contact with that friend. Can your package wait until morning, or is it urgent to be delivered now?"

"The package, tomorrow. It can wait until then."

"However, you, my friend, cannot. Let's get you some help. I know a good medic . . ."

MI'KAIL DIDN'T have much to go on, only what he'd picked up from here and there, and he was far from home in this unfamiliar part of the station. He glanced down the corridor, counting doors. At least the arrangements for personal quarters were the same throughout the station. Even though this was far from his familiar territory near the operations center, L'Rene's room had been relatively easy to find.

Standing outside the door, raising his hand to knock, he paused, then pressed his ear to the surface. L'Rene's voice he recognized, but the other wasn't Jer'son. The man could not have possibly beat him here from the medic's quarters. The raucous sounds of amorous play were clear, though.

He stepped back, hesitating, private time being just that onboard the station. To intrude could be reason for a severe reprimand, or even the thrust of a knife from some of the internees. However, if this was what he suspected . . .

He took a deep breath, raising his hand to knock. Closing his eyes, he was reminded of his wife from all those years ago, a day that was to have been so special for them both.

He had just returned from a month-long posting off-world, one of what had become many. To his delight, he'd managed to catch an early shuttle. He held an enormous bouquet of flowers in his hands as he crept to the bedroom door. She'd be in there now, possibly at the mirror, maybe putting on the necklace he'd sent to her, the one he'd never seen her wear. He knocked and cracked the door.

"Not now, Ker'nt. You're early. Come back in fifteen minutes. Veldn's not finished."

Mi'Kail pushed the door open to find his wife amorously engaged with one of his closest coworkers.

"Oh, hi, Mi'Kail." Her words were casual and cheery, belying the flush of arousal on her skin. "You know I always like you to call. I'm glad you finally know, though. It'll be so much easier. Please close the door. Veldn's getting nervous, and he almost had me there. I don't want him to stop now."

That was when Mi'Kail saw red. Later, he was never sure if it was the anger or the blood. It didn't matter, anyway. Either way, they were both just as dead.

He opened his eyes, studying L'Rene's door just in front of him, knowing he could not let this go, that Jer'son could not be allowed to face the same betrayal he had endured all those years ago. He would see to that, although not quite in the way he'd taken care of his wife and her lover. No, his anger was something he'd long ago learned to control.

He raised his hand to the door once again. When someone stepped around a corner and into the corridor, he paused as they sauntered by, wondering what he would say if he was mistaken. I'm sorry, L'Rene. There's a surprise station inspection going on, and I'm looking for Jer'son.

In some twisted sense, it would be true.

Then, rather than knocking, he took a deep breath, input the override code and pressed his hand against the pad. He closed his eyes, not wanting to see what he knew he must. He threw the door wide and stepped inside, quickly turning to face the corridor as if intending to push the door shut once more.

"Hey! What do you think you're doing?"

It was L'Rene's voice, and Mi'Kail chuckled apologetically. "I'm so sorry, L'Rene." He took a deep breath. "This is an emergency, and I need Jer'son immediately in the operations center. Jer'son? I'll step outside and wait on you." He grabbed the door, ready to do just that, just hoping he hadn't made a fool of himself.

"Mi'Kail, you are so stupid. Open your eyes. This is not Jer'son, so wait as long as you want. He won't be coming through that door."

Mi'Kail looked to find exactly what he'd suspected: Barn't next to L'Rene, frantically grabbing at rumpled bedding to cover himself.

"L'Rene, let him at least close the door." Barn't's frantic

whisper betrayed his dismay. Louder, he called, "Go away, Mi'Kail."

"Don't you dare, Mi'Kail." She hissed at Barn't, "I can have anyone I want sharing my quarters, and I don't care who watches. If you don't like it, you can get up and leave. I need to take a shower, anyway, because you've got me all sweaty."

"But I'm not finished." His plaintive voice, heavy with arousal, pleaded, whining more than anything, that of a little boy denied another taste of his favorite flavor candy, and he shifted on the bed, sending the remains of the bedding sliding away to expose bare skin.

"Get away, Barn't!" L'Rene shoved him, and the man toppled to the floor on top of the crumpled bedding.

Mi'Kail grabbed Barn't's clothes and flung them at him in disgust. He stood with his arms crossed, glaring as the man struggled to pull his pants on. When he didn't move fast enough, Mi'Kail grabbed his arm and pulled him toward the corridor with his clothing still around his knees.

Stumbling through the doorway, Barn't muttered angrily, his voice still coarse with the remains of his assignation, "Can't you slow down? You can see I'm not actually dressed."

"That should bother you?" Mi'Kail snorted in disgust. "Move!" He gave him a shove, glaring when the half-dressed man tried to cover himself as two middle-aged women walked past them, one reaching out to tug at his ill-arranged clothing with a suggestive laugh.

"Gods, that was embarrassing." Barn't finally got his pants to his waist and stepped into his shoes. His shirt fought him as Mi'Kail grabbed his arm once again.

Hauling Barn't down the corridor, the boy tripping on untied shoes, his pants unfastened, and his hands still doing up his shirt, Mi'Kail growled at him, "I don't care how embarrassed you are. You should be ashamed to have stomped on Jer'son like that."

Stopping, he slammed Barn't to the wall, attracting the attention of several people who quickly melted away. "You are a fool. The best man on this station sacrifices everything, even his girl, to help you, and you cheat on him with her. Is this the first time, or have you been at her all along?" He watched Barn't shake his head yes, while keeping his eyes glued to the floor. "Look at me, Barn't." Mi'Kail's voice was hard, and it yanked Barn't's eyes upwards. "Jer'son's my friend, too, and I'm not about to see him treated this way. If you don't want him for your friend, tell me. Better yet, tell him, because I'll take a friend like Jer'son any day, got it? Now, how often has this been going on?" Seeing that Barn't was near to tears, but no longer caring about the young man's feelings, Mi'Kail shook him and slammed him to the wall again. "How often, Barn't?"

Cracking, his voice barely understood, Barn't whispered, "Every day."

"Gods! I can't stand the sight of you!" Mi'Kail released him, and with the flat of his hand, shoved his shoulder to get him moving down the corridor. "March your ugly carcass to the operations center."

Barn't turned pleadingly to look at him. "You're not going to tell him, are you, Mi'Kail?"

"No, Barn't. No, I'm not." He grinned at the relieved

look on Barn't's face. "You are."

"I can't. I just can't." Tears pooled in Barn't's eyes. He looked up to see they had arrived, and with panic, he grabbed at the waist of his pants, holding them firmly. "Not inside. Not here. I'll wait on him in my quarters. Please."

Mi'Kail triggered the door and pointed. "There, Barn't. Have a seat. I'll have Jer'son here pronto."

"Can't I tell him later? Please, Mi'Kail. I promise I really will."

"After what I saw—and I swear to you I hope I never again see what I just saw, because I'll cut your tool off if I do—I don't trust you any further than you can spit, from either end of you. Get it?"

"I understand." Barn't melted into a chair.

Mi'Kail hit the comm switch, sending an all call for Jer'son to return to the operations center. It was only a few minutes before he appeared on the comm feeds, striding down the adjacent corridor. As he walked in the door, he turned to see Barn't, who immediately tried to disappear into his seat.

"Barn't!" he cried, his eyes frantic.

Mi'Kail began, "Jer'son, Barn't has something to share—"

Jer'son interrupted. "Mi'Kail, can it wait? I have to speak to him urgently, and I need it to be now. Okay?"

Mi'Kail looked at them and laughed. "Sure, Boss. He's *your* friend. I'm just glad I could get you two back together again."

Jer'son grabbed Barn't's arm and pulled him from the room, talking as he dragged him along.

"YOU'RE A mess, Barn't. Are you okay?" Jer'son grabbed Barn't's face in one hand and wiped sweat from it. "You're flushed and hotter than the sun. You're not sick, are you?"

He simply responded, "Where are we going?"

Jer'son pulled his face close and whispered, "We need to talk. I found something out today about you and me. You have no idea how important this is. It involves someone we both know, and we've got to work this out before tonight. I want to warn you, it's going to hurt a lot." He patted his face before throwing an arm across his shoulders.

Barn't wailed, "I'm sorry, Jer'son. Please don't hurt me."

"Shush! I don't think we can do it any other way, but let's get to my room first. I don't want anyone else to know. Now, be quiet."

"Gods, Jer'son. I'm so sorry!"

Jer'son gave him a what's-that-all-about look as he pushed him inside and closed the door. "Now, Barn't. Pull your shirt off."

Barn't stood and closed his eyes. "Just hit me, Jer'son. I deserve it. As hard as you want."

"Quit clowning and get your shirt off. Here," and he began undoing the clasps for him.

"I can do it." He pushed his friend's hands away and started loosening the fasteners.

"Now, pull it off and turn around. Bend over and let me look." With Barn't bent over, Jer'son ran his hand over his friend's back to find the small scar where the tracker had been injected. He pressed on the dimple with his thumb, leaving an imprint. "Gods, this is going to hurt. I'm sorry,

Barn't."

"Okay, Jer'son, I'm ready. Start any time."

"What are you talking about? Barkeen's going to do it. Not me."

"She knows, too?" Barn't whipped around and looked at him in dismay.

Jer'son gave his old friend a puzzled look. "She's the one who told me. She said to let you know."

Barn't looked like he was going to cry. "But it was Mi'Kail who found me."

"And I'm glad he did. I was looking for you everywhere. I didn't know where you were or who you were with."

"He didn't tell you?"

"Barn't, I'm beginning to think I should have just let those uppercadets beat you up back on the training ship. What are you talking about?"

"Um, you tell me first," he suggested.

"Tonight Barkeen is taking these hated trackers out of our lungs so we can get off Rant someday. It won't be tomorrow or even this week, but when the time comes, we can be free." He reached into a small drawer along the wall and pulled out the syringe he'd been given by Barkeen. "I have to inject this just where they inserted the tracker. It will help Barkeen find and remove it quickly."

"What about Renhant?"

"We're still working on that. If we do this, and my 'if' means you have a choice, then it has to be tonight, it will hurt, and it may take a while to heal. Do you want to do this?" Jer'son held the syringe up for him to see, then he put his hands on his shoulders, watching his face intently for a truthful answer.

"If it's going to hurt, you could do it, and I could stay here."

"We're a team, Barn't. Both or none."

Barn't took a deep breath, and with a pained expression, answered, "Both."

Jer'son let out a deep breath, relieved that the little fool was willing to go along. Then he spun him around and placed the syringe against his bare skin at the injection site. With a grimace, he triggered the device; and with a whoosh of compressed air, it was done.

When Barn't stood, Jer'son handed him the syringe and reached to unbutton his own shirt. He was next.

—Chapter 17—

*Station Position Open: medical training
preferred; must have extensive knowledge of
the human body; experience a must; apply in
person*

—Posted onworld

RENHANT RUBBED his chin with his hand, cutting his
eyes to the man at his side. He studied the bandages, and
around that, the darkening bruises. Then he looked closer to
see if he could judge his reaction. If Chr's wasn't a hundred
percent onboard, involving Racket wouldn't do.

"So," Chr's said softly, "you have a man you can contact.
This is a man who used to work for the company you now
run, a company that's not even a Rant organization."

"That about sums it up."

He leaned forward in his chair. "What is that company
doing here on Rant? We're told this world is run solely by
prisoners incarcerated here." He shook his head. "There are
layers within layers, Renhant. I thought we were so clever,

319

Barkeen, Bird, and me. We intended to save all the worlds out there from MegaCorp, and all with just our own little subterfuges. Now, I find there are more layers within the layers than I can count. What do you know about this man that you know? How well do you know him?"

Renhant stood and walked across the room. He looked back at Chr's. Patched up by the medic, the man looked better, but Renhant definitely didn't see the scholar he knew him to be. A ruffian, maybe. Streetwise. He gave a small chuckle. Maybe after he healed, then the look of the scholar would come out.

"Your limp, Chr's. That's from yesterday's brawl? You hide it well, but it's there." His question was real, but it was also a distraction from the man's probing. A mere affirmation was not what he needed to understand how much Renhant trusted Racket. Renhant needed to offer a deeper assurance, and he could if Chr's would talk to him.

Chr's laughed a laugh telling of an old hurt that was now a reminder only. "Your friend, our mutual friend, this Jer'son. This was his salvation." He stood. "Now that I see I cannot hide it from you, I can feel free to give in to it. It still pains me."

"Jer'son? His salvation?" Renhant let out a disbelieving chuckle, the mirth showing a long association of memories. Inside, he was pleased with the sudden turn of the conversation; already he had his idea of how to offer the reassurance Chr's needed to hear, how to drive it home to him. "How is it that our friend was involved with your leg?"

Chr's massaged his thigh and smiled the smile of the resigned. "The story is an old one that needs time to tell.

Instead, tell me of your unknown man."

"I worked with him when I came here. Not for long, but long enough. However, this man was an old friend of a much better friend, and I trusted this much better friend with my life."

"This much better friend, was he the one who left you here as he went on to a new life elsewhere?" The bemused expression on Chr's' face showed his opinion of someone who would do such a thing.

Renhant changed his tack, certain he could find a way to make this man understand. "Do you have a family, Chr's? Or, since this is Rant, did you have a family?" He watched the man's face for what he needed to see there.

Chr's licked his lips and looked anywhere but at Renhant for a moment, and then turned with red-rimmed eyes. "This is Rant. The old world doesn't follow, no matter how much we want it to." He paused, looking at his feet for a time, then back to Renhant's face. "It was a long time ago, and with what I know now, I hope they were told I died. At first, though, I had dreams of seeing them again. Two little ones."

"Your children." Renhant nodded.

"A scholar's pay is like the stars in the heavens." Chr's worked his mouth as if the words and memories were hard for him to drag from their long-sequestered hiding place. He laughed. "No matter how many the stars, the space they need to fill is always so much greater. I was brilliant."

He stood, walking with his limp to look out a window, the new day just starting to crawl into the sky. He turned back, grabbing a table for balance and support. "I was the crème de la crème. Research. The corporate environment.

Any university in the arm. I had offers by the hundreds." He took a deep breath and dropped his head, shaking it from side to side. "By the hundreds."

"And, Chr's? What happened?"

"My wife's family. She was so beautiful. Her little world was distant and out of circulation, and yet that's where she wanted to be. So, we went. I got a position at a small school, and that was that." He took a deep breath and returned to the chair.

"Your family, I can see. What happened, though? I'm still confused."

"I stagnated. I loved my family, but we had nothing, and I was nothing. When I found I could access MegaCorp's files through an algorithm I had created, suddenly I could give my family all I wanted them to have. I felt so superior that I had broken into MegaCorp, and MegaCorp didn't even know."

He laughed sourly. "One day, finally, they knew. And, here I am. My family?" He clasped his hands in front of him, rubbed them together, and threw them up in the air with a smile that belied the redness in his eyes. "I have no idea."

"You knew their importance to you, right?"

Chr's closed his eyes, squeezing them hard, then wiped a tear from his cheek. "I *know* their importance to me. If I didn't put it aside, I couldn't live every day."

Renhant spoke with feeling. "Then you know why I trust this friend of a friend. Let me contact him. He will be what we need, I'm sure of that."

"Now. Do it." Chr's waved his hand at him.

Renhant smiled.

ONCE AGAIN, as it had so many times in the dark of night, a hand grabbed Barn't's shoulder. He glanced up, and it was Jer'son with a smile on his face. Before he could react, Jer'son spun him around, putting his hand on his side, a familiar touch from a familiar friend, one who was more family than acquaintance.

"Barn't! You can't just pass me by in the corridor. I looked for you where I left you. I was so angry. After I stepped away, I realized just how important you are to me. You are my very closest friend, and I know you would only do what's best for me. I can trust you, Barn't. I know I can. You would never let me down, no matter how badly I treated you. We're a team, aren't we, just like always, protecting each other, no matter who gets hurt?"

He cringed as Jer'son wrapped his arms around him, a brother's hug, and one that he never once remembered from his father. The news of Bird's illness was gone, and the anger over whether he could go down to the planet or not was now a moot issue. Other things had crowded those concerns from his thoughts. Friendship. Jer'son. *L'Rene.*

As he stood with his friend's arms around him, all Barn't could think of was the smell of L'Rene in his nostrils, his sweat mixed with hers, and the dampness of their union soaking the clothes he still wore. Surely he could tell. Surely he would step back and ask the hard, pointed questions. *Where have you been, Barn't? Why are you just getting dressed, Barn't? Why are your clothes so damp, Barn't? Why does your skin smell like L'Rene, Barn't?*

He hated what he'd just done, and he hated himself. He pulled away from Jer'son's hug. Then, he was yanked from the corridor, back to the present, to his bunk, and to wakefulness.

"It's time, Barn't. Come alive."

Jer'son's hand grabbed his shoulder, shaking him hard, and he opened his eyes to his friend's face, still feeling the betrayal that had been so strong in the dream. He rolled back into his pillow, his eyes burning, even as Jer'son punched his shoulder.

"I've missed you in here. This room hasn't been the same with you gone. We've got business to attend to, though. Are you ready for this?"

Barn't turned his head, squinting into the light, then swung his feet to the floor before Jer'son could question him further. His head spun, and he put his hands over his face to hide the shame. It didn't stop the longing, though.

"Friend, there's no time to lose. You must move now." Jer'son slapped his shoulder encouragingly.

They stepped into a darkened corridor, Barn't nervous, filled with regret for agreeing to this, the only lights those of personnel access panels and security indicators providing comfort and convenience to those who must wander at night. Reaching the examination room door after a long, hurried walk, Barn't stood to the side, glancing up and down the corridor as Jer'son rapped quietly. It opened immediately.

"Shush! Not a sound." Barkeen quickly drew them inside. The light from the examination room door spilled into the darkness of the corridor for only a moment. She closed the door behind them, sealing the light into the room.

"We have this window of time, only. I have altered my records to reflect two damaged trackers that will then be disposed of. Yours. Boys, I have locals only, but they are the strongest I can procure. Expect some disorientation. Afterward, you must not let anyone see your bandages or know of any pain you may later experience. With the meds I must give, you may not remember returning to your rooms afterward, but be quiet when doing so. When I am done, I will give you a drink to speed the healing. Secrecy. Am I clear?" Barkeen was already moving swiftly around the room, preparing her tools. "This examination room is not my preferred place for this procedure, but the only space possible."

"It will be fine." Jer'son nodded.

"It will have to be. First?" She slapped the table.

Barn't jumped when Jer'son pushed him forward, and his skin prickled as Barkeen efficiently removed his shirt, pushing him on the table, and covering his back with absorbent toweling.

Turning to Jer'son, she spoke with urgency. "Watch the time. This is more than just reaching in and pulling out. I have only one hour each. Just one. The examination room surveillance systems are offline for the self-repair algorithms to run just for that time. Only this one night have I been able to adjust them to my needs. This opportunity will not arise again. I cannot afford to still be working when they return to online status. Do not talk to me once I begin."

Barn't turned to see her eyes riveting Jer'son's, and it was as if something electric passed between them. Then, seemingly satisfied, she picked up a long needle. Her hand covered his face, and he felt the instrument jab deep into his back. As he felt it slip greasily out, her fingers pressed around the spot for a few moments, but before he felt more, his head spun, and the world around him shifted.

"Here, dear." Barn't looked up. His mother was playing with him this time. She was really here on the beach.

"Well, don't you want it?" She reached out and handed him the ice cream.

"Thank you, Mommy." He had been afraid to take it. Sometimes when his mommy played with him, taking something she gave him broke the spell. Then, she would go away, and he didn't want her to go away.

"Mommy, you look pretty in your swimsuit. I like it when you come to the beach with me." She was pleased when he said nice things to her.

She twirled around, making several complete circles. "Do you like my new hat? It keeps the sun out of my eyes." Her laughter tinkled as she spun around in a circle another time. "What do you want to do today, Je'main?"

"Is Daddy coming?" His mommy was always more fun without his daddy.

She bent over him, her hat nearly touching his face. "Why is that? Don't you want your daddy to come?" She reached down and touched his nose, and then answered his question with a smile. "No, my wonderful son. Your daddy isn't coming today. Now, I asked you. What would you like to do?"

He didn't like that question. Sometimes when he chose something she didn't like, she would get sad and go away. He knew one thing, though. She wouldn't want to sit today. Not with her new hat.

"Do you want to watch me swim? I could splash for you,

and you could clap for me."

He watched his mother stop and look at him. She gave him her slow smile, as if she had to pull it from way deep inside. He liked the smile that was right there on the outside, the one that was quick and easy, showing she really liked his ideas.

"Mommy, we can do something else instead. You don't have to watch me swim." His words were suddenly frantic as he looked at her, her attention now on something else down the beach. He looked and couldn't see anything. When his mommy gave that look, sometimes she was getting ready to go away. "Mommy, look at me, please. Mommy." He had to get her attention. She couldn't go away yet.

In desperation, he jumped up, sending sand flying everywhere. His mother looked down at the small grains stuck all over her suit.

"Oh, Je'main! You got sand all over my new suit. Now, why did you go and do that?" She began brushing it off. She looked to him, her smile brightening. "I'm meeting someone today."

"Mommy, stay with me. Please play with me today."

She looked off again, her hand poised under the brim of her hat, shading her eyes as if she really could see something in the distance. He saw a smile start at the corner of her lips. Without looking at him, she waved her hand his direction. "Aren't you going to swim for Mommy?"

"Yes, Mommy. Mommy, are you going to watch?"

She turned her eyes to him with a look of bemusement. "Why, of course, Je'main. Would I ask you to swim, otherwise? Now, scoot to the water, dear. The day won't last forever." She was already looking off down the beach again.

He ran to the water, yelling so his mother would know he was there. He wanted her to turn to look at him and see him playing. If she saw how much fun he was having, she might want to swim, too.

He didn't know why no one else was in the water. It was so warm today. The water felt good. He jumped into a deep spot and felt something on his back. It touched him, then it started to sting and burn. He jumped and tried to get away from the burning, but it just got worse. He heard his mother talking to someone.

"I always tell him to watch for jellyfish. Sometimes he's a silly boy, and he doesn't pay attention. If he'd just come up out of the water, the jellyfish would leave him alone."

He ran to the sound of her voice, the water splashing at his feet. The burning didn't stop when he got out of the water. The running just made it worse. It hurt so much. When he got on the beach, he looked for his mommy.

"Mommy, this burns. Please help me. My back. It hurts so much." There was no one there. Then he realized the beach was gone, also.

"Barn't! You're yelling again. Keep it down."

He felt a hand on his shoulder, Jer'son's, shaking it gently as he handed him a pouch.

"Drink this."

He sat up and nearly choked on the pain. "Gods! Can anything hurt so much?"

"Mine does, too. Drink that. You'll heal faster." Jer'son was dressed with a shirt on. "We have to get you clothed before you go out."

"Clothed?" Barn't looked down at the bandage wrapped around his chest. "Do you have one of these?" He looked to Jer'son who pulled his shirt up to show him. "I don't think I can go out. It hurts to even breathe."

Jer'son moved, and immediately he coughed, making a pained face. "Does it hurt any less to be stuck here on Rant?"

Barn't looked at him, taking a deep breath of his own, and his chest knotted into an explosive fireball. It came out as a violent cough.

"Awk!" he spit out. "I should have paid attention to you when you coughed. That was a starstrike detonation." He glanced up. "I get what you mean. This is better than staying here. Winning the contest would have been even better, though."

Jer'son closed his eyes and leaned his head back against the wall. "In five years, Barn't, how many people have you ever seen win?"

"None."

He smiled a mirthless smile. "But, yeah, winning the contest would have been better, that's for sure."

"RACKET! WHAT is this? What about that report I turned in about five years ago? That transport that got blown up? I used to ride on this thing." Renhant walked around the old machine, not really believing he was seeing it in one piece. He ran his hand over where Cornerstone's stamping machine had been attached to the back of the transport, and he looked at Racket with a bemused expression. "I know Cornerstone's transport."

Renhant also knew the remains of a destroyed transport

had been cleared away from the explosion site all those years ago. Yet, it was obviously not this one. Somehow, Racket had managed that, it would seem.

"It was a good machine, ser. I had one that wasn't a good machine. I moved a VIN plate, switched some ID tags, and blew up mine instead. This one is slow, but it will last a long time." He smiled at his ingenuity.

Renhant glanced at Chr's and back to Racket. Not entirely sure what had been meant by the cryptic message that Racket was a friend, but sure it was meant for an emergency like this, he knew he had to take this chance. The rescued transport? That proved something to him. Cornerstone's old friend could think on his own, and that was a very good thing on a planet like this.

Now was the time to find out just where that thinking would take them.

"Racket, I know you've made your own business, and I believe you still have your girl, too." Racket nodded. "What about adventure? Are you up for a risk or two?"

Racket broke into a grin. "You do not know where I got my name, I think. Back on my world, I was into the numbers, you see. It was a thing of mine. Pretty soon, I got with a friend, and we got this little racket going. Well, I may not have my racket anymore, but that is still my name. Racket. Get it? Now, ser, you tell me the odds, and I will tell you if I wish to play."

Chr's broke in with a sour chuckle. "The odds? There's a good chance that either MegaCorp will discover what we are doing, or that we will not see any result in our lifetimes. Those are the odds in this."

"So," Racket said, a pensive look on his face. "The odds are very poor?"

"Yes. The odds are very poor, indeed." Renhant was not encouraged by his expression.

However, Racket burst into a huge smile. "Why then, I am counted in. When do we start?"

Chr's and Renhant clapped him on the back as Renhant interjected, "Right now, Racket. The first order of business is getting a package to the orbital station. We know of no other way there than the regular methods, and those don't provide the opportunities we need. How can we do that? Is there perhaps a way to gain access to the station other than the scheduled runs? Also, who can we trust in all this?"

Turning to Racket, Chr's suggested, "An accident is my best idea. I started a fight to get emergency transportation to the city." He paused, holding out his arms, the injuries still very apparent. "How about to the station? I'd be willing to do that. I don't want to, understand. It could be a mishap with machinery, perhaps. I'd let myself be injured if that's what it takes. Is that possible? Would that be enough to get the medic to commandeer the shuttle for an emergency case?"

"Boss." Racket chuckled. "May I call you that? It seems we will be working together. This is so exciting, much like when I was home. Boss, I always look at the obvious, first. So, before we beat you up or run you over, let us think. Easy solutions. Your friend. He could come get it. What do you say?"

"I'm glad you're thinking on the same lines as we've been. That was our first idea, but that friend is who the package goes to, and he must be on the station to use what we send him. Coming to Rant isn't a risk we can take. Another idea?"

"Boss, now that the obvious plan is gone, let's look at the easy one. It is easy to see that the station and the planet are interdependent. We ship things up; they ship things down. All the time. Foods, fabrics, etc. Bake your friend a cake, so to speak. Put it in the cake."

Renhant was growing amused by Racket's rendition of possibilities, and he looked at Chr's and laughed before turning his eyes back to his old coworker. "I now see why I had that message, Racket. I understand why Cornerstone trusted you so."

"Then we can put it in the cake?" Racket looked at them hopefully.

"Is there no way for a direct delivery by a person we can trust?" Chr's leaned forward, his question cutting to the chase.

Racket looked at the two men for a time. "Perhaps it is time to tell Racket just what is so important about the message, so Racket can begin to decide just how much his two bosses should know."

Chr's and Renhant grinned at each other. This was getting interesting.

—Chapter 18—

When at first you don't succeed, try, try again.

—Mid-Twentieth Century old-Earth saying

"BARN'T."

It was L'Rene's voice, and he refused to turn. He closed the stor'lok. He could be in the activities room at mealtime if he wanted to be. Even alone. She had caused him enough problems already. She should just go away.

"Barn't, you aren't listening to me."

"Go away, L'Rene." There. He had said the words. He leaned his forehead against the stor'lok and wished her gone. His side hurt, and he and Jer'son weren't even off the station. He wasn't sure this had been a good idea anymore. It had gotten him and Jer'son back together, but the pain. It hurt so often, and he couldn't even tell anyone.

"Barn't."

Closer now, once again L'Rene interrupted his private

misery. Her words reminded him of the cruel things he'd done to his best friend.

"It's been a long time, Barn't. Come back to my quarters with me. No one else does it like you do." She wrapped her hand around his arm and pulled him to face her. "I'm still pretty, aren't I?"

"Very pretty." In that moment, Barn't knew he shouldn't have looked. Just seeing her made his body want to do things his mind found disgusting. When he thought about her being Jer'son's girl, he knew it was disgusting to be with her. Still, when he thought about the times he had been with her already, he didn't care. Just seeing her face, he could already feel that ache that said he wanted her again.

Yet, the pain in his side kept reminding him of Jer'son. He closed his eyes, determined not to betray his friend once again. He had to break this off and for good.

"You were a really nice girl five standards ago, L'Rene." He opened his eyes, intending to look her in the face, but she was there, all woman, just under the fabric of her clothing, and every time she breathed, she made him want her more. "I don't know what's happened to you since then. You've changed, and I don't like what you're doing to Jer'son. He doesn't deserve that."

He had been prepared to own up that day, what with Mi'Kail finding him with L'Rene. He couldn't actually deny what he'd done, could he? After all, Mi'Kail had opened the door; and he had seen them together. It was only later that he'd realized Jer'son didn't know. So, as long as L'Rene kept quiet, he never had to know. Mi'Kail wouldn't tell. He'd already told Barn't that.

L'Rene put her hand against his face. "Oh, look, Barn't. You're blushing. How sweet. Am I still your only girl? That makes me really want you. I don't count that Y'rae, you know. I've heard she's no fun at all. Can I just touch you? More than just your face. Please? It's been days."

"No," he began, but his body was calling, and what could it hurt if he didn't do anything, if he just stood here and let her hold him? That would feel good, and he needed to feel good for a while.

He closed his eyes as L'Rene caressed his cheekbone, running her hands down his neck, then across his shoulders and his arms. He licked his lips and sensed his breath quickening as he felt her arms start down his chest. Her touch was no longer unwelcome to him, and if she asked him now, he would have to go with her.

She ran her hands down his sides, and then she slapped his chest hard.

"Ouch, L'Rene! What'd you do that for?" He coughed as he reached to rub where she had hit him.

"What is that under your shirt?" She was no longer fun and games. "Jer'son has one of these, and now I find you do, too. Fess up, Barn't." She glared at him. "Is this why I can't get either of you to come back to my rooms with me? Have you had something done?"

"L'Rene, I'm not supposed to talk about it. What did Jer'son tell you?"

"He told me he'd cracked a rib or something, and he couldn't come to see me for a while. You didn't even tell him, did you Barn't?" She started unfastening his shirt. "I want to know what this is for, and if you don't show me, I'm telling Jer'son about us. Then you'll see just how good a friend you've got. He'll turn on you like a snap. Just you wait and see."

"L'Rene." He didn't know what to do. He and Jer'son were just now friends again, and until his back healed, he was even staying with him in the quarters that had been theirs. Y'rae hadn't even acted sorry to see him go. He couldn't return there.

"L'Rene, I'm not supposed to show anyone." However, if she knew, surely she would be glad he no longer had the tracker in him. Anyway, he never went off the station. What good did the tracker do in him, anyway?

He pushed her gently away. "Stop, L'Rene. I'll take it off. You can't tell, though." With fumbling fingers, he began undoing his shirt one fastener at a time.

AS SOON AS L'Rene saw the fresh wound on Barn't's back, she knew what it was from. She also knew who had done it.

Barkeen! That witch! She wouldn't save my poor brother, beaten and raped by the guards right in front of my eyes, but she'd save these two traitors. How dare she! I'll take care of this! Barkeen, I know how to get even!

To Barn't she sounded very different, though. "Thank you, Barn't. I won't tell anyone. You can count on me." She helped him wrap the bandage back up and put his shirt on.

She was very nice to him, indeed.

"THERE IS ONE other possibility, Boss." Racket looked between the two men, not focusing specifically on either one.

"Are these plans so very important as to take a very great risk? Are they worth a life if we fail?" He pursed his lips, knowing the value of a good ace in the hole, even if that was a card game that had been forgotten for over five hundred years. He also knew not to reveal his ace in the hole unless the situation was very desperate.

Chr's was the one who answered.

"These plans have by this time already cost lives. We have completed and implemented the design changes these alternate plans reflect. They will be compared within the day. They must be in place. These adjustments will precipitate a destruction of such magnitude that important powers will have to take notice of what MegaCorp is doing. The corporation will be brought to its knees."

Racket looked from one of the cohorts to another. He knew of Cornerstone and Cornerstone's father. He knew of MegaCorp's overwhelming power, as well as the greed that would wield that muscle shamelessly and without regard for human rights. He had also made a comfortable home on Rant, and still, he knew the desire to make MegaCorp pay. Even before he asked, he had known his decision was made.

"Well, then this path we must do. Hitch up your suspenders, Bosses."

Renhant stopped him with a puzzled frown. "What does that mean, Racket? I've never heard of suspenders."

Racket just shrugged. "Neither have I, Boss. But, my eldest great-grandfather used to say it before doing a hard task, and the task always got done. I think it must be a good luck saying."

Chr's slapped Renhant on the back. "Then, for luck,

Renhant, hitch up your suspenders."

He grinned. "I'm hitching as we go."

"It will be a very long ride, Bosses. Do you have your plans?"

"Yes, right here, Racket. Just where are we going?"

Racket paused as he pursed his lips, then he continued with a mischievous grin. "To do something very dangerous. Very dangerous, indeed."

BARN'T FOUND Jer'son already sprawled on the top bunk. They'd hoped to coordinate sleeping schedules so both could use the bottom one—with the surgery, climbing up was difficult—but that didn't work out this night. He immediately began pulling his clothes off, the shoes and the shirt the most difficult because of Barkeen's work. He talked as he went. Although things had been better since he'd come back, neither one of the friends felt comfortable with silence. Rambling conversation seemed the best option to fill the void.

"I saw someone from downsides we know, Jer'son. You might remember her. She worked at that eating place by Bird's. You remember the one with the fried cakes? She's taken Trainer's place. She said she's seen you."

Jer'son's face was turned towards the wall, and for a moment it was just like old times. Jer'son's bandage had caught a portion of his shirt, twisting it, and Barn't asked, "How'd you get up there? I couldn't have climbed up alone. You should have waited on me for help." When he didn't answer, Barn't tapped his shoulder.

Jer'son jerked violently away from his hand, hissing,

"Ouch! Gods, that hurts!" He curled up in a tight ball, still facing the wall. "You are a fool, Barn't!"

"Did I do something wrong?" The world went flat and colorless around Barn't, and he knew L'Rene had told in spite of her promise. He stood rock still, only breaking the silence with one word. "Jer'son?"

Jer'son whipped around to face him, the sudden movement writing pain across his face. "Gods, I shouldn't have listened to her. I shouldn't have asked you to have your tracker taken out, too. Then, Barkeen would have refused to do mine. She insisted, though, so I just had to ask you. I should have let it go. I would have been all right here for the rest of my life. It's no worse than the academy. So much for friendship."

"Jer'son?" Barn't felt like ice. That certainly wasn't what he had expected.

"Don't Jer'son me. You're not simple minded. I didn't want to ask you. When I finally got my chance to escape, I wanted to leave you here." With difficulty, he was finally sitting, hunched, his arms holding his side. "Why did L'Rene come by today and tell me she knew you had your chest bandaged like mine? Tell me that, Barn't. How would she know that? Make this good, man. Little lies don't impress me anymore. Make it whopping good, then I can at least get a laugh out of all this." His face wasn't laughing at all.

"Um, what did she tell you?" Now he knew. Everything was out.

Jer'son spat, "What should she have told me, best-friend-we're-a-team-no-matter-who-gets-hurt?"

"I don't know. I wasn't there." He felt a whine at the

339

edges of his voice, and he hated it. Then his eyes turned gritty, and he blinked them to keep from crying.

Jer'son snapped out even more barbs. "Don't you pull that crying thing on me. You're twenty-two standards, and I'm so mad at you that you can cry until your body shrivels up and blows away, and I'll just help the wind sweep you out the door."

"Jer'son, you've always been my friend. I've always counted on you."

"Focus, runt. What would L'Rene be doing under your shirt?"

"Gods, Jer'son. Won't you just tell me what you know?" He couldn't tell if he really knew about him and L'Rene, or if he was upset that L'Rene knew about what Barkeen did. He did know he didn't want to lose Jer'son for a friend again, and he may already have done that.

"I know enough. That's all you need to know. If Barkeen suffers, don't expect me to help you ever again." He flipped back onto his bunk, and in a sudden blast, he slammed the wall with his fist and barked, "Gods, it still hurts when I do that."

Barn't turned off the light and lay on his bunk in the dark for a long time. Finally, he whispered, "Jer'son? Jer'son, are you awake? I have something I want to tell you. Everything you thought is true."

As he continued, he fulfilled his promise to Mi'Kail. He told everything, from the time he lashed out about not getting to go see Bird for the last time and how long he'd sat there waiting for Jer'son to return, to what L'Rene had threatened tonight when he showed her his wound. Barn't told it all. He just hoped Jer'son was listening, because he wasn't sure he was brave enough to tell it again.

"BOSSES, THIS is it." Racket rubbed his hand down the side of a machine that shouldn't be on this world. "It works, but it is very old."

The small ship he admired looked like it had long ago seen its better days. The finish was worn, and there were stress marks in the canopy. Obviously this was no military model. It was not finished with indestructible glassine designed to shelter the pilot from the hazards of deepest space.

"What's it for?" Renhant looked at it askance. "I'm hoping it's not for taking someone to the station. It might get us to the city, but offworld?" He shuddered.

"Will it truly fly?" Chr's walked around the ship. It was very small with room for maybe two people, if one could crowd in back. "You know, the shape of this looks familiar. Years ago I flew a small ship, although without the canopy this one has. With the canopy, the lines are different, but I'm certain this is the same." He looked up and smiled. "This might do, Renhant. This might be perfect."

"Perfect for what? Perfect for a crash landing?" Renhant turned to Racket. "Why is this here at all? I don't get that."

"Cornerstone's father brought this with him. It was old, then, with room for barely the two men. Then, Reenna. There was no room, so there was a new ship, not new, of course." He laughed at his joke. "This one was not worth selling. So, it sits. I keep it running just for old times, because I like to tinker, Boss. I didn't tell you. I didn't want to have to change the VIN numbers when you decided to blow it up."

341

"So, this is yours, Renhant?" Chr's was working to get the compartment open, and he wrestled with a control panel on the side.

"I guess. Racket?" He looked at his old work partner. "Is this mine?"

When Racket nodded in affirmation, Chr's asked, "Can you fly it, Renhant?'

"Once it's up, probably. Remember, while Racket says it's mine, I've never seen it before. In fact, I've never even seen a model like this. If I do manage to get it up, it's gonna be a rough landing. How about you? You said you flew a similar one. Can you operate it?"

Finally getting the hatch open, Chr's climbed inside. He grinned and looked out at the other two men. "This is exactly the same as the one I had. Mine didn't really fly, not into space, but I did get it off the ground from time to time. I would limp it to the mountains and back, hoping it wouldn't break down on the way."

"So, one boss is familiar with the controls." Racket looked satisfied.

"Absolutely. I'm certain I can fly it, perhaps even land it." Chr's grinned broader, looking at Renhant hopefully.

"It is settled. Boss Chr's, you will go to the station. Boss Renhant, you will go with me to let your friend up in the sky know to expect a visitor. The ship is ready now. When I tinker, I always leave it ready to fly. You never know when an emergency might come along." He gave them both a wink.

"Chr's, what message should I send to the ship? Who should get it? Jer'son? Or should I try to contact Barkeen?"

Climbing out, Chr's reached in a pocket and pulled out a small slip of paper. He handed it to Renhant. "It's all on this." He laughed. "Paper is easier to destroy when you're done with it. Send it to Medic Barkeen. Include just what the paper says. *The scholar is arriving to meet an old friend. Please have the welcome mat out.* She'll know what to do." At a whirring sound, he turned, realizing the ship's hatch had begun to close.

Racket grinned. "Automatic. I like to tinker."

Chr's threw one arm across Renhant's shoulder and slapped him heartily on the back. "I know you for one night, and I feel I can trust you with my life. You are truly the good friend my good friend deserved. Take care. If this goes as I suspect, I may not return." He turned to thrust a hand to Racket. "I will try to see your marvelous ship somehow gets back to you, my good man, one way or another."

Racket tried to stifle a grin. "I would not worry, Boss. The ship will return when it is time. Just make sure you are inside." He slapped the side and released the hatch. Reaching inside, with several quick touches to the control panel, he backed out. "You must go now, Boss. The destination is set."

"Once I arrive?"

"You will be expected. Your message will be delivered by us long before then."

He stepped back as Chr's climbed into the old ship and engaged the starting mechanism. When its noises began to build in volume, Racket yelled enthusiastically through the open hatch, "Purrs like a kitten!" He slammed the hatch and backed away as Chr's put it in motion.

Renhant grinned at Ratchet. "What's a kitten?"

"I do not know, Boss. My great-grandfather used to say that when something worked really well. When he said that, it never broke down." They backed away as the small vessel rose steadily into the night sky. "Ready for a long ride back to town? We have a message to send."

UNEXPECTED BANGING on the door jarred Jer'son from a fitful sleep. Flipping the light on, his eyes bleary and his injury hurting, he yelled at whoever was making the noise to go away and leave them alone.

An imperative voice could be heard through the door. "Barkeen. Examination A. Double stat." Then the thudding of feet faded away.

With groans of pain, Jer'son dragged Barn't from his bunk, and both men slipped on clothing, the silence of the previous evening filling the room. The anger that had flared between them thickened into a soup of bitterness that made the room stink.

Yet, even so, they were in this together, and together they ran the distance to find Medic Barkeen on the examination table, her pale assistant desperately trying to staunch bleeding from a wound in her side.

"Barkeen!" Jer'son shot through the room, calling to her. Seeing the extent of the injuries, he leveled narrowed eyes at Barn't. He had warned him. "How bad is it?"

"Bad enough." Barkeen grasped the blood-soaked cloth at her side and motioned the young assistant to leave. The weakness in her voice and movements told more than her words.

"Medic Barkeen, I cannot. You must have treatment

344

now." The girl pulled bandaging and surgical supplies from a cart near the table.

"Girl, you must go immediately, or I will deal with you in the afterlife. Go!"

"As you wish, Medic Barkeen." The girl tearfully backed from the room, looking at the two men and calling out, "I will be just outside. Help her, please."

"Barkeen." Jer'son moved to her and lifted her hand in his, forcing the assistant's towel against the wound. "Oh, Barkeen!"

"My wound is unimportant. This I expected long ago. At least now I know when it will come." She barked out a laugh, spitting up blood. "I will not leave this room alive, although you must." She raised her hand. "A message of a lifetime was sent to me tonight. It was you I thought at the door, and so I freely opened it. My past swept in, instead, and you see the damage that has been done. However, you have arrived in time. All my hopes have come together, and they depend on you, my boy."

She held out an old-fashioned piece of paper with a series of numbers on it. "This will override the landing bay. It must be opened." She coughed, blood running from her mouth. She smiled thinly as she weakly patted Jer'son's arm. "An old friend of yours is making a call. Be sure you greet him for me." She coughed again, more blood spilling with each wracking shake of her body. Jer'son reached with one end of the towel to wipe it clean.

"Who did this? You must tell me. They will pay," Jer'son growled. He cut his eyes to Barn't and watched him cringe at the look. If L'Rene did this, Barn't would suffer, also. He would make sure of that.

Barkeen squeezed her eyes tightly, and her hand grasped at his arm, a jagged slash of pain darting across her face. Then, she relaxed for a moment, barely able to speak. "This was to right an old wrong. It is of no concern to you. The bay. It must be opened! Go!"

With tears gathering in his eyes, his most trusted ally bleeding profusely in his arms, Jer'son knew many people had axes to grind here on Rant, but he didn't understand who could find fault with Barkeen. He looked in her half-closed eyes, and with a steely determination, he whispered his demand. "Not without knowing the who, I will not. Tell me, or I will not go."

"If you must. L'Rene." She grabbed his arm in a death grip and squeezed; and she made her position clear. "That girl has caused bad blood between the two of you. Your bond goes deeper than her evil. You must remain friends no matter what she has done. Help each other. Tonight may be your night. Take your chance when it is given. Do not let her come in your way."

As she sagged onto the table, choking, blood began to foam from her lips in a red soup of death.

"Barkeen, you have to tell me how to help you." Jer'son put his hand to her face to comfort her. Her sightless eyes were his only answer, and seeing that, he knew he could do nothing more.

—Chapter 19—

*Va•li•um (val' ē əm) a trademark for a
tranquilizing drug; often used for people with
personality disorders; its use was
discontinued when personality reconstruction
became popular: archaic term*

—New Galactic Dictionary

THE SMALL FLYER whistled through the atmosphere, protected by a battered canopy that was not entirely airtight. After a time, the sky began to glow along the horizon. Somewhere on Rant, the sun was beginning to rise.

However, the controls were locked, and until Chr's got closer to the station, there was nothing for him to do. Remembering all the times he'd flown his small ship, limping it across the surface of his wife's beloved world, he closed his eyes and reached for the control panel, letting the past flood over him.

"Chr's, do you have all your free day homework done?" His mother's voice still echoed in his ears.

"Mommy, all the other kids don't have to. I don't even get to play outside at school. I have to do my independent projects." He dropped his head onto the desk. "I'm tired, and I want to go with Daddy today. He promised, and I didn't get to go last time. Please let me go. It's free day, and no one else has school." Daddy had said he could ride in his ship. He drove the shuttle that carried people from the port to the big ship that he could see at night in the sky. Then, he brought them back again. Most people never got to go to the big ship, but his daddy got to go there all the time.

"Now, Chr's. It doesn't matter if it's your free day; the extra work is because you're in the accelerated class. You have to set the pace. You know getting your assignments completed is more important than what your father has planned. He'll understand you can't go if you've been careless and your work isn't complete. Now, get busy. If you apply yourself, you can get everything finished."

He couldn't, though. It was too much. He put his head down and looked out the window, the sky drawing his attention. He idly pushed icons over his glass, not really caring about his assignments. The math problems he had to do were too hard. How should he know how many times a scout ship had to circle a world to map the continents if the scout ship had a subsonic gamma-enhanced beam n^3 degrees in width?

He looked at the clock. Sometimes he could get away with finishing just the first and the last sections. Of course, he would get in trouble later, but it would be okay as long as he got to go with Daddy. He'd never been on Daddy's ship before.

He looked at the clock again. Maybe he could hide some of the work. He could download it to his spare glass and put it under his mattress. That's what he would do. He'd show her what was already finished, and no one would know.

He pulled the completed work from his stack and pushed all the rest onto the old glass he never used anymore. Then, he shoved it between the mattress and the bottom of the bed. When his mother came in, everything on the glass he held out was finished.

"See, Mommy." He stood right in front of where he'd stuffed the old glass. "Do I get to go with Daddy?"

"Chr's, I thought you had more work than this. What happened to the rest?" She picked up his glass, flipping through the assignments. "Well, I don't see any not done. So, yes, I guess you can go, dear." She closed out the work and laid it on his bed.

Chr's knew why she put it back on his bed. He had to check over all the answers a second time to make sure they were all correct. But not now. She wouldn't make him do that now.

"Run to get ready. If you're not prepared, you won't be able to go." She watched him dash off, his excitement carrying him in a run.

It had been the best night of his life, and that was when he knew what he had been born to do. He just never had the chance until now. In this ship, he felt he could fly right across deepest space.

Then reality came rushing back. The little ship had no jumpdrive. With that thought, he laughed, picturing traveling 400 years at sublight speeds across the depths of space. He also had no foodstuffs, and he still carried a tracker. After the first thirtyday, it wouldn't matter, anyway. He'd be dead one way or the other. However, it was the idea, the possibility of freedom that had his adrenalin running so high.

There was something else, also, perhaps even more meaningful. He was following in his dad's footsteps, flying the little ship that went to the giant ship in the sky.

THAT OLD WITCH will die, now. She deserved what I did to her. My brother didn't have to go down there. That witch could have saved him, could have kept him on the ship just like she did me. He was half of me. Half of me died down there.

L'Rene carried a bloodied knife in her hand as she stalked the station corridors.

Jer'son sided with Barkeen, and so did Barn't. They shouldn't have done that. I promise, they'll hurt as much as I do.

She knew they were on the station, and she'd find them no matter where they went. There wasn't any way for them to get away. No way at all.

MI'KAIL PROPPED his feet on the console, the lighted displays across the wall giving him a fractured look. Tapping his finger on the counter in a syncopated beat, he pondered the call that had prompted him to send that messenger to Jer'son's quarters. Why might Medic Barkeen think Jer'son was on night rotation this cycle? She was the station's medic, and she had unprecedented access to duty assignments.

He tapped a control on the console, and the duty rosters

rolled across the screens. "Barkeen," he called into the room. The information on the screens shifted, and one line remained. She wasn't on duty, after all. He frowned. The request had come in over her line, possibly from Barkeen's assistant. However, Barkeen's new assistant didn't have Barkeen's level of access, and that made him wonder. If Barkeen wasn't there, why would the assistant be on duty at this time? Everything about this reeked of an emergency in the making.

"That's strange." He leaned over to check a blinking status icon. "The docking bay doors are being accessed." He sat back, tapping the console for a moment. No transports were due in until morning. He pulled up the corridor cameras to see Barn't kneeling in front of the access panel. He zoomed in to see his face sweating. Barn't placed a trembling hand on the panel, and it turned red. The man fumbled a piece of paper in his hand and wiped sweat from his face. Mi'Kail ran through the rest of the feeds looking for Jer'son but didn't locate him. One camera caught his eye: L'Rene, striding down a corridor, and it looked like blood on her clothing.

"Gods," he murmured to himself. "Looks like trouble tonight."

He stood, running through the facts as he knew them. First, there had been the weirdness between Jer'son and Barn't. Then, Barkeen had made that emergency call to meet with Jer'son. Earlier today, Jer'son had moved like someone with a broken rib. Now, Barkeen—or someone using her comm code—hadn't even known where to find him.

L'Rene was the clincher. He could smell the evil in that

woman. Hitting a switch to flip the controls into remote mode, he picked up a glass and watched the icons swirl down the walls and shrink across its surface. It was time to do just what his job required him to do, get out and take care of things.

"I'm headed to check on a malfunctioning indicator," he called into his glass, reaching to gather his gear, including Jer'son's override key. It would be useful if the panel at the airlock wasn't accepting input codes. Almost as an afterthought, he snapped open a cabinet and pulled out an official, station-issue weapon. He felt his adrenalin surge.

With a casualness that belied the urgency he felt inside, he hitched up his weapon, and he headed into the night.

JER'SON STOOD in a darkened recess and watched Barn't as he crouched in front of the access panel, repeatedly trying to input the code Barkeen had given him. Each time he placed his palm to the panel, it blinked a warning red. Jer'son snorted, disgusted, and he stepped to the glassine panels that made up the doors, searching the empty landing bay beyond. On the opposite side rose the giant exterior access doors, their surfaces covered with the massive gears and connecting chains that would ratchet them open when the time came.

He really had no idea what Barkeen had meant by meeting an old friend. Renhant was coming up? At night? He couldn't imagine that. He had no way to get up here and no pass that Jer'son knew of. Anyway, the transport wouldn't run again until morning, and even if he had managed to requisition it, the transport unlocked the bay doors automatically upon arrival. Renhant's sister? She and Cornerstone had gone offworld; at least that had been their plan.

He glanced at Barn't wiping his face and starting the sequence once again. He'd sworn that if Barkeen got hurt because of him, he'd never help him again. Now, they were here side by side, and the man was a fool! He'd never been able to think for himself. Never. It was always Renhant and him planning everything, following through, and picking up the pieces for the little weasel. He knew one thing. If Barn't had been paying attention, those "incidences" down on Rant wouldn't have happened. He was so tired of picking up after the little snot. He'd do what Barkeen asked this one last time, but if Barn't screwed up again, he was gone.

"Jer'son, it won't take the code. Don't you have your key?" Barn't looked at him, ashen and broken.

"Fine, Barn't. Barkeen's dead, and you want me to hike back to the control center, interrupt Mi'Kail and retrieve the override key, just because you can't enter a simple code? The override gets us in the bay. It doesn't open the outer doors." He was too angry to offer his help. Let him suffer.

Even more irritating, something had been grinding on him. In their bunks, had the fool really thought he was asleep? Whispering about L'Rene like he was dead to the world simply to get it off his chest. Did he really think it made him feel better to know Barn't had just come from her that night in the corridor? No wonder L'Rene had been so pleased with herself.

"Gods, Barn't. Do it the way I showed you. Just enter one number right after the other. Then press your palm to it. It's very straightforward." The little idiot couldn't do anything right.

I HEARD what Barkeen said. I think someone's coming to pick us up. I'll bet it's Renhant. He runs those ground transports down there. I bet he could just get on the transport for here and use it anytime he wants. I bet he knows how hard it is up here for me right now.

I hope he leaves Jer'son. I saw him look at me when Barkeen died. He thinks I did it. I was with him. He should give his mean looks to L'Rene. She's the bad person. I just don't see how she can be a bad person, though, when she feels so good when we're together.

If all this weren't going on, I'd be with her right now. I'd lock out the override so no one could come in, and I'd do that to L'Rene, and if she wanted me to be angry, I'd be fast and rough with her. I'd think about what those men did to me, even if I did have nightmares afterwards, but I wouldn't go to Jer'son.

Barn't placed his palm to the sensor, and he groaned when it blinked red once again. With sweat making his eyes burn, he refused to look up. Instead, he wiped his face on his sleeve and tried to focus on the numbers.

I bet he's known all along about me and L'Rene. I bet he smelled her on me in the corridor that first time, and he's been laughing at me because he knows, and he probably even told L'Rene to do that to me so I'd feel really bad, except it backfired on him, because it felt really good, except that I saw him again, and that made me sorry, but when I went back to her again, I forgot about him because it felt so good.

I can't get this code to work!

It was only that first time I thought about Jer'son the whole time I was with L'Rene, except not after I started doing that, because then it felt so good, I didn't want to think about him.

He glanced up, only to find Jer'son watching him with contempt on his face. He felt his chest tighten, as if the air in the station were crushing him. He began to enter the numbers once more. *I wish he'd quit watching me do this code. I think this input panel is broken. Gods, I never do anything right.*

"WHAT NOW, Barn't?" The kid was blubbering, and Jer'son was about to grab the paper and do this himself.

"It's got to be Renhant coming." Barn't looked up from the flashing pad, his eyes red and his cheeks showing wet streaks. "I can't face him. You know all about what I did, but he doesn't. I know you'll tell him, and I don't want to be here when you do."

"Just enter the code, Barn't. You're being a baby." He had to force him to focus, or else he'd lose him. It would be just like him to run away and hide again, and Jer'son would have betrayed Barkeen's last trust. However, he wasn't staying on this station, not if there was a way to get off, even if it meant leaving the slobbering fool behind.

Barn't visibly collapsed at the verbal attack. He reached and wiped the moisture from his face, drying his hand on the fabric of his clothing. "I'm sorry I did that to you, but I can't face Renhant, too." Standing, he started to back down the corridor leading away from the landing bay.

Jer'son stepped to him and grabbed his arm, yanking it harder than necessary. "Get back here. I don't think it is

355

Renhant coming in. Finish the code, or we'll never know."

Fool. Can't do anything right. Jer'son snorted his disgust.

"I'm sorry, Jer'son. You go." Barn't jerked his arm away, his face panic stricken. "I don't deserve to leave. I've been everything bad I could be, and I don't want anyone else to know. Please don't tell Renhant. I want at least one person to still like me." He turned and lurched away, dragging his hand along the wall like a little boy as he slowed for a shift in the corridor, then speeding up as he rounded a curve.

"Idiot." Jer'son watched him for a moment, and then he twisted away in disgust. "He couldn't even stand in one spot and finish one thing, this code."

Blinking and looking around, he reached to the panel to input the rest of the override code only to realize Barn't had taken Barkeen's slip of paper with him. Frustration overwhelmed him. "That was all he had to do, just stay here and do this simple thing. Now, I cannot even finish this for him. Gods! I wish . . . I don't know what I wish."

"Hey, Jer'son, you talking to me?" Mi'Kail tapped him on the back.

He jerked and turned, slamming his back against the wall. "Oh, Mi'Kail, it's you. Barn't's a fool, that's all." He glanced down the corridor where Barn't had disappeared. "Let me explain what's going on here."

"Nope. I do not want to hear it. I trust you and respect you. If you're here doing something, it's bound to need doing. I just want to help." He peered into the landing bay, the well-lighted area telling of the activity at the control panel. "Lights are on. Trying to get inside? I have my magic tool here." He held up the override key. "I bet this will work."

Jer'son looked at his friend with amazement. "I cannot believe you brought that, Mi'Kail. Gods, I'm glad you're here. Do you mean that about wanting to help?"

"I'm yours to command."

"And you've got," Jer'son laughed shakily as he pulled Mi'Kail's shirt aside, "a weapon? You don't know how welcome that is. What prompted this?"

"L'Rene. I don't know what's going on with her, but it seemed I might find this handy." He slipped the override key into the panel and placed his palm onto it. It turned green. "We're ready, Boss." The locking mechanism on the interior door unlocked with a hiss.

"No, we're not. I don't need in. I need the outer doors open, and Barn't took my override code." Jer'son took a deep breath and ran his hands through his hair. He wanted to spit, he was so angry at the twit.

"This, by any chance? It was on the floor back there." Mi'Kail held out a wadded slip of paper. "I saw Barn't with this on the corridor camera, and when it was on the floor, I thought it might be important."

"You are a lifesaver." Jer'son clapped his forearm with his hand, and he took the paper and began to input the final digits of the code. As the warning lights began to flash in the massive landing bay, and as the enormous gears on the doors shifted with a bone-jarring thud, preparing to turn on their stanchions, powerful pumps began to remove the air from the compartment.

"Expecting someone, are we?" Mi'Kail pocketed the override key, and he checked to ensure his weapon was live and ready to fire.

"Thanks, Mi'Kail. I don't know exactly. However, my part is done. Now we get to wait and see," Jer'son said, wiping his face with his hand. He didn't know just what they would find. He might be inviting a MegaCorp battalion in, for all he knew.

"Just want to help, Boss. All you have to do is let me know what you need." Mi'Kail clapped his hand on his shoulder, and he squeezed it firmly before letting go.

"THERE, JUST like Dad used to do."

The station expanded in all its rough majesty just ahead of Chr's. He pulled the memory crystal from his pocket. So much was riding on this alteration to the original design plan. Without these filed and logged, the changes would be spotted and corrected. This new ship they were building was the latest in design and technology, and it was supposed to be very secret. Bring this ship down with a big enough bang, and the galaxy would notice. He was certain.

When a light on the console blinked a warning yellow, he took the controls, looking for the landing bay. He'd only been to the station once, and had only ridden the transport one time, down. But, there it was. It was open, too. Good old Barkeen. He'd be so glad to see her.

Guiding the ship, he eased it in and set it down. He was pleased that it was no trouble at all. It helped that the bay was large enough to land the regular transport, and here he was in a tiny one-man, maybe with room behind him for a second person to squeeze inside in a pinch.

"Did you see that, Dad?" Chr's smiled, speaking to a

358

memory.

He glanced up as the bay doors began closing him in, faced with the realization that he was back on the station he'd been working for years to bring down. He smiled again at that. He didn't really care about the station. He wanted to bring down its owner, MegaCorp. That's what this was all about.

"FIRST, YOU can stop calling me Boss." Jer'son looked inside the bay, the expansive interior glassine doors still firmly sealed and protecting the station from the vacuum of space. A small ship now rested inside, but it was too far away to identify its occupant. A sharp hissing of air told of pumps forcing breathable atmosphere through the bay's massive vents.

He turned back and placed his fist gently on Mi'Kail's chest, a warning to the man who was so eager to help. "Second, Mi'Kail, you don't even know what's going on. I only understand part of it, but if you get involved, you're in all the way, whatever it is."

A wry grin spread across Mi'Kail's face. "You don't know what I've already endured for you, Boss. Barn't does. I've seen things no man ought to be forced to see, and I've done it out of respect and friendship for you. Don't cut me out. I want to be in."

With a quick laugh, Jer'son opened his fist and clasped Mi'Kail's shoulder. "So, I can't get you to drop the Boss. Here's what's going on. I've got a visitor out there, and I'm not sure just who it is. I do know there's a good chance this will be be a life or death issue. Have you heard about Barkeen?"

"No, Boss. What?" He frowned. "She just sent for you a little bit ago. Is there a medical emergency brewing?"

"It was an emergency, all right. That's why I'm here. Barkeen needed me to do this, a last bequest. L'Rene killed her."

"No, Boss. Say it's not so. Not Barkeen." His face dropped.

"She was killed over whatever's happening now, and that's why this, whatever it is, is so important. So, I'm going in."

"I've got your back, Boss." Mi'Kail grabbed his shoulder and squeezed.

Jer'son looked to him and grinned. Hearing the doors at his side release, he turned to see the small ship far across the enormous bay. Behind it, the outside doors were completing their final kiss of life-giving lockdown, and he could see the residual tufts of condensation in the air that still swirled into the bay though the vents in the walls and floor. He stepped through the glassine doors, and with no hesitation, he strode towards the waiting ship.

As the ship's hatch opened, out stepped a visitor. At first glance, Jer'son didn't recognize him, but then, astonished, he called with enthusiasm, "Chr's! What are you doing here, and where did you get a ship?"

"It's a loaner, and you know those suggestions you made from way back about those actuator arm modifications? That's why I'm here." He grabbed Jer'son by the shoulders, grinning broadly, and then he gripped his hand in a firm shake.

"Modifications? The actuator arm?" He shook his head. "I remember that ridiculous story, but that was five years ago. You're up here about that?"

"We've done it, my friend." Excitement poured from every pore in the man's body. "All your suggestions have been built into the battleship. It will fail. But we need one more thing."

"Name it, if I can do it." Jer'son called to his second-in-command, "This fool saved my life when I first came here. Now he needs my help. You in, Mi'Kail?"

"With you, Boss." He grinned.

Chr's pulled out the memory crystal. "This needs to be loaded as an update to the official plans, so that what we've done will be part and parcel of the design. Can you do that?"

Jer'son turned to Mi'Kail. "Well? Can we?"

He winked with delight. "That's my specialty, Boss." He motioned to Chr's. "If this is what I think it is, follow me, and we'll start to correct many years' worth of wrongs."

L'RENE STARTED at Barn't's and Jer'son's quarters. She even found the door still open. There was no one there. "Fools," she called aloud. Still, she knew they had to be somewhere. Even so, the station would soon be coming alive for the day shift, and she needed clean clothes, ones without blood on them. For now she needed to head to her rooms.

Rounding the corner to her quarters, she was pleasantly surprised to find someone waiting for her.

"Barn't!"

"L'Rene." He ducked his head and mumbled her name almost unintelligibly. His hands were in his pockets, and his eyes were on the floor. "Can I come in?"

She smiled. "Sure, of course, you can." She laid the knife just outside the room, lowering it carefully onto the corridor floor before triggering the door lock.

Shutting the door behind her, Barn't saw the blood. "You have blood on your clothes. Is that from Barkeen?"

She looked down, dismayed. "I was trying to help her, and she sent me to find you. And Jer'son. Where is he?"

He grinned. "He's at the landing bay. Do you want me to go there with you? We can explain everything to him. He thinks you hurt Barkeen, and we can tell him you were only trying to help. I knew that's how it had to be."

"Would you do that with me? Let me put on a fresh shirt."

She reached up and slipped her top off, and as she expected, she saw Barn't's eyes widen. He would do anything she asked, just for the chance to mount her afterward.

"Did you like them?" She grinned. "Maybe later you can have them for your own."

"I'd like that." He grinned back.

He was a fool, and L'Rene knew she would have no trouble at all using him to get at Jer'son. Then, they both could die.

CHR'S FOLLOWED Mi'Kail as they ran the darkened corridors to the operations center. As soon as they were inside, Mi'Kail held out his hand for the information crystal.

"Now that we're here, this will be a snap." Mi'Kail reached his hands over the station's main glass display and shifted several icons. The displays lighted up with recognition. With a brisk series of jabs and several tugs and twists, he had the battleship's plans pulled up and ready for an update. He opened a small panel, and he slipped the crystal into its appropriate slot. They turned to the progress display on the wall, watching the icon spin.

"How is old Barkeen doing these days?" Chr's glanced at Mi'Kail expectantly. He wondered if it might be possible to greet his friend while aboard the station.

"You haven't heard." Mi'Kail closed his eyes and let out a disgusted breath.

"Tell me." Chr's saw the look on the man's face, and it said nothing good.

"Dead, although I don't know the reason. Only the who."

"Gods!" Chr's slammed a fist against the console. Just then, the display chimed briskly, the update complete. Chr's breathed a sigh of relief. Retrieving the crystal, he looked Mi'Kail in the eyes. "Barkeen will have to wait. Thanks, friend. People have given their lives for this. You do not even know me, and still, you have done more good than you realize. I have no words with which to thank you."

Mi'Kail reached out to shake his hand. Chr's didn't even flinch. The familiar motion had been taught them by a mutual friend. He returned the handshake as Mi'Kail pulled him towards the corridor, encouraging him to follow.

"I think our shared friend might need help. Perhaps we should return."

With the staccato rhythm of a rapidly firing machine, the movement of both men's feet harmonized in a steady cadence as they traveled back to where they had left their companion all alone with the landing craft. In the adrenalinfueled excitement of the moment, Chr's' injured leg didn't slow him down at all.

JER'SON TURNED at the sound of feet coming down the corridor. When he saw who it was, he froze, taking a deep breath. Barn't had fled, and now he returned, bringing a murderer with him. He was a bigger fool than Jer'son had given him credit for.

Then, his eyes caught the knife rudely concealed at L'Rene's side. Had Barn't been involved in her scheme to murder Barkeen? He couldn't imagine it, even of Barn't.

"Hey, Jer'son. I've brought L'Rene." Barn't waved. "It wasn't like Barkeen thought at all. L'Rene got there after she was hurt and was trying to help her."

Jer'son yelled, "Get away from her, Barn't. She's got a knife."

"You're wrong, Jer'son. She told me." He looked confused, as he touched her shoulder. "L'Rene, tell him."

Instead, she whirled around, brandishing the knife for him to see for the first time, a demonic look on her face. The bloody blade flashed through the air, catching the lights in the corridor, and gleaming with the wickedness of the evil intent that L'Rene had slashed across the station earlier that night.

"Stars, L'Rene," Barn't croaked, his eyes wide, as he threw himself against the wall. "Be careful."

"Careful?" Her face twisted with fury as she crouched, with her eyes glued to Jer'son. She called louder, "Careful? You'll think careful when I come for you, Jer'son!" She yelled that.

Jer'son caught a movement just behind them and yelled out as Chr's and Mi'Kail rounded the hallway. "Watch out! L'Rene's got a knife!"

"KNIFE?" Mi'Kail, at least, had the presence of mind to freeze, and he grabbed Chr's' arm. "Up ahead. Careful."

"That I can see." Chr's' voice echoed against the metal walls. He fell into a quick crouch, one leg bent more sharply than the other. A fleeting expression passed over his face, telling of the pain the abrupt action knifed through his leg.

"We should go easy." Mi'Kail motioned with a hand for his companion to keep his voice down as they watched the knife-wielding woman glance back and forth, her eyes glassy. He had seen that look, and he knew she was about to explode. He had no doubt she intended someone other than Barkeen to die. "She's outnumbered, and she knows it. That can be used against her, I think, although if she becomes desperate, who knows what she might do."

Chr's whispered back, "It's clear to me that this must be Barkeen's killer." His words were hard and spoke of no sympathy and less mercy. He glanced at the hard metal walls, and his tightening expression spoke the thoughts in his head. "We have no advantage in this corridor. The space is too tight. If we can work her into the bay, we may be able to maneuver to her disadvantage and disarm her."

Mi'Kail shot him a thumbs-up as he pulled his weapon.

"So," L'Rene yelled, her head in constant motion as she attempted to track all those against her. "You think three of you can take one of me?"

"Four!" Mi'Kail yelled. The word was harsh in the metal

environment, and it echoed.

"I count three. Are you all idiots?" She knelt as if ready to pounce, the knife now held in front of her. "Barn't's with me."

"My weapon's number four, L'Rene." Mi'Kail called to her loudly and firmly, letting the reverberations carry his voice. He held up the weapon for her to see, hoping she would retreat.

"Careful, man," Chr's hissed. "Let's make that our last option. We are in a pressurized tin can, after all."

"Understood," and Mi'Kail chuckled. Still, his weapon did not waver.

Barn't stepped back, his face a puzzled mask. "L'Rene? Put that knife away. You said you didn't kill Barkeen. What are you doing now?"

"Fool," she spat. "I may just kill you first if you don't shut up."

Chr's shifted position, motioning for Jer'son to head towards the landing bay. As L'Rene caught her quarry moving, she called out, "Hey, Jer'son! Running away? Afraid? I'll teach you afraid." She grabbed Barn't by the shoulder, then threw her arm violently around his neck, thrusting the knife hard and fast at his throat. "I'll take him out. I'll do it."

"Come and get me," Jer'son yelled, as he paused at the bay door. "It's me you want to fight. Barn't's not your enemy. Leave him out of this."

"I'll kill him, Jer'son," she screamed at him.

"L'Rene, you don't have to do this," cajoled Mi'Kail from behind her, his words calm and steady. He had moved closer without her seeing.

She jerked her head around. "Stay back, Mi'Kail. You're not on my side. You're Jer'son's friend." Her face grew hard as her eyes flicked one way up the corridor, then back again the other way. She growled with frustration when she saw Jer'son disappear into the bay.

"I'm everyone's friend. Just put the knife down. Let Barn't go. We can work this out."

"Work it out?" Her voice was razor edged. "Put me in a pod is more like it. Get Jer'son back out here."

"He's in the bay so we have room to talk. Just follow him, L'Rene."

"I'll kill him, Mi'Kail. I'll kill Barn't. I swear I'll do it."

"You won't have to. We'll talk this out, like I said." He motioned for Chr's to move her direction as he stepped forward. He had worked out the angles, and if the other man could move on the right track, they could act as a pinscher.

As they did, she started backing away, frantically looking back and forth, keeping her distance from the approaching men. Finally, the wall disappearing behind her, she dodged into the landing bay, whipping around, and pulling Barn't inside after her.

"JER'SON! WHERE are you? I'll kill him! I will! Barn't's dead right now, if you don't come out." She would not be beaten, not yet. Damn that old woman for living long enough to tell her tale. She should have stabbed her more times, and she would have if not for that pesky aide.

"Let him go, L'Rene. He's not your enemy." He stepped from behind the small ship. "Let Barn't come to me."

Stepping forward, her arm still tightly around Barn't's neck, she called out, "What are you trying? I'm not falling for it. Barkeen's probably dead by now. They'll space me for sure. What have I got to lose?" She saw Jer'son's eyes dart sideways and back again. She turned just in time to see Chr's slap the Emergency Pressure Seal and Exterior Door Release panel before leaping through the door directly into her, knocking her legs out from under her.

Her grip on Barn't broken, she threw herself at her attacker. Her face a twisted knot, she spat at him, "You're going to wish you had never met me!"

"Scum. You're a foul excuse for a woman," he spat back at her. "I've seen you below. I always thought you were animal fodder." He grabbed her in a bear hug, his legs twisting around hers and taking her to the floor.

"How dare you!" Furious, with a yell of rage, she thrust her knife deep into his side. This fool would die, and if she never learned his name, so much for that. They would all die, and then perhaps her anger would be salved.

"Chr's!" Jer'son started toward him, only making it half-way across the metal planking before Barn't intercepted him, grabbing his arm, terror written in his eyes.

"Get off, Barn't! Chr's needs me." Jer'son attempted to push him away.

"No! Go! The ship! Get the canopy open!" Chr's yelled, pointing overhead. The massive gears had already started to turn. Each time one engaged, the sound thudded noisily, drowning out everything else.

"Fool! Shut up!" L'Rene struggled to pull the knife from his side, cursing him at every step of the way. "You will die today, cur," she hissed into his ear. She meant it, too, each and every one of them.

"NO, CHR'S!" Jer'son was frozen with disbelief. What was L'Rene doing? Did she intend to kill everyone he knew?

"Ship?" Barn't twisted around in shocked awareness, releasing Jer'son, as if seeing the small craft for the first time. Confusion was written on his bloodless face.

"Damn you! Get off me!" L'Rene raised the knife and drove it into Chr's' side once again. By this time, he had begun to cough up blood.

Jer'son realized this had to be what Chr's intended when he sealed the landing bay. It was then he noticed the great gears were indeed in motion, as one of the monstrosities engaged with a resounding bang. Time was of the essence. With no other choice, he threw himself back along the way he had come. The small ship was his only option if he wanted to live. The craft was unfamiliar, but the controls to open the canopy weren't. He slapped his hand to them, relieved to see the seal separate and invite him in. Pulling himself up and putting one leg inside, he turned to see Barn't's eyes on him, true understanding dawning on his face. He hadn't been invited onboard.

Barn't yelled against the clanking of the massive overhead gears, desperation lacing every word, "You aren't taking me, are you, Jer'son?" Already the wind around the doors had begun to whistle, and his clothes whipped against his legs and arms.

Pausing for what seemed an eternity, and then with narrowed eyes, Jer'son jumped from the ship and ran to him, grabbing his shoulders. "Now. For Barkeen." Together they leaped toward the unfamiliar ship.

"Can you fly this thing?" Barn't called out as he squeezed in back.

Not certain his decision to honor Barkeen's last mandate was one he'd be glad he made, Jer'son snapped, "It's not a T404, but I can try." Then, he reached for a grip on the canopy and pulled the cockpit hatch down, sealing it from the rising vacuum. Immediately, the air around them seemed thicker, and within the small craft, a fan whirred into motion, the rush of oxygen sweet to hungry lungs.

"That was close." Barn't's hand came to rest on Jer'son's shoulder.

Jer'son looked at it. "Entirely too close. You can say that again."

ON THE FAR side of the bay, as Chr's' lifeless arms fell away from her, releasing her from their grasp, L'Rene stood, victorious, searching for her next victims. Seeing them sitting in the small ship, she ran at them, yelling, her knife in hand.

"You won't get away so easily!"

She leaped, landing against the canopy, grabbing for a handhold. Her foot found a step, and she drew back her arm, slamming the blade of her knife against the transparent cover. It ricocheted off, leaving a long, bloody mark. She cursed. She began to dig the blade between the metal and the canopy, digging out chunks of rubbery stripping. "You'll die one way or another," she screamed at them.

Just then, the exterior doors split fully open, rolling on

their great tracks, and the remaining air in the bay was evacuated ruthlessly into the emptiness outside of the station. L'Rene wailed, helpless against the forces thrusting her toward the darkness. With a mighty tearing vortex of torrential wind, both she and the man she had killed were exhausted into the void like jetsam, their bodies drifting away from the station.

THE SMALL SHIP remained, though. Watching Mi'Kail in the pressurized corridor, the two men ensconced in the small vessel saw him motioning. Jer'son had no doubt what his friend meant for them to do. Their time on the station was done.

He called to Barn't, "How do I start this thing?"

"Try that one," he called, pointing to a red sensor pad.

As the engines whirred to life with a high-pitched whine, Jer'son called back, "That was a very good guess. I should thank you."

"You're welcome, but I sure hope you can fly this." He leaned back, bumping his head in the cramped space. "Let's get away from here. I hate this place."

Jer'son moved the old-fashioned control stick, the altitude and the attitude markers clearly familiar to him. With a few false starts, the small craft began to rise.

He called back to Barn't, "We're underway. Let's see how much of this I remember. You know, it's been a few years since I sat in a sim'lator." The small craft lurched and then turned as he fiddled with controls that were barely familiar to him, and never in this configuration. "Hold onto the seat of your pants when we get there. I was never trained to actually land the T404's, just to fly them."

There was a span of silence as the ship exited the lighted bay and was washed with the stars overhead. Below was the void of Rant. No artificial lights brought it to life. It was indeed a black hole from which none could hope to return.

"For a moment there, Jer'son, I thought you were going to leave me in the docking bay." Barn't's voice was strained. "I wasn't sure I was welcome."

Jer'son didn't reply, remembering Barkeen and L'Rene. He couldn't reply. He had no words to say that Barn't wanted to hear. He had indeed been ready to leave him, but to say that now would only make a bad situation worse. For Barkeen's sake, he would not do that.

"You weren't, were you, Jer'son?" Barn't's words grew ragged. "Jer'son? You wouldn't have left me, would you?"

Jer'son called over his shoulder, "Since we're going to be dead when I can't land this thing, it won't hurt me to welcome you along. It's just for the sake of an old friend, though. Barkeen wanted us together. So, welcome aboard." *That was for you, Barkeen. I've done what you've asked, old friend. Am I released, now?* He wanted to spit the sour taste of forgiveness from his lips. Even the tears he had seen in Barn't's eyes didn't make him feel sorry for the cuckolding ex-friend he had been forced to bring along.

Once a short distance out of the station, the ship suddenly took on a life of its own. Jer'son threw his hands up when he could no longer get the controls to respond. He twisted around to frown at the man sitting behind him.

"Barn't, did you do anything? I have no control."

"Gods, no," he cried, and he grasped Jer'son's shoulder

in fear. "Are we about to crash?" Outside, the planet rushed at them faster and faster.

Jer'son searched his memory. Onboard MegaCorp's training ships, automated landings had been the norm. Here? On this forgotten world? He searched the console for something that suggested automation, but he saw nothing he recognized. His heart raced, knowing for certain they were heading to sure death. In that moment of clarity, things fell into a different perspective. Inside that small ship were no longer two men torn apart by the cruelties of a woman who had used them both. Instead, there was a lifetime of friendship against a few sevendays of L'Rene. This craft was going down, and what he needed was starkly clear to him. He needed to die with a friend, not an enemy.

Reaching up to clasp the hand on his shoulder, he whispered under his breath, "This time I forgive you, Barn't, and not just for Barkeen. I forgive you for me."

"What?" Barn't leaned forward. "What about Barkeen?"

Jer'son called louder, "I said this is not like the T404 sim'lator. They never showed us this." He was relieved to feel landing gear disengage from the underbelly, finally coming to rest on the surface of the world that had been theirs for mere days five years before.

"I think we're there, Jer'son."

"We're at least somewhere, Barn't, and we're still alive." He turned to him, his heart still unsettled. A laugh tore itself from his throat as he leaned his head back on the seat. "It looks like we might still be a team after all."

"Thank you for standing by me, even when I let you down."

Barn't didn't see the tears Jer'son blinked away, his emotions torn with what he'd almost done. Sitting there, adrenalin still coursing through his veins, Jer'son heard something click, and with a low whirring sound, the hatch lifted itself to show an unexpected face staring back at them.

"Oh, no. Two more bosses."

When Racket grinned, Jer'son finally let himself relax with a chuckle.

"Did you like my ship? I like to tinker, and the first boss who flew it was not good with directions. I built in a homing device. She always comes straight back home." He finally looked closely at the face in the back of the ship and scratched his head. Then, his grin erupted again. "Barn't? Little Barn't?" He laughed. "No one will ever pick on you again, I think." He reached a hand to help him climb out of the tight confines in the back of the small ship.

Jer'son was too drained to move, however, and he sat immobile as Barn't scrambled out. In a moment they were out of his view.

He took a deep breath and closed his eyes. Opening them finally and looking up into the sky, he murmured, "I almost didn't forgive you, Barn't. I almost let you fly the sky without any wings." Casting his eyes across the darkness above him, looking for the station and knowing he wouldn't really be able to see it, he said more softly, "Thank you, Barkeen. You really did save two of us tonight."

As he watched, he caught two falling stars. He saluted one of them, knowing just what he was seeing. With his hand at his forehead, he whispered quietly, "You saved this kid twice, Chr's. Once for each of your own. Thanks, friend."

He stood and stepped from the small ship, patting it on its side before following the other two men. Here, he knew, was where his future lay. The station had been his home for a short time, but he now had no tracker inside his body to let the authorities know he was back onworld. He was free, as he had never been before.

"Welcome home," he called aloud, and with a wave to the sky, he strode inside to find his friends.

MI'KAIL SAT at his new desk. He turned on the station's central comm system and made the following announcements:

"For those of you who are up, in a few moments we will see two of the brightest meteors visible this century falling into the upper atmosphere of Rant directly under this orbital platform. That's our new word for our home up here. Rant Orbital Platform. Learn it. Also, three of our crew have been transferred offstation. We wish them the best. Finally, we regret the passing of our station medic who died in her sleep last night. The position will be opening up for qualified planetary applicants. The new title for the job will be Platform Medic Prime. Recommendations are welcome. All out.

"I think I might make these announcements a daily thing. In fact, I know I will." He turned and smiled at the girl beside him, reaching and putting his arm around her. He whispered to her, "And the pretty medic's assistant never said a word."

Then, she reached over and kissed him directly on the lips.

SOME MONTHS later, three men with a long history sat

over a shared drink, with Renhant's improving fortunes picking up the tab. One of them was tracked constantly by the system, his presence there to be read by those with the knowledge or know-how. The other two were invisible, a fact known only to them.

Jer'son turned from his drink to his two friends. "Years ago, I swore I'd sabotage that ship they are building out there, if I just knew Bofsky'd be on board when it blew. Well, half that, at least, has come true."

"Sometimes I'm not even angry, anymore." Renhant ran his finger around the rim of his container. "We're making a life here."

"Yeah, but guys," Barn't's eyes gleamed, "what if? Imagine he *is* on that ship when it blows. Wouldn't that be great?"

"Grow up, Barn't. That's about as likely as you or me getting off this planet in one piece." Renhant glanced to Jer'son, and then he snorted a rough sort of laugh, finding black humor in his words.

Barn't laughed. He didn't take offense. He knew these men were truly his friends. He teased with them, throwing out an insane prediction. "You don't know. There's a first time for everything. Maybe this time, it'll happen just that way."

Jer'son looked at him appraisingly. "You know, Barn't. It might do it at that. It just might do it at that."

The three men raised their drinks in a toast, tossing them back, just three friends sharing a quiet moment of companionship.

As if.

Glossary:

Aain'sl	first guard on jumpship
abilities class	physical training class
airlock	provides safe passage between a ship and a space station
armscans	tracks workers and jobs worked; jobsite term
Barn't	Je'main Winterd Barn't; one of three boys sent to the prisonplanet, Rant
behavioral algorithms	computer program that can predict what people are doing under certain circumstances
bunkie, bunkmate .	shares a tiered bunk
Chr's	Chr's Zi'ggratson, once a well-known scholar; works with Jer'son at the jobsite
comm device	intercom
conscripts	drafted labor; work teams
Cornerstone	Sam'elton Welt'n Rhnnesty III; on the transport with Renhant
crikin'	invective
cryofreeze	suspended animation process
dorm leader	given de facto control
downside	on a planet
duty roster	duty assignment
Examination A	examination room on the space station

377

Medic Barkeen	part of an underground movement; space station doctor
midmeal	lunch
Mi'Kail	Mi'Kail Tranderkov; station second-in-command under Jer'son
nanobot	termite; nanobot that keeps comm feeds clean
night rotation	duty assignment
nonresuscitation . . .	cannot be brought out of cryofreeze
obsat	observation satellite
one-day	single day job
operations overseer	Jer'son's job; runs general station operations
overjacket	formal clothing
overnights	multiple day jobs; jobsite term
override emergency	allows supervisory control of numerous systems by one controller
payshare	portion of a job's profits
personal palm-approval delivery . .	requires personal palm print ID before delivery can be completed
priv'tshorts	underwear
Racket	drove transport for Cornerstone and Renhant
Rant	prison; entire planet; for all practical purposes also includes Rant Orbital Station

reader	like a barcode reader
realtime	live information feed
receiving hangar . . .	stationside landing bay
Reenna	Reenna Chi'lita Renhant; Renhant's sister
rejuv ward	medical facility for an age reversal process
Renhant	Steph'ni B'ltn Renhant; one of three boys sent to the prisonplanet, Rant
rikers	invective
Sam'elton Welt'n Rhnnesty III	a.k.a. Cornerstone
scout ship	small vessel
security feeds	visuals on an internal link
sonic imagers	type of radar
stationside	on Rant Orbital Station
struck in dirt	seals a deal
subsonic gamma-enhanced beam n^3 degrees in width . . .	Chr's' homework problem
Tan'sn	guard on jumpship who likes his boys young and tender
tenday	shipboard week
tracker	security device shot into the lung; contains contraceptives
Trainer	old man on station
Trikeen	where Renhant's sister, Reenna, was reportedly killed
uppercadets	high ranking academy students

Read all the books in this vibrant new series!

The Se'Yan't Chronicles

Get Yours At:

www.ThreeSkilletPublishing.com

www.ingramcontent.com/pod-product-compliance
Lightning Source LLC
Chambersburg PA
CBHW071202250626

47159CB00001B/169